GALACTIC NORTH

Also by Alastair Reynolds from Gollancz:

Chasm City
Revelation Space
Redemption Ark
Absolution Gap
Century Rain
Pushing Ice
The Prefect

Short Story Collections

Diamond Dogs, Turquoise Days
Galactic North

GALACTIC NORTH

Alastair Reynolds

Copyright © Alastair Reynolds 2006
All rights reserved

The right of Alastair Reynolds to be identified as the author
of this work has been asserted by him in accordance with
the Copyright, Designs and Patents Act 1988.

First published in Great Britain in 2006 by
Gollancz
An imprint of the Orion Publishing Group
Orion House, 5 Upper St Martin's Lane, London WC2H 9EA
An Hachette Livre UK Company

This edition published in Great Britain in 2007 by Gollancz

3 5 7 9 10 8 6 4 2

A CIP catalogue record for this book is available
from the British Library

ISBN 978 0 57507 9 847

Typeset at The Spartan Press Ltd,
Lymington, Hants

Printed in Great Britain at
Mackays of Chatham plc, Chatham, Kent

The Orion Publishing Group's policy is to use papers that
are natural, renewable and recyclable products and made
from wood grown in sustainable forests. The logging and
manufacturing processes are expected to conform to the
environmental regulations of the country of origin.

www.orionbooks.co.uk

For David Pringle

CONTENTS

'You realise you might die down there,' said Warren.

Nevil Clavain looked into his brother's one good eye; the one the Conjoiners had left him with after the Battle of Tharsis Bulge. 'Yes, I know,' he said. 'But if there's another war, we might all die. I'd rather take that risk, if there's a chance for peace.'

Warren shook his head, slowly and patiently. 'No matter how many times we've been over this, you just don't seem to get it, do you? There can't ever be any kind of peace while they're still down there. That's what you don't understand, Nevil. The only long-term solution here is . . .' he trailed off.

'Go on,' Clavain goaded. 'Say it. Genocide.'

Warren might have been about to answer when there was a bustle of activity along the docking tube, at the far end from the waiting spacecraft. Through the door Clavain saw a throng of media people, then someone gliding through them, fielding questions with only the curtest of answers. That was Sandra Voi, the Demarchist woman who would be accompanying him to Mars.

'It's not genocide when they're just a faction, not an ethnically distinct race,' Warren said, before Voi was within earshot.

'What is it, then?'

'I don't know. Prudence?'

Voi approached. She carried herself stiffly, her face a mask of quiet resignation. Her ship had only just docked from Circum-Jove after a three-week transit at maximum burn. During that time the prospects for a peaceful resolution of the current crisis had steadily deteriorated.

'Welcome to Deimos,' Warren said.

'Marshals,' she said, addressing them both. 'I wish the circumstances were better. Let's get straight to business. Warren – how long do you think we have to find a solution?'

'Not long. If Galiana maintains the pattern she's been following for the last six months, we're due another escape attempt in . . .' Warren glanced at a read-out buried in his cuff. 'About three days. If she does try to get another shuttle off Mars, we'll really have no option but to escalate.'

They all knew what would mean: a military strike against the Conjoiner nest.

'You've tolerated her attempts so far,' Voi said, 'and each time you've successfully destroyed her ship with all the people in it. The net risk of a successful breakout hasn't increased. So why retaliate now?'

'It's very simple,' Warren said. 'After each violation we issued Galiana a stronger warning than the one before. Our last was absolute and final.'

'You'll be in violation of treaty if you attack.'

Warren's smile was one of quiet triumph. 'Not quite, Sandra. You may not be completely conversant with the treaty's fine print, but we've discovered that it allows us to storm Galiana's nest without breaking any terms. The technical phrase is a "police action", I believe.'

Clavain saw that Voi was momentarily lost for words. That was hardly surprising. The treaty between the Coalition and the Conjoiners – which Voi's neutral Demarchists had helped draft – was the longest document in existence, apart from some obscure, computer-generated mathematical proofs. It was supposed to be watertight, though only machines had ever read it from beginning to end, and only machines had ever stood a chance of finding the kind of loophole Warren was now brandishing.

'No . . .' she said. 'There's some mistake.'

'I'm afraid he's right,' Clavain said. 'I've seen the natural-language summaries, and there's no doubt about the legality of a police action. But it needn't come to that. I'm sure I can persuade Galiana not to make another escape attempt.'

'But if we should fail?' Voi looked at Warren now. 'Nevil and I could still be on Mars in three days.'

'Don't be, is my advice.'

Disgusted, Voi turned and stepped into the green cool of the shuttle. Clavain was left alone with his brother for a moment. Warren fingered the leathery patch over his ruined eye with the chrome gauntlet of his prosthetic arm, as if to remind Clavain of what the war had cost him; how little love he had for the enemy, even now.

'We haven't got a chance of succeeding, have we?' Clavain said. 'We're only going down there so you can say you explored all avenues of negotiation before sending in the troops. You actually want another damned war.'

'Don't be so defeatist,' Warren said, shaking his head sadly, forever the older brother disappointed at his sibling's failings. 'It really doesn't become you.'

'It's not me who's defeatist,' Clavain said.

'No, of course not. Just do your best, little brother.'

Warren extended his hand for his brother to shake. Hesitating, Clavain looked again into his brother's good eye. What he saw there was an interrogator's eye: as pale, colourless and cold as a midwinter sun. There was hatred in it. Warren despised Clavain's pacifism; Clavain's belief that any kind of peace, even a peace that consisted only of stumbling episodes of mistrust between crises, was always better than war. That schism had fractured any lingering fraternal feelings they might have retained. Now, when Warren reminded Clavain that they were brothers, he never entirely concealed the disgust in his voice.

'You misjudge me,' Clavain whispered, before quietly shaking Warren's hand.

'No. I honestly don't think I do.'

Clavain stepped through the airlock just before it sphinctered shut. Voi had already buckled herself in; she had a glazed look now, as if staring into infinity. Clavain guessed she was uploading a copy of the treaty through her implants, scrolling it across her visual field, trying to find the loophole; probably running a global search for any references to police actions.

The ship recognised Clavain, its interior shivering to his preferences. The green was closer to turquoise now, the read-outs and controls minimalist in layout, displaying only the most mission-critical systems. Though the shuttle was the tiniest peacetime vessel Clavain had been in, it was a cathedral compared to the dropships he had flown during the war; vessels so small that they were assembled around their occupants like medieval armour before a joust.

'Don't worry about the treaty,' Clavain said. 'I promise you Warren won't get his chance to exploit that loophole.'

Voi snapped out of her trance irritatedly. 'You'd better be right, Nevil. Is it me, or is your brother hoping we fail?' She was speaking Quebecois French now, Clavain shifting mental gears to follow her. 'If my people discover there's a hidden agenda here, there'll be hell to pay.'

'The Conjoiners gave Warren plenty of reasons to hate them after the Battle of the Bulge,' Clavain said. 'And he's a tactician, not a field specialist. After the ceasefire, my knowledge of worms was even more valuable than before, so I had a role. But Warren's skills were a lot less transferable.'

'So that gives him a right to edge us closer to another war?' The way Voi spoke, it was as if her own side had not been neutral during the last exchange. But Clavain knew she was right. If hostilities between the Conjoiners and the Coalition re-ignited, the Demarchy would not be able to stand on the sidelines as they

4

had fifteen years ago. And it was anyone's guess how they would align themselves this time around.

'There won't be war.'

'And if you can't reason with Galiana? Or are you going to play on your personal connection?'

'I was just her prisoner, that's all.' Clavain took the controls – Voi said piloting was a bore – and unlatched the shuttle from Deimos. They dropped away at a tangent to the rotation of the equatorial ring that girdled the moon, instantly in free fall. Clavain sketched a porthole in the wall with his fingertip, outlining a rectangle that instantly became transparent.

For a moment he saw his reflection in the glass: older than he felt he had any right to look, the grey beard and hair making him appear ancient rather than patriarchal; a man deeply wearied by recent circumstance. With some relief he darkened the cabin so that he could see Deimos, dwindling at surprising speed. The higher of the two Martian moons was a dark, bristling lump infested with armaments, belted by the bright, window-studded band of the moving ring. For the last nine years, Deimos was all he had known, but now he could encompass it within the arc of his fist.

'Not just her prisoner,' Voi said. 'No one else came back sane from the Conjoiners. She never even tried to infect you with her machines.'

'No, she didn't, but only because the timing was on my side.' Clavain was reciting an old argument now, as much for his own benefit as Voi's. 'I was the only prisoner she had. She was losing the war by then; one more recruit to her side wouldn't have made any real difference. The terms of ceasefire were being thrashed out and she knew she could buy herself favours by releasing me unharmed. There was something else, too: Conjoiners weren't supposed to be capable of anything so primitive as mercy. They were Spiders, as far as we were concerned. Galiana's act threw a wrench into our thinking. It divided alliances within high command. If she hadn't released me, they might well have nuked her out of existence.'

'So there was absolutely nothing personal?'

'No,' Clavain said. 'There was nothing personal about it at all.'

Voi nodded, without in any way suggesting that she actually believed him. It was a skill some women had honed to perfection, Clavain reflected.

Of course, he respected Voi completely. She had been one of the first human beings to enter Europa's ocean, decades back. Now they were planning fabulous cities under the ice, efforts she had spearheaded. Demarchist society was supposedly flat in structure, non-hierarchical; but someone of Voi's brilliance ascended through echelons of her own making. She had been instrumental in brokering the peace between the Conjoiners and Clavain's own Coalition. That was why she was coming along now: Galiana had only agreed to Clavain's mission provided he was accompanied by a neutral observer, and Voi had been the obvious choice. Respect was easy. Trust, however, was more difficult: it required that Clavain ignore the fact that, with her head dotted with implants, the Demarchist woman's condition was not very far removed from that of the enemy.

The descent to Mars was hard and steep.

Once or twice they were queried by the automated tracking systems of the Satellite Interdiction Network. Dark weapons hovering in Mars-synchronous orbit above the nest locked on to the ship for a few instants, magnetic railguns powering up, before the shuttle's diplomatic nature was established and it was allowed to proceed. The Interdiction was very efficient; as well it might be, given that Clavain had designed much of it himself. In fifteen years no ship had entered or left the Martian atmosphere, nor had any surface vehicle ever escaped from Galiana's nest.

'There she is,' Clavain said, as the Great Wall rose over the horizon.

'Why do you call "it" a "she"?' Voi asked. 'I never felt the urge to personalise it, and I designed it. Besides . . . even if it was alive once, it's dead now.'

She was right, but the Wall was still awesome to behold. Seen from orbit, it was a pale, circular ring on the surface of Mars, two thousand kilometres wide. Like a coral atoll, it entrapped its own weather system: a disc of bluer air flecked with creamy white clouds that stopped abruptly at the boundary.

Once, hundreds of communities had sheltered inside that cell of warm, thick, oxygen-rich atmosphere. The Wall was the most audacious and visible of Voi's projects. The logic had been inescapable: a means to avoid the millennia-long timescales needed to terraform Mars via such conventional schemes as cometary bombardment or ice-cap thawing. Instead of modifying the whole atmosphere at once, the Wall allowed the initial effort to be concentrated in a relatively small region, at first only a thousand kilometres across. There were no craters deep enough, so the Wall had been completely artificial: a vast ring-shaped atmospheric dam designed to move slowly outward, encompassing ever more surface area at a rate of twenty kilometres per year. The Wall needed to be very tall because the low Martian gravity meant that the column of atmosphere was higher for a fixed surface pressure than on Earth. The ramparts were hundreds of metres thick, dark as glacial ice, sinking great taproots deep into the lithosphere to harvest the ores needed for the Wall's continual growth. Yet two hundred kilometres higher, the wall was a diaphanously thin membrane only microns wide, completely invisible except when rare optical effects made it hang like a frozen aurora against the stars. Eco-engineers had seeded the liveable area circumscribed by the Wall with terran genestocks deftly altered in orbital labs. Flora and fauna had moved out in vivacious waves, lapping eagerly against the constraints of the Wall.

But the Wall was dead.

It had stopped growing during the war, hit by some sort of viral weapon that crippled its replicating subsystems, and now even the ecosystem within it was failing; the atmosphere cooling, oxygen bleeding into space, pressure declining inevitably towards the Martian norm of one seven-thousandth of an atmosphere.

He wondered how it must look to Voi; whether in any sense she saw it as her murdered child.

'I'm sorry we had to kill it,' Clavain said. He was about to add that it had been the kind of act that war normalised, but decided the statement would have sounded hopelessly defensive.

'You needn't apologise,' Voi said. 'It was only machinery. I'm surprised it's lasted as long as it has, frankly. There must still be some residual damage-repair capability. We Demarchists build for posterity, you know.'

Yes, and it worried Clavain's own side. There was talk of challenging the Demarchist supremacy in the outer solar system; perhaps even an attempt to gain a Coalition foothold around Jupiter.

They skimmed the top of the Wall and punched through the thickening layers of atmosphere within it, the shuttle's hull morphing to an arrowhead shape. The ground had an arid, bleached look to it, dotted here and there with ruined shacks, broken domes, gutted vehicles and shot-down shuttles. There were patches of shallow-rooted, mainly dark-red tundra vegetation: cotton grass, saxifrage, arctic poppies and lichen. Clavain knew each species by its distinct infrared signature, but many of the plants were in recession now that the imported bird species had died. Ice lay in great silver swathes, and what few expanses of open water remained were warmed by buried thermopiles. Elsewhere whole zones had reverted to almost sterile permafrost. It could have been a kind of paradise, Clavain thought, had the war not ruined everything. Yet what had happened here could only be a foretaste of the devastation that would follow across the system, on Earth as well as Mars, if another war was allowed to happen.

'Do you see the nest yet?' Voi said.

'Wait a second,' Clavain said, requesting a head-up display that boxed the nest. 'That's it. A nice fat thermal signature, too. Nothing else for kilometres around – nothing inhabited, anyway.'

'Yes. I see it now.'

The Conjoiner nest lay a third of the way from the Wall's edge, not far from the footslopes of Arsia Mons. The entire encampment was only a kilometre across, circled by a dyke piled high with regolith dust on one side. The area within the Great Wall was large enough to have an appreciable weather system: spanning enough Martian latitude for significant Coriolis effects; enough longitude for diurnal warming and cooling to cause thermal currents.

He could see the nest much more clearly now, details leaping out of the haze.

Its external layout was crushingly familiar. Clavain's side had been studying the nest from the vantage point of Deimos ever since the ceasefire. Phobos with its lower orbit would have been even better, of course – but there was no helping that, and perhaps the Phobos problem might actually prove useful in his negotiations with Galiana. She was somewhere in the nest, he knew: somewhere beneath the twenty varyingly sized domes emplaced within the rim, linked together by pressurised tunnels or merged at their boundaries like soap bubbles. The nest extended several tens of levels beneath the Martian surface; maybe deeper.

'How many people do you think are inside?' Voi said.

'Nine hundred or so,' said Clavain. 'That's an estimate based on my experiences as a prisoner, and the hundred or so who've died trying to escape since. The rest, I have to say, is pretty much guesswork.'

'Our estimates aren't dissimilar. A thousand or less here, and perhaps another three or four spread across the system in smaller nests. I know your side thinks we have better intelligence than that, but it happens not to be the case.'

'Actually, I believe you.' The shuttle's airframe was flexing around them, morphing to a low-altitude profile with wide, bat-like wings. 'I was just hoping you might have some clue as to why Galiana keeps wasting valuable lives on pointless escape attempts.'

Voi shrugged. 'Maybe to her the lives aren't anywhere near as valuable as you'd like to think.'

'Do you honestly believe that?'

'I'm not sure we can even begin to guess the thinking of a true hive-mind society, Clavain. Even from a Demarchist standpoint.'

There was a chirp from the console: Galiana signalling them. Clavain opened the channel allocated for Coalition–Conjoiner diplomacy.

'Nevil Clavain?' he heard.

'Yes.' He tried to sound as calm as possible. 'I'm with Sandra Voi. We're ready to land as soon as you show us where.'

'Okay,' Galiana said. 'Vector your ship towards the westerly rim wall. And please, be careful.'

'Thank you. Any particular reason for the caution?'

'Just be quick about it, Nevil.'

They banked over the nest, shedding height until they were skimming only a few tens of metres above the weatherworn Martian surface. A wide rectangular door had opened in the concrete dyke revealing a hangar bay aglow with yellow lights.

'That must be where Galiana launches her shuttles from,' Clavain whispered. 'We always thought there had to be some kind of opening on the western side of the rim, but we never had a good view of it before.'

'Which still doesn't tell us why she does it,' Voi said.

The console chirped again – the link poor even though they were so close. 'Nose up,' Galiana said. 'You're too low and slow. Get some altitude or the worms will lock on to you.'

'You're telling me there are worms here?' Clavain said.

'I thought you were the worm expert, Nevil.'

He nosed the shuttle up, but fractionally too late. Ahead of them something coiled out of the ground with lightning speed, metallic jaws opening in its blunt, armoured head. He recognised the type immediately: Ouroborus class. Worms of this form still infested a hundred niches across the system. Not quite as smart as the type infesting Phobos, but still adequately dangerous.

'Shit,' Voi said, her veneer of Demarchist cool cracking for an instant.

'You said it,' Clavain answered.

The Ouroborus passed underneath them and then there was a spine-jarring series of bumps as the jaws tore into the shuttle's belly. Clavain felt the shuttle lurch down sickeningly; no longer a flying thing but an exercise in ballistics. The cool, minimalist turquoise interior shifted liquidly into an emergency configuration, damage read-outs competing for attention with weapons-status options. Their seats ballooned around them.

'Hold on,' he said. 'We're going down.'

Voi's calm returned. 'Do you think we can reach the rim in time?'

'Not a cat in hell's chance.' He wrestled with the controls all the same, but it was no good. The ground was coming up fast and hard. 'I wish Galiana had warned us a bit sooner—'

'I think she thought we already knew.'

They hit. The impact was harder than Clavain had been expecting, but the shuttle stayed in one piece and the seat cushioned him from the worst of it. They skidded for a few metres and then nosed up against a sandbank. Through the window Clavain saw the white worm racing towards them with undulating waves of its segmented robot body.

'I think we're finished,' Voi said.

'Not quite,' Clavain said. 'You're not going to like this, but . . .' Biting his tongue, he brought the shuttle's hidden weapons online. An aiming scope plunged down from the ceiling; he brought his eyes to it and locked crosshairs onto the Ouroborus. Just like old times . . .

'Damn you,' Voi said. 'This was meant to be an unarmed mission!'

'You're welcome to lodge a formal complaint.'

Clavain fired, the hull shaking from the recoil. Through the side window they watched the white worm blow apart into stubby segments. The parts wriggled beneath the dust.

'Good shooting,' Voi said, almost grudgingly. 'Is it dead?'

'For now,' Clavain said. 'It'll take several hours for the segments to fuse back into a functional worm.'

'Good,' Voi said, pushing herself out of her seat. 'But there will be a formal complaint, take my word.'

'Maybe you'd rather the worm had eaten us?'

'I just hate duplicity, Clavain.'

He tried the radio again. 'Galiana? We're down – the ship's history, but we're both unharmed.'

'Thank God.' Old verbal mannerisms died hard, even amongst the Conjoined. 'But you can't stay where you are. There are more worms in the area. Do you think you can make it overland to the nest?'

'It's only two hundred metres,' Voi said. 'It shouldn't be a problem.'

Two hundred metres, yes, Clavain thought – but two hundred metres across treacherous, potholed ground riddled with enough soft depressions to hide a dozen worms. And then they would have to climb up the rim's side to reach the entrance to the hangar bay – ten or fifteen metres above the soil, at least.

'Let's hope it isn't,' Clavain said.

He unbuckled, feeling light-headed as he stood for the first time in Martian gravity. He had adapted entirely too well to the one gee of the Deimos ring, constructed for the comfort of Earthside tacticians. He went to the emergency locker and found a mask, which slithered eagerly across his face; another for Voi. They plugged in air-tanks and went to the shuttle's door. This time when it sphinctered open there was a glistening membrane stretched across the doorway, a recently licensed item of Demarchist technology. Clavain pushed through the membrane and the stuff enveloped him with a wet, sucking sound. By the time he hit the dirt, the membrane had hardened itself around his soles and had begun to contour itself around his body, forming ribs and accordioned joints while remaining transparent.

Voi exited behind him, gaining her own m-suit.

They loped away from the crashed shuttle, towards the dyke. The worms would be locking on to their seismic patterns already, if there were any nearby. They might be more interested in the shuttle for now, but they couldn't count on it. Clavain knew the behaviour of worms intimately, knew the major routines that drove them; but that expertise did not guarantee his survival. It had almost failed him in Phobos.

The mask felt clammy against his face. The air at the base of the Great Wall was technically breathable even now, but there was no point in taking chances when speed was of the essence. His feet scuffed through the topsoil, and while he felt as if he was crossing ground, the dyke obstinately refused to come any closer. It was larger than it had looked from the crash site; the distance further.

'Another worm,' Voi said.

White coils erupted through sand to the west. The Ouroborus was making undulating progress towards them, zigzagging with predatory calm, knowing that it could afford to take its time. In the tunnels of Phobos, they had never had the luxury of knowing when a worm was close. They struck from ambush, quick as pythons.

'Run,' Clavain said.

Dark figures appeared in the opening high in the rim wall. A rope ladder unfurled down the side of the structure. Clavain, making for the base of it, made no effort to quieten his footfalls. He knew that the worm almost certainly had a lock on him by now.

He looked back.

The worm paused by the downed shuttle, then smashed its diamond-jawed head into the ship, impaling the hull on its body.

The worm reared up, wearing the ship like a garland. Then it shivered and the ship flew apart like a rotten carcass. The worm returned its attention to Clavain and Voi. Like a sidewinder, it pulled its thirty-metre-long body from the sand and rolled towards them on wheeling coils.

Clavain reached the base of the ladder.

Once, he could have ascended the ladder with his arms alone, in one gee, but now the ladder felt alive beneath his feet. He began to climb, then realised that the ground was dropping away much faster than he was passing rungs. The Conjoiners were hauling him aloft.

He looked back in time to see Voi stumble.

'Sandra! No!'

She made to stand up, but it was too late by then. As the worm descended on her, Clavain could do nothing but turn his gaze away and pray for her death to be quick. If it had to be meaningless, he thought, at least let it be swift.

Then he started thinking about his own survival. 'Faster!' he shouted, but the mask reduced his voice to a panicked muffle. He had forgotten to assign the ship's radio frequency to the suit.

The worm thrashed against the base of the wall, then began to rear up, its maw opening beneath him: a diamond-ringed orifice like the drill of a tunnelling machine. Then something eye-hurtingly bright cut into the worm's hide. Craning his neck, Clavain saw a group of Conjoiners leaning over the lip of the opening, aiming guns downward. The worm writhed in intense robotic irritation. Across the sand, he could see the coils of other worms coming closer. There must have been dozens ringing the nest. No wonder Galiana's people had made so few attempts to leave by land.

They had hauled him within ten metres of safety. The injured worm showed cybernetic workings where its hide had been flensed away by weapons impacts. Enraged, it flung itself against the rim wall, chipping off scabs of concrete the size of boulders.

Clavain felt the vibration of each impact through the wall as he was dragged upwards.

The worm hit again and the wall shook more violently than before. To his horror, Clavain watched one of the Conjoiners lose his footing and tumble over the edge of the rim towards him. Time oozed to a crawl. The falling man was almost upon him. Without thinking, Clavain hugged closer to the wall, locking his limbs around the ladder. Suddenly, he had seized the man by the arm. Even in Martian gravity, even allowing for the Conjoiner's willowy build, the impact almost sent both of them careering towards the Ouroborus. Clavain felt his bones pop out of location, tearing at gristle, but he managed to keep his grip on both the Conjoiner and the ladder.

Conjoiners breathed the air at the base of the Wall without difficulty. The man wore only lightweight clothes, grey silk pyjamas belted at the waist. With his sunken cheeks and bald skull, the man's Martian physique lent him a cadaverous look. Yet somehow he had managed not to drop his gun, still holding it in his other hand.

'Let me go,' the man said.

Below, the worm inched higher despite the harm the Conjoiners had inflicted on it. 'No,' Clavain said, through clenched teeth and the distorting membrane of his mask. 'I'm not letting you go.'

'You've no option.' The man's voice was placid. 'They can't haul both of us up fast enough, Clavain.'

Clavain looked into the Conjoiner's face, trying to judge the man's age. Thirty, perhaps – maybe not even that, since his cadaverous visage probably made him appear older than he really was. Clavain was easily twice his age; had surely lived a richer life; had comfortably cheated death on three or four previous occasions.

'I'm the one who should die, not you.'

'No,' the Conjoiner said. 'They'd find a way to blame your death on us. They'd make it a pretext for war.' Without any fuss, the man pointed the gun at his own head and blew his brains out.

As much in shock as recognition that the man's life was no longer his to save, Clavain released his grip. The dead man tumbled down the rim wall, into the mouth of the worm that had just killed Sandra Voi.

Numb, Clavain allowed himself to be pulled to safety.

When the armoured door to the hangar was shut, the Conjoiners attacked his m-suit with enzymic sprays. The sprays digested the fabric of the m-suit in seconds, leaving Clavain wheezing in a pool of slime. Then a pair of Conjoiners helped him unsteadily to his feet and waited patiently while he caught his breath through the mask. Through tears of exhaustion he saw that the hangar was racked full of half-assembled spacecraft: skeletal geodesic shark-shapes designed to punch out of an atmosphere, fast.

'Sandra Voi is dead,' he said, removing the mask to speak.

There was no way the Conjoiners could not have seen that for themselves, but it felt inhuman not to acknowledge what had happened.

'I know,' Galiana said. 'But at least you survived.'

He thought of the man falling into the Ouroborus. 'I'm sorry about your . . .' But then he trailed off, because for all his depth of knowledge concerning the Conjoiners, he had no idea what the appropriate term was.

'You placed your life in danger trying to save him.'

'He didn't have to die.'

Galiana nodded sagely. 'No; in all likelihood he didn't. But the risk to you was too great. You heard what he said – your death would be made to appear our fault; justification for a pre-emptive strike against our nest. Even the Demarchists would turn against us if we were seen to murder a diplomat.'

Taking another suck from the mask, he looked into her face. He had spoken to her over low-bandwidth video-links, but only in person was it obvious that Galiana had hardly aged in fifteen years. A decade and a half of habitual expression should have engraved existing lines deeper into her face – but Conjoiners were not known for their facial expression. Galiana had seen little sunlight in the intervening time, cooped up there in the nest, and Martian gravity was much kinder to bone structure than the one gee of Deimos. She still had the cruel beauty he remembered from his time as a prisoner. The only real evidence of ageing lay in the filaments of grey threading her hair; raven-black when she had been his captor.

'Why didn't you warn us about the worms?'

'Warn you?' For the first time something like doubt crossed her face, but it was only fleeting. 'We assumed you were fully aware of the Ouroborus infestation. Those worms have been dormant – waiting – for years, but they've always been there. It was only when I saw how low your approach was that I realised—'

'That we might not have known?'

Worms were area-denial devices; autonomous prey-seeking mines. The war had left many pockets of the solar system still riddled with active worms. The machines were intelligent, in a one-dimensional way. Nobody ever admitted to deploying them and it was usually impossible to convince them that the war was over and that they should quietly deactivate.

'After what happened to you in Phobos,' Galiana said, 'I assumed there was nothing you needed to be taught about worms.'

He never liked thinking about Phobos: the pain was still too deeply engraved. But if it had not been for the injuries he had sustained there he would never have been sent to Deimos to recuperate; would never have been recruited into his brother's intelligence wing to study the Conjoiners. Out of that phase of deep immersion in everything concerning the enemy had come his peacetime role as negotiator – and now diplomat – on the eve of another war. Everything was circular, ultimately. And now

Phobos was central to his thinking because he saw it as a way out of the impasse – maybe the last chance for peace. But it was too soon to put his idea to Galiana. He was not even sure the mission could still continue, after what had happened.

'We're safe now, I take it?'

'Yes; we can repair the damage to the dyke. Mostly, we can ignore their presence.'

'We should have been warned. Look, I need to talk to my brother.'

'Warren? Of course. It's easily arranged.'

They walked out of the hangar, away from the half-assembled ships. Somewhere deeper in the nest, Clavain knew, was a factory where the components for the ships were made, mined out of Mars or winnowed from the fabric of the nest. The Conjoiners managed to launch one every six weeks or so; had been doing so for six months. Not one of the ships had ever managed to escape the Martian atmosphere before being shot down . . . but sooner or later he would have to ask Galiana why she persisted with this provocative folly.

Now, though, was not the time – even if, by Warren's estimate, he only had three days before Galiana's next provocation.

The air elsewhere in the nest was thicker and warmer than in the hangar, which meant he could dispense with the mask. Galiana took him down a short, grey-walled, metallic corridor that ended in a circular room containing a console. He recognised the room from the times he had spoken to Galiana from Deimos. Galiana showed him how to use the system, then left him in privacy while he established a connection with Deimos.

Warren's face soon appeared on a screen, thick with pixels like an impressionist portrait. Conjoiners were only allowed to send kilobytes a second to other parts of the system. Much of that bandwidth was now being sucked up by this one video link.

'You've heard, I take it,' Clavain said.

Warren nodded, his face ashen. 'We had a pretty good view

from orbit, of course. Enough to see that Voi didn't make it. Poor woman. We were reasonably sure you'd survived, but it's good to have it confirmed.'

'Do you want me to abandon the mission?'

Warren's hesitation was more than just timelag. 'No . . . I thought about it, of course, and high command agrees with me. Voi's death was tragic – no escaping that. But she was only along as a neutral observer. If Galiana consents for you to stay, I suggest you do so.'

'But you still say I only have three days?'

'That's up to Galiana, isn't it? Have you learned much?'

'You must be kidding. I've seen shuttles ready for launch, that's all. I haven't raised the Phobos proposal yet, either. The timing wasn't exactly ideal, after what happened to Voi.'

'Yes. If only we'd known about that Ouroborus infestation.'

Clavain leaned closer to the screen. 'Yes. Why the hell didn't we? Galiana assumed that we would, and I don't blame her for that. We've had the nest under constant surveillance for fifteen years. Surely in all that time we'd have seen evidence of the worms?'

'You'd have thought so, wouldn't you?'

'Meaning what?'

'Meaning, maybe the worms weren't always there.'

Conscious that there could be nothing private about this conversation – but unwilling to drop the thread – Clavain said, 'You think the Conjoiners put them there to ambush us?'

'I'm saying we shouldn't disregard any possibility, no matter how unpalatable.'

'Galiana would never do something like that.'

'No, I wouldn't.' She had just stepped back into the room. 'And I'm disappointed that you'd even debate the possibility.'

Clavain terminated the link with Deimos. 'Eavesdropping's not a very nice habit, you know.'

'What did you expect me to do?'

'Show some trust? Or is that too much of a stretch?'

'I never had to trust you when you were my prisoner,' Galiana said. 'That made our relationship infinitely simpler. Our roles were completely defined.'

'And now? If you distrust me so completely, why did you ever agree to my visit? Plenty of other specialists could have come in my place. You could even have refused any dialogue.'

'Voi's people pressured us to allow your visit,' Galiana said. 'Just as they pressured your side into delaying hostilities a little longer.'

'Is that all?'

She hesitated slightly now. 'I . . . knew you.'

'Knew me? Is that how you sum up a year of imprisonment? What about the thousands of conversations we had; the times when we put aside our differences to talk about something other than the damned war? You kept me sane, Galiana. I've never forgotten that. It's why I've risked my life to come here to talk you out of another provocation.'

'It's completely different now.'

'Of course!' He forced himself not to shout. 'Of course it's different. But not fundamentally. We can still build on that bond of trust and find a way out of this crisis.'

'But does your side really want a way out of it?'

He did not answer her immediately, wary of what the truth might mean. 'I'm not sure. But I'm not sure you do either, or else you wouldn't keep pushing your luck.' Something snapped inside him and he asked the question he had meant to ask in a million better ways. 'Why do you keep doing it, Galiana? Why do you keep launching those ships when you know they'll be shot down as soon as they leave the nest?'

Her eyes locked on to his, unflinchingly. 'Because we can. Because sooner or later one will succeed.'

Clavain nodded. It was exactly the sort of thing he had feared she would say.

*

She led him through more grey-walled corridors, descending several levels deeper into the nest. Light poured from snaking strips embedded into the walls like arteries. It was possible that the snaking design was decorative, but Clavain thought it much more likely that the strips had simply grown that way, expressing biological algorithms. There was no evidence that the Conjoiners had attempted to enliven their surroundings, to render them in any sense human.

'It's a terrible risk you're running,' Clavain said.

'And the status quo is intolerable. I've every desire to avoid another war, but if it came to one, we'd at least have the chance to break these shackles.'

'If you didn't get exterminated first—'

'We'd avoid that. In any case, fear plays no part in our thinking. You saw the man accept his fate on the dyke, when he understood that your death would harm us more than his own. He altered his state of mind to one of total acceptance.'

'Fine. That makes it all right, then.'

She halted. They were alone in one of the snakingly lit corridors; he had seen no other Conjoiners since the hangar. 'It's not that we regard individual lives as worthless, any more than you would willingly sacrifice a limb. But now that we're part of something larger—'

'Transenlightenment, you mean?'

It was the Conjoiners' term for the state of neural communion they shared, mediated by the machines swarming in their skulls. Whereas Demarchists used implants to facilitate real-time democracy, Conjoiners used them to share sensory data, memories – even conscious thought itself. That was what had precipitated the war. Back in 2190, half of humanity had been hooked into the system-wide data nets via neural implants. Then the Conjoiner experiments had exceeded some threshold, unleashing a transforming virus into the nets. Implants had begun to change, infecting millions of minds with the templates of Conjoiner thought.

Instantly the infected had become the enemy. Earth and the other inner planets had always been more conservative, preferring to access the nets via traditional media.

Once they saw communities on Mars and in the asteroid belts fall prey to the Conjoiner phenomenon, the Coalition powers hurriedly pooled their resources to prevent it from spreading to their own states. The Demarchists, out around the gas giants, had managed to get firewalls up before many of their habitats were lost. They had chosen neutrality while the Coalition tried to contain – some said sterilise – zones of Conjoiner takeover. Within three years – after some of the bloodiest battles in human experience – the Conjoiners had been pushed back to a clutch of hideaways dotted around the system. Yet all along they professed a kind of puzzled bemusement that their spread was being resisted. After all, no one who had been assimilated seemed to regret it. Quite the contrary. The few prisoners whom the Conjoiners had reluctantly returned to their pre-infection state had sought every means to re-enter the fold. Some had even chosen suicide rather than be denied Transenlightenment. Like acolytes given a vision of heaven, they devoted their entire waking existence to the search for another glimpse.

'Transenlightenment blurs our sense of self,' Galiana said. 'When the man elected to die, the sacrifice was not absolute for him. He understood that much of what he was had already achieved preservation amongst the rest of us.'

'But he was just one man. What about the hundred lives you've thrown away with your escape attempts? We know – we've counted the bodies.'

'Replacements can always be cloned.'

Clavain hoped that he hid his disgust satisfactorily. Amongst his people, the very notion of cloning was an unspeakable atrocity, redolent with horror. To Galiana it would be just another technique in her arsenal. 'But you don't clone, do you? And you're losing people. We thought there would be nine hundred of you in this nest, but that was a gross overestimate, wasn't it?'

'You haven't seen much of it yet,' Galiana said.

'No, but this place smells deserted. You can't hide absence, Galiana. I bet there aren't more than a hundred of you left here.'

'You're wrong,' Galiana said. 'We have cloning technology, but we've hardly ever used it. What would be the point? We don't aspire to genetic unity, no matter what your propagandists think. The pursuit of optima leads only to local minima. We honour our errors. We actively seek persistent disequilibrium.'

'Right.' The last thing he needed now was a dose of Conjoiner rhetoric. 'So where the hell is everyone?'

In a while he had part of the answer, if not the whole of it. At the end of the maze of corridors – deep under the Martian surface now – Galiana brought him to a nursery.

It was shockingly unlike his expectations. Not only did it not match what he had imagined from the vantage point of Deimos, but it jarred against his predictions based on what he had seen so far of the nest. In Deimos, he had assumed a Conjoiner nursery would be a place of grim medical efficiency: all gleaming machines with babies plugged in like peripherals, like a monstrously productive doll factory. Within the nest, he had revised his model to allow for the depleted numbers of Conjoiners. If there was a nursery, it was obviously not very productive. Fewer babies, then – but still a vision of hulking grey machines, bathed in snaking light.

The nursery was nothing like that.

The huge room Galiana showed him was almost painfully bright and cheerful: a child's fantasy of friendly shapes and primary colours. The walls and ceiling projected a holographic sky: infinite blue and billowing clouds of heavenly white. The floor was an undulating mat of synthetic grass forming hillocks and meadows. There were banks of flowers and forests of bonsai trees. There were robot animals: fabulous birds and rabbits just slightly too anthropomorphic to fool Clavain. They were like the animals in children's books: big-eyed and happy-looking. Toys were scattered on the grass.

And there were children. They numbered between forty and fifty, spanning by his estimate ages from a few months to six or seven standard years. Some were crawling amongst the rabbits; other, older children were gathered around tree stumps whose sheared-off surfaces flickered rapidly with images, underlighting their faces. They were talking amongst themselves, giggling or singing. He counted perhaps half a dozen adult Conjoiners kneeling with the children. The children's clothes were a headache of bright, clashing colours and patterns. The Conjoiners crouched amongst them like ravens. Yet the children looked at ease with them, listening attentively when the adults had something to say.

'This isn't what you thought it would be like, is it?'

'No . . . not at all.' There was no point lying to her. 'We thought you'd raise your young in a simplified version of the machine-generated environment you experience.'

'In the early days, that's more or less what we did.' Subtly, Galiana's tone of voice had changed. 'Do you know why chimpanzees are less intelligent than humans?'

He blinked at the change of tack. 'I don't know – are their brains smaller?'

'Yes – but a dolphin's brain is larger, and they're scarcely more intelligent than dogs.' Galiana stooped next to a vacant tree stump. Without apparently doing anything, she made a diagram of mammal brain anatomies appear on the trunk's upper surface, then sketched her finger across the relevant parts. 'It's not overall brain volume that counts so much as the developmental history. The difference in brain volume between a neonatal chimp and an adult is only about twenty per cent. By the time the chimp receives any data from beyond the womb, there's almost no plasticity left to use. Similarly, dolphins are born with almost their complete repertoire of adult behaviour already hardwired.

A human brain, on the other hand, keeps growing through years of learning. We inverted that thinking. If data received during post-natal growth was so crucial to intelligence, perhaps we could boost our intelligence even further by intervening during the earliest phases of brain development.'

'In the womb?'

'Yes.' Now she made the tree stump show a human embryo running through cycles of cell division until the faint fold of a rudimentary spinal nerve began to form, nubbed with the tiniest of emergent minds. Droves of subcellular machines swarmed in, invading the nascent nervous system. Then the embryo's development slammed forward, until Clavain was looking at an unborn human baby.

'What happened?'

'It was a grave error,' Galiana said. 'Instead of enhancing normal neural development, we impaired it terribly. All we ended up with were various manifestations of savant syndrome.'

Clavain looked around him. 'So you let these kids develop normally?'

'More or less. There's no family structure, of course, but then again there are plenty of human and primate societies where the family is less important in child development than the cohort group. So far we haven't seen any pathologies.'

Clavain watched as one of the older children was escorted out of the grassy room, through a door in the sky. When the Conjoiner reached the door the child hesitated, tugging against the man's gentle insistence. The child looked back for a moment, then followed the man through the gap.

'Where's that child going?'

'To the next stage of its development.'

Clavain wondered what the chances were of him seeing the nursery just as one of the children was being promoted. Small, he judged – unless there was a crash programme to rush as many of them through as quickly as possible. As he thought about this,

Galiana took him into another part of the nursery. While this room was smaller and dourer, it was still more colourful than any other part of the nest he had seen before the grassy room. The walls were a mosaic of crowded, intermingling displays, teeming with moving images and rapidly scrolling text. He saw a herd of zebra stampeding through the core of a neutron star. Elsewhere an octopus squirted ink at the face of a twentieth-century despot. Other display facets rose from the floor like Japanese paper screens, flooded with data. Children – up to early teenagers – sat on soft black toadstools next to the screens in little groups, debating.

A few musical instruments lay around unused: holoclaviers and air-guitars. Some of the children had grey bands around their eyes and were poking their fingers through the interstices of abstract structures, exploring the dragon-infested waters of mathematical space. Clavain could see what they were manipulating on the flat screens: shapes that made his head hurt even in two dimensions.

'They're nearly there,' Clavain said. 'The machines are outside their heads, but not for long. When does it happen?'

'Soon; very soon.'

'You're rushing them, aren't you? Trying to get as many children Conjoined as you can. What are you planning?'

'Something . . . has arisen, that's all. The timing of your arrival is either very bad or very fortunate, depending on one's point of view.' Before he could query this, Galiana added, 'Clavain, I want you to meet someone.'

'Who?'

'Someone very precious to us.'

She took him through a series of childproof doors until they reached a small circular room. The walls and ceiling were veined grey; tranquil after the last place. A child sat cross-legged on the floor in the middle of the room. Clavain estimated the girl's age as ten standard years – perhaps fractionally older. But she did not respond to Clavain's presence in any way an adult, or even a normal child, would have. She just kept on doing the thing she had been doing when they stepped inside, as if they were not really present at all. It was not particularly clear what she was doing. Her hands moved before her in slow, precise gestures. It was as if she were playing a holoclavier or working a phantom puppet show. Now and then she would pivot around until she was facing another direction and carry on making the hand movements.

'Her name's Felka,' Galiana said.

'Hello, Felka . . .' Clavain waited for a response, but none came. 'I can see there's something wrong with her.'

'She's one of the savants. Felka developed with machines in her head. She was the last to be born before we realised our failure.'

Something about Felka disturbed him. Perhaps it was the way she carried on regardless, engrossed in an activity to which she appeared to attribute the utmost significance, yet which had to be without any sane purpose.

'She doesn't seem aware of us.'

'Her deficits are severe,' Galiana said. 'She has no interest in other human beings. She has prosopagnosia: the inability to distinguish faces. We all look alike to her. Can you imagine something stranger than that?'

He tried, and failed. Life from Felka's viewpoint must have been a nightmarish thing, surrounded by identical clones whose inner lives she could not begin to grasp. No wonder she was so engrossed in her game.

'Why is she so precious to you?' Clavain asked, not really wanting to know the answer.

'She's keeping us alive,' Galiana said.

Of course, he asked Galiana what she meant by that. Galiana's only response was to tell him that he was not yet ready to be shown the answer.

'And what exactly would it take for me to reach that stage?'

'A simple procedure.'

Oh yes, he understood that part well enough. Just a few machines in the right parts of his brain and the truth could be his. Politely, doing his best to mask his distaste, Clavain declined. Fortunately, Galiana did not press the point, for the time had arrived for the meeting he had been promised before his arrival on Mars.

He watched a subset of the nest file into the conference room. Galiana was their leader only inasmuch as she had founded the lab from which the original experiment had sprung and was accorded some respect deriving from seniority. She was also the most obvious spokesperson amongst them. But they all had areas of expertise that could not easily be shared amongst other Conjoined, which distinguished them from the hive mind of identical clones that still figured in the Coalition's propaganda. If the nest was in any way like an ant colony, then it was an ant colony in which every ant fulfilled a role distinct from all the others. Naturally, no individual could be solely entrusted with a particular skill essential to the nest – that would have been dangerous over-specialisation – but neither had individuality been completely subsumed into the group mind.

The conference room must have dated back to the days when the nest was a research outpost, or even earlier, when it was some kind of mining base in the early 2100s. It was much too big for the dour handful of Conjoiners who stood around the main table. Tactical read-outs around the table showed the build-up of strike forces above the Martian exclusion zone; probable drop trajectories for ground-force deployment.

'Nevil Clavain,' Galiana said, introducing him to the others. Everyone sat down. 'I'm just sorry that Sandra Voi can't be with us now. We all feel the tragedy of her death. But perhaps out of this terrible event we can find some common ground. Nevil – before you came here you told us you had a proposal for a peaceful resolution to the crisis.'

'I'd really like to hear it,' one of the others murmured audibly.

Clavain's throat was dry. Diplomatically, this was quicksand. 'My proposal concerns Phobos—'

'Go on,' Galiana invited.

'I was injured there,' he said. 'Very badly. Our attempt to clean out the worm infestation failed and I lost some good friends. That makes it personal between me and the worms. But I'd accept anyone's help to finish them off.'

Galiana glanced quickly at her compatriots before answering. 'A joint assault operation?'

'It could work.'

'Yes . . .' Galiana looked lost, momentarily. 'I suppose it could be a way out of the impasse. Our own attempt failed, too – and the Interdiction's stopped us from trying again.' Again, she seemed to fall into reverie. 'But who would really benefit from the flushing out of Phobos? We'd still be quarantined here.'

Clavain leaned forward. 'A cooperative gesture might be exactly the thing to lead to a relaxation in the terms of the Interdiction. But don't think of it that way. Think instead of reducing the current threat from the worms.'

'Threat?'

Clavain nodded. 'It's possible that you haven't noticed.' He leaned further forward, elbows on the table. 'We're concerned about the Phobos worms. They've begun altering the moon's orbit. The shift is tiny at the moment, but too large to be anything other than deliberate.'

Galiana looked away from him for an instant, as if weighing her options, then said, 'We were aware of this, but you weren't to know that.'

Was that an indication of gratitude from Galiana?

He had assumed the worms' activity could not have escaped Galiana. 'We've seen odd behaviour from other worm infestations across the system, things that begin to look like emergent intelligence, but never anything this purposeful. This infestation must have come from a batch with some subroutines we never even guessed existed. Do you have any ideas about what they might be up to?'

Again, there was the briefest of hesitations, as if she was communing with her compatriots for the right response. Then she nodded towards a male Conjoiner sitting opposite her, Clavain guessing that the gesture was entirely for his benefit. His hair was black and curly, his face as smooth and untroubled by expression as Galiana's, with something of the same beautifully symmetrical bone structure.

'This is Remontoire,' said Galiana. 'He's our specialist on the Phobos situation.'

Remontoire nodded politely. 'In answer to your question, we currently have no viable theories as to what they're doing, but we do know one thing: they're raising the apocentre of the moon's orbit.' Apocentre, Clavain knew, was the Martian equivalent of apogee for an object orbiting Earth: the point of highest altitude in an elliptical orbit. Remontoire continued, his voice as preternaturally calm as a parent reading slowly to a child, 'The natural orbit of Phobos is actually inside the Roche limit for a gravitationally bound moon; Phobos is raising a tidal bulge on Mars but, because of friction, the bulge can't quite keep up with Phobos. It's causing Phobos to spiral slowly closer to Mars, by about two metres a century. In a few tens of millions of years, what's left of the moon will crash into Mars.'

'You think the worms are elevating the orbit to avoid a cataclysm so far in the future?'

'I don't know,' Remontoire said. 'I suppose the orbital alterations could also be a by-product of some less meaningful worm activity.'

'I agree,' Clavain said. 'But the danger remains. If the worms can elevate the moon's apocentre – even accidentally – we can assume they also have the means to lower its pericentre. They could drop

Phobos on top of your nest. Does that scare you sufficiently that you'd consider cooperation with the Coalition?'

Galiana steepled her fingers before her face; a human gesture of deep concentration that her time as a Conjoiner had not quite eroded. Clavain could almost feel the web of thought looming the room: ghostly strands of cognition reaching between each Conjoiner at the table, and beyond into the nest proper.

'A winning team, is that your idea?' she said at length.

'It's got to be better than war,' Clavain said. 'Hasn't it?'

Galiana might have been about to answer him when her face grew troubled. Clavain saw the wave of discomposure sweep over the others almost simultaneously. Something told him that it was nothing to do with his proposal.

Around the table, half the display facets switched automatically over to another channel. The face that Clavain was looking at was much like his own, except that the face on the screen was missing an eye. It was his brother. Warren was overlaid with the official insignia of the Coalition and a dozen system-wide media cartels.

He was in the middle of a speech. '. . . express my shock,' Warren said. 'Or, for that matter, my outrage. It's not just that they've murdered a valued colleague and a deeply experienced member of my team. They've murdered my brother.'

Clavain felt the deepest of chills. 'What is this?'

'A live transmission from Deimos,' Galiana breathed. 'It's going out to all the nets, right out to the trans-Pluto habitats.'

'What they did was an act of unspeakable treachery,' Warren said. 'Nothing less than the premeditated, cold-blooded murder of a peace envoy.' And then a video clip sprang up to replace Warren. The image must have been snapped from Deimos or one of the Interdiction satellites. It showed Clavain's shuttle, lying in the dust close to the dyke. He watched the Ouroborus destroy the shuttle, then saw the image zoom in on himself and Voi, running for sanctuary. The Ouroborus took Voi. But this time there was no ladder lowered down for him. Instead, he saw weapon beams scythe out from the nest towards him, knocking him to the ground. Horribly wounded, he tried to get up, to crawl a few centimetres nearer to his tormentors, but the worm was already upon him.

He watched himself get eaten.

Warren was back again. 'The worms around the nest were a Conjoiner trap. My brother's death must have been planned days – maybe even weeks – in advance.' His face was a granite-like mask of military composure. 'There can only be one outcome from such an act – something the Conjoiners must have well understood. For months they've been goading us towards hostile action.' He paused, then nodded at an unseen audience. 'Well, now they're going to get it. In fact, our response has already commenced.'

'Dear God, no,' Clavain said, but the evidence was everywhere now: all around the table he could see the updating orbital spread of the Coalition's dropships, knifing down towards Mars.

'I think it's war,' Galiana said.

Conjoiners stormed onto the roof of the nest, taking up defensive positions around the domes and the dyke's edge. Most of them carried the same guns they had used against the Ouroborus. Smaller numbers were setting up automatic cannon on tripods. One or two were manhandling large anti-assault weapons into position. Most of it was war surplus. Fifteen years ago the Conjoiners had avoided extinction by deploying weapons of awesome ferocity – but those ship-to-ship armaments were simply too destructive to use against a nearby foe. Now it would be more visceral, closer to the primal templates of combat, and none of what the Conjoiners were marshalling would be much use against the kind of assault Warren had prepared, Clavain knew. They could slow an attack, but not much more than that.

Galiana had given him another breather mask, made him don lightweight chameleoflage armour and then forced him to carry one of the smaller guns. The gun felt alien in his hands;

something he had never expected to carry again. The only possible justification for carrying it was to use it against his brother's forces – against his own side.

Could he do that?

It was clear that Warren had betrayed him; he had surely been aware of the worms around the nest. So his brother was capable not just of contempt, but of treacherous murder. For the first time, Clavain felt genuine hatred for Warren. He must have hoped that the worms would destroy the shuttle completely and kill Clavain and Voi in the process. It must have pained him to see Clavain make it to the dyke . . . pained him even more when Clavain called to talk about the tragedy. But Warren's larger plan had not been affected. The diplomatic link between the nest and Deimos was secure – even the Demarchists had no immediate access to it. So Clavain's call from the surface could be quietly ignored; spysat imagery doctored to make it appear as if he had never reached the dyke . . . had in fact been repelled by Conjoiner treachery. Inevitably the Demarchists would unravel the deception given time . . . but if Warren's plan succeeded, they would all be embroiled in war long before then. That, thought Clavain, was all that Warren had ever wanted.

Two brothers, Clavain thought. In many ways so alike. Both had embraced war once, but like a fickle lover Clavain had wearied of its glories. He had not even been injured as severely as Warren . . . but perhaps that was the point, too. Warren needed another war to avenge what one had stolen from him.

Clavain despised and pitied him in equal measure.

He searched for the safety clip on the gun. The rifle, now that he studied it more closely, was not all that different from those he had used during the war. The read-out said the ammo-cell was fully charged.

He looked into the sky.

The attack wave broke orbit hard and steep above the Wall: five hundred fireballs screeching towards the nest. The insertion scorched centimetres of ablative armour from most of the ships; fried a few others that came in just fractionally too hard. Clavain knew exactly what was happening: he had studied possible attack scenarios for years, the range of outcomes burned indelibly into his memory.

The anti-assault guns were already working – locking on to the plasma trails as they flowered overhead, swinging down to find the tiny spark of heat at the head, computing refraction paths for laser pulses, spitting death into the sky. The unlucky ships flared a white that hurt the back of the eye and rained down in a billion dulling sparks. A dozen – then a dozen more. Maybe fifty in total before the guns could no longer acquire targets. It was nowhere near enough. Clavain's memory of the simulations told him that at least four hundred units of the attack wave would survive both re-entry and the Conjoiner's heavy defences.

Nothing that Galiana could do would make any difference.

And that had always been the paradox. Galiana was capable of running the same simulations. She must always have known that her provocations would bring down something she could never hope to defeat.

Something that was always going to destroy her.

The surviving members of the wave were levelling out now, commencing long, ground-hugging runs from all directions. Cocooned in their dropships, the soldiers would be suffering punishing gee-loads, but it was nothing they were not engineered to withstand: their cardiovascular systems had been augmented with the sort of non-neural implants the Coalition grudgingly tolerated.

The first of the wave came arcing in at supersonic speeds. All around, worms struggled to snatch them out of the sky, but mostly they were too slow to catch the dropships. Galiana's people manned their cannon positions and did their best to fend off as many as they could. Clavain clutched his gun, not firing yet.

34

Best to save his ammo-cell power for a target he stood a chance of injuring.

Above, the first dropships made hairpin turns, nosing suicidally down towards the nest. Then they fractured cleanly apart, revealing falling pilots clad in bulbous armour. Just before the moment of impact, each pilot's armour exploded into a mass of black shock-absorbing balloons, looking something like a blackberry, bouncing across the nest before the balloons deflated just as swiftly to leave the pilot standing on the ground. By then the pilot – now properly a soldier – would have a comprehensive computer-generated map of the nest's nooks and crannies; enemy positions graphed in real-time from the down-looking spysats.

Clavain fell behind the curve of a dome before the nearest soldier got a lock on him. The firefight was beginning now. He had to hand it to Galiana's people – they were fighting like devils. And they were at least as well coordinated as the attackers. But their weapons and armour were simply inadequate. Chameleoflage was only truly effective against a solitary enemy, or a massed enemy moving in from a common direction. With Coalition forces surrounding him, Clavain's suit was going crazy trying to match every background, like a chameleon in a house of mirrors.

The sky overhead looked strange now – darkening purple. And the purple was spreading in a mist across the nest. Galiana had deployed some kind of chemical smokescreen: infrared and optically opaque, he guessed. It would occlude the spysats and might be primed to adhere only to enemy chameleoflage. That had never been in Warren's simulations. Galiana had just given herself the slightest of edges.

A soldier stepped out of the mist, the obscene darkness of a gun muzzle trained on Clavain. His chameleoflage armour was dappled with vivid purple patches, ruining its stealthiness. The man fired, but his discharge wasted itself against Clavain's armour. Clavain returned the compliment, dropping his compatriot. What he had done, he thought, was not technically treason. Not yet. All he had done was act in self-preservation.

The man was wounded, but not yet dead. Clavain stepped through the purple haze and knelt down beside the soldier. He tried not to look at the man's wound.

'Can you hear me?' he said. There was no answer from the man, but beneath his visor, Clavain thought he saw the man's lips shape a word. The man was just a kid – hardly old enough to remember much of the last war. 'There's something you have to know,' Clavain continued. 'Do you realise who I am?' He wondered how recognisable he was, under the breather mask. Then something made him relent. He could tell the man he was Nevil Clavain – but what would that achieve? The soldier would be dead in minutes; maybe sooner than that. Nothing would be served by the soldier knowing that the basis for his attack was a lie; that he would not in fact be laying down his life for a just cause. The universe could be spared a single callous act.

'Forget it,' Clavain said, turning away from his victim.

And then he moved deeper into the nest, to see who else he could kill before the odds took him.

But the odds never did.

'You were always were lucky,' Galiana said, leaning over him. They were somewhere underground again – deep in the nest. A medical area, by the look of things. He was on a bed, fully clothed apart from the outer layer of chameleoflage armour. The room was grey and kettle-shaped, ringed by a circular balcony.

'What happened?'

'You took a head wound, but you'll survive.'

He groped for the right question. 'What about Warren's attack?'

'We endured three waves. We took casualties, of course.'

Around the circumference of the balcony were thirty or so grey couches, slightly recessed into archways studded with grey medical equipment. They were all occupied. There were more

Conjoiners in this room than he had seen so far in one place. Some of them looked very close to death.

Clavain reached up and examined his head, gingerly. There was some dried blood on the scalp, matted with his hair, some numbness, but it could have been a lot worse. He felt normal – no memory drop-outs or aphasia. When he pushed himself up to sitting and tried to stand, his body obeyed his will with only a tinge of dizziness.

'Warren won't stop at just three waves, Galiana.'

'I know.' She paused. 'We know there'll be more.'

He walked to the railing on the inner side of the balcony and looked over the edge. He had expected to see something – some chunk of incomprehensible surgical equipment, perhaps – but the middle of the room was only an empty, smooth-walled, grey pit. He shivered. The air was colder than in any part of the nest he had visited so far, with a medicinal tang that reminded him of the convalescence ward on Deimos. What made him shiver even more was the realisation that some of the injured – some of the dead – were barely older than the children he had visited only hours ago. Perhaps some of them were those children, conscripted from the nursery since his visit, uploaded with fighting reflexes through their new implants.

'What are you going to do? You know you can't win. Warren lost only a tiny fraction of his available force in those waves. You look as if you've lost half your nest.'

'It's much worse than that,' Galiana said.

'What do you mean?'

'You're not quite ready yet. But I can show you in a moment.'

He felt colder than ever now. 'What do you mean, "not quite ready"?'

Galiana looked deeply into his eyes now. 'You suffered a serious head injury, Clavain. The entry wound was small, but the internal bleeding . . . it would have killed you, had we not intervened.' Before he could ask the inevitable question she answered it for him. 'We injected a small cluster of medichines into your head. They undid the damage very easily. But it seemed provident to allow them to grow.'

'You've put replicators in my head?'

'You needn't sound so horrified. They're already growing – spreading out and interfacing with your existing neural circuitry – but the total volume of glial mass they will consume is tiny: only a few cubic millimetres in total, across your entire brain.'

He wondered if she was calling his bluff. 'I don't feel anything.'

'You won't – not for a minute or so.' Now she pointed into the empty pit in the middle of the room. 'Stand here and look into the air.'

'There's nothing there.'

But as soon as he had spoken, he knew he was wrong. There was something in the pit. He blinked and directed his attention somewhere else, but when he returned his gaze to the pit, the thing he imagined he had seen – milky, spectral – was still there, and becoming sharper and brighter by the second. It was a three-dimensional structure, as complex as an exercise in protein-folding. A tangle of loops and connecting branches and nodes and tunnels, embedded in a ghostly red matrix.

Suddenly he saw it for what it was: a map of the nest, dug into Mars. Just as the Coalition had suspected, the base was far more extensive than the original structure, reaching deeper and further out than anyone had imagined. Clavain made a mental effort to retain some of what he was seeing in his mind, the intelligence-gathering reflex stronger than the conscious knowledge that he would never see Deimos again.

'The medichines in your brain have interfaced with your visual cortex,' Galiana said. 'That's the first step on the road to Trans-enlightenment. Now you're privy to the machine-generated imagery encoded by the fields through which we move – most of it, anyway.'

'Tell me this wasn't planned, Galiana. Tell me you weren't intending to put machines in me at the first opportunity.'

'No, I wasn't planning it. But nor was I going to let your phobias prevent me from saving your life.'

The image grew in complexity. Glowing nodes of light appeared in the tunnels, some moving slowly through the network.

'What are they?'

'You're seeing the locations of the Conjoiners,' Galiana said. 'Are there as many as you imagined?'

Clavain judged that there were no more than seventy lights in the whole complex now. He searched for a cluster that would identify the room in which he stood. There: twenty-odd bright lights, accompanied by one much fainter than the rest. Himself, of course. There were few people near the top of the nest – the attack must have collapsed half the tunnels, or maybe Galiana had deliberately sealed entrances herself.

'Where is everyone? Where are the children?'

'Most of the children are gone now.' She paused. 'You were right to guess that we were rushing them to Transenlightenment, Clavain.'

'Why?'

'Because it's the only way out of here.'

The image changed again. Now each of the bright lights was connected to another by a shimmering filament. The topology of the network was constantly shifting, like a pattern seen in a kaleidoscope. Occasionally, too swiftly for Clavain to be sure, it coalesced towards a mandala of elusive symmetry, only to dissolve into the flickering chaos of the ever-changing network. He studied Galiana's node and saw that – even as she was speaking to him – her mind was in constant rapport with the rest of the nest.

Now something very bright appeared in the middle of the image, like a tiny star, against which the shimmering network paled almost to invisibility. 'The network is abstracted now,' Galiana said. 'The bright light represents its totality: the unity of Transenlightenment. Watch.'

He watched. The bright light – as beautiful and alluring as anything Clavain had ever imagined – was extending a ray towards the isolated node that represented himself. The ray was extending itself through the map, coming closer by the second.

'The new structures in your mind are nearing maturity,' Galiana said. 'When the ray touches you, you will experience partial integration with the rest of us. Prepare yourself, Nevil.'

Her words were unnecessary. His fingers were already clenched sweating on the railing as the light inched closer and engulfed his node.

'I should hate you for this,' Clavain said.

'Why don't you? Hate's always the easier option.'

'Because . . .' Because it made no difference now. His old life was over. He reached out for Galiana, needing some anchor against what was about to hit him. Galiana squeezed his hand and an instant later he knew something of Transenlightenment. The experience was shocking; not because it was painful or fearful, but because it was profoundly and totally new. He was literally thinking in ways that had not been possible microseconds earlier.

Afterwards, when Clavain tried to imagine how he might describe it, he found that words were never going to be adequate for the task. And that was no surprise: evolution had shaped language to convey many concepts, but going from a single to a networked topology of self was not amongst them. But if he could not convey the core of the experience, he could at least skirt its essence with metaphor. It was like standing on the shore of an ocean, being engulfed by a wave taller than himself. For a moment he sought the surface; tried to keep the water from his lungs. But there happened not to be a surface. What had consumed him extended infinitely in all directions. He could only submit to it. Yet as the moments slipped by, it turned from something terrifying in its unfamiliarity to something he could begin to adapt to; something that even began in the tiniest way to feel comforting. Even then he glimpsed that it was only a shadow of what Galiana was experiencing every instant of her life.

'All right,' Galiana said. 'That's enough for now.'

The fullness of Transenlightenment retreated, like a fading vision of Godhead. What he was left with was purely sensory, lacking any direct rapport with the others. His state of mind came crashing back to normality.

'Are you all right, Nevil?'

'Yes . . .' His mouth was dry. 'Yes, I think so.'

'Look around you.'

He did.

The room had changed completely. So had everyone in it.

His head reeling, Clavain walked in light. The formerly grey walls oozed beguiling patterns, as if a dark forest had suddenly become enchanted. Information hung in veils in the air: icons and diagrams and numbers clustering around the beds of the injured, thinning out into the general space like fantastically delicate neon sculptures. As he walked towards the icons they darted out of his way, mocking him like schools of brilliant fish. Sometimes they seemed to sing, or tickle the back of his nose with half-familiar smells.

'You can perceive things now,' Galiana said, 'but none of it will mean much to you. You'd need years of education, or deeper neural machinery, for that – building cognitive layers. We read all this almost subliminally.'

Galiana was dressed differently now. He could still see the vague shape of her grey outfit, but layered around it were billowing skeins of light, unravelling at their edges into chains of Boolean logic. Icons danced in her hair like angels. He could see, faintly, the web of thought linking her with the other Conjoiners.

She was inhumanly beautiful.

'You said things were much worse,' Clavain said. 'Are you ready to show me now?'

She took him to see Felka again, passing on the way through deserted nursery rooms, populated now only by bewildered mechanical animals. Felka was the only child left in the nursery.

Clavain had been deeply disturbed by Felka when he had seen her before, but not for any reason he could easily express. Something about the purposefulness of her actions, performed with ferocious concentration, as if the fate of creation hung on the outcome of her game. Felka and her surroundings had not changed at all since his previous visit. The room was still austere to the point of oppressiveness. Felka looked the same. In every respect it was as if only an instant had passed since their first meeting; as if the onset of war and the assaults against the nest – the battle in which this was only an interlude – were only figments from someone else's troubling dream; nothing that need concern Felka in her devotion to the task at hand.

And the task awed Clavain.

Before, he had watched her make strange gestures in the empty air in front of her. Now the machines in his head revealed the purpose those gestures served. Around Felka – cordoning her like a barricade – was a ghostly representation of the Great Wall.

She was doing something to it.

It was not a scale representation, Clavain knew. The Wall looked much higher here in relation to its diameter. And the surface was not the nearly invisible membrane of the real thing, but something like etched glass. The etching was a filigree of lines and junctions, descending down to smaller and smaller scales in fractal steps until the blur of detail was too fine for his eyes to discriminate. It was shifting and altering colour, and Felka was responding to these alterations with what he now saw was frightening efficiency. It was as if the colour changes warned of some malignancy in part of the Wall, and by touching it – expressing some tactile code – Felka was able to restructure the etching to block and neutralise the malignancy before it spread.

'I don't understand,' Clavain said. 'I thought we destroyed the Wall, completely killed its systems.'

'You only ever injured it,' Galiana said, 'stopped it from growing, and from managing its own repair processes correctly . . . but you never truly killed it.'

Sandra Voi had guessed, Clavain realised. She had wondered how the Wall had survived this long.

Galiana told him the rest: how they had managed to establish control pathways to the Wall from the nest, fifteen years earlier – optical cables sunk deep below the worm zone. 'We stabilised the Wall's degradation with software running on dumb machines,' she said. 'But when Felka was born we found that she managed the task just as efficiently as the computers; in some ways better than they ever did. In fact, she seemed to thrive on it. It was as if in the Wall she found . . .' Galiana trailed off. 'I was going to say a friend.'

'Why don't you?'

'Because the Wall's just a machine. If Felka recognised kinship with it . . . what would that make her?'

'Someone lonely, that's all.' Clavain watched the girl's motions. 'She seems faster than before. Is that possible?'

'I told you things had deteriorated. She's having to work harder to hold the Wall together.'

'Warren must have attacked it.' Clavain said. 'The possibility of knocking down the Wall always figured in our contingency plans for another war. I just never thought it would happen so soon.' Then he looked at Felka. Maybe it was his imagination, but she seemed to be working even faster than when he had entered the room, not just since his last visit. 'How long do you think she can keep it together?'

'Not much longer,' Galiana said. 'As a matter of fact, I think she's already failing.'

It was true. Now that he looked closely at the ghost Wall, he saw that the upper edge was not the mathematically smooth ring it should have been: there were scores of tiny ragged bites eating down from the top. Felka's activities were increasingly directed to these opening cracks, instructing the crippled structure to divert energy and raw materials to these critical failure points. Clavain knew that the distant processes Felka directed were awesome. Within the Wall lay a lymphatic system whose peristaltic feed-pipes ranged in size from metres across to the submicroscopic, all flowing with myriad tiny repair machines. Felka chose where to send those machines, her hand gestures establishing pathways between damage points and the factories sunk into the Wall's ramparts that made the required types of machine. For more than a decade, Galiana said, Felka had kept the Wall from crumbling – but for most of that time her adversaries had been only natural decay and accidental damage. It was a different game now that the Wall had been attacked again. It was not one she could ever win.

Felka's movements became swifter, less fluid. Her face remained impassive, but in the quickening way that her eyes darted from point to point it was possible to read the first hints of panic. No surprise, either: the deepest cracks in the structure now reached a quarter of the way to the surface, and they were too wide to be repaired. The Wall was unzipping along those flaws. Cubic kilo-metres of atmosphere would be howling out through the open-ings. The loss of pressure would be immeasurably slow at first, for near the top the trapped cylinder of atmosphere was only frac-tionally thicker than the rest of the Martian atmosphere. But only at first . . .

'We have to get deeper,' Clavain said. 'Once the Wall goes, we won't have a chance in hell if we're anywhere near the surface. It'll be like the worst tornado in history.'

'What will your brother do? Will he nuke us?'

'No, I don't think so. He'll want to get hold of any technologies you've hidden away. He'll wait until the dust storms have died down, then he'll raid the nest with a hundred times as many troops as you've seen so far. You won't be able to resist, Galiana. If you're lucky you may just survive long enough to be taken prisoner.'

'There won't be any prisoners,' Galiana said.

'You're planning to die fighting?'

'No. And mass suicide doesn't figure in our plans either. Neither will be necessary. By the time your brother reaches here, there won't be anyone left in the nest.'

Clavain thought of the worms encircling the area; how small the chances were of reaching any kind of safety if it involved getting past them. 'Secret tunnels under the worm zone, is that it? I hope you're serious.'

'I'm deadly serious,' Galiana said. 'And yes, there is a secret tunnel. The other children have already gone through it now. But it doesn't lead under the worm zone.'

'Where, then?'

'Somewhere a lot further away.'

When they passed through the medical centre again it was empty, save for a few swan-necked robots patiently waiting for further casualties. They had left Felka behind tending the Wall, her hands a manic blur as she tried to slow the rate of collapse. Clavain had tried to make her come with them, but Galiana had told him he was wasting his time: that she would sooner die than be parted from the Wall.

'You don't understand,' Galiana said. 'You're placing too much humanity behind her eyes. Keeping the Wall alive is the single most important fact of her universe – more important than love, pain, death – anything you or I would consider definitively human.'

'Then what happens to her when the Wall dies?'

'Her life ends,' Galiana said.

Reluctantly he had left without her, the taste of shame bitter in his mouth. Rationally it made sense: without Felka's help, the Wall would collapse much sooner and there was a good chance all their lives would end, not just that of the haunted girl. How deep would they have to go before they were safe from the suction of the escaping atmosphere? Would any part of the nest be safe?

The regions through which they were descending now were as cold and grey as any Clavain had seen. There were no entoptic generators buried in these walls to supply visual information to the implants Galiana had put in his head, and even her own aura of light was gone. They only met a few other Conjoiners, and they were all moving in the same general direction: down to the nest's basement levels. This was unknown territory for Clavain.

Where was Galiana taking him?

'If you had an escape route all along, why did you wait so long before sending the children through it?'

'I told you, we couldn't bring them to Transenlightenment too soon. The older they were, the better,' Galiana said. 'Now, though—'

'There was no waiting any longer, was there?'

Eventually they reached a chamber with the same echoing acoustics as the topside hangar. The chamber was dark except for a few pools of light, but in the shadows Clavain made out discarded excavation equipment and freight pallets; cranes and deactivated robots. The air smelled of ozone. Something was still going on there.

'Is this the factory where you make the shuttles?' Clavain said.

'We manufactured parts of them here, yes,' Galiana said, 'but that was a side-industry.'

'Of what?'

'The tunnel, of course.' Galiana made more lights come on. At the far end of the chamber – they were walking towards it – waited a series of cylindrical things with pointed ends, like huge bullets. They rested on rails, one after the other. The tip of the very first bullet was next to a dark hole in the wall. Clavain was about to say something when there was a sudden loud buzz and the first bullet slammed into the hole. The remaining three bullets eased slowly forward and halted. Conjoiners were waiting to board them.

He remembered what Galiana had said about no one being left behind.

'What am I seeing here?'

'A way out of the nest,' Galiana said. 'And a way off Mars, though I suppose you figured that part out for yourself.'

'There is no way off Mars,' Clavain said. 'The Interdiction guarantees that. Haven't you learned that with your shuttles?'

'The shuttles were only ever a diversionary tactic,' Galiana said. 'They made your side think we were still striving to escape, whereas our true escape route was already fully operational.'

'A pretty desperate diversion.'

'Not really. I lied to you when I said we didn't clone. We did – but only to produce braindead corpses. The shuttles were full of corpses before we ever launched them.'

For the first time since leaving Deimos, Clavain smiled, amused by the sheer obliquity of Galiana's thinking.

'Of course, the shuttles performed another function,' she said. 'They provoked your side into a direct attack against the nest.'

'So this was deliberate all along?'

'Yes. We needed to draw your side's attention; to concentrate your military presence in low orbit, near the nest. Of course, we were hoping the offensive would come later than it did . . . but we reckoned without Warren's conspiracy.'

'Then you are planning something.'

'Yes.' The next bullet slammed into the wall, ozone crackling from its linear induction rails. Now only two remained. 'We can talk later. There isn't much time left.' She projected an image into his visual field: the Wall, now veined by titanic fractures down half its length. 'It's collapsing.'

'And Felka?'

'She's still trying to save it.'

He looked at the Conjoiners boarding the leading bullet; tried to imagine where they were going. Was it to any kind of sanctuary he might recognise – or to something so beyond his experience that it might as well be death? Did he have the nerve to find out? Perhaps. He had nothing to lose now, after all: he certainly could not return home. But if he was going to follow Galiana's exodus, it could not be with the sense of shame he now felt in abandoning Felka.

The answer, when it came, was simple. 'I'm going back for her. If you can't wait for me, don't. But don't try to stop me doing this.'

Galiana looked at him, shaking her head slowly. 'She won't thank you for saving her life, Clavain.'

'Maybe not now,' he said.

He had the feeling he was running back into a burning building. Given what Galiana had said about the girl's deficiencies – that by any reasonable definition she was hardly more than an automaton – what he was doing was very likely pointless, if not suicidal. But if he turned his back on her, he would become something less than human himself. He had misread Galiana badly when she said the girl was precious to them. He had assumed some bond of affection . . . whereas what Galiana meant was that the girl was precious in the sense of a vital component. Now – with the nest being abandoned – the component had no further use. Did that make Galiana as cold as a machine herself – or was she just being unfailingly realistic?

He found the nursery after only one or two false turns, and then Felka's room. The implants Galiana had given him were once again throwing phantom images into the air. Felka sat within the crumbling circle of the Wall. Great fissures now reached to the surface of Mars. Shards of the Wall, as big as icebergs, had fractured away and now lay like vast sheets of broken glass across the regolith.

She was losing, and she knew it. This was not just some more difficult phase of the game. This was something she could never win, and her realisation was now plainly evident in her face. She was still moving her arms frantically, but her face was red, locked into a petulant scowl of anger and fear.

For the first time, she seemed to notice him.

Something had broken through her shell, Clavain thought. For the first time in years, something was happening that was beyond her control; something that threatened to destroy the neat, geometric universe she had made for herself. She might not have distinguished his face from all the other people who came to see her, but she surely recognised something . . . that now the adult world was bigger than she was, and it was only from the adult world that any kind of salvation could come.

Then she did something that shocked him beyond words. She looked deep into his eyes and reached out a hand.

But there was nothing he could do to help her.

Later – it felt like hours, but in fact could only have been tens of minutes – Clavain found that he was able to breathe normally again. They had escaped Mars now: Galiana, Felka and himself, riding the last bullet.

And they were still alive.

The bullet's vacuum-filled tunnel cut deep into Mars; a shallow arc curving under the crust before rising again, thousands of kilometres away, well beyond the Wall, where the atmosphere was as thin as ever. For the Conjoiners, boring the tunnel had not been especially difficult. Such engineering would have been impossible on a planet that had plate tectonics, but beneath its lithosphere, Mars was geologically quiet. They had not even had to worry about tailings. What they excavated, they compressed and fused and used to line the tunnel, maintaining rigidity against awesome pressure with some trick of piezoelectricity. In the tunnel, the bullet accelerated continuously at three gees for ten minutes. Their seats had tilted back and wrapped around them, applying pressure to their legs to maintain bloodflow to their brains. Even so, it was difficult to think, let alone move, but Clavain knew that it was no worse than what the earliest space explorers had endured climbing away from Earth. And he had undergone similar tortures during the war, in combat insertions.

They were moving at ten kilometres a second when they reached the surface again, exiting via a camouflaged trap door. For a moment the atmosphere snatched at them . . . but almost as soon as Clavain had registered the deceleration, it was over. The surface of Mars was dropping below them very quickly indeed.

In half a minute, they were in true space.

'The Interdiction's sensor web can't track us,' Galiana said. 'You placed your best spysats directly over the nest. That was a mistake, Clavain – even though we did our best to reinforce your thinking with the shuttle launches. But now we're well outside your sensor footprint.'

Clavain nodded. 'But that won't help us once we're far from the surface. Then we'll just look like another ship trying to reach deep space. The web may be late locking on to us, but it'll still get us in the end.'

'It would,' Galiana said, 'if deep space was where we were going.'

Felka stirred next to him. She had withdrawn into some kind of catatonia. Separation from the Wall had undermined her entire existence; now she was free-falling through an abyss of meaninglessness. Perhaps, Clavain thought, she would fall for ever. If that was the case, he had only postponed her fate. Was that much of a cruelty? Perhaps he was deluding himself, but with time, was it out of the question that Galiana's machines could undo the harm they had inflicted ten years earlier? Surely they could try. It depended, of course, on where exactly they were headed. One of the system's other Conjoiner nests had been Clavain's initial guess – even though it seemed unlikely that they would ever survive the crossing. At ten klicks per second it would take years . . .

'Where are you taking us?' he asked.

Galiana issued some neural command that made the bullet's skin become transparent.

'There,' she said.

Something lay distantly ahead. Galiana made the forward view zoom in until the object was much clearer.

Dark – misshapen. Like Deimos without fortifications.

'Phobos,' Clavain said, wonderingly. 'We're going to Phobos.'

'Yes,' Galiana said.

'But the worms—'

'Don't exist any more.' She spoke with the same tutorly patience with which Remontoire had addressed him on the same subject not long before. 'Your attempt to oust the worms failed. You assumed our subsequent attempt failed, but that was only what we wanted you to think.'

For a moment he was lost for words. 'You've had people in Phobos all along?'

'Ever since the ceasefire, yes. They've been quite busy, too.'

Phobos altered. Layers of it were peeled away, revealing the glittering device that lay hidden in its heart, poised and ready for flight. Clavain had never seen anything like it, but the nature of the thing was instantly obvious. He was looking at something wonderful; something that had never existed before in the whole of human experience.

He was looking at a starship.

'We'll be leaving soon,' Galiana said. 'They'll try to stop us, of course. But now that their forces are concentrated near the surface of Mars, they won't succeed. We'll leave Phobos and Mars behind, and send messages to the other nests. If they can break out and meet us, we'll take them as well. We'll leave this whole system behind.'

'Where are you going?'

'Shouldn't that be where are *we* going? You're coming with us, after all.' She paused. 'There are a number of candidate systems.

Our choice will depend on the trajectory the Coalition forces upon us.'

'What about the Demarchists?'

'They won't stop us.' She spoke with total assurance – implying . . . what? That the Demarchy knew of this ship? Perhaps. It had long been rumoured that the Demarchists and the Conjoiners were closer than they admitted.

Clavain thought of something. 'What about the worms' altering the orbit?'

'That was our doing,' Galiana said. 'We couldn't help it. Every time we send up one of these canisters, we nudge Phobos into a different orbit. Even after we sent up a thousand canisters, the effect was tiny – we changed Phobos's velocity by less than one-tenth of a millimetre per second – but there was no way to hide it.' Then she paused and looked at Clavain with something like apprehension. 'We'll be arriving in two hundred seconds. Do you want to live?'

'I'm sorry?'

'Think about it. The tube in Mars was a thousand kilometres long, which allowed us to spread the acceleration over ten minutes. Even then it was three gees. But there simply isn't room for anything like that in Phobos. We'll be slowing down much more abruptly.'

Clavain felt the hairs on the back of his neck prickle. 'How much more abruptly?'

'Complete deceleration in one-fifth of a second.' She let that sink home. 'That's around five thousand gees.'

'I can't survive that.'

'No, you can't. Not the way you are right now, anyway. But there are machines in your head now. If you allow it, there's time for them to establish a structural web across your brain. We'll flood the cabin with foam. We'll all die temporarily, but there won't be any damage they can't fix in Phobos.'

'It won't just be a structural web, will it? I'll be like you, then. There won't be any difference between us.'

'You'll become Conjoined, yes.' Galiana offered the faintest of smiles. 'The procedure is reversible. It's just that no one's ever wanted to go back.'

'And you still tell me none of this was planned?'

'It wasn't, but I don't expect you to believe me. For what it's worth, though . . . you're a good man, Nevil. The Transenlightenment could use you. Maybe at the back of my mind . . . at the back of our mind—'

'You always hoped it might come to this?'

Galiana smiled.

He looked at Phobos. Even without Galiana's magnification, it was clearly bigger. They would be arriving very shortly. He would have liked longer to think about it, but the one thing not on his side now was time. Then he looked at Felka, and wondered which of them was about to embark on the stranger journey. Felka's search for meaning in a universe without her beloved Wall, or his passage into Transenlightenment? Neither would necessarily be easy. But together, perhaps, they might even find a way to help each other. That was all he could hope for now.

Clavain nodded assent, preparing for the loom of machines to embrace his mind.

He was ready to defect.

GLACIAL

Nevil Clavain picked his way across a mosaic of shattered ice. The field stretched away in all directions, gouged by sleek-sided crevasses. They had mapped the largest cracks before landing, but he was still wary of surprises; his breath caught every time his booted foot cracked through a layer of ice. He was aware of how dangerous it would be to wander from the red path his implants were painting across the glacier field.

He only had to remind himself of what had happened to Martin Setterholm.

They had found his body a month ago, shortly after their arrival on the planet. It had been near the main American base; a stroll from the perimeter of the huge, deserted complex of stilted domes and ice-walled caverns. Clavain's friends had found dozens of dead within the buildings, and most of them had been easily identified against the lists of base personnel that the expedition had pieced together. But Clavain had been troubled by the gaps, and had wondered if any further dead might be found in the surrounding ice fields. He had explored the warrens of the base until he found an airlock that had never been closed, and though snowfalls had long since obliterated any footprints, there was little doubt in which direction a wanderer would have set off.

Long before the base had vanished over the horizon behind him, Clavain had run into the edge of a deep, wide crevasse. And there at the bottom – just visible if he leaned over the edge – was a man's outstretched arm and hand. Clavain had gone back to the others and had them return with a winch to lower him into the depths, descending thirty or forty metres into a cathedral of stained and sculpted ice. The body had come into view: a figure in an old-fashioned atmospheric survival suit. The man's legs were bent in a horrible way, like those of a strangely articulated alien. Clavain knew it was a man because the fall had jolted his helmet from its neck-ring; the corpse's well-preserved face was pressed halfway into a pillow of ice. The helmet had ended up a few metres away.

No one died instantly on Diadem. The air was breathable for short periods, and the man had clearly had time to ponder his predicament. Even in his confused state of mind he must have known that he was going to die.

'Martin Setterholm,' Clavain had said aloud, picking up the helmet and reading the nameplate on the crown. He felt sorry for him, but could not deny himself the small satisfaction of accounting for another of the dead. Setterholm had been amongst the missing, and though he had waited the better part of a century for it, he would at least receive a proper funeral now.

There was something else, but Clavain very nearly missed it. Setterholm had lived long enough to scratch out a message in the ice. Sheltered at the base of the glacier, the marks he had gouged were still legible. Three letters, it seemed to Clavain: an 'I', a 'V' and an 'F'.

IVF.

The message meant nothing to Clavain, and even a deep search of the Conjoiner collective memory threw up only a handful of vaguely plausible candidates. The least ridiculous was '*in vitro* fertilisation', but even that seemed to have no immediate connection with Setterholm. But then again, he had been a biologist, according to the base records. Did the message spell out the chilling truth about what had happened to the colony on

Diadem: a biology lab experiment that had gone terribly wrong? Something to do with the worms, perhaps?

But after a while, overwhelmed by the sheer number of dead, Clavain had allowed the exact details of Setterholm's death to slip from his mind. He was hardly unique anyway, just one more example of the way most of them had died: not by suicide or violence but through carelessness, recklessness or just plain stupidity. Basic safety procedures – like not wandering into a crevasse zone without the right equipment – had been forgotten or ignored. Machines had been used improperly. Drugs had been administered incorrectly. Sometimes the victim had taken only themselves to the grave, but in other cases the death toll had been much higher. And it had all happened swiftly.

Galiana talked about it as if it was some kind of psychosis, while the other Conjoiners speculated about an emergent neural condition, buried in the gene pool of the entire colony, lurking for years until it was activated by an environmental trigger.

Clavain, while not discounting his friends' theories, could not help but think of the worms. They were everywhere, after all, and the Americans had certainly been interested in them – Setterholm especially. Clavain himself had pressed his faceplate against the ice and observed that the worms reached down to the depth where the man had died. Their fine burrowing trails scratched into the vertical ice walls like the branchings of a river delta, with dark nodes of breeding tangles at the intersections of the larger tunnels. The tiny black worms had infested the glacier completely, and this would only be one distinct colony out of the millions that existed throughout Diadem's frozen regions. The worm biomass in this single colony must have been several dozen tonnes at the very least. Had the Americans' studies of the worms unleashed something that shattered the mind, turning them all into stumbling fools?

He sensed Galiana's quiet presence at the back of his thoughts, where she had not been a moment earlier.

'Nevil,' she said. 'We're ready to leave again.'

'You're done with the ruin already?'

'It isn't very interesting – just a few equipment shacks. There are still some remains to the north we have to look over, and it'd be good to get there before nightfall.'

'But I've only been gone half an hour or—'

'Two hours, Nevil.'

He checked his wrist display disbelievingly, but Galiana was right: he had been out alone on the glacier for all that time. Time away from the others always seemed to fly by, like sleep to an exhausted man. Perhaps the analogy was accurate, at that: sleep was when the mammalian brain took a rest from the business of processing the external universe, allowing the accumulated experience of the day to filter down into long-term memory; collating useful memories and discarding what did not need to be remembered. And for Clavain – who still needed normal sleep – these periods away from the others were when his mind took a rest from the business of engaging in frantic neural communion with the other Conjoiners. He could almost feel his neurons breathing a vast collective groan of relief, now that all they had to do was process the thoughts of a single mind.

Two hours was nowhere near enough.

'I'll be back shortly,' Clavain said. 'I just want to pick up some more worm samples, then I'll be on my way.'

'You've picked up hundreds of the damned things already, Nevil, and they're all the same, give or take a few trivial differences.'

'I know. But it can't hurt to indulge an old man's irrational fancies, can it?'

As if to justify himself, he knelt down and began scooping surface ice into a small sample container. The leech-like worms riddled the ice so thoroughly that he was bound to have picked up a few individuals in this sample, even though he would not know for sure until he got back to the shuttle's lab. If he was lucky, the sample might even hold a breeding tangle: a knot of several dozen worms engaged in a slow, complicated orgy of cannibalism and sex. There, he would complete the same comprehensive scans he had run on all the other worms he had picked up, trying to guess just why the Americans had devoted so much effort to studying them. And doubtless he would get exactly the same results he had found previously. The worms never changed; there was no astonishing mutation buried in every hundredth or even thousandth specimen; no stunning biochemical trickery going on inside them. They secreted a few simple enzymes and they ate pollen grains and ice-bound algae and they wriggled their way through cracks in the ice, and when they met other worms they obeyed the brainless rules of life, death and procreation.

That was all they did.

Galiana, in other words, was right: the worms had simply become an excuse for him to spend time away from the rest of the Conjoiners.

At the beginning of the expedition, a month ago, it had been much easier to justify these excursions. Even some of the true Conjoined had been drawn by a primal human urge to walk out into the wilderness, surrounding themselves with kilometres of beautifully tinted, elegantly fractured, unthinking ice. It was good to be somewhere quiet and pristine after the war-torn solar system they had left behind.

Diadem was an Earth-like planet orbiting the star Ross 248. It had oceans, ice caps, plate tectonics and signs of reasonably advanced multi-cellular life. Plants had already invaded Diadem's land, and some animals – the equivalents of arthropods, molluscs and worms – had begun to follow in their wake. The largest land-based animals were still small by terrestrial standards, since nothing in the oceans had yet evolved an internal skeleton. There was nothing that showed any signs of intelligence, but that was only a minor disappointment. It would still take a lifetime's study just to explore the fantastic array of body-plans, metabolisms and survival strategies Diadem life had blindly evolved.

Yet even before Galiana had sent down the first survey shuttles, a shattering truth had become apparent.

Someone had reached Diadem before them.

The signs were unmistakable: glints of refined metal on the surface, picked out by radar. Upon inspection from orbit they turned out to be ruined structures and equipment, obviously of human origin.

'It's not possible,' Clavain had said. 'We're the first. We have to be the first. No one else has ever built anything like the *Sandra Voi*; nothing capable of travelling this far.'

'Somewhere in there,' Galiana had answered, 'I think there might be a mistaken assumption, don't you?'

Meekly, Clavain had nodded.

Now – later still than he had promised – Clavain made his way back to the waiting shuttle. The red carpet of safety led straight to the access ramp beneath the craft's belly. He climbed up and stepped through the transparent membrane that spanned the entrance door, most of his suit slithering away on contact with the membrane. By the time he was inside the ship he wore only a lightweight breather mask and a few communications devices. He could have survived outside naked for many minutes – Diadem's atmosphere now had enough oxygen to support humans – but Galiana refused to allow any intermingling of micro-organisms.

He returned the equipment to a storage locker, placed the worm sample in a refrigeration rack and clothed himself in a paper-thin black tunic and trousers, before moving into the aft compartment where Galiana was waiting.

She and Felka were sitting facing each other across the blank-walled, austerely furnished room. They were staring into the space between them without quite meeting each other's eyes. They looked like a mother and daughter locked in argumentative stalemate, but Clavain knew better.

He issued the mental command, well rehearsed now, that opened his mind to communion with the others. It was like opening a tiny aperture in the side of a dam: he was never adequately prepared for the force with which the flow of data hit him. The room changed: colour bleeding out of the walls, lacing itself into abstract structures that permeated the room's volume. Galiana and Felka, dressed dourly a moment earlier, were now veiled in light, and appeared superhumanly beautiful. He could feel their thoughts, as if he were overhearing a heated conversation in the room next door. Most of it was non-verbal; Galiana and Felka were playing an intense, abstract game. The thing floating between them was a solid lattice of light, resembling the plumbing diagram of an insanely complex refinery. It was constantly adjusting itself, with coloured flows racing this way and that as the geometry changed. About half the volume was green, the remainder lilac, but suddenly the former encroached dramatically on the latter.

Felka laughed; she was winning.

Galiana conceded and crashed back into her seat with a sigh of exhaustion, but she was smiling as well.

'Sorry. I appear to have distracted you,' Clavain said.

'No; you just hastened the inevitable. I'm afraid Felka was always going to win.'

The girl smiled again, still enjoying something through Clavain sensed her victory; a hard-edged thing, which for a moment outshone all other thoughts from her direction, eclipsing even Galiana's air of weary resignation.

Felka had been a failed Conjoiner experiment in the manipulation of foetal brain development; a child with a mind more machine than human. When he had first met her – in Galiana's nest on Mars – he had encountered a girl absorbed in a profound, endless game: directing the faltering self-repair processes of the terraforming structure known as the Great Wall of Mars, in which the nest sheltered. She had no interest in people – indeed, she could not even discriminate between faces. But when the nest was being evacuated, Clavain had risked his life to save hers, even though Galiana had told him that the kindest thing would be to let her die. As Clavain had struggled to adjust to life as part of Galiana's commune, he had set himself the task of helping Felka to develop her latent humanity. She had begun to show signs of recognition in his presence, perhaps sensing on some level that they had a kinship; that they were both strangers stumbling towards a mysterious new light.

Galiana rose from her chair, carpets of light wrapping around her. 'It was time to end the game, anyway. We've got work to do.' She looked down at the girl, who was still staring at the lattice. 'Sorry, Felka. Later, maybe.'

Clavain said, 'How's she doing?'

'She's laughing, Nevil. That has to be progress, doesn't it?'

'I'd say that depends what she's laughing about.'

'She beat me. She thought it was funny. I'd say that was a fairly human reaction, wouldn't you?'

'I'd still be happier if I could convince myself she recognised my face, and not my smell, or the sound my footfalls make.'

'You're the only one of us with a beard, Nevil. It doesn't take vast amounts of neural processing to spot *that*.'

Clavain scratched his chin self-consciously as they stepped through into the shuttle's flight deck. He liked his beard, even though it was trimmed to little more than grey stubble so that he could slip a breather mask on without difficulty. It was as much a link to his past as his memories, or the wrinkles Galiana had studiously built into his remodelled body.

'You're right, of course. Sometimes I just have to remind myself how far we've come.'

Galiana smiled – she was getting better at that, though there was still something a little forced about it – and pushed her long, grey-veined black hair behind her ears. 'I tell myself the same things when I think about you, Nevil.'

'Mm. But I have come some way, haven't I?'

'Yes, but that doesn't mean you haven't got a considerable distance ahead of you. I could have put that thought into your head in a microsecond, if you allowed me to do so – but you still insist that we communicate by making noises in our throats, the way monkeys do.'

'Well, it's good practice for you,' Clavain said, hoping that his irritation was not too obvious.

They settled into adjacent seats while avionics displays slithered into take-off configuration. Clavain's implants allowed him to fly the machine without any manual inputs at all, but – old soldier that he was – he generally preferred tactile controls. So his implants obliged, hallucinating a joystick inset with buttons and levers, and when he reached out to grasp it his hands appeared to close around something solid. He shuddered to think how thoroughly his perceptions of the real world were being doctored to support this illusion; but once he had been flying for a few minutes he generally forgot about it, lost in the joy of piloting.

He got them airborne, then settled the shuttle into level flight towards the fifth ruin they would be visiting that day. Kilometres of ice slid beneath them, only occasionally broken by a protruding ridge or a patch of dry, boulder-strewn ground.

'Just a few shacks, you said?'

Galiana nodded. 'A waste of time, but we had to check it out.'

'Any closer to understanding what happened to them?'

'They died, more or less overnight. Mostly through incidents related to the breakdown of normal thought – although one or two may simply have died, as if they had some greater susceptibility to a toxin than the others.'

Clavain smiled, feeling that a small victory was his. 'Now you're looking at a toxin, rather than a psychosis?'

'A toxin's difficult to explain, Nevil.'

'From Martin Setterholm's worms, perhaps?'

'Not very likely. Their biohazard containment measures weren't as good as ours – but they were still adequate. We've analysed those worms and we know they don't carry anything obviously hostile to us. And even if there was a neurotoxin, how would it affect everyone so quickly? Even if the lab workers had caught something, they'd have fallen ill before anyone else did, sending a warning to the others – but nothing like that happened.' She paused, anticipating Clavain's next question. 'And no, I don't think that what happened to them is necessarily something we need worry about, though that doesn't mean I'm going to rule anything out. But even our oldest technology's a century ahead of the best they had – and we have the *Sandra Voi* to retreat to if we run into anything the medichines in our heads can't handle.'

Clavain always did his best not to think too much about the swarms of subcellular machines lacing his brain – supplanting much of it, in fact – but there were times when it was unavoidable. He still had a squeamish reaction to the idea, though it was becoming milder. Now, though, he could not help but view the machines as his allies; as intimately a part of him as his immune system. Galiana was right: they would resist anything that tried to interfere with what now passed as the 'normal' functioning of his mind.

'Still,' he said, not yet willing to drop his pet theory, 'you've got to admit something: the Americans – Setterholm especially – were interested in the worms. Too interested, if you ask me.'

'Look who's talking.'

'Ah, but my interest is strictly forensic. And I can't help but put the two things together. They were interested in the worms. And they went mad.'

This was an oversimplification, of course: it was clear enough that the worms had preoccupied only some of the Americans: those who were most interested in xeno-biology. According to the evidence the Conjoiners had so far gathered, the effort had been largely spearheaded by Setterholm, the man Clavain had found dead at the bottom of the crevasse. Setterholm had travelled widely across Diadem's snowy wastes, gathering a handful of allies to assist in his work. He had found worms in dozens of ice fields, grouped into vast colonies. For the most part the other members of the expedition had let him get on with his activities, even as they struggled with the day-to-day business of staying alive in what was still a hostile, alien environment.

Even before they had all died, things had been far from easy. The self-replicating robots that had brought them there in the first place had failed years before, leaving the delicate life-support systems of their shelters to slowly collapse; each malfunction a little more difficult to rectify than the last. Diadem was getting colder, too – sliding inexorably into a deep ice age. It had been the Americans' misfortune to arrive at the onset of a great, centuries-long winter. Now, Clavain thought, it was colder still; the polar ice caps rushing towards each other like long-separated lovers.

'It must have been fast, whatever it was,' Clavain mused. 'They'd already abandoned most of the outlying bases by then, huddling together back at the main settlement. By that point they only had enough spare parts and technical know-how to run a single fusion power plant.'

'Which failed.'

'Yes – but that doesn't mean much. It couldn't run itself, not by then – it needed constant tinkering. Eventually the people with the right know-how must have succumbed to the . . . whatever it was – and then the reactor stopped working and they all died of the cold. But they were in trouble long before the reactor failed.'

Galiana seemed on the point of saying something. Clavain could always tell when she was about to speak: it was as if some leakage from her thoughts reached his brain even as she composed what she would say.

'Well?' he said, when the silence had stretched long enough.

'I was just thinking,' she said. 'A reactor of that type – it doesn't need any exotic isotopes, does it? No tritium, or deuterium?'

'No. Just plain old hydrogen. You could get all you needed from sea water.'

'Or ice,' Galiana said.

They vectored in for the next landing site. Toadstools, Clavain thought: half a dozen black metal towers of varying height surmounted by domed black habitat modules, interlinked by a web of elevated, pressurised walkways. Each of the domes was thirty or forty metres wide, perched a hundred or more metres above the ice, festooned with narrow, armoured windows, sensors and communications antennas. A tongue-like extension from one of the tallest domes was clearly a landing pad. In fact, as he came closer, he saw that there was an aircraft parked on it: one of the blunt-winged machines that the Americans had used to get around in. It was dusted with ice, but it would probably still fly with a little persuasion.

He inched the shuttle down, one of its skids coming to rest only just inside the edge of the pad. Clearly the landing pad had only really been intended for one aircraft at a time.

'Nevil . . .' Galiana said. 'I'm not sure I like this.'

He felt tension leaking into his head, but could not be sure if it was his own or Galiana's.

'What don't you like?'

'There shouldn't be an aircraft here,' Galiana said.

'Why not?'

She spoke softly, reminding him that the evacuation of the outlying settlements had been orderly, compared to the subsequent crisis. 'This base should have been shut down and mothballed with all the others.'

'Then maybe someone stayed behind here,' Clavain suggested.

Galiana nodded. 'Or someone came back.'

There was a third presence with them now; another hue of

thought bleeding into his mind. Felka had come into the cockpit. He could taste her apprehension.

'You sense it, too,' he said wonderingly, looking into the face of the terribly damaged girl. 'Our discomfort. And you don't like it any more than we do, do you?'

Galiana took the girl's hand. 'It's all right, Felka.'

She must have spoken aloud just for Clavain's benefit. Before her mouth had even opened Galiana would have planted reassuring thoughts in Felka's mind, attempting to still the disquiet with the subtlest of neural adjustments. Clavain thought of an expert ikebana artist minutely altering the placement of a single flower in the interests of harmony.

'Everything will be okay,' Clavain said. 'There's nothing here that can harm you.'

Galiana took a moment, blank-eyed, to commune with the other Conjoiners in and around Diadem. Most of them were still in orbit, observing things from the ship. She told them about the aircraft and notified them that she and Clavain were going to enter the structure.

He saw Felka's hand tighten around Galiana's wrist.

'She wants to come as well,' Galiana said.

'She'll be safer if she stays here.'

'She doesn't want to be alone.'

Clavain chose his words carefully. 'I thought Conjoiners – I mean we – could never be truly alone, Galiana.'

'There might be a communicational block inside the structure. It'll be better if she stays physically close to us.'

'Is that the only reason?'

'No, of course not.' For a moment he felt a sting of her anger, prickling his mind like sea-spray. 'She's still human, Nevil – no matter what we've done to her mind. We can't erase a million years of evolution. She may not be very good at recognising faces, but she recognises the need for companionship.'

He raised his hands. 'I never doubted it.'

'Then why are you arguing?'

Clavain smiled. He'd had this conversation so many times before, with so many women. He had been married to some of them. It was oddly comforting to be having it again, light-years from home, wearing a new body, his mind clotted with machines and confronting the matriarch of what should have been a feared and hated hive mind. At the epicentre of so much strangeness, a tiff was almost to be welcomed.

'I just don't want anything to hurt her.'

'Oh. And I do?'

'Never mind,' he said, gritting his teeth. 'Let's just get in and out, shall we?'

The base, like all the American structures, had been built for posterity. Not by people, however, but by swarms of diligent self-replicating robots. That was how the Americans had reached Diadem: they had been brought there as frozen fertilised cells in the armoured, radiation-proofed bellies of star-crossing von Neumann robots. The robots had been launched towards several solar systems about a century before the *Sandra Voi* had left Mars. Upon arrival on Diadem they had set about breeding, making copies of themselves from local ores. When their numbers had reached some threshold, they had turned over their energies to the construction of bases: luxurious accommodation for the human children who would then be grown in their wombs.

'The entrance door's intact,' Galiana said when they had crossed from the shuttle to the smooth black side of the dome, stooping against the wind. 'And there's still some residual power in its circuits.'

That was a Conjoiner trick that always faintly unnerved Clavain. Like sharks, Conjoiners were sensitive to ambient electrical fields. Mapped into her vision, Galiana would see the energised circuits superimposed on the door like a ghostly neon maze. Now she extended her hand towards the lock, palm first.

'I'm accessing the opening mechanism. Interfacing with it now.' Behind her mask, her saw her face scrunch in concentration. Galiana only ever frowned when having to think hard. With her hand outstretched she looked like a wizard attempting some particularly demanding enchantment.

'Hmm,' she said. 'Nice old software protocols. Nothing too difficult.'

'Careful,' Clavain said. 'I wouldn't put it past them to have installed some kind of trap here—'

'There's no trap,' she said. 'But there is – ah, yes – a verbal entry code. Well, here goes.' She spoke louder, so that her voice would travel through the air to the door even above the howl of the wind. 'Open sesame.'

Lights flicked from red to green; dislodging a frosting of ice, the door slid ponderously aside to reveal a dimly lit interior chamber. The base must have been running on a trickle of emergency power for decades.

Felka and Clavain lingered while Galiana crossed the threshold.

'Well?' she challenged, turning around. 'Are you two sissies coming or not?'

Felka offered a hand. He took hers and the two of them – the old soldier and the girl who could barely grasp the difference between two human faces – took a series of tentative steps inside.

'What you just did, that business with your hand and the password . . .' Clavain paused. 'That was a joke, wasn't it?'

Galiana looked at him, blank-faced. 'How could it have been? Everyone knows Conjoiners haven't got anything remotely resembling a sense of humour.'

Clavain nodded gravely. 'That was my understanding, but I just wanted to be sure.'

There was no trace of the wind inside, but it would still have been too cold to remove their suits, even had they not been concerned about contamination. They worked their way along a series of winding corridors, some of which were dark, others bathed in feeble, pea-green lighting. Now and then they passed the entrance to a room full of equipment, but nothing that looked like a laboratory or living quarters. Then they descended a series of stairs and found themselves crossing one of the sealed walkways between the toadstools. Clavain had seen a few other American settlements built like this one; they were designed to remain useful even as they sank slowly into the ice.

The bridge led to what was obviously the main habitation section. Now there were lounges, bedrooms, laboratories and kitchens – enough for a crew of perhaps fifty or sixty. But there were no signs of any bodies, and the place did not look as if it had been abandoned in a hurry. The equipment was neatly packed away and there were no half-eaten meals on the tables. There was frost everywhere, but that was just the moisture that had frozen out of the air when the base cooled down.

'They were expecting to come back,' Galiana said.

Clavain nodded. 'They couldn't have had much of an idea of what lay ahead of them.'

They moved on, crossing another bridge, until they arrived in a toadstool almost entirely dedicated to bio-analysis laboratories. Galiana had to use her neural trick again to get them inside, the machines in her head sweet-talking the duller machines entombed in the doors. The low-ceilinged labs were bathed in green light, but Galiana found a wall panel that brought the lighting up a notch and even caused some bench equipment to wake up, pulsing with stand-by lights.

Clavain looked around, recognising centrifuges, gene-sequencers, gas chromatographs and scanning-tunnelling microscopes. There were at least a dozen other hunks of gleaming machinery whose function eluded him. A wall-sized cabinet held dozens of pull-out drawers, each of which contained hundreds of culture dishes, test tubes and gel slides. Clavain glanced at the samples, reading the tiny labels. There were bacteria and single-cell cultures with unpronounceable codenames, most of which were marked with

Diadem map coordinates and a date. But there were also drawers full of samples with Latin names, comparison samples which must have come from Earth. The robots could easily have carried the tiny parent organisms from which these larger samples had been grown or cloned. Perhaps the Americans had been experimenting with the hardiness of Earth-born organisms, with a view to terraforming Diadem at some point in the future.

He closed the drawer silently and moved to a set of larger sample tubes racked on a desk. He picked one from the rack and raised it to the light, examining the smoky things inside. It was a sample of worms, indistinguishable from those he had collected on the glacier a few hours earlier. A breeding tangle, probably: harvested from the intersection point of two worm tunnels. Some of the worms in the tangle would be exchanging genes; others would be fighting; others would be allowing themselves to be digested by adults or newly hatched young; all behaving according to rigidly deterministic laws of caste and sex. The tangle looked dead, but that meant nothing with the worms. Their metabolism was fantastically slow, each individual easily capable of living for thousands of years. It would take them months just to crawl along some of the longer cracks in the ice, let alone move between some of the larger tangles.

But the worms were not really all that alien. They had a close terrestrial analogue: the sun-avoiding ice-worms that had first been discovered in the Malaspina Glacier in Alaska towards the end of the nineteenth century. The Alaskan ice-worms were a lot smaller than their Diadem counterparts, but they also nourished themselves on the slim pickings that drifted onto the ice, or had been frozen into it years earlier. Like the Diadem worms, their most notable anatomical feature was a pore at the head end, just above the mouth. In the case of the terrestrial worms, the pore served a single function: secreting a salty solution that helped the worms melt their way into ice when there was no tunnel already present – an escape strategy that helped them get beneath the ice before the sun dried them up. The Diadem worms had a similar structure, but according to Setterholm's notes they had evolved a second use for it: secreting a chemically rich 'scent trail' which helped other worms navigate through the tunnel system. The chemistry of that scent trail turned out to be very complex, with each worm capable of secreting not merely a unique signature but a variety of flavours. Conceivably, more complex message schemes were embedded in some of the other flavours: not just 'follow me' but 'follow me only if you are female' – the Diadem worms had at least three sexes – 'and this is breeding season'. There were many other possibilities, which Setterholm seemed to have been attempting to decode and catalogue when the end had come.

It was interesting . . . up to a point. But even if the worms followed a complex set of rules dependent on the scent trails they were picking up, and perhaps other environmental cues, it would still only be rigidly mechanistic behaviour.

'Nevil, come here.'

It was Galiana's voice, but it had a tone he had barely heard before. It was one that made him run to where Felka and Galiana were waiting on the other side of the lab.

They were facing an array of lockers occupying an entire wall. A small status panel was set into each locker, but only one locker – placed at chest height – showed any activity. Clavain looked back towards the door through which they had entered, but from there it was hidden by intervening lab equipment. They would not have seen this locker even if it had been illuminated before Galiana brought the room's power back on.

'It might have been on all along,' he said.

'I know,' Galiana agreed.

She reached a hand up to the panel, tapping the control keys with unnerving fluency. Machines to Galiana were like musical instruments to a prodigy. She could pick one up cold and play it like an old friend.

The array of status lights changed configuration abruptly, then there was a bustle of activity somewhere behind the locker's metal face – latches and servomotors clicking after decades of stasis.

'Stand back,' Galiana said.

A rime of frost shattered into a billion sugary pieces. The locker began to slide out of the wall, the unhurried motion giving them adequate time to digest what lay inside. Clavain felt Felka grip his hand, and then noticed that her other hand was curled tightly around Galiana's wrist. For the first time, he began to wonder if it had really been such a good idea to allow the girl to join them.

The locker was two metres in length and half that in width and height; just sufficient to contain a human body. It had probably been designed to hold animal specimens culled from Diadem's oceans, but it was equally capable of functioning as a mortuary tray. That the man inside the locker was dead was beyond question, but there was no sign of injury. His composure – flat on his back, his blue-grey face serenely blank, his eyes closed and his hands clasped neatly just below his ribcage – suggested to Clavain a saint lying in grace. His beard was neatly pointed and his hair long, frozen into a solid sculptural mass. He was still wearing several heavy layers of thermal clothing.

Clavain knelt closer and read the name-tag above the man's heart.

'Andrew Iverson. Ring a bell?'

A moment passed while Galiana established a link to the rest of the Conjoiners, ferreting the name out of some database. 'Yes. One of the missing. Seems he was a climatologist with an interest in terraforming techniques.'

Clavain nodded shrewdly. 'That figures, with all the micro-organisms I've seen in this place. Well: the trillion dollar question – how do you think he got in there?'

'I think he climbed in,' Galiana said, and nodded at something Clavain had missed, almost tucked away beneath the man's shoulder. Clavain reached into the gap, his fingers brushing against the rock-hard fabric of Iverson's outfit. A cannula vanished into the man's forearm, where he had cut away a square of fabric. The cannula's black feed-line reached back into the cabinet, vanishing into a socket at the rear.

'You're saying he killed himself?' Clavain asked.

'He must have put something in that which would stop his heart. Then he probably flushed out his blood and replaced it with glycerol, or something similar, to prevent ice crystals forming in his cells. It would have taken some automation to make it work, but I'm sure everything he needed was here.'

Clavain thought back to what he knew about the cryonic immersion techniques that had been around a century or so earlier. They left something to be desired now, but back then they had not been much of an advance over mummification.

'When he sank that cannula into himself, he can't have been certain we'd ever find him,' Clavain remarked.

'Which would still have been preferable to suicide.'

'Yes, but . . . the thoughts that must have gone through his head. Knowing he had to kill himself first, to stand a chance of living again – and then hope someone else stumbled on Diadem.'

'You made a harder choice than that, once.'

'Yes. But at least I wasn't alone when I made it.'

Iverson's body was astonishingly well preserved, Clavain thought. The skin tissue looked almost intact, even if it had a deathly, granite-like colour. The bones of his face had not ruptured under the strain of the temperature drop. Bacterial processes had stopped dead. All in all, things could have been a lot worse.

'We shouldn't leave him like this,' Galiana said, pushing the locker so that it began to slide back into the wall.

'I don't think he cares much about that now,' Clavain said.

'No. You don't understand. He mustn't warm – not even to the ambient temperature of the room. Otherwise we won't be able to wake him up.'

*

It took five days to bring him back to consciousness.

The decision to reanimate had not been taken lightly; it had only been arrived at after intense discussion amongst the Conjoined, debates in which Clavain participated to the best of his ability. Iverson, they all agreed, could probably be resurrected with current Conjoiner methods. *In-situ* scans of his mind had revealed preserved synaptic structures that a scaffold of machines could coax back towards consciousness. However, since they had not yet identified the cause of the madness that had killed Iverson's colleagues – and the evidence was pointing towards some kind of infectious agent – Iverson would be kept on the surface; reborn on the same world where he had died.

They had, however, moved him: shuttling him halfway across the world back to the main base. Clavain had travelled with the corpse, marvelling at the idea that this solid chunk of man-shaped ice – tainted, admittedly, with a few vital impurities – would soon be a breathing, thinking human being with memories and feelings. To him it was astonishing that this was possible; that so much latent structure had been preserved across the decades. Even more astonishing that the infusions of tiny machines the Conjoiners were brewing would be able to stitch together damaged cells and kick-start them back to life. And out of that inert loom of frozen brain structure – a thing that was at this moment nothing more than a fixed geometric entity, like a finely eroded piece of rock – something as malleable as consciousness would emerge.

But the Conjoiners were blasé at the prospect, viewing Iverson the way expert picture-restorers might view a damaged old master. Yes, there would be difficulties ahead – work that would require great skill – but nothing to lose sleep over.

Except, Clavain reminded himself, none of them slept anyway.

While the others were working to bring Iverson back to life, Clavain wandered the outskirts of the base, trying to get a better feel for what it must have been like during the last days. The debilitating mental illness must have been terrifying as it struck even those who might have stood a chance of developing some kind of counter-agent to it. Perhaps in the old days, when the base had been under the stewardship of the von Neumann machines, something might have been done . . . but in the end it must have been like trying to crack a particularly tricky algebra problem while growing steadily more drunk; losing first the ability to focus sharply, then to focus on the problem at all, and then to remember what was so important about it anyway. The labs in the main complex had an abandoned look to them: experiments half-finished; notes scrawled on the wall in ever more incoherent handwriting.

Down in the lower levels – the transport bays and storage areas – it was almost as if nothing had happened. Equipment was still neatly racked, surface vehicles neatly parked, and – with the base sub-systems back on – the place was bathed in light and not so cold as to require extra clothing. It was quite therapeutic, too: the Conjoiners had not extended their communicational fields into these regions, so Clavain's mind was mercifully isolated again; freed of the clamour of other voices. Despite that, he was still tempted by the idea of spending some time outdoors.

With that in mind he found an airlock, one that must have been added late in the base's history as it was absent from the blue-prints. There was no membrane stretched across this one; if he stepped through it he would be outside as soon as the doors cycled, with no more protection than the clothes he was wearing now. He considered going back into the base proper to find a membrane suit, but by the time he did that, the mood – the urge to go outside – would be gone.

Clavain noticed a locker. Inside, to his delight, was a rack of old-style suits such as Setterholm had been wearing. They looked brand new, alloy neck-rings gleaming. Racked above each one was a bulbous helmet. He experimented until he found a suit that fitted him, then struggled with the various latches and seals that coupled the suit parts together. Even when he thought he had donned the suit properly, the airlock detected that one of his gloves wasn't latched correctly. It refused to let him outside until he reversed the cycle and fixed the problem.

But then he was outside, and it was glorious.

He walked around the base until he found his bearings, and then – always ensuring that the base was in view and that his air supply was adequate – he set off across the ice. Above, Diadem's sky was a deep enamelled blue, and the ice – though fundamentally white – seemed to contain a billion nuances of pale turquoise, pale aquamarine; even hints of the palest of pinks. Beneath his feet he imagined the crack-like networks of the worms, threading down for hundreds of metres; and he imagined the worms, wriggling through that network, responding to and secreting chemical scent trails. The worms themselves were biologically simple – almost dismayingly so – but that network was a vast, intricate thing. It hardly mattered that the traffic along it – the to-and-fro motions of the worms as they went about their lives – was so agonisingly slow. The worms, after all, had endured longer than human comprehension. They had seen people come and go in an eyeblink.

He walked on until he arrived at the crevasse where he had found Setterholm. They had long since removed Setterholm's body, of course, but the experience had imprinted itself deeply on Clavain's mind. He found it easy to relive the moment at the lip of the crevasse when he had first seen the end of Setterholm's arm. At the time he had told himself that there must be worse places to die; surrounded by beauty that was so pristine; so utterly untouched by human influence. Now, the more he thought about it, the more that Setterholm's death played on his mind – he wondered if there could be any worse place. It was undeniably beautiful, but it was also crushingly dead; crushingly oblivious to life. Setterholm must have felt himself draining away, soon to become as inanimate as the palace of ice that was to become his tomb.

Clavain thought about it for many more minutes, enjoying the silence and the solitude and the odd awkwardness of the suit. He thought back to the way Setterholm had been found, and his mind niggled at something not quite right; a detail that had not seemed wrong at the time but which now troubled him.

It was Setterholm's helmet.

He remembered the way it had been lying away from the man's corpse, as if the impact had knocked it off. But now that Clavain had locked an identical helmet onto his own suit, that was more difficult to believe. The latches were sturdy, and he doubted that the drop into the crevasse would have been sufficient to break the mechanism. He considered the possibility that Setterholm had put his suit on hastily, but even that seemed unlikely now. The airlock had detected that Clavain's glove was badly attached; it – or any of the other locks – would surely have refused to allow Setterholm outside if his helmet had not been correctly latched.

Clavain wondered if Setterholm's death had been something other than an accident.

He thought about it, trying the idea on for size, then slowly shook his head. There were myriad possibilities he had yet to rule out. Setterholm could have left the base with his suit intact and then – confused and disoriented – he could have fiddled with the latch, depriving himself of oxygen until he stumbled into the crevasse. Or perhaps the airlocks were not as foolproof as they appeared; the safety mechanism capable of being disabled by people in a hurry to get outside.

No. A man had died, but there was no need to assume it had been anything other than an accident. Clavain turned, and began to walk back to the base.

'He's awake,' Galiana said, a day or so after the final wave of machines had swum into Iverson's mind. 'I think it might be better if he spoke to you first, Nevil, don't you? Rather than one of us?' She bit her tongue. 'I mean, rather than someone who's been Conjoined for as long as the rest of us?'

Clavain shrugged. 'Then again, an attractive face might be preferable to a grizzled old relic like myself. But I take your point. Is it safe to go in now?'

'Perfectly. If Iverson was carrying anything infectious, the machines would have flagged it.'

'I hope you're right.'

'Well, look at the evidence. He was acting rationally up to the end. He did everything to ensure we'd have an excellent chance of reviving him. His suicide was just a coldly calculated attempt to escape his situation.'

'Coldly calculated,' Clavain echoed. 'Yes, I suppose it would have been. Cold, I mean.'

Galiana said nothing, but gestured towards the door into Iverson's room.

Clavain stepped through the opening. And it was as he crossed the threshold that a thought occurred to him. He could once again see, in his mind's eye, Martin Setterholm's body lying at the bottom of the crevasse, his fingers pointing to the letters 'IVF'.

In-vitro fertilisation.

But suppose Setterholm had been trying to write 'IVERSON', but had died before finishing the word? If Setterholm had been murdered – pushed into the crevasse – he might have been trying to pass on a message about his murderer. Clavain imagined his pain, legs smashed; knowing with absolute certainty he was going to die alone and cold, but willing himself to write Iverson's name . . .

But why would the climatologist have wanted to kill Setterholm? Setterholm's fascination with the worms was perplexing but harmless. The information Clavain had collected pointed to Setterholm being a single-minded loner; the kind of man who would inspire pity or indifference in his colleagues rather than hatred. And everyone was dying anyway – against such a back-ground, a murder seemed almost irrelevant.

Maybe he was attributing too much to the six faint marks a dying man had scratched on the ice.

Forcing suspicion from his mind – for now – Clavain walked further into Iverson's room. The room was spartan but serene, with a small blue holographic window set high in one white wall. Clavain was responsible for that. Left to the Conjoiners – who had taken over an area of the main American base and filled it with their own pressurised spaces – Iverson's room would have been a grim, grey cube. That was fine for the Conjoiners – they moved through informational fields draped like an extra layer over reality. But though Iverson's head was now drenched with their machines, they were only there to assist his normal patterns of thought; reinforcing weak synaptic signals and compensating for a far-from-equilibrium mix of neurotransmitters.

So Clavain had insisted on cheering the place up a bit; Iverson's sheets and pillow were now the same pure white as the walls, so that his head bobbed in a sea of whiteness. His hair had been trimmed, but Clavain had made sure that no one had done more than neaten Iverson's beard.

'Andrew?' he said. 'I'm told you're awake now. I'm Nevil Clavain. How are you feeling?'

Iverson wet his lips before answering. 'Better, I suspect, than I have any reason to feel.'

'Ah.' Clavain beamed, feeling as if a large burden had just been lifted from his shoulders. 'Then you've some recollection of what happened to you.'

'I died, didn't I? Pumped myself full of antifreeze and hoped for the best. Did it work, or is this just some weird-ass dream as I'm sliding towards brain death?'

'No, it sure as hell worked. That was one weird-heck-ass of a risk . . .' Clavain halted, not entirely certain that he could emulate

Iverson's century-old speech patterns. 'That was quite some risk you took. But it did work, you'll be glad to hear.'

Iverson lifted a hand from beneath the sheets, examining his palm and the pattern of veins and tendons on the back. 'This is the same body I went under with? You haven't stuck me in a robot, or cloned me, or hooked up my disembodied brain to a virtual-reality generator?'

'None of those things, no. Just mopped up some cell damage, fixed a few things here and there and – um – kick-started you back into the land of the living.'

Iverson nodded, but Clavain could tell he was far from convinced. Which was unsurprising: Clavain, after all, had already told a small lie.

'So how long was I under?'

'About a century, Andrew. We're an expedition from back home. We came by starship.'

Iverson nodded again, as if this was mere incidental detail. 'We're aboard it now, right?'

'No . . . no. We're still on the planet. The ship's parked in orbit.'

'And everyone else?'

No point sugaring the pill. 'Dead, as far as we can make out. But you must have known that would happen.'

'Yeah. But I didn't know for sure, even at the end.'

'So what happened? How did you escape the infection, or whatever it was?'

'Sheer luck.' Iverson asked for a drink. Clavain fetched him one, and at the same time had the room extrude a chair next to the bed.

'I didn't see much sign of luck,' Clavain said.

'No; it was terrible. But I was the lucky one – that's all I meant. I don't know how much you know. We had to evacuate the outlying bases towards the end, when we couldn't keep more than one fusion reactor running.' Iverson took a sip from the glass of water Clavain had brought him. 'If we'd still had the machines to look after us—'

'Yes. That's something we never really understood.' Clavain leaned closer to the bed. 'Those von Neumann machines were built to self-repair themselves, weren't they? We still don't see how they broke down.'

Iverson eyed him. 'They didn't. Break down, I mean.'

'No? Then what happened?'

'We smashed them up. Like rebellious teenagers overthrowing parental control. The machines were nannying us, and we were sick of it. In hindsight, it wasn't such a good idea.'

'Didn't the machines put up a fight?'

'Not exactly. I don't think the people who designed them ever thought they'd get trashed by the kids they'd lovingly cared for.'

So, Clavain thought – whatever had happened here, whatever he went on to learn, it was clear that the Americans had been at least partially the authors of their own misfortunes. He still felt sympathy for them, but now it was cooler, tempered with something close to disgust. He wondered if that feeling of disappointed appraisal would have come so easily without Galiana's machines in his head. *It would be just a tiny step to go from feeling that way towards Iverson's people to feeling that way about the rest of humanity . . . and then I'd know that I'd truly attained Transenlightenment . . .*

Clavain snapped out of his morbid line of thinking. It was not Transenlightenment that engendered those feelings, just ancient, bone-deep cynicism.

'Well, there's no point dwelling on what was done years ago. But how did you survive?'

'After the evacuation, we realised that we'd left something behind – a spare component for the remaining fusion reactor. So I went back for it, taking one of the planes. I landed just as a bad weather front was coming in, which kept me grounded there for two days. That was when the others began to get sick. It happened pretty quickly, and all I knew about it was what I could figure out from the comm links back to the main base.'

'Tell me what you did figure out.'

'Not much,' Iverson said. 'It was fast, and it seemed to attack the central nervous system. No one survived it. Those that didn't die of it directly went on to get themselves killed through accidents or sloppy procedure.'

'We noticed. Eventually someone died who was responsible for keeping the fusion reactor running properly. It didn't blow up, did it?'

'No. Just spewed out a lot more neutrons than normal; too much for the shielding to contain. Then it went into emergency shutdown mode. Some people were killed by the radiation, but most died of the cold that came afterwards.'

'Hm. Except you.'

Iverson nodded. 'If I hadn't had to go back for that component, I'd have been one of them. Obviously, I couldn't risk returning. Even if I could have got the reactor working again, there was still the problem of the contaminant.' He breathed in deeply, as if steeling himself to recollect what had happened next. 'So I weighed my options and decided dying – freezing myself – was my only hope. No one was going to come from Earth to help me, even if I could have kept myself alive. Not for decades, anyway. So I took a chance.'

'One that paid off.'

'Like I said, I was the lucky one.' Iverson took another sip from the glass Clavain had brought him. 'Man, that tastes better than anything I've ever drunk in my life. What's in this, by the way?'

'Just water. Glacial water. Purified, of course.'

Iverson nodded, slowly, and put the glass down next to his bed. 'Not thirsty now?'

'Quenched my thirst nicely, thank you.'

'Good.' Clavain stood up. 'I'll let you get some rest, Andrew. If there's anything you need, anything we can do – just call out.'

'I'll be sure to.'

Clavain smiled and walked to the door, observing Iverson's obvious relief that the questioning session was over for now. But Iverson had said nothing incriminating, Clavain reminded himself, and his responses were entirely consistent with the fatigue and confusion anyone would feel after so long asleep – or dead, depending on how you defined Iverson's period on ice. It was unfair to associate him with Setterholm's death just because of a few indistinct marks gouged in ice, and the faint possibility that Setterholm had been murdered.

Still, Clavain paused before leaving the room. 'One other thing, Andrew – just something that's been bothering me, and I wondered if you could help.'

'Go ahead.'

'Do the initials "I", "V" and "F" mean anything to you?'

Iverson thought about it for a moment, then shook his head. 'Sorry, Nevil. You've got me there.'

'Well, it was just a shot in the dark,' Clavain said.

Iverson was strong enough to walk around the next day. He insisted on exploring the rest of the base, not simply the parts the Conjoiners had taken over. He wanted to see for himself the damage that he had heard about, and look over the lists of the dead – and the manner in which they had died – that Clavain and his friends had assiduously compiled. Clavain kept a watchful eye on the man, aware of how emotionally traumatic the whole experience must be. He was bearing it well, but that might easily have been a front. Galiana's machines could tell a lot about how his brain was functioning, but they were unable to probe Iverson's state of mind at the resolution needed to map emotional well-being.

Clavain, meanwhile, strove as best he could to keep Iverson in the dark about the Conjoiners. He did not want to overwhelm Iverson with strangeness at this delicate time; did not want to shatter the man's illusion that he had been rescued by a group of 'normal' human beings. But it turned out to be easier than he had expected, as Iverson showed surprisingly little interest in the history he had missed. Clavain had gone as far as telling him that the *Sandra Voi* was technically a ship full of refugees, fleeing the aftermath of a war between various factions of solar-system humanity – but Iverson had done little more than nod, never probing Clavain for more details about the war. Once or twice Clavain had even alluded accidentally to the Transenlightenment – that shared consciousness state the Conjoiners had reached – but Iverson had shown the same lack of interest. He was not even curious about the *Sandra Voi* herself, never once asking Clavain what the ship was like. It was not quite what Clavain had been expecting.

But there were rewards, too.

Iverson, it turned out, was fascinated by Felka, and Felka herself seemed pleasantly amused by the newcomer. It was, perhaps, not all that surprising: Galiana and the others had been busy helping Felka grow the neural circuitry necessary for normal human interactions, adding new layers to supplant the functional regions that had never worked properly – but in all that time, they had never introduced her to another human being she had not already met. And here was Iverson: not just a new voice but a new smell; a new face; a new way of walking – a deluge of new input for her starved mental routines. Clavain watched the way Felka latched on to Iverson when he entered a room, her attention snapping to him, her delight evident. And Iverson seemed perfectly happy to play the games that so wearied the others, the kinds of intricate challenge Felka adored. For hours on end Clavain watched the two of them lost in concentration; Iverson pulling mock faces of sorrow or – on the rare occasions when he beat her – extravagant joy. Felka responded in kind, her face more animated – more plausibly human – than Clavain had ever believed possible. She spoke more often in Iverson's presence than she had ever done in his, and the utterances she made more closely approximated well-formed, grammatically sound sentences than the disjointed shards of language Clavain had grown to recognise. It was like watching a difficult, backward child suddenly come alight in the presence of a skilled teacher. Clavain thought back to the time when he had rescued Felka from Mars, and how unlikely it had seemed then that she would ever grow into something resembling a normal adult human, as sensitised to others' feelings as she was to her own. Now, he could almost believe it would happen – yet half the distance she had come had been due to Iverson's influence, rather than his own.

Afterwards, when even Iverson had wearied of Felka's ceaseless demands for games, Clavain spoke to him quietly, away from the others.

'You're good with her, aren't you?'

Iverson shrugged, as if the matter was of no great consequence to him. 'Yeah. I like her. We both enjoy the same kinds of game. If there's a problem—'

He must have detected Clavain's irritation. 'No – no problem at all.' Clavain put a hand on his shoulder. 'There's more to it than just games, though, you have to admit—'

'She's a pretty fascinating case, Nevil.'

'I don't disagree. We value her highly.' He flinched, aware of how much the remark sounded like one of Galiana's typically flat statements. 'But I'm puzzled. You've been revived after nearly a century asleep. We've travelled here on a ship that couldn't even have been considered a distant possibility in your own era. We've undergone massive social and technical upheavals in the last hundred years. There are things about us – things about me – I haven't told you yet. Things about *you* I haven't even told you yet.'

'I'm just taking things one step at a time, that's all.' Iverson shrugged and looked distantly past Clavain, through the window behind him. His gaze must have been skating across kilometres of ice towards Diadem's white horizon, unable to find a purchase. 'I admit, I'm not really interested in technological innovations. I'm sure your ship's really nice, but . . . it's just applied physics. Just engineering. There may be some new quantum principles underlying your propulsion system, but if that's the case, it's probably just an elaborate curlicue on something that was already pretty baroque to begin with. You haven't smashed the light barrier, have you?' He read Clavain's expression accurately. 'No – didn't think so. Maybe if you had—'

'So what exactly does interest you?'

Iverson seemed to hesitate before answering, but when he did speak Clavain had no doubt that he was telling the truth. There was a sudden, missionary fervour in his voice. 'Emergence. Specifically, the emergence of complex, almost unpredictable patterns from systems governed by a few simple laws. Consciousness is an excellent example. A human mind's really just a web of simple neuronal cells wired together in a particular way. The laws governing the functioning of those individual cells aren't all that difficult to grasp – a cascade of well-studied electrical, chemical and enzymic processes. The tricky part is the wiring diagram. It certainly isn't encoded in DNA in any but the crudest sense. Otherwise why would a baby bother growing neural connections that are pruned down before birth? That'd be a real waste – if you had a perfect blueprint for the conscious mind you'd only bother forming the connections you needed. No; the mind organises itself during growth, and that's why it needs so many more neurons than it'll eventually incorporate into functioning networks. It needs the raw material to work with as it gropes its way toward a functioning consciousness. The pattern emerges, bootstrapping itself into existence, and the pathways that aren't used – or aren't as efficient as others – are discarded.' Iverson paused. 'But how this organisation happens really isn't understood in any depth. Do you know how many neurons it takes to control the first part of a lobster's gut, Nevil? Have a guess, to the nearest hundred.'

Clavain shrugged. 'I don't know. Five hundred? A thousand?'

'No. Six. Not six hundred, just six. Six damned neurons. You can't get much simpler than that. But it took decades to understand how those six worked together, let alone how that particular network evolved. The problems aren't inseparable, either. You can't really hope to understand how ten billion neurons organise themselves into a functioning whole unless you understand how the whole actually functions. Oh, we've made some progress – we can tell you exactly which spinal neurons fire to make a lamprey swim, and how that firing pattern maps into muscle motion – but we're a long way from understanding how something as elusive as the concept of "I" emerges in the developing human mind. Well, at least we were before I went under. You may be about to reveal that you've achieved stunning progress in the last century, but something tells me you were too busy with social upheaval for that.'

Clavain felt an urge to argue – angered by the man's tone – but suppressed it, willing himself into a state of serene acceptance. 'You're probably right. We've made progress in the other direction – augmenting the mind as it is – but if we genuinely understood brain development, we wouldn't have ended up with a failure like Felka.'

'Oh, I wouldn't call her a failure, Nevil.'

'I didn't mean it like that.'

'Of course not.' Now it was Iverson's turn to place a hand on Clavain's shoulder. 'But you must see now why I find so Felka so fascinating. Her mind is damaged – you told me that yourself, and there's no need to go into the details – but despite that damage, despite the vast abysses in her head, she's beginning to self-assemble the kinds of higher-level neural routines we all take for granted. It's as if the patterns were always there as latent potentials, and it's only now that they're beginning to emerge. Isn't that fascinating? Isn't it something worthy of study?'

Delicately, Clavain removed the man's hand from his shoulder. 'I suppose so. I had hoped, however, that there might be something more to it than study.'

'I've offended you, and I apologise. My choice of phrase was poor. Of course I care for her.'

Clavain felt suddenly awkward, as if he had misjudged a fundamentally decent man. 'I understand. Look, ignore what I said.'

'Yeah, of course. It – um – will be all right for me to see her again, won't it?'

Clavain nodded. 'I'm sure she'd miss you if you weren't around.'

Over the next few days, Clavain left the two of them to their games, only rarely eavesdropping to see how things were going. Iverson had asked permission to show Felka around some of the other areas of the base, and after a few initial misgivings Clavain and Galiana had both agreed to his request. After that, long hours went by when the two of them were not to be found. Clavain had tracked them once, watching as Iverson led the girl into a disused lab and showed her intricate molecular models. They clearly delighted her; vast fuzzy holographic assemblages of atoms and chemical bonds that floated in the air like Chinese dragons. Wearing cumbersome gloves and goggles, Iverson and Felka were able to manipulate the mega molecules, forcing them to fold into minimum-energy configurations that brute-force computation would have struggled to predict. As they gestured into the air and made the dragons contort and twist, Clavain watched for the inevitable moment when Felka would grow bored and demand something more challenging. But it never came. Afterwards – when she had returned to the fold, her face shining with wonder – it was as if Felka had undergone a spiritual experience. Iverson had shown her something her mind could not instantly encompass; a problem too large and subtle to be stormed in a flash of intuitive insight.

Seeing that, Clavain again felt guilty about the way he had spoken to Iverson, and knew that he had not completely put aside his doubts about the message Setterholm had left in the ice. But – the riddle of the helmet aside – there was no reason to think that Iverson might be a murderer beyond those haphazard marks. Clavain had looked into Iverson's personnel records from the time before he was frozen, and the man's history was flawless. He had been a solid, professional member of the expedition, well liked and trusted by the others. Granted, the records were patchy, and since they were stored digitally they could have been doctored to almost any extent. But then much the same story was told by the hand-written diary and verbal log entries of some of the other victims. Andrew Iverson's name came up again and again as a man regarded with affection by his fellows; most certainly not someone capable of murder. Best, then, to discard the evidence of the marks and give him the benefit of the doubt.

Clavain spoke of his fears to Galiana, and while she listened to him, she only came back with exactly the same rational counter-arguments he had already provided for himself.

'The problem is,' Galiana said, 'that the man you found in the crevasse could have been severely confused, perhaps even hallucinatory. That message he left – if it was a message, and not just a set of random gouge marks he made while convulsing – could mean anything at all.'

'We don't know that Setterholm was confused,' Clavain protested.

'We don't? Then why didn't he make sure his helmet was on properly? It can't have been latched fully, or it wouldn't have rolled off him when he hit the bottom of the crevasse.'

'Yes,' Clavain said. 'But I'm reasonably sure he wouldn't have been able to leave the base if his helmet hadn't been latched.'

'In which case he must have undone it afterwards.'

'Yes, but there's no reason for him to have done that, unless . . .'

Galiana gave him a thin-lipped smile. 'Unless he was confused. Back to square one, Nevil.'

'No,' he said, conscious that he could almost see the shape of something; something that was close to the truth if not the truth itself. 'There's another possibility, one I hadn't thought of until now.'

Galiana squinted at him, that rare frown appearing. 'Which is?'

'That someone else removed his helmet for him.'

They went down into the bowels of the base. In the dead space of the equipment bays Galiana became ill at ease. She was not used to being out of communicational range of her colleagues. Normally systems buried in the environment picked up neural signals from individuals, amplifying and rebroadcasting them to other people, but there were no such systems here. Clavain could hear Galiana's thoughts, but they came in weakly, like a voice from the sea almost drowned by the roar of surf.

'This had better be worth it,' Galiana said.

'I want to show you the airlock,' Clavain answered. 'I'm sure Setterholm must have left here with his helmet properly attached.'

'You still think he was murdered?'

'I think it's a remote possibility that we should be very careful not to discount.'

'But why would anyone kill a man whose only interest was a lot of harmless ice-worms?'

'That's been bothering me as well.'

'And?'

'I think I have an answer. Half of one, anyway. What if his interest in the worms brought him into conflict with the others? I'm thinking about the reactor.'

Galiana nodded. 'They'd have needed to harvest ice for it.'

'Which Setterholm might have seen as interfering with the

worms' ecology. Maybe he made a nuisance of himself and someone decided to get rid of him.'

'That would be a pretty extreme way of dealing with him.'

'I know,' Clavain said, stepping through a connecting door into the transport bay. 'I said I had half an answer, not all of one.'

As soon as he was through he knew something was amiss. The bay was not as it had been before, when he had come down here scouting for clues. He dropped his train of thought immediately, focusing only on the now.

The room was much, much colder than it should have been. And brighter. There was an oblong of chill blue daylight spilling across the floor from the huge open door of one of the vehicle exit ramps. Clavain looked at it in mute disbelief, wanting it to be a temporary glitch in his vision. But Galiana was with him, and she had seen it, too.

'Someone's left the base,' she said.

Clavain looked out across the ice. He could see the wake the vehicle had left in the snow, arcing out towards the horizon. For a long moment they stood at the top of the ramp, frozen into inaction. Clavain's mind screamed with the implications. He had never really liked the idea of Iverson taking Felka away with him elsewhere in the base, but he had never considered the possibility that he might take her into one of the blind zones. From here, Iverson must have known enough little tricks to open a surface door, start a rover and leave, without any of the Conjoiners realising.

'Nevil, listen to me,' Galiana said. 'He doesn't necessarily mean her any harm. He might just want to show her something.'

He turned to her. 'There isn't time to arrange a shuttle. That party trick of yours – talking to the door? Do you think you can manage it again?'

'I don't need to. The door's already open.'

Clavain nodded at one of the other rovers, hulking behind them. 'It's not the door I'm thinking about.'

Galiana was disappointed: it took her three minutes to convince the machine to start, rather than the few dozen seconds she said it should have taken. She was, she told Clavain, in serious danger of getting rusty at that sort of thing. Clavain just thanked the gods that there had been no mechanical sabotage to the rover; no amount of neural intervention could have fixed that.

'That's another thing that makes it look as if this is just an innocent trip outside,' Galiana said. 'If he'd really wanted to abduct her, it wouldn't have taken much additional effort to stop us following him. If he'd closed the door, as well, we might not even have noticed he was gone.'

'Haven't you ever heard of reverse psychology?' Clavain said.

'I still can't see Iverson as a murderer, Nevil.' She checked his expression, her own face calm despite the effort of driving the machine. Her hands were folded in her lap. She was less isolated now, having used the rover's comm systems to establish a link back to the other Conjoiners. 'Setterholm, maybe. The obsessive loner and all that. Just a shame he's the dead one.'

'Yes,' Clavain said, uneasily.

The rover itself ran on six wheels, a squat, pressurised hull perched low between absurd-looking balloon tyres. Galiana gunned them hard down the ramp and across the ice, trusting the machine to glide harmlessly over the smaller crevasses. It seemed reckless, but if they followed the trail Iverson had left, they were almost guaranteed not to hit any fatal obstacles.

'Did you get anywhere with the source of the sickness?' Clavain asked.

'No breakthroughs yet—'

'Then here's a suggestion. Can you read my visual memory accurately?' Clavain did not need an answer. 'While you were finding Iverson's body, I was looking over the lab samples. There were a lot of terrestrial organisms there. Could one of those have been responsible?'

'You'd better replay the memory.'

Clavain did so: picturing himself looking over the rows of culture dishes, test tubes and gel slides; concentrating especially on those that had come from Earth rather than the locally obtained samples. In his mind's eye the sample names refused to snap into clarity, but the machines Galiana had seeded through his head would already be locating the eidetically stored short-term memories and retrieving them with a clarity beyond the capabilities of Clavain's own brain.

'Now see if there's anything there that might do the job.'

'A terrestrial organism?' Galiana sounded surprised. 'Well, there might be something there, but I can't see how it could have spread beyond the laboratory unless someone wanted it to.'

'I think that's exactly what happened.'

'Sabotage?'

'Yes.'

'Well, we'll know sooner or later. I've passed the information to the others. They'll get back to me if they find a candidate. But I still don't see why anyone would sabotage the entire base, even if it was possible. Overthrowing the von Neumann machines is one thing . . . mass suicide is another.'

'I don't think it was mass suicide. Mass murder, maybe.'

'And Iverson's your main suspect?'

'He survived, didn't he? And Setterholm scrawled a message in the ice just before he died. It must have been a warning about him.' But even as he spoke, he knew there was a second possibility; one that he could not quite focus on.

Galiana swerved the rover to avoid a particularly deep and yawning chasm, shaded with vivid veins of turquoise blue.

'There's a small matter of missing motive.'

Clavain looked ahead, wondering if the thing he saw glinting in the distance was a trick of the eye. 'I'm working on that,' he said.

Galiana halted them next to the other rover. The two machines were parked at the lip of a slope-sided depression in the ice. It was not really steep enough to call a crevasse, although it was at least thirty or forty metres deep. From the rover's cab it was not possible to see all the way into the powdery blue depths, although Clavain could certainly make out the fresh footprints descending into them. Up on the surface, marks like that would have been scoured away by the wind in days or hours, so these prints were very fresh. There were, he observed, two sets – someone heavy and confident and someone lighter, less sure of their footing.

Before they had taken the rover they had made sure there were two suits aboard it. They struggled into them, fiddling with the latches.

'If I'm right,' Clavain said, 'this kind of precaution isn't really necessary. Not for avoiding the sickness, anyway. But better safe than sorry.'

'Excellent timing,' Galiana said, snapping down her helmet and giving it a quarter twist to lock into place. 'They've just pulled something from your memory, Nevil. There's a family of single-celled organisms called dinoflagellates, one of which was present in the lab where we found Iverson. Something called *Pfiesteria piscicida*. Normally it's an ambush predator that attacks fish.'

'Could it have been responsible for the madness?'

'It's at least a strong contender. It has a taste for mammalian tissue as well. If it gets into the human nervous system it produces memory loss, disorientation – as well as a host of physical effects. It could have been dispersed as a toxic aerosol, released into the base's air system. Someone with access to the lab's facilities could have turned it from something merely nasty into something deadly, I think.'

'We should have pinpointed it, Galiana. Didn't we swab the air ducts?'

'Yes, but we weren't looking for something terrestrial. In fact we were excluding terrestrial organisms, only filtering for the basic biochemical building blocks of Diadem life. We just weren't think-ing in criminal terms.'

'More fool us,' Clavain said.

Suited now, they stepped outside. Clavain began to regret his haste in leaving the base so quickly; at having to make do with these old suits and lacking any means of defence. Wanting something in his hand for moral support, he examined the equipment stowed around the outside of the rover until he found an ice pick. It would not be much of a weapon, but he felt better for it.

'You won't need that,' Galiana said.

'What if Iverson turns nasty?'

'You still won't need it.'

But he kept hold of it anyway – an ice pick was an ice pick, after all – and the two of them walked to the point where the icy ground began to curve over the lip of the depression. Clavain examined the wrist of his suit, studying the cryptic and old-fashioned matrix of keypads that controlled the suit's functions. On a whim he pressed something promising and was gratified when he felt crampons spike from the soles of his boots, anchoring him to the ice.

'Iverson!' he shouted. 'Felka!'

But sound carried poorly beyond his helmet, and the ceaseless, whipping wind would have snatched his words away from the crevasse. There was nothing for it but to make the difficult trek into the blue depths. He led the way, his heart pounding in his chest, the old suit awkward and top-heavy. He almost lost his footing once or twice, and had to stop to catch his breath when he reached the level bottom of the depression, sweat running into his eyes.

He looked around. The footprints led horizontally for ten or fifteen metres, weaving between fragile, curtain-like formations of opal ice. On some clinical level he acknowledged that the place had a sinister charm – he imagined the wind breathing through those curtains of ice, making ethereal music – but the need to find Felka eclipsed such considerations. He focused only on the low, dark-blue hole of a tunnel in the ice ahead of them. The footprints vanished into the tunnel.

'If the bastard's taken her . . .' Clavain said, tightening his grip on the pick. He switched on his helmet light and stooped into the tunnel, Galiana behind him. It was hard going; the tunnel wriggled, rose and descended for many tens of metres, and Clavain was unable to decide whether it was some weird natural feature – carved, perhaps, by a hot sub-glacial river – or whether it had been dug by hand, much more recently. The walls were veined with worm tracks: a marbling like an immense magnification of the human retina. Here and there Clavain saw the dark smudges of worms moving through cracks that were very close to the surface, though he knew it would be necessary to stare at them for long seconds before any movement was discernible. He groaned, the stooping becoming painful, and then the tunnel widened out dramatically. He realised that he had emerged into a much larger space.

It was still underground, although the ceiling glowed with the blue translucence of filtered daylight. The covering of ice could not have been more than a metre or two thick; a thin shell stretched like a dome over tens of metres of yawing nothing. Nearly sheer walls of delicately patterned ice rose up from a level, footprint-dappled floor.

'Ah,' said Iverson, who was standing near one wall of the chamber. 'You decided to join us.'

Clavain felt a stab of relief seeing that Felka was standing not far from him, next to a piece of equipment Clavain failed to recognise. Felka appeared unharmed. She turned towards him, the peculiar play of light and shade on her helmeted face making her look older than she was.

'Nevil,' he heard Felka say. 'Hello.'

He crossed the ice, fearful that the whole marvellous edifice was about to come crashing down on them all.

'Why did you bring her here, Iverson?'

'There's something I wanted to show her. Something I knew she'd like, even more than the other things.' He turned to the smaller figure near him. 'Isn't that right, Felka?'

'Yes.'

'And do you like it?'

Her answer was matter of fact, but it was closer to conversation than anything Clavain had ever heard from her lips.

'Yes. I do like it.'

Galiana stepped ahead of him and extended a hand to the girl. 'Felka? I'm glad you like this place. I like it, too. But now it's time to come back home.'

Clavain steeled himself for an argument, some kind of show-down between the two women, but to his immense relief Felka walked casually towards Galiana.

'I'll take her back to the rover,' Galiana said. 'I want to make sure she hasn't had any problems breathing with that old suit on.'

A transparent lie, but it would suffice.

Then she spoke to Clavain. It was a tiny thing, almost inconsequential, but she placed it directly in his head.

And he understood what he would have to do.

When they were alone, Clavain said, 'You killed him.'

'Setterholm?'

'No. You couldn't have killed Setterholm because you *are* Setterholm.' Clavain looked up, the arc of his helmet light tracing the filamentary patterning until it became too tiny to resolve; blurring into an indistinct haze of detail that curved over into the ceiling itself. It was like admiring a staggeringly ornate fresco.

'Nevil – do me a favour? Check the settings on your suit, in case you're not getting enough oxygen.'

'There's nothing wrong with my suit.' Clavain smiled, the irony of it all delicious. 'In fact, it was the suit that tipped me off. When you pushed Iverson into the crevasse, his helmet came off. That couldn't have happened unless it wasn't fixed on properly in the first place – and *that* couldn't have happened unless someone had removed it after the two of you left the base.'

Setterholm – he was sure the man was Setterholm – snorted derisively, but Clavain continued speaking.

'Here's my stab at what happened, for what it's worth. You needed to swap identities with Iverson because Iverson had no obvious motive for murdering the others, whereas Setterholm certainly did.'

'And I don't suppose you have any idea what that motive might have been?'

'Give me time; I'll get there eventually. Let's just deal with the lone murder first. Changing the electronic records was easy enough – you could even swap Iverson's picture and medical data for your own – but that was only part of it. You also needed to get Iverson into your clothes and suit, so that we'd assume the body in the crevasse belonged to you, Setterholm. I don't know exactly how you did it.'

'Then perhaps—'

Clavain carried on. 'But my guess is you let him catch a dose of the bug you let loose in the main base – *Pfiesteria*, wasn't it? – then followed him when he went walking outside. You jumped him, knocked him down on the ice and got him out of his suit and into yours. He was probably unconscious by then, I suppose. But then he must have started coming round, or you panicked for another reason. You jammed the helmet on and pushed him into the crevasse. Maybe if all that had happened was his helmet coming off, I wouldn't have dwelled on it. But he wasn't dead, and he lived long enough to scratch a message in the ice. I thought it concerned his murderer, but I was wrong. He was trying to tell me who he was. Not Setterholm, but Iverson.'

'Nice theory.' Setterholm glanced down at a display screen in the back of the machine squatting next to him. Mounted on a tripod, it resembled a huge pair of binoculars, pointed with a slight elevation towards one wall of the chamber.

'Sometimes a theory's all you need. That's quite a toy you've got there, by the way. What is it, some kind of ground-penetrating radar?'

Setterholm brushed aside the question. 'If I was him – why would I have done it? Just because I was interested in the ice-worms?'

'It's simple,' Clavain said, hoping the uncertainty he felt was not apparent in his voice. 'The others weren't as convinced as you were of the worms' significance. Only you saw them for what they were.' He was treading carefully here; masking his ignorance of Setterholm's deeper motives by playing on the man's vanity.

'Clever of me if I did.'

'Oh, yes. I wouldn't doubt that at all. And it must have driven you to distraction, that you could see what the others couldn't. Naturally, you wanted to protect the worms, when you saw them under threat.'

'Sorry, Nevil, but you're going to have to try a lot harder than that.' He paused and patted the machine's matt-silver casing, clearly unable to pretend that he did not know what it was. 'It's radar, yes. It can probe the interior of the glacier with sub-centi-metre resolution, to a depth of several tens of metres.'

'Which would be rather useful if you wanted to study the worms.'

Setterholm shrugged. 'I suppose so. A climatologist interested in glacial flow might also have use for the information.'

'Like Iverson?' Clavain took a step closer to Setterholm and the radar equipment. He could see the display more clearly now: a fibrous tangle of mainly green lines slowly spinning in space, with a denser structure traced out in red near its heart. 'Like the man you killed?'

'I told you, I'm Iverson.'

Clavain stepped towards him with the ice pick held double-handed, but when he was a few metres from the man he veered past and made his way to the wall. Setterholm had flinched, but he had not seemed unduly worried that Clavain was about to try to hurt him.

'I'll be frank with you,' Clavain said, raising the pick. 'I don't really understand what it is about the worms.'

'What are you going to do?'

'This.'

Clavain smashed the pick against the wall as hard as he was able. It was enough: a layer of ice fractured noisily away, sliding down like a miniature avalanche to land in pieces at his feet; each fist-sized shard was veined with worm trails.

'Stop,' Setterholm said.

'Why? What do you care, if you're not interested in the worms?'

Clavain smashed the ice again, dislodging another layer.

'You . . .' Setterholm paused. 'You could bring the whole place down on us if you're not careful.'

Clavain raised the pick again, letting out a groan of effort as he swung. This time he put all his weight behind the swing, all his fury, and a chunk the size of his upper body calved noisily from the wall.

'I'll take that risk,' Clavain said.

'No. You've got to stop.'

'Why? It's only ice.'

'No!'

Setterholm rushed him, knocking him off his feet. The ice pick spun from his hand and the two of them crashed into the ground, Setterholm landing on his chest. He pressed his faceplate close to Clavain's, every bead of sweat on his forehead gleaming like a precise little jewel.

'I told you to stop.'

Clavain found it difficult to speak with the pressure on his chest, but forced out the words with effort. 'I think we can dispense with the charade that you're Iverson now, can't we?'

'You shouldn't have harmed it.'

'No . . . and neither should the others, eh? But they needed that ice very badly.'

Now Setterholm's voice held a tone of dull resignation. 'For the reactor, you mean?'

'Yes. The fusion plant.' Clavain allowed himself to feel some small satisfaction before adding, 'Actually, it was Galiana who made the connection, not me. That the reactor ran on ice, I mean. And after all the outlying bases had been evacuated, they had to keep everyone alive back at the main one. And that meant more load on the reactor. Which meant it needed more ice, of which there was hardly a shortage in the immediate vicinity.'

'But they couldn't be allowed to harvest the ice. Not after what I'd discovered.'

Clavain nodded, observing that the reversion from Iverson to Setterholm was now complete.

'No. The ice is precious, isn't it? Infinitely more so than anyone else realised. Without that ice the worms would have died—'

'You don't understand either, do you?'

Clavain swallowed. 'I think I understand more than the others, Setterholm. You realised that the worms—'

'It wasn't the damned worms!' He had shouted – Setterholm had turned on a loudspeaker function in his suit that Clavain had not yet located – and for a moment the words crashed around the great ice chamber, threatening to start the tiny chain reaction of fractures that would collapse the whole structure. But when silence had returned – disturbed only by the rasp of Clavain's breathing – nothing had changed.

'It wasn't the worms?'

'No.' Setterholm was calmer now, as if the point had been made. 'No – not really. They were important, yes – but only as low-level elements in a much more complex system. Don't you understand?'

Clavain strove for honesty. 'I never really understood what it was that fascinated you about them. They seem quite simple to me.'

Setterholm removed his weight from Clavain and rose up onto his feet again. 'That's because they are. A child could grasp the biology of a single ice-worm in an afternoon. Felka did, in fact. Oh, she's wonderful, Nevil.' Setterholm's teeth flashed a smile that chilled Clavain. 'The things she could unravel . . . she isn't a failure; not at all. I think she's something miraculous we barely comprehend.'

'Unlike the worms.'

'Yes. They're like clockwork toys, programmed with a few simple rules.' Setterholm stooped down and grabbed the ice pick for himself. 'They always respond in exactly the same way to the same input stimulus. And the kinds of stimuli they respond to are simple in the extreme: a few gradations of temperature; a few biochemical cues picked up from the ice itself. But the emergent properties . . .'

Clavain forced himself to a sitting position. 'There's that word again.'

'It's the network, Nevil. The system of tunnels the worms dig through the ice. Don't you understand? That's where the real complexity lies. That's what I was always more interested in. Of course, it took me years to see it for what it is—'

'Which is?'

'A self-evolving network. One that has the capacity to adapt; to learn.'

'It's just a series of channels bored through ice, Setterholm.'

'No. It's infinitely more than that.' The man craned his neck as far as the architecture of his suit would allow, revelling in the palatial beauty of the chamber. 'There are two essential elements in any neural network, Nevil. Connections and nodes are necessary, but not enough. The connections must be capable of being weighted; adjusted in strength according to usefulness. And the nodes must be capable of processing the inputs from the

102

connections in a deterministic manner, like logic gates.' He gestured around the chamber. 'Here, there is no absolutely sharp distinction between the connections and the nodes, but the essences remain. The worms lay down secretions when they travel, and those secretions determine how other worms make use of the same channels; whether they utilise one route or another. There are many determining factors – the sexes of the worms, the seasons, others I won't bore you with. But the point is simple. The secretions – and the effect they have on the worms – mean that the topology of the network is governed by subtle emergent principles. And the breeding tangles function as logic gates; processing the inputs from their connecting nodes according to the rules of worm sex, caste and hierarchy. It's messy, slow and biological – but the end result is that the worm colony as a whole functions as a neural network. It's a program that the worms themselves are running, even though any given worm hasn't a clue that it's a part of a larger whole.'

Clavain absorbed all that and thought carefully before asking the question that occurred to him. 'How does it change?'

'Slowly,' Setterholm said. 'Sometimes routes fall into disuse because the secretions inhibit other worms from using them. Gradually, the glacier seals them shut. At the same time other cracks open by chance – the glacier's own fracturing imposes a constant chaotic background on the network – or the worms bore new holes. Seen in slow motion – our time frame – almost nothing ever seems to happen, let alone change. But imagine speeding things up, Nevil. Imagine if we could see the way the network has changed over the last century, or the last thousand years . . . imagine what we might find. A constantly evolving loom of connections, shifting and changing eternally. Now – does that remind you of anything?'

Clavain answered in the only way that he knew would satisfy Setterholm. 'A mind, I suppose. A newborn one, still forging neural connections.'

'Yes. Oh, you'd doubtless like to point out that the network is isolated, so it can't be responding to stimuli beyond itself – but we can't know that for certain. A season is like a heartbeat here, Nevil! What we think of as geologically slow processes – a glacier cracking, two glaciers colliding – those events could be as forceful as caresses and sounds to a blind child.' He paused and glanced at the screen in the back of the imaging radar. 'That's what I wanted to find out. A century ago, I was able to study the network for a handful of decades, and I found something that astonished me. The colony moves, reshapes itself constantly, as the glacier shifts and breaks up. But no matter how radically the network changes its periphery, no matter how thoroughly the loom evolves, there are deep structures inside the network that are always preserved.' Setterholm's finger traced the red mass at the heart of the green tunnel map. 'In the language of network topology, the tunnel system is scale-free rather than exponential. It's the hallmark of a highly organised network with a few rather specialised processing centres – hubs, if you like. This is one. I believe its function is to cause the whole network to move away from a widening fracture in the glacier. It would take me much more than a century to find out for sure, although everything I've seen here confirms what I originally thought. I mapped other structures in other colonies, too. They can be huge, spread across cubic kilometres of ice. But they always persist. Don't you see what that means? The network has begun to develop specialised areas of function. It's begun to process information, Nevil. It's begun to creep its way towards thought.'

Clavain looked around him once more, trying to see the chamber in the new light that Setterholm had revealed. Think not of the worms as entities in their own right, he thought, but as electrical signals, ghosting along synaptic pathways in a neural network made of solid ice . . .

He shivered. It was the only appropriate response.

'Even if the network processes information . . . there's no reason to think it could ever become conscious.'

'Why not, Nevil? What's the fundamental difference between perceiving the universe via electrical signals transmitted along nerve tissue, and via fracture patterns moving through a vast block of ice?'

'I suppose you have a point.'

'I had to save them, Nevil. Not just the worms, but the network they were a part of. We couldn't come all this way and just wipe out the first thinking thing we'd ever encountered in the universe, simply because it didn't fit into our neat little pre-conceived notions of what alien thought would actually be like.'

'But saving the worms meant killing everyone else.'

'You think I didn't realise that? You think it didn't agonise me to do what I had to do? I'm a human being, Nevil – not a monster. I knew exactly what I was doing and I knew exactly what it would make me look like to anyone who came here afterwards.'

'But you still did it.'

'Put yourself in my shoes. How would you have acted?'

Clavain opened his mouth, expecting an easy answer to spring to mind. But nothing came; not for several seconds. He was thinking about Setterholm's question, more thoroughly than he had done so far. Until then he had satisfied himself with the quiet, unquestioned assumption that he would not have acted the way Setterholm had done. But could he really be so sure? Setterholm, after all, had truly believed that the network formed a sentient whole; a thinking being. Possessing that knowledge must have made him feel divinely chosen; sanctioned to commit any act to preserve the fabulously rare thing he had found. And he had, after all, been right.

'You haven't answered me.'

'That's because I thought the question warranted something more than a flippant answer, Setterholm. I like to think I wouldn't have acted the way you did, but I don't suppose I can ever be sure of that.'

Clavain stood up, inspecting his suit for damage; relieved that the scuffle had not injured him.

'You'll never know.'

'No. I never will. But one thing's clear enough. I've heard you talk; heard the fire in your words. You believe in your network, and yet you still couldn't make the others see it. I doubt I'd have been able to do much better, and I doubt that I'd have thought of a better way to preserve what you'd found.'

'Then you'd have killed everyone, just like I did?'

The realisation of it was like a heavy burden someone had just placed on his shoulders. It was so much easier to feel incapable of such acts. But Clavain had been a soldier. He had killed more people than he could remember, even though those days had been a long time ago. It was really a lot less difficult to do when you had a cause to believe in.

And Setterholm had definitely had a cause.

'Perhaps,' Clavain said. 'Perhaps I might have, yes.'

He heard Setterholm sigh. 'I'm glad. For a moment there—'

'For a moment what?'

'When you showed up with that pick, I thought you were planning to kill me.' Setterholm hefted the pick, much as Clavain had done earlier. 'You wouldn't have done that, would you? I don't deny that what I did was regrettable, but I had to do it.'

'I understand.'

'But what happens to me now? I can stay with you all, can't I?'

'We probably won't be staying on Diadem, I'm afraid. And I don't think you'd really want to come with us; not if you knew what we're really like.'

'You can't leave me alone here, not again.'

'Why not? You'll have your worms. And you can always kill yourself again and see who shows up next.' Clavain turned to leave.

'No. You can't go now.'

'I'll leave your rover on the surface. Maybe there are some supplies in it. Just don't come anywhere near the base again. You won't find a welcome there.'

'I'll die out here,' Setterholm said.

'Start getting used to it.'

He heard Setterholm's feet scuffing across the ice; a walk breaking into a run. Clavain turned around calmly, unsurprised to see Setterholm coming towards him with the pick raised high, as a weapon.

Clavain sighed.

He reached into Setterholm's skull, addressing the webs of machines that still floated in the man's head, and instructed them to execute their host in a sudden, painless orgy of neural deconstruction. It was not a trick he could have done an hour ago, but after Galiana had planted the method in his mind, it was easy as sneezing. For a moment he understood what it must feel like to be a god.

And in that same moment Setterholm dropped the ice pick and stumbled, falling forward onto one end of the pick's blade. It pierced his faceplate, but by then he was dead anyway.

'What I said was the truth,' Clavain said. 'I might have killed them as well, just like I said. I don't want to think so, but I can't say it isn't in me. No; I don't blame you for that; not at all.'

With his boot he began to kick a dusting of frost over the dead man's body. It would be too much bother to remove Setterholm from this place, and the machines inside him would sterilise his body, ensuring that none of his cells ever contaminated the glacier. And, as Clavain had told himself only a few days earlier, there were worse places to die than here. Or worse places to be left for dead, anyway.

When he was done, when what remained of Setterholm was just an ice-covered mound in the middle of cavern, Clavain addressed him one final time.

'But that doesn't make it right, either. It was still murder, Setterholm.' He kicked a final divot of ice over the corpse. 'Someone had to pay for it.'

A SPY IN EUROPA

Marius Vargovic, agent of Gilgamesh Isis, savoured an instant of free fall before the flitter's engines kicked in, slamming it away from the *Deucalion*. His pilot gunned the craft towards the moon below, quickly outrunning the other shuttles that the Martian liner had disgorged. Europa enlarged perceptibly: a flattening arc the colour of nicotine-stained wallpaper.

'Boring, isn't it.'

Vargovic turned around in his seat, languidly. 'You'd rather they were shooting at us?'

'I'd rather they were doing *something*.'

'Then you're a fool,' Vargovic said, making a tent of his fingers. 'There's enough armament buried in that ice to give Jupiter a second red spot. What it would do to us doesn't bear thinking about it.'

'Only trying to make conversation, friend.'

'Don't bother – it's an overrated activity at the best of times.'

'All right, Marius – I get the message. In fact I intercepted it, parsed it, filtered it, decrypted it with the appropriate one-time pad and wrote a fucking two-hundred-page report on it. Satisfied?'

'I'm never satisfied, Mishenka. It just isn't in my nature.'

But Mishenka was right: Europa was an encrypted document; complexity masked by a surface of fractured and refrozen ice. Its surface grooves were like the capillaries in a vitrified eyeball; faint as the structure in a raw surveillance image. But once within the airspace boundary of the Europan Demarchy, traffic-management co-opted the flitter, vectoring it into a touchdown corridor. In three days Mishenka would return, but then he would disable the avionics, kissing the ice for less than ten minutes.

'Not too late to abort,' Mishenka said, a long time later.

'Are you out of your tiny mind?'

The younger man dispensed a frosty Covert Ops smile. 'We've all heard what the Demarchy does to spies, Marius.'

'Is this a personal grudge or are you just psychotic?'

'I'll leave being psychotic to you, Marius – you're so much better at it.'

Vargovic nodded. It was the first sensible thing Mishenka had said all day.

They landed an hour later. Vargovic adjusted his Martian businesswear, tuning his holographically inwoven frock coat to project red sandstorms; lifting the collar in what he had observed from the liner's passengers was a recent Martian fad. Then he grabbed his bag – nothing incriminating there, no gadgets or weapons – and exited the flitter, stepping through the gasket of locks. A slitherwalk propelled him forward, massaging the soles of his slippers. It was a single cultured ribbon of octopus skin, stimulated to ripple by the timed firing of buried squid axons.

To get to Europa you either had to be sickeningly rich or sickeningly poor. Vargovic's cover was the former: a lie excusing the single-passenger flitter. As the slitherwalk advanced he was joined by other arrivals: businesspeople like himself, and a sugaring of the merely wealthy. Most of them had dispensed with holographics, instead projecting entoptics beyond their personal space: machine-generated hallucinations decoded by the implant hugging Vargovic's optic nerve. Hummingbirds and seraphim were in sickly vogue. Others were attended by autonomous perfumes that subtly altered the moods of those around them. Slightly lower down the social scale, Vargovic observed a clique of noisy tourists – antlered brats from Circum-Jove. Then there was a discontinuous jump: to squalid-looking Maunder refugees who must have accepted indenture to the Demarchy. The refugees were quickly segregated from the more affluent immigrants, who found themselves within a huge geodesic dome resting above the ice on refrigerated stilts. The walls of the dome glittered with duty-free shops, boutiques and bars. The floor was bowl-shaped, slitherwalks and spiral stairways descending to the nadir where a quincunx of fluted marble cylinders waited. Vargovic observed that the newly arrived were queuing for elevators that terminated in the cylinders. He joined a line and waited.

'First time in Cadmus-Asterius?' asked the bearded man ahead of him, iridophores in his plum-coloured jacket projecting Boolean propositions from Sirikit's *Machine Ethics in the Transenlightenment*.

'First time on Europa, actually. First time Circum-Jove, you want the full story.'

'Down-system?'

'Mars.'

The man nodded gravely. 'Hear it's tough.'

'You're not kidding.' And he wasn't. Since the sun had dimmed – the second Maunder Minimum, repeating the behaviour the sun had exhibited in the seventeenth century – the entire balance of power in the First System had altered. The economies of the inner worlds had found it difficult to adjust; agriculture and power-generation handicapped, with concomitant social upheaval. But the outer planets had never had the luxury of solar energy in the first place. Now Circum-Jove was the benchmark of First System economic power, with Circum-Saturn trailing behind. Because of this, the two primary Circum-Jove superpowers – the Demarchy, which controlled Europa and Io, and Gilgamesh Isis, which controlled Ganymede and parts of Callisto – were vying for dominance.

The man smiled keenly. 'Here for anything special?'

'Surgery,' Vargovic said, hoping to curtail the conversation at the earliest juncture. 'Very extensive anatomical surgery.'

They hadn't told him much.

'Her name is Cholok,' Control had said, after Vargovic had skimmed the dossiers back in the caverns that housed the Covert Operations section of Gilgamesh Isis security, deep in Ganymede. 'We recruited her ten years ago, when she was on Phobos.'

'And now she's Demarchy?'

Control had nodded. 'She was swept up in the brain-drain, once Maunder Two began to bite. The smartest got out while they could. The Demarchy – and us, of course – snapped up the brightest.'

'And also one of our sleepers.' Vargovic glanced down at the portrait of the woman, striped by video lines. She looked mousy to him, with a permanent bone-deep severity of expression.

'Cheer up,' Control said. 'I'm asking you to contact her, not sleep with her.'

'Yeah, yeah. Just tell me her background.'

'Biotech.' Control nodded at the dossier. 'On Phobos she led one of the teams working in aquatic transform work – modifying the human form for submarine operations.'

Vargovic nodded diligently. 'Go on.'

'Phobos wanted to sell their know-how to the Martians, before their oceans froze. Of course, the Demarchy also appreciated her talents. Cholok took her team to Cadmus-Asterius, one of their hanging cities.'

'Mm.' Vargovic was getting the thread now. 'By which time we'd already recruited her.'

'Right,' Control said, 'except we had no obvious use for her.'

'Then why this conversation?'

Control smiled. Control always smiled when Vargovic pushed the envelope of subservience. 'We're having it because our sleeper won't lie down.' Then Control reached over and touched the image of Cholok, making her speak. What Vargovic was seeing was an intercept: something Gilgamesh had captured, riddled with edits and jump-cuts.

She appeared to be sending a verbal message to an old friend in Isis. She was talking rapidly from a white room, inert medical servitors behind her. Shelves displayed flasks of colour-coded medichines. A cruciform bed resembled an autopsy slab with ceramic drainage sluices.

'Cholok contacted us a month ago,' Control said. 'The room's part of her clinic.'

'She's using Phrase-Embedded Three,' Vargovic said, listening to her speech patterns, siphoning content from otherwise normal Canasian.

'Last code we taught her.'

'All right. What's her angle?'

Control chose his words – skating around the information excised from Cholok's message. 'She wants to give us something,' he said. 'Something valuable. She's acquired it accidentally. Someone good has to smuggle it out.'

'Flattery will get you everywhere, Control.'

The muzak rose to a carefully timed crescendo as the elevator plunged through the final layer of ice. The view around and below was literally dizzying, and Vargovic registered exactly as much awe as befitted his Martian guise. He knew the Demarchy's history, of course – how the hanging cities had begun as points of entry into the ocean; air-filled observation cupolas linked to the surface by narrow access shafts sunk through the kilometre-thick crustal ice. Scientists had studied the unusual smoothness of the crust, noting that its fracture patterns echoed those on Earth's ice shelves, implying the presence of a water ocean. Europa was further from the sun than Earth, but something other than solar energy maintained the ocean's liquidity. Instead, the moon's orbit around Jupiter created stresses that flexed the moon's silicate core, tectonic heat bleeding into the ocean via hydrothermal vents.

Descending into the city was a little like entering an amphitheatre – except that there was no stage; merely an endless succession of steeply tiered lower balconies. They converged towards a light-filled infinity, seven or eight kilometres below, where the city's conic shape constricted to a point. The opposite side was half a kilometre away, levels rising like geologic strata. A wide glass tower threaded the atrium from top to bottom, aglow with smoky-green ocean and a mass of kelp-like flora, cultured by gilly swimmers. Artificial sun lamps burned in the kelp like Christmas tree lights. Above, the tower branched, peristaltic feeds reaching out to the ocean proper. Offices, shops, restaurants and residential units were stacked atop each other, or teetered into the abyss on elegant balconies, spun from lustrous sheets of bulk-chitin polymer, the Demarchy's major construction material. Gossamer bridges arced across the atrium space, dodging banners, projections and vast translucent sculptures moulded from a silky variant of the same chitin polymer. Every visible surface was overlaid by neon, holographics and entoptics. People were everywhere, and in every face Vargovic detected a slight absence, as if their minds were not entirely focused on the here and now. No wonder: all citizens had an implant that constantly interrogated them, eliciting their opinions on every aspect of Demarchy life, both within Cadmus-Asterius and beyond. Eventually, it was said, the implant's nagging presence faded from consciousness, until the act of democratic participation became near-involuntary.

It revolted Vargovic as much as it intrigued him.

'Obviously,' Control said, with judicial deliberation, 'what Cholok has to offer isn't merely a nugget – or she'd have given it via PE3.'

Vargovic leaned forward. 'She hasn't told you what it is?'

'Only that it could endanger the hanging cities.'

'You trust her?'

Vargovic felt one of Control's momentary indiscretions coming on. 'She may have been sleeping, but she hasn't been completely valueless. She's assisted in defections . . . like the Maunciple job – remember that?'

'If you're calling that a success, perhaps it's time I defected.'

'Actually, it was Cholok's information that persuaded us to get Maunciple out via the ocean rather than the front door. If Demarchy security had taken Maunciple alive they'd have learned ten years of tradecraft.'

'Whereas instead Maunciple got a harpoon in his back.'

'So the operation had its flaws.' Control shrugged. 'But if you're thinking all this points to Cholok having been compromised . . . Naturally, the thought entered our heads. But if Maunciple had acted otherwise it would have been worse.' Control folded his arms. 'And of course, he might have made it, in which case even you'd have to admit Cholok's safe.'

'Until proven otherwise.'

Control brightened. 'So you'll do it?'

'Like I have a choice.'

'There's always a choice, Vargovic.'

Yes, Vargovic thought. There was always a choice, between doing whatever Gilgamesh Isis asked of him and being deprogrammed, cyborgised and sent to work in the sulphur projects around the slopes of Ra Patera. It just wasn't a particularly good one.

'One other thing . . .'

'Yes?'

'When I've got whatever Cholok has—'

Control half-smiled, the two of them sharing a private joke that did not need illumination. 'I'm sure the usual will suffice.'

The elevator slowed into immigration.

Demarchy guards hefted big guns, but no one took any interest in him. His story about coming from Mars was accepted; he was subjected to only the usual spectrum of invasive procedures: neural and genetic patterns scanned for pathologies, body bathed

115

in eight forms of exotic radiation. The final formality consisted of drinking a thimble of chocolate. The beverage consisted of billions of medichines which infiltrated his body, searching for concealed drugs, weapons and illegal biomodifications. He knew that they would find nothing, but was still relieved when they reached his bladder and requested to be urinated back into the Demarchy.

The entire procedure lasted six minutes. Outside, Vargovic followed a slitherwalk to the city zoo, and then barged through crowds of schoolchildren until he arrived at the aquarium where Cholok was meant to meet him. The exhibits were devoted to Europan biota, most of which depended on the ecological niches of the hydrothermal vents, carefully reproduced here. There was nothing very exciting to look at, since most Europan predators looked marginally less fierce than hat stands or lampshades. The commonest were called ventlings: large and structurally simple animals whose metabolisms hinged on symbiosis. They were pulpy, funnelled bags planted on a tripod of orange stilts, moving with such torpor that Vargovic almost nodded off before Cholok arrived at his side.

She wore an olive-green coat and tight emerald trousers, projecting a haze of medicinal entoptics. Her clenched jaw accentuated the dourness he had gleaned from the intercept.

They kissed.

'Good to see you Marius. It's been – what?'

'Nine years, thereabouts.'

'How's Phobos these days?'

'Still orbiting Mars.' He deployed a smile. 'Still a dive.'

'You haven't changed.'

'Nor you.'

At a loss for words, Vargovic found his gaze returning to the informational read-out accompanying the ventling exhibit. Only half-attentively, he read that the ventlings, motile in their juvenile phase, gradually became sessile in adulthood, stilts thickening with deposited sulphur until they were rooted to the ground like stalagmites. When they died, their soft bodies dispersed into the ocean, but the tripods remained; eerily regular clusters of orange spines concentrated around active vents.

'Nervous, Marius?'

'In your hands? Not likely.'

'That's the spirit.'

They bought two mugs of mocha from a nearby servitor, then returned to the ventling display, making what sounded like small talk. During indoctrination, Cholok had been taught Phrase-Embedded Three. The code allowed the insertion of secondary information into a primary conversation by means of careful deployment of word order, hesitation and sentence structure.

'What have you got?' Vargovic asked.

'A sample,' Cholok answered, one of the easy, pre-set words that did not need to be laboriously conveyed. But what followed took nearly five minutes to put over, freighted via a series of rambling reminiscences of the Phobos years. 'A small shard of hyperdiamond.'

Vargovic nodded. He knew what hyperdiamond was: a topologically complex interweave of tubular fullerene; structurally similar to cellulose or bulk chitin but thousands of times stronger; its rigidity artificially maintained by some piezoelectric trick that Gilgamesh lacked.

'Interesting,' Vargovic said. 'But unfortunately not interesting enough.'

She ordered another mocha and downed it, replying, 'Use your imagination. Only the Demarchy knows how to synthesise it.'

'It's also useless as a weapon.'

'Depends. There's an application you should know about.'

'What?'

'Keeping this city afloat – and no, I'm not talking about economic solvency. Do you know about Buckminster Fuller? He lived about four hundred years ago; believed absolute democracy could be achieved through technological means.'

'The fool.'

'Maybe. But Fuller also invented the geodesic lattice that determines the structure of the buckyball: the closed allotrope of tubular fullerene. The city owes him on two counts.'

'Save the lecture. How does the hyperdiamond come into it?'

'Flotation bubbles,' she said. 'Around the outside of the city. Each one is a hundred-metre-wide sphere of hyperdiamond, holding vacuum. A hundred-metre-wide molecule, in fact, since each sphere is composed of one endless strand of tubular fullerene. Think of that, Marius: a molecule you could park a ship inside.'

While he absorbed that, another part of his mind continued to read the ventling caption: how their biochemistry had many similarities with the gutless tube worms that lived around Earth's ocean vents. The ventlings drank hydrogen sulphide through their funnels, circulating it via a modified form of haemoglobin, passing it through a bacteria-saturated organ in the lower part of their bags. The bacteria split and oxidised the hydrogen sulphide, manufacturing a molecule similar to glucose. The glucose-analogue nourished the ventling, enabling it to keep living and occasionally make slow perambulations to other parts of the vent, or even to swim between vents, until the adult phase rooted it to the ground. Vargovic read this, and then read it again, because he had just remembered something: a puzzling intercept passed to him from cryptanalysis several months earlier; something about Demarchy plans to incorporate ventling biochemistry into a larger animal. For a moment he was tempted to ask Cholok about it directly, but he decided to force the subject from his mind until a more suitable time.

'Any other propaganda to share with me?'

'There are two hundred of these spheres. They inflate and deflate like bladders, maintaining C-A's equilibrium. I'm not sure how the deflation happens, except that it's something to do with changing the piezoelectric current in the tubes.'

'I still don't see why Gilgamesh needs it.'

'Think. If you can get a sample of this to Ganymede, they might be able to find a way of attacking it. All you'd need would be a molecular agent capable of opening the gaps between the fullerene strands so that a molecule of water could squeeze through, or something that impedes the piezoelectric force.'

Absently Vargovic watched a squid-like predator nibble a chunk from the bag of a ventling. The squid's blood ran thick with two forms of haemoglobin, one oxygen-bearing, one tuned for hydrogen sulphide. They used glycoproteins to keep their blood flowing and switched metabolisms as they swam from oxygen-dominated to sulphide-dominated water.

He snapped his attention back to Cholok. 'I can't believe I came all this way for . . . what? Carbon?' He shook his head, slotting the gesture into the primary narrative of their conversation. 'How did you obtain this?'

'An accident, with a gilly.'

'Go on.'

'An explosion near one of the bubbles. I was the surgeon assigned to the gilly; had to remove a lot of hyperdiamond from him. It wasn't difficult to save a few splinters.'

'Forward-thinking of you.'

'Hard part was persuading Gilgamesh to send you. Especially after Maunciple—'

'Don't lose any sleep over him,' Vargovic said, consulting his coffee. 'He was a fat bastard who couldn't swim fast enough.'

The surgery took place the next day. Vargovic woke with his mouth furnace-dry.

He felt . . . odd. They had warned him of this. He had even interviewed subjects who had undergone similar procedures in Gilgamesh's experimental labs. They told him he would feel fragile, as if his head was no longer adequately coupled to his body. The periodic flushes of cold around his neck only served to increase that feeling.

'You can speak,' Cholok said, looming over him in surgeon's whites. 'But the cardiovascular modifications – and the amount of reworking we've done to your laryngeal area – will make your voice sound a little strange. Some of the gilled are really only comfortable talking to their own kind.'

He held a hand before his eyes, examining the translucent webbing that now spanned between his fingers. There was a dark patch in the pale tissue of his palm: Cholok's embedded sample. The other hand held another.

'It worked, didn't it?' His voice sounded squeaky. 'I can breathe water.'

'And air,' Cholok said. 'Though what you'll now find is that really strenuous exercise only feels natural when you're submerged.'

'Can I move?'

'Of course,' she said. 'Try standing up. You're stronger than you feel.'

He did as she suggested, using the moment to assess his surroundings. A neural monitor clamped his crown. He was naked, in a brightly lit revival room; one glass-walled side faced the exterior ocean. It was from here that Cholok had first contacted Gilgamesh.

'This place is secure, isn't it?'

'Secure?' she said, as if the word itself was obscene. 'Yes, I suppose so.'

'Then tell me about the Denizens.'

'What?'

'Demarchy codeword. Cryptanalysis intercepted it recently – supposedly something about an experiment in radical biomodification. I was reminded of it in the aquarium.' Vargovic fingered the gills in his neck. 'Something that would make this look like cosmetic surgery. We heard the Demarchy had tailored the sulphur-based metabolism of the ventlings for human use.'

She whistled. 'That would be quite a trick.'

'Useful, though – especially if you wanted a workforce who could tolerate the anoxic environments around the vents, where the Demarchy happens to have certain mineralogical interests.'

'Maybe.' Cholok paused. 'But the changes required would be beyond surgery. You'd have to script them in at the developmental level. And even then . . . I'm not sure that what you'd end up with would necessarily be human any more.' It was as if she shivered, though Vargovic was the one who felt cold, still standing naked beside the revival table. 'All I can say is, if it happened, no one told me.'

'I thought I'd ask, that's all.'

'Good.' She brandished a white medical scanner. 'Now can I run a few more tests? We have to follow procedure.'

Cholok was right: quite apart from the fact that Vargovic's operation was completely real – and therefore susceptible to complications that had to be looked for and monitored – any deviation from normal practice was undesirable.

After the first hour or so, the real strangeness of his transformation hit home. He had been blithely unaffected by it until then, but when he saw himself in a full-body mirror, in the corner of Cholok's revival room, he knew that there was no going back.

Not easily, anyway. The Gilgamesh surgeons had promised him they could undo the work – but he didn't believe them. After all, the Demarchy was ahead of Ganymede in the biosciences, and even Cholok had told him reversals were tricky. He'd accepted the mission in any case: the pay tantalising; the prospect of the sulphur projects rather less so.

Cholok spent most of the day with him, only breaking off to talk to other clients or confer with her team. Breathing exercises occupied most of that time: prolonged periods spent underwater, nulling the brain's drowning response. Unpleasant, but Vargovic had done worse things in training. They practised fully submerged swimming, using his lungs to regulate buoyancy, followed by instruction about keeping his gill-openings – what Cholok called his opercula – clean, which meant ensuring the health of the colonies of commensal bacteria that thrived in the openings and crawled over the fine secondary flaps of his lamellae. He'd read the brochure: what she'd done was to surgically sculpt his anatomy towards a state somewhere between human and air-breathing fish: incorporating biochemical lessons from lungfish and walking-catfish. Fish breathed water through their mouths and returned it to the sea via their gills, but it was the gills in Vargovic's neck that served the function of a mouth. His true gills were below his thoracic cavity: crescent-shaped gashes below his ribs.

'Compared to your body size,' she said, 'these gill-openings are never going to give you the respiratory efficiency you'd have if you went in for more dramatic changes—'

'Like a Denizen?'

'I told you, I don't know anything about that.'

'It doesn't matter.' He flattened the gill-flaps down, watching – only slightly nauseated – as they puckered with each exhalation. 'Are we finished?'

'Just some final bloodwork,' she said, 'to make sure everything's still functioning properly. Then you can go and swim with the fishes.'

While she was busy at one of her consoles, surrounded by false-colour entoptics of his gullet – he asked her, 'Do you have the weapon?'

Cholok nodded absently and opened a drawer, fishing out a hand-held medical laser. 'Not much,' she said. 'I disabled the yield-suppresser, but you'd have to aim it at someone's eyes to do much damage.'

Vargovic hefted the laser, scrutinising the controls in its con-toured haft. Then he grabbed Cholok's head and twisted her around, dousing her face with the laser's actinic-blue beam. There were two consecutive popping sounds as her eyeballs evaporated.

'What, like that?'

*

Conventional scalpels did the rest.

He rinsed off the blood, dressed and left the medical centre alone, travelling kilometres down-city, to where Cadmus-Asterius narrowed to a point. Even though there were many gillies moving freely through the city – they were volunteers, by and large, with full Demarchy rights – he did not linger in public for long. Within a few minutes he was safe inside a warren of collagen-walled service tunnels, frequented only by technicians, servitors or other gill-workers. The late Cholok had been right: breathing air was more difficult now. It felt too thin.

'Demarchy security advisory,' said a bleak machine voice emanating from the wall. 'A murder has occurred in the medical sector. The suspect may be an armed gill-worker. Approach with extreme caution.'

They'd found Cholok. Risky, killing her. But Gilgamesh preferred to burn its bridges, removing the possibility of any sleeper turning traitor after they had fulfilled their usefulness. In the future, Vargovic mulled, they might be better using a toxin, rather than the immediate kill. He made a mental note to insert that in his report.

He entered the final tunnel, not far from the waterlock that was his destination. At the tunnel's far end a technician sat on a crate, listening with a stethoscope to something going on behind an access panel. For a moment Vargovic considered passing the man, hoping he was engrossed in his work. He began to approach him, padding on bare webbed feet, which made less noise than the shoes he had just removed. Then the man nodded to himself, uncoupled from the listening post and slammed the hatch. Grabbing his crate, he stood and made eye contact with Vargovic.

'You're not meant to be here,' he said. Then offered, almost plaintively, 'Can I help you? You've just had surgery, haven't you? I always recognise new ones like you: always a little red around the gills.'

Vargovic drew his collar higher, then relented because that

made it harder to breathe. 'Stay where you are,' he said. 'Put down the crate and freeze.'

'Christ, that advisory – it was you, wasn't it?' the man said.

Vargovic raised the laser. Blinded, the man blundered into the wall, dropping the crate. He made a pitiful moan. Vargovic crept closer, the man stumbling into the scalpel. Not the cleanest of killings, but that hardly mattered.

Vargovic was sure the Demarchy would shortly seal off access to the ocean – especially when his latest murder came to light. For now, however, the locks were accessible. He moved into the air-filled chamber, his lungs now aflame for water. High-pressure jets filled the room, and he quickly transitioned to water-breathing, feeling his thoughts clarify. The secondary door clammed open, revealing ocean. He was kilometres below the ice, and the water here was both chillingly cold and under crushing pressure – but it felt normal; pressure and cold registered only as abstract qualities of the environment. His blood was inoculated with glycoproteins now, molecules which would lower its freezing point below that of water.

The late Cholok had done well.

Vargovic was about to leave the city when a second gill-worker appeared in the doorway, returning to the city after completing a shift. He killed her efficiently, and she bequeathed him a thermally inwoven wetsuit, for working in the coldest parts of the ocean. The wetsuit had octopus ancestry, and when it slithered onto him it left apertures for his gill-openings. She had been wearing goggles that had infrared and sonar capability, and carried a hand-held tug. The thing resembled the still-beating heart of a vivisected animal, its translucent components nobbed with dark veins and ganglia. But it was easy to use: Vargovic set its pump to maximum thrust and powered away from the lower levels of C-A. Even in the relatively uncontaminated water of the Europan ocean, visibility was low; he would not have been able to see anything were the city not abundantly illuminated on all its levels. Even so, he could see no more than half a kilometre upwards; the higher parts of C-A were lost in golden haze and then deepening darkness. Although its symmetry was upset by protrusions and accretions, the city's basic conic form was still evident, tapering at the narrowest point to an inlet mouth which ingested ocean. The cone was surrounded by a haze of flotation bubbles, black as caviar. He remembered the chips of hyper-diamond in his hands. If Cholok was right, Vargovic's people might find a way to make it water-permeable; opening the full-erene weave sufficiently so that the spheres' buoyant properties would be destroyed. The necessary agent could be introduced into the ocean by ice-penetrating missiles. Some time later – Vargovic was uninterested in the details – the Demarchy cities would begin to groan under their own weight. If the weapon worked sufficiently quickly, there might not even be time to act against it. The cities would fall from the ice, sinking down through the black kilometres of ocean below them.

He swam on.

Near C-A, the rocky interior of Europa climbed upwards to meet him. He had travelled three or four kilometres north, and was comparing the visible topography – lit by service lights installed by Demarchy gill-workers – with his own mental maps of the area. Eventually he found an outcropping of silicate rock. Beneath the overhang was a narrow ledge on which a dozen or so small boulders had fallen. One was redder than the others. Vargovic anchored himself to the ledge and hefted the red rock, the warmth of his fingertips activating its latent biocircuitry. A screen appeared in the rock, filling with Mishenka's face.

'I'm on time,' Vargovic said, his own voice sounding even less recognisable through the distorting medium of the water. 'I presume you're ready?'

'Problem,' Mishenka said. 'Big fucking problem.'

'What?'

'Extraction site's compromised.' Mishenka – or rather the

simulation of Mishenka that was running in the rock – anticipated Vargovic's next question: 'A few hours ago the Demarchy sent a surface team out onto the ice, ostensibly to repair a transponder. But the spot they're covering is right where we planned to pull you out.' He paused. 'You did – uh – kill Cholok, didn't you? I mean, you didn't just grievously injure her?'

'You're talking to a professional.'

The rock did a creditable impression of Mishenka looking pained. 'Then the Demarchy got to her.'

Vargovic waved his hand in front of the rock. 'I got what I came for, didn't I?'

'You got something.'

'If it isn't what Cholok said it was, then she's accomplished nothing except get herself dead.'

'Even so . . .' Mishenka appeared to entertain a thought briefly, before discarding it. 'Listen, we always had a back-up extraction point, Vargovic. You'd better get your ass there.' He grinned. 'Hope you can swim faster than Maunciple.'

It was thirty kilometres south.

He passed a few gill-workers on the way, but they ignored him and once he was more than five kilometres from C-A there was increasingly less evidence of human presence. There was a head-up display in the goggles. Vargovic experimented with the read-out modes before calling up a map of the whole area. It showed his location, and also three dots following him from C-A.

He was being tailed by Demarchy security.

They were at least three kilometres behind him now, but they were perceptibly narrowing the distance. With a cold feeling gripping his gut, it occurred to Vargovic that there was no way he could make it to the extraction point before the Demarchy caught him.

Ahead, he noticed a thermal hot spot: heat bubbling up from the relatively shallow level of the rock floor. The security operatives were probably tracking him via the gill-worker's appropriated equipment. But once he was near the vent he could ditch it: the water was warmer there; he wouldn't need the suit, and the heat, light and associated turbulence would confuse any other tracking system. He could lie low behind a convenient rock, stalk them while they were preoccupied with the homing signal.

It struck Vargovic as a good plan. He covered the distance to the vent quickly, feeling the water grow warmer around him, noticing how the taste of it changed, turning brackish. The vent was a fiery red fountain surrounded by bacteria-crusted rocks and the colourless Europan equivalent of coral. Ventlings were everywhere, their pulpy bags shifting as the currents altered. The smallest were motile, ambling on their stilts like animated bagpipes, navigating around the triadic stumps of their dead relatives.

Vargovic ensconced himself in a cave, after placing the gill-worker's equipment near another cave on the far side of the vent, hoping that the security operatives would look there first. While they did so, he would be able to kill at least one of them; maybe two. Once he had their weapons, taking care of the third would be a formality.

Something nudged him from behind.

What Vargovic saw when he turned around was something too repulsive even for a nightmare. It was so wrong that for a faltering moment he could not quite assimilate what he was looking at, as if the thing was a three-dimensional perception test; a shape that refused to stabilise in his head. The reason he could not hold it still was because part of him refused to believe that this thing had any connection with humanity. But the residual traces of human ancestry were too obvious to ignore.

Vargovic knew – beyond any reasonable doubt – that what he was seeing was a Denizen. Others loomed from the cave's depths – five more of them, all roughly similar, all aglow with faint bioluminescence, all regarding him with darkly intelligent eyes. Vargovic had seen pictures of mermaids in books when he was a child; what he was looking at now were macabre corruptions of those innocent illustrations. These things were the same fusions of human and fish as in those pictures – but every detail had been twisted towards ugliness, and the true horror of it was that the fusion was total; it was not simply that a human torso had been grafted to a fish's tail, but that the splice had been made – it was obvious – at the genetic level, so that in every aspect of the creature there was something simultaneously and grotesquely piscine. The faces were the worst, bisected by a lipless down-curved slit of a mouth, almost shark-like. There was no nose, not even a pair of nostrils; just an acreage of flat, sallow fish-flesh. The eyes were forward facing; all expression compacted into their dark depths.

The first creature had touched him with one of its arms, which terminated in an obscenely human hand. And then – to compound the horror – it spoke, its voice perfectly clear and calm despite the water.

'We've been expecting you, Vargovic.'

The others behind murmured, echoing the sentiment.

'What?'

'So glad you were able to complete your mission.'

Vargovic began to get a grip, shakily. He reached up and dislodged the Denizen's hand from his shoulder. 'You aren't why I'm here,' he said, forcing authority into his voice, drawing on every last drop of Gilgamesh training to suppress his nerves. 'I wanted to know about you . . . that was all—'

'No,' the lead Denizen said, opening its mouth to expose an alarming array of teeth. 'You misunderstand. Coming here was always your mission. You have brought us something we want very much. That was always your purpose.'

'Brought you something?' His mind was reeling now.

'Concealed within you.' The Denizen nodded: a human gesture that only served to magnify the horror of what it was. 'The means by which we will strike at the Demarchy; the means by which we will take the ocean.'

He thought of the chips in his hands. 'I think I understand,' he said slowly. 'It was always intended for you, is that what you mean?'

'Always.'

Then he'd been lied to by his superiors – or they had at least drastically simplified the matter. He filled in the gaps himself, making the necessary mental leaps: evidently Gilgamesh was already in contact with the Denizens – bizarre as it seemed – and the chips of hyperdiamond were meant for the Denizens, not his own people. Presumably – although he couldn't begin to guess at how this might be possible – the Denizens had the means to examine the shards and fabricate the agent that would unravel the hyperdiamond weave. They'd be acting for Gilgamesh, saving it the bother of actually dirtying its hands in the attack. He could see why this might appeal to Control. But if that was the case . . . why had Gilgamesh ever faked ignorance about the Denizens? It made no sense. But on the other hand, he could not concoct a better theory to replace it.

'I have what you want,' he said, after due consideration. 'Cholok said removing it would be simple.'

'Cholok can always be relied upon,' the Denizen said.

'You knew – know – her, then?'

'She made us what we are today.'

'You hate her, then?'

'No; we love her.' The Denizen flashed its shark-like smile again, and it seemed to Vargovic that as its emotional state changed, so did the coloration of its bioluminescence. It was scarlet now, no longer the blue-green hue it had displayed upon its first appearance. 'She took the abomination that we were and made us something better. We were in pain, once. Always in pain. But Cholok took it away, made us strong. For that they punished her, and then us.'

'If you hate the Demarchy,' Vargovic said, 'why have you waited until now before attacking it?'

'Because we can't leave this place,' one of the other Denizens said, the tone of its voice betraying femininity. 'The Demarchy hated what Cholok had done to us. She brought our humanity to the fore, made it impossible for them to treat us as animals. We thought they would kill us, rather than risk our existence becoming known to the rest of Circum-Jove. Instead, they banished us here.'

'They thought we might come in handy,' said another of the lurking creatures.

Just then, another Denizen entered the cave, having swum in from the sea.

'Demarchy agents have followed him,' it said, its coloration blood red, tinged with orange, pulsing lividly. 'They'll be here in a minute.'

'You'll have to protect me,' Vargovic said.

'Of course,' the lead Denizen said. 'You're our saviour.'

Vargovic nodded vigorously, no longer convinced that he could handle the three operatives on his own. Ever since he had arrived in the cave he had felt his energy dwindling, as if he was succumbing to slow poisoning. A thought tugged at the back of his mind, and for a moment he almost paid attention to it; almost considered seriously the possibility that he was being poisoned. But what was going on beyond the cave was too distracting. He watched the three Demarchy agents approach, pulled forward by the tugs they held in front of them. Each agent carried a slender harpoon gun, tipped with a vicious barb.

They didn't stand a chance.

The Denizens moved too quickly, lancing out from the shadows, cutting through the water. The creatures moved faster than the Demarchy agents, even though they only had their own muscles and anatomy to propel them. But it was more than enough. They had no weapons, either – not even harpoons. But sharpened rocks more than sufficed – that and their teeth.

Vargovic was impressed by their teeth.

Afterwards, the Denizens returned to the cave to join their cousins. They moved more sluggishly now, as if the fury of the fight had drained them. For a few moments they were silent, their bioluminescence curiously subdued.

Slowly, though, Vargovic watched their colour return.

'It was better that they not kill you,' the leader said.

'Damn right,' Vargovic said. 'They wouldn't just have killed me, you know.' He opened his fists, exposing his palms. 'They'd have made sure you never got this.'

The Denizens – all of them – looked momentarily towards his open hands, as if there ought to have been something there.

'I'm not sure you understand,' the leader said, eventually.

'Understand what?'

'The nature of your mission.'

Fighting his fatigue – it was a black slick lapping at his consciousness – Vargovic said, 'I understand perfectly well. I have the samples of hyperdiamond, in my hands—'

'That isn't what we want.'

He didn't like this, not at all. It was the way the Denizens were slowly creeping closer to him, sidling around him to obstruct his exit from the cave.

'What then?'

'You asked why we haven't attacked them before,' the leader said, with frightening charm. 'The answer's simple: we can't leave the vent.'

'You can't?'

'Our haemoglobin. It's not like yours.' Again that awful shark-like smile – and now he was well aware of what those teeth could do, given the right circumstances. 'It was tailored to allow us to work here.'

'Copied from the ventlings?'

'Adapted, yes. Later it became the means of imprisoning us. The DNA in our bone marrow was manipulated to limit the production of normal haemoglobin; a simple matter of suppressing a few beta-globin genes while retaining the variants that code for ventling haemoglobin. Hydrogen sulphide is poisonous to you, Vargovic. You probably already feel weak. But we can't survive without it. Oxygen kills us.'

'You leave the vent . . .'

'We die, within a few hours. There's more. The water's hot here, so hot that we don't need the glycoproteins. We have the genetic instructions to synthezise them, but they've also been turned off. But without the glycoproteins we can't swim into colder water. Our blood freezes.'

Now he was surrounded by them; looming aquatic devils, flushed a florid shade of crimson. And they were coming closer.

'But what do you expect me to do about it?'

'You don't have to do anything, Vargovic.' The leader opened its chasmic jaw wide, as if tasting the water. It was a miracle an organ like that was capable of speech in the first place . . .

'I don't?'

'No.' And with that the leader reached out and seized him, while at the same time he was pinned from behind by another of the creatures. 'It was Cholok's doing,' the leader continued. 'Her final gift to us. Maunciple was her first attempt at getting it to us – but Maunciple never made it.'

'He was too fat.'

'All the defectors failed – they just didn't have the stamina to make it this far from the city. That was why Cholok recruited you – an outsider.'

'Cholok recruited me?'

'She knew you'd kill her – you have, of course – but that didn't stop her. Her life mattered less than what she was about to give us. It was Cholok who tipped off the Demarchy about your primary extraction site, forcing you to come to us.'

He struggled, but it was pointless. All he could manage was a feeble, 'I don't understand—'

'No,' the Denizen said. 'Perhaps we never expected you to. If you had understood, you might have been less than willing to follow Cholok's plan.'

'Cholok was never working for us?'

'Once, maybe. But her last clients were us.'

'And now?'

'We take your blood, Vargovic.' Their grip on him tightened. He used his last draining reserves of strength to try to work loose, but it was futile.

'My blood?'

'Cholok put something in it. A retrovirus – a very hardy one, capable of surviving in your body. It reactivates the genes that were suppressed by the Demarchy. Suddenly, we'll be able to make oxygen-carrying haemoglobin. Our blood will fill up with glyco-proteins. It's no great trick: all the cellular machinery for making those molecules is already present; it just needs to be unshackled.'

'Then you need . . . what? A sample of my blood?'

'No,' the Denizen said, with genuine regret. 'Rather more than a sample, I'm afraid. Rather a lot more.'

And then – with magisterial slowness – the creature bit into his arm, and as his blood spilled out, the Denizen drank. For a moment the others waited – but then they too came forward, and bit, and joined in the feeding frenzy.

All around Vargovic, the water was turning red.

WEATHER

We were at one-quarter of the speed of light, outbound from Shiva-Parvati with a hold full of refugees, when the *Cockatrice* caught up with us. She commenced her engagement at a distance of one light-second, seeking to disable us with long-range weapons before effecting a boarding operation. Captain Van Ness did his best to protect the *Petronel*, but we were a lightly armoured ship and Van Ness did not wish to endanger his passengers by provoking a damaging retaliation from the pirates. As coldly calculated as it might appear, Van Ness knew that it would be better for the sleepers to be taken by another ship than suffer a purposeless death in interstellar space.

As shipmaster, it was my duty to give Captain Van Ness the widest choice of options. When it became clear that the *Cockatrice* was on our tail, following us out from Shiva-Parvati, I recommended that we discard fifty thousand tonnes of nonessential hull material, in order to increase the rate of acceleration available from our Conjoiner drives. When the *Cockatrice* ramped up her own engines to compensate, I identified a further twenty thousand tonnes of material we could discard until the next orbitfall, even though the loss of the armour would marginally increase the radiation dosage we would experience during the flight. We gained a little, but the pirates still had power in reserve: they'd stripped back their ship to little more than a husk, and they didn't have the mass handicap of our sleepers. Since we could not afford to lose any more hull material, I advised Van Ness to eject two of our three heavy shuttles, each of which massed six thousand tonnes when fully fuelled. That bought us yet more time, but to my dismay the pirates still found a way to squeeze a little more out of their engines.

Whoever they had as shipmaster, I thought, they were good at their work.

So I went to the engines themselves, to see if I could better my nameless opponent. I crawled out along the pressurised access tunnel that pierced the starboard spar, out to the coupling point where the foreign technology of the starboard Conjoiner drive was mated to the structural fabric of the *Petronel*. There I opened the hatch that gave access to the controls of the drive itself: six stiff dials, fashioned in blue metal, arranged in hexagon formation, each of which was tied to some fundamental aspect of the engine's function. The dials were set into quadrant-shaped recesses, all now glowing a calm blue-green.

I noted the existing settings, then made near-microscopic alterations to three of the six dials, fighting to keep my hands steady as I applied the necessary effort to budge them. Even as I made the first alteration, I felt the engine respond: a shiver of power as some arcane process occurred deep inside it, accompanied by a shift in my own weight as the thrust increased by five or six per cent. The blue-green hue was now tinted with orange.

The *Petronel* surged faster, still maintaining her former heading. It was only possible to make adjustments to the starboard engine, since the port engine had no external controls. That didn't matter, because the Conjoiners had arranged the two engines to work in perfect synchronisation, despite them being a kilometre apart. No one had ever succeeded in detecting the signals that passed between two matched C-drives, let alone in understanding the messages those signals carried. But everyone who worked with them knew what would happen if, by accident or design, the engines were allowed to get more than sixteen hundred metres apart.

I completed my adjustments, satisfied that I'd done all I could without risking engine malfunction. Three of the five dials were now showing orange, indicating that those settings were now outside what the Conjoiners deemed the recommended envelope of safe operation. If any of the dials were to show red, or if more than three showed orange, than we'd be in real danger of losing the *Petronel*.

When Ultras meet on friendly terms, to exchange data or goods, the shipmasters will often trade stories of engine settings. On a busy trade route, a marginal increase in drive efficiency can make all the difference between one ship and its competitors. Occasionally you hear about ships that have been running on three orange, even four orange, for decades at a time. By the same token, you sometimes hear about ships that went nova when only two dials had been adjusted away from the safety envelope. The one thing every shipmaster agrees upon is that no lighthugger has ever operated for more than a few days of shiptime with one dial in the red. You might risk that to escape aggressors, but even then some will insist that the danger is too great; that those ships that lasted days were the lucky ones.

I left the starboard engine and retreated back into the main hull of the *Petronel*. Van Ness was waiting to greet me. I could tell by the look on his face – the part of it that I could read – that the news wasn't good.

'Good lad, Inigo,' he said, placing his heavy gauntleted hand on my shoulder. 'You've bought us maybe half a day, and I'm grateful for that, no question of it. But it's not enough to make a difference. Are you sure you can't sweet-talk any more out of them?'

'We could risk going to two gees for a few hours. That still wouldn't put us out of reach of the *Cockatrice*, though.'

'And beyond that?'

I showed Van Ness my handwritten log book, with its

meticulous notes of engine settings, compiled over twenty years of shiptime. Black ink for my own entries, the style changing abruptly when I lost my old hand and slowly learned how to use the new one; red annotations in the same script for comments and know-how gleaned from other shipmasters, dated and named. 'According to this, we're already running a fifteen per cent chance of losing the ship within the next hundred days. I'd feel a lot happier if we were already throttling back.'

'You don't think we can lose any more mass?'

'We're stripped to the bone as it is. I can probably find you another few thousand tonnes, but we'll still only be looking at prolonging the inevitable.'

'We'll have the short-range weapons,' Van Ness said resignedly. 'Maybe they'll make enough of a difference. At least now we have an extra half-day to get them run out and tested.'

'Let's hope so,' I agreed, fully aware that it was hopeless. The weapons were antiquated and underpowered, good enough for fending off orbital insurgents but practically useless against another ship, especially one that had been built for piracy. The *Petronel* hadn't fired a shot in anger in more than fifty years. When Van Ness had the chance to upgrade the guns, he'd chosen instead to spend the money on newer reefersleep caskets for the passenger hold.

People have several wrong ideas about Ultras. One of the most common misconceptions is that we must all be brigands, every ship bristling with armaments, primed to a state of nervous readiness the moment another vessel comes within weapons range.

It isn't true. For every ship like that, there are a thousand like the *Petronel*: just trying to ply an honest trade, with a decent, hardworking crew under the hand of a fair man like Van Ness. Some of us might look like freaks, by the standards of planetary civilisation. But spending an entire life aboard a ship, hopping from star to star at relativistic speed, soaking up exotic radiation from the engines and from space itself, is hardly the environment for which the human form was evolved. I'd lost my old hand in an accident, and much of what had happened to Van Ness was down to time and misfortune in equal measure.

He was one of the best captains I'd ever known, maybe the best ever. He'd scared the hell out of me the first time we met, when he was recruiting for a new shipmaster in a carousel around Greenhouse. But Van Ness treated his crew well, kept his word in a deal and always reminded us that our passengers were not frozen 'cargo' but human beings who had entrusted themselves into our care.

'If it comes to it,' Van Ness said, 'we'll let them take the passengers. At least that way some of them might survive, even if they won't necessarily end up where they were expecting. We put up too much of a fight, even after we've been boarded, the *Cockatrice*'s crew may just decide to burn everything, sleepers included.'

'I know,' I said, even though I didn't want to hear it.

'But here's my advice to you, lad.' Van Ness's iron grip tightened on my shoulder. 'Get yourself to an airlock as soon as you can. Blow yourself into space rather than let the bastards get their hands on you. They might be in mind for a bit of cruelty, but they won't be in need of new crew.'

I winced, before he crushed my collarbone. He meant well, but he really didn't know his own strength.

'Especially not a shipmaster, judging by the way things are going.'

'Aye. He's good, whoever he is. Not as good as you, though. You've got a fully laden ship to push; all they have is a stripped-down skeleton.'

It was meant well, but I knew better than to underestimate my adversary. 'Thank you, Captain.'

'We'd best start waking those guns, lad. If you're done with the engines, the weaponsmaster may appreciate a helping hand.'

I barely slept for the next day. Coaxing the weapons back to operational readiness was a fraught business, and it all had to be done without alerting the *Cockatrice* that we had any last-minute defensive capability. The magnetic coils on the induction guns had to be warmed and brought up to operational field strength, and then tested with slugs of recycled hull material. One of the coils fractured during warm-up and took out its entire turret, injuring one of Weps' men in the process. The optics on the lasers had to be aligned and calibrated, and then the lasers had to be test-fired against specks of incoming interstellar dust, hoping that the *Cockatrice* didn't spot those pinpoint flashes of gamma radiation as the lasers found their targets.

All the while this was going on, the enemy continued their long-range softening-up bombardment. The *Cockatrice* was using everything in her arsenal, from slugs and missiles to beam-weapons. The *Petronel* was running an evasion routine, swerving to exploit the sadly narrowing timelag between the two ships, but the routine was old and with the engines already notched up to close-on maximum output, there was precious little reserve power. No single impact was damaging, but as the assault continued, the cumulative effect began to take its toll. Acres of hull shielding were now compromised, and there were warnings of structural weakness in the port drive spar. If this continued, we would soon be forced to dampen our engines, rather than be torn apart by our own thrust loading. That was exactly what the *Cockatrice* wanted. Once they'd turned us into a lame duck, they could make a forced hard docking and storm our ship.

By the time they were eighty thousand kilometres out, things were looking very bad for us. Even the *Cockatrice* must have been nervous of what would happen if the port spar gave way, since they'd begun to concentrate their efforts on our midsection instead. Reluctantly I crawled back along the starboard spar and confronted the engine settings again. I was faced with two equally numbing possibilities. I could turn the dials even further into the orange, making the engines run harder still. Even if the engines held, the ship wouldn't, but at least we'd go out in a flash when the spar collapsed and the two engines drifted apart. Or I could return the dials to blue-green and let the *Cockatrice* catch us up without risk of further failure. One option might ensure the future survival of the passengers. Neither looked very attractive from the crew's standpoint.

Van Ness knew it, too. He'd begun to go around the rest of the crew, all two dozen of us, ordering those who weren't actively involved in the current crisis to choose an empty casket in the passenger hold and try to pass themselves off as cargo. Van Ness was wise enough not to push the point when no one took him up on his offer.

At fifty thousand kilometres, the *Cockatrice* was in range of our own weapons. We let her slip a little closer and then rotated our hull through forty-five degrees to give her a full broadside, all eleven working slug-cannons discharging at once, followed by a burst from the lasers. The recoil from the slugs was enough to generate further warnings of structural failure in a dozen critical nodes. But we held, somehow, and thirty per cent of that initial salvo hit the *Cockatrice* square-on. By then the lasers had already struck her, vaporising thousands of tonnes of ablative ice from her prow in a scalding white flash. When the steam had fallen astern of the still-accelerating ship, we got our first good look at the damage.

It wasn't enough. We'd hurt her, but barely, and I knew we couldn't sustain more than three further bursts of fire before the *Cockatrice*'s own short-range weapons found their lock and returned the assault. As it was, we only got off another two salvos before the slug-cannons suffered a targeting failure. The lasers continued to fire for another minute, but once they'd burned off the *Cockatrice*'s ice (which she could easily replenish from our own shield, once we'd been taken) they could inflict little further damage.

By twenty thousand kilometres, all our weapons were inoperable. Fear of breakup had forced me to throttle our engines back down to zero thrust, leaving only our in-system fusion motors running. At ten thousand kilometres, the *Cockatrice* released a squadron of pirates, each of whom would be carrying hull-penetrating gear and shipboard weapons, in addition to their thruster packs and armour. They must have been confident that we had nothing else to throw at them.

We knew then it was over.

It was, too: but for the *Cockatrice*, not us. What took place happened too quickly for the human eye to see. It was only later, when we had the benefit of footage from the hull cameras, that we were able to piece together what had occurred.

One instant, the *Cockatrice* was creeping closer to us, her engines doused to a whisper now to match our own feeble rate of acceleration. The next instant, she was still *there*, but everything about her had changed. The engines were shut down completely and the hull had begun to come apart, flaking away in a long lateral line that ran the entire four kilometres from bow to stern. The *Cockatrice* began to crab, losing axial stabilisation. Pieces of her were drifting away. Vapour was jetting from a dozen apertures along her length. Where the hull had scabbed away, the brassy orange glow of internal fire was visible. One engine spar was seriously buckled.

We didn't know it at the time – didn't know it until much later, when we'd actually boarded her – but the *Cockatrice* had fallen victim to the oldest hazard in space: collision with debris. There isn't a lot of it out there, but when it hits . . . at a quarter of the speed of light, it doesn't take much to inflict crippling damage. The impactor might only have been the size of a fist, or a fat thumb, but it had rammed its way right through the ship like a bullet, and the momentum transfer had almost ripped the engines off.

It was bad luck for the crew of the *Cockatrice*. For us, it was the most appalling piece of good luck imaginable. Except it wasn't even luck, really. Every now and then, ships will encounter something like that. Deep-look radar will identify an incoming shard and send an emergency steer command to the engines. Or the radar will direct anti-collision lasers to vaporise the object before it hits. Even if it does hit, most of its kinetic energy will be soaked up by the ablation ice. Ships don't carry all that deadweight for nothing.

But the *Cockatrice* had lost her ice under our lasers. She'd have replaced it sooner or later, but without it she was horribly vulnerable. And her own anti-collision system was preoccupied dealing with our short-range weapons. One little impactor was all it took to remove her from the battle.

It gave us enough of a handhold to start fighting back. With the *Cockatrice* out of the fight, our own crew were able to leave the protection of the ship without fear of being fried or pulverised. Van Ness was the first out of the airlock, with me not far behind him. Within five minutes there were twenty-three of us outside, our suits bulked out with armour and antiquated weapons. There were at least thirty incoming pirates from the *Cockatrice*, and they had better gear. But they'd lost the support of their mother ship, and all of them must have been aware that the situation had undergone a drastic adjustment. Perhaps it made them fight even more fiercely, given that ours was now the only halfway-intact ship. They'd been planning to steal our cargo before, and strip the *Petronel* for useful parts; now they needed to take the *Petronel* and claim her as her own. But they didn't have back-up from the *Cockatrice* and – judging by the way the battle proceeded – they seemed handicapped by more than just the lack of covering fire. They fought as well as they could, which was with a terrible individual determination, but no overall coordination. Afterwards, we concluded that their suit-to-suit communications, even their spatial-orientation systems, must have been reliant on signals routed through their ship. Without her they were deaf and blind.

We still lost good crew. It took six hours to mop up the last resistance from the pirates, by which point we'd taken eleven fatalities, with another three seriously wounded. But by then the pirates were all dead, and we were in no mood to take prisoners.

But we were in a mood to take what we needed from the *Cockatrice*.

If we'd expected to encounter serious resistance aboard the damaged ship, we were wrong. As Van Ness led our boarding party through the drifting wreck, the scope of the damage became chillingly clear. The ship had been gutted from the inside out, with almost no intact pressure-bearing structures left anywhere inside her main hull. For most of the crew left aboard when the impactor hit, the end would have come with merciful swiftness. Only a few had survived the initial collision, and most of them must have died shortly afterwards, as the ship bled through its wounds. We found no sign that the *Cockatrice* had been carrying frozen passengers, although – since entire internal bays had been blasted out of existence, leaving only an interlinked chain of charred, blackened caverns – we probably wouldn't ever know for sure. Of the few survivors we did encounter, none attempted surrender or requested parley. That made it easier for us. If they stood still, we shot them. If they fled, we still shot them.

Except for one.

We knew there was something different about her as soon as we saw her. She didn't look or move like an Ultra. There was something of the cat or snake about the way she slinked out of the illumination of our lamps, something fluid and feral, something sleek and honed that did not belong aboard a ship crewed by pirates. We held our fire from the moment her eyes first flashed at us, for we knew she could not be one of them. Wide, white-edged eyes in a girl's face, her strong-jawed expression one of ruthless self-control and effortless superiority. Her skull was hairless, her forehead rising to a bony crest rilled on either side by shimmering coloured tissue.

The girl was a Conjoiner.

It was three days before we found her again. She knew that ship with animal cunning, as if the entire twisted and blackened warren was a lair she had made for herself. But her options were diminishing with every hour that passed, as more and more air drained out of the wreck. Even Conjoiners needed to breathe, and that meant there was less and less of the ship in which she could hide.

Van Ness wanted to move on. Van Ness – a good man, but never the most imaginative of souls – wasn't interested in what a stray Conjoiner could do for us. I'd warned him that the *Cockatrice*'s engines were in an unstable condition, and that we wouldn't have time to back off to a safe distance if the buckled drive spar finally gave way. Now that we'd harvested enough of the other ship's intact hull to repair our own damage, Van Ness saw no reason to hang around. But I managed to talk him into letting us hunt down the girl.

'She's a Conjoiner, Captain. She wouldn't have been aboard that ship of her own free will. That means she's a prisoner that we can free and return to her people. They'll be grateful. That means they'll want to reward us.'

Van Ness fixed me with an indulgent smile. 'Lad, have you ever had close dealings with Spiders?'

He still called me 'lad' even though I'd been part of his crew for twenty years, and had been born another twenty before that, by shiptime reckoning. 'No,' I admitted. 'But the Spiders – the Conjoiners – aren't the bogey men some people like to make out.'

'I've dealt with 'em,' Van Ness said. 'I'm a lot older than you, lad. I go right back to when things weren't so pretty between the Spiders and the rest of humanity, back when my wife was alive.'

It took a lot to stir up the past for Rafe Van Ness. In all our years together, he'd only mentioned his wife a handful of times. She'd been a botanist, working on the Martian terraforming programme. She'd been caught by a flash flood when she was working in one of the big craters, testing plant stocks for the Demarchists. All I knew was that after her death, Van Ness had left the system, on one of the first passenger-carrying starships. It had been his first step on the long road to becoming an Ultra.

'They've changed since the old days,' I said. 'We trust them enough to use their engines, don't we?'

'We trust the engines. Isn't quite the same thing. And if they didn't have such a monopoly on making the things, maybe we wouldn't have to deal with them at all. Anyway, who is this girl? What was she doing aboard the *Cockatrice*? What makes you think she wasn't helping them?'

'Conjoiners don't condone piracy. And if we want answers, we have no option but to catch her and find out what she has to say.'

Van Ness sounded suddenly interested. 'Interrogate her, you mean?'

'I didn't say that, Captain. But we might want to ask her a few questions.'

'We'd be playing with fire. You know they can make things happen just by thinking about them.'

'She'll have no reason to hurt us. We'll have saved her life just by taking her off the *Cockatrice*.'

'Maybe she doesn't want it saved. Have you thought of that?'

'We'll cross that bridge when we find her, Captain.'

He pulled a face, that part of his visage still capable of making expressions, at least. 'I'll give you another twelve hours, lad. That's my limit. Then we put as much distance between us and that wreck as God and physics will allow.'

I nodded, knowing that it was pointless to expect more of Van Ness. He'd already shown great forbearance in allowing us to delay the departure for so long. Given his feelings regarding Conjoiners, I wasn't going to push for any more time.

We caught her eleven hours later. We'd driven her as far as she could go, blocking her escape routes by blowing the few surrounding volumes that were still pressurised. I was the first to speak to her, when we finally had her cornered.

I pushed up the visor of my helmet, breathing stale air so that we could speak. She was huddled in a corner, compressed like some animal ready to bolt or strike.

'Stop running from us,' I said, as my lamp pinned her down and forced her to squint. 'There's nowhere left to go, and even if there was, we don't want to hurt you. Whatever these people did to you, whatever they made you do, we're not like them.'

She hissed back, 'You're Ultras. That's all I need to know.'

'We're Ultras, yes, but we still want to help you. Our captain just wants to get away from this time bomb as quickly as possible. I talked him into giving us a few extra hours to find you. You can come with us whenever you like. But if you'd rather stay aboard this ship . . .'

She stared back at me and said nothing. I couldn't guess her age. She had the face of a girl, but there was a steely resolution in her olive-green eyes that told me she was older than she looked.

'I'm Inigo, the shipmaster from the *Petronel*,' I said, hoping that my smile looked reassuring rather than threatening. I reached out my hand, my right one, and she flinched back. Even suited, even hidden under a glove, my hand was obviously mechanical. 'Please,' I continued, 'come with us. We'll treat you well and get you back to your people.'

'Why?' she snarled. 'Why do *you* care?'

'Because we're not all the same,' I said. 'And you need to believe it, or you're going to die here when we leave. Captain wants us to secure for thrust in less than an hour. So *come on*.'

'What happened?' she asked, looking around at the damaged

compartment in which she had been cornered. 'I know the *Cockatrice* was attacking another ship . . . how did you do this?'

'We didn't. We just got very, very lucky. Now it's your turn.'

'I can't leave here. I need to be with this ship.'

'This ship is going to blow up if one of us sneezes. Do you really want to be aboard when that happens?'

'I still need to be here. Leave me alone, I'll survive by myself. Conjoiners will find me again.'

I shook my head firmly. 'That isn't going to happen. Even if this ship doesn't blow up, you're still drifting at twenty-five per cent of the speed of light. That's too fast to get you back to Shiva-Parvati, even if there's a shuttle aboard this thing. Too fast for anyone around Shiva-Parvati to come out and rescue you, too.'

'I know this.'

'Then you also know that you're not moving anywhere near fast enough to actually get anywhere before your resources run out. Unless you think you can survive fifty years aboard this thing, until you swing by the next colonised system with no way of slowing down.'

'I'll take my chances.'

A voice buzzed in my helmet. It was Van Ness, insisting that we return to the *Petronel* as quickly as possible. 'I'm sorry,' I said, 'but if you don't come willingly, I'm going to have to bring you in unconscious.' I raised the blunt muzzle of my slug-gun.

'If there's a tranquiliser dart in there, it won't work on me. My nervous system isn't like yours. I only sleep when I choose to.'

'That's what I figured. It's why I dialled the dose to five times its normal strength. I don't know about you, but I'm willing to give it a try and see what happens.'

Panic crossed her face. 'Give me a suit,' she said. 'Give me a suit and then leave me alone, if you really want to help.'

'What's your name?'

'We don't have names, Inigo. At least nothing *you* could get your tongue around.'

'I'm willing to try.'

'Give me a suit. Then leave me alone.'

Van Ness started screaming in my ears again. I'd had enough. I pointed the muzzle at her, aiming for the flesh of her thigh, where she had her legs tucked under her. I squeezed the trigger and delivered the stun fléchette.

'You fool,' she said. 'You don't understand. You have to leave me here, with this . . .'

That was all she managed before slumping into unconsciousness. She'd gone down much faster than I'd expected, as if she'd already been on her last reserves of strength. I just hoped I hadn't set the stun dose too high. It was already strong enough to kill any normal human being.

Van Ness had been right to be concerned about our proximity to the *Cockatrice*. We'd barely doubled the distance between the two ships when her drive spar failed, allowing the port engine to drift away from its starboard counterpart. Several agonising minutes later, the distance between the two engine units exceeded sixteen hundred metres and the drives went up in a double burst that tested our shielding to its limits. The flash must have been visible all the way back to Shiva-Parvati.

The girl had been unconscious right up until that moment, but when the engines went up she twitched on the bunk where we'd placed her, just as if she'd been experiencing a vivid and disturbing dream. The rilled structures on the side of her crest throbbed with vivid colours, each chasing the last. Then she was restful again, for many hours, and the play of colours calmer.

I watched her sleeping. I'd never been near a Conjoiner before, let alone one like this. Aboard the ship, when we had been hunting her, she had seemed strong and potentially dangerous. Now she looked like some half-starved animal, driven to the brink of madness by hunger and something infinitely worse. There were awful bruises all over her body, some more recent than others.

There were fine scars on her skull. One of her incisors was missing a point.

Van Ness still wasn't convinced of the wisdom of bringing her aboard, but even his dislike of Conjoiners didn't extend to the notion of throwing her back into space. All the same, he insisted that she be bound to the bunk by heavy restraints, in an armoured room under the guard of a servitor, at least until we had some idea of who she was and how she had ended up aboard the pirate ship. He didn't want heavily augmented crew anywhere near her, either: not when (as he evidently believed) she had the means to control any machine in her vicinity, and might therefore over-power or even commandeer any crewperson who had a skull full of implants. It wasn't like that, I tried to tell him: Conjoiners could talk to machines, yes, but not all machines, and the idea that they could work witchcraft on anything with a circuit inside it was just so much irrational fearmongering.

Van Ness heard my reasoned objections, and then ignored them. I'm glad that he did, though. Had he listened to me, he might have put some other member of the crew in charge of questioning her, and then I wouldn't have got to know her as well as I did. Because I only had the metal hand, the rest of me still flesh and blood, he deemed me safe from her influence.

I was with her when she woke.

I placed my left on her shoulder as she squirmed under the restraints, suddenly aware of her predicament. 'It's all right,' I said softly. 'You're safe now. Captain made us put these on you for the time being, but we'll get them off you as soon as we can. That's a promise. I'm Inigo, by the way, shipmaster. We met before, but I'm not sure how much of that you remember.'

'Every detail,' she said. Her voice was low, dark-tinged, un-trusting.

'Maybe you don't know where you are. You're aboard the *Petronel*. The *Cockatrice* is gone, along with everyone aboard her.

Whatever they did to you, whatever happened to you aboard that ship, it's over now.'

'You didn't listen to me.'

'If we'd listened to you,' I said patiently, 'you'd be dead by now.'

'No, I wouldn't.'

I'd been ready to give her the benefit of the doubt, but my reservoir of sympathy was beginning to dry up. 'You know, it wouldn't hurt to show a little gratitude. We put ourselves at considerable risk to get you to safety. We'd taken everything we needed from the pirates. We only went back in to help you.'

'I didn't need you to help me. I could have survived.'

'Not unless you think you could have held that spar on by sheer force of will.'

She hissed back her reply. 'I'm a Conjoiner. That means the rules were different. I could have changed things. I could have kept the ship in one piece.'

'To make a point?'

'No,' she said, with acid slowness, as if that was the only speed I was capable of following. 'Not to make a point. We don't *make* points.'

'The ship's gone,' I said. 'It's over, so you may as well deal with it. You're with us now. And no, you're not our prisoner. We'll do everything I said we would: take care of you, get you to safety, back to your people.'

'You really think it's that simple?'

'I don't know. Why don't you tell me? I don't see what the problem is.'

'The problem is I can't ever go back. Is that simple enough for you?'

'Why?' I asked. 'Were you exiled from the Conjoiners, or something like that?'

She shook her elaborately crested head, as if my question was the most naive thing she had ever heard. 'No one gets exiled.'

'Then tell me what the hell happened!'

Anger burst to the surface. 'I was taken, all right? I was stolen, snatched away from my people. Captain Voulage took me prisoner around Yellowstone, when the *Cockatrice* was docked near one of our ships. I was part of a small diplomatic party visiting Carousel New Venice. Voulage's men ambushed us, split us up, then took me so far from the other Conjoiners that I dropped out of neural range. Have you any idea what that means to one of us?'

I shook my head, not because I didn't understand what she meant, but because I knew I could have no proper grasp of the emotional pain that severance must have caused. I doubted that pain was a strong enough word for the psychic shock associated with being ripped away from her fellows. Nothing in ordinary human experience could approximate the trauma of that separation, any more than a frog could grasp the loss of a loved one. Conjoiners spent their whole lives in a state of gestalt consciousness, sharing thoughts and experiences via a web of implant-mediated neural connections. They had individual personalities, but those personalities were more like the blurred identities of atoms in a metallic solid. Beyond the level of individual self was the state of higher mental union that they called Transenlightenment, analogous to the fizzing sea of dissociated electrons in that same metallic lattice. And the girl had been ripped away from that, forced to come to terms with existence as a solitary mind, an island once more.

'I understand how bad it must have been,' I said. 'But now you can go back. Isn't that something worth looking forward to?'

'You only *think* you understand. To a Conjoiner, what happened to me is the worst thing in the world. And now I can't go back: not now, not ever. I've become damaged, broken, useless. My mind is permanently disfigured. It can't be allowed to return to Transenlightenment.'

'Why ever not? Wouldn't they be glad to get you back?'

She took a long time answering. In the quiet, I studied her face, watchful for anything that would betray the danger Van Ness clearly believed she posed. Now his fears seemed groundless. She looked smaller and more delicately boned than when we'd first glimpsed her on the *Cockatrice*. The strangeness of her, the odd shape of her hairless crested skull, should have been off-putting. In truth I found her fascinating. It was not her alienness that drew my furtive attention, but her very human face: her small and pointed chin, the pale freckles under her eyes, the way her mouth never quite closed, even when she was silent. The olive green of her eyes was a shade so dark that from certain angles it became a lustrous black, like the surface of coal.

'No,' she said, answering me finally. 'It wouldn't work. I'd upset the purity of the others, spoil the harmony of the neural connections, like a single out-of-tune instrument in an orchestra. I'd make everyone else start playing out of key.'

'I think you're being too fatalistic. Shouldn't we at least try to find some other Conjoiners and see what they say?'

'That isn't how it works,' she said. 'They'd have to take me back, yes, if I presented myself to them. They'd do it out of kindness and compassion. But I'd still end up harming them. It's my duty not to allow that to happen.'

'Then you're saying you have to spend the rest of your life away from other Conjoiners, wandering the universe like some miserable excommunicated pilgrim?'

'There are more of us than you realise.'

'You do a good job keeping out of the limelight. Most people only see Conjoiners in groups, all dressed in black like a flock of crows.'

'Maybe you aren't looking in the right places.'

I sighed, aware that nothing I said was going to convince her that she would be better off returning to her people. 'It's your life, your destiny. At least you're alive. Our word still holds: we'll drop you at the nearest safe planet, when we next make orbitfall. If that isn't satisfactory to you, you'd be welcome to remain aboard ship until we arrive somewhere else.'

'Your captain would allow that? I thought he was the one who wanted to leave the wreck before you'd found me.'

'I'll square things with the captain. He isn't the biggest fan of Conjoiners, but he'll see sense when he realises you aren't a monster.'

'Does he have a reason not to like me?'

'He's an old man,' I said simply.

'Riven with prejudice, you mean?'

'In his way,' I said, shrugging. 'But don't blame him for that. He lived through the bad years, when your people were first coming into existence. I think he had some first-hand experience of the trouble that followed.'

'Then I envy him those first-hand memories. Not many of us are still alive from those times. To have lived through those years, to have breathed the same air as Remontoire and the others . . .' She looked away sadly. 'Remontoire's gone now. So are Galiana and Nevil. We don't know what happened to any of them.'

I knew she must have been talking about pivotal figures from earlier Conjoiner history, but the people of whom she spoke meant nothing to me. To her, cast so far downstream from those early events on Mars, the names must have held something of the resonance of saints or apostles. I thought I knew something of Conjoiners, but they had a long and complicated internal history of which I was totally ignorant.

'I wish things hadn't happened the way they did,' I said. 'But that was then and this is now. We don't hate or fear you. If we did, we wouldn't have risked our necks getting you out of the *Cockatrice*.'

'No, you don't hate or fear me,' she replied. 'But you still think I might be useful to you, don't you?'

'Only if you wish to help us.'

'Captain Voulage thought that I might have the expertise to improve the performance of his ship.'

'Did you?' I asked innocently.

'By increments, yes. He showed me the engines and . . . encouraged me to make certain changes. You told me you are a shipmaster, so you doubtless have some familiarity with the principles involved.'

I thought back to the adjustments I had made to our own engines, when we still had ambitions of fleeing the pirates. The memory of my trembling hand on those three critical dials felt as if it had been dredged from deepest antiquity, rather than something that had happened only days earlier.

'When you say "encouraged" . . .' I began.

'He found ways to coerce me. It is true that Conjoiners can control their perception of pain by applying neural blockades. But only to a degree, and then only when the pain has a real physical origin. If the pain is generated in the head, using a reverse-field trawl, our defences are useless.' She looked at me with a sudden hard intensity, as if daring me to imagine one-tenth of what she had experienced. 'It is like locking a door when the wolf is already in the house.'

'I'm sorry. You must have been through hell.'

'I only had the pain to endure,' she said. 'I'm not the one anyone needs to feel sorry about.'

The remark puzzled me, but I let it lie. 'I have to get back to our own engines now,' I said, 'but I'll come to see you later. In the meantime, I think you should rest.' I snapped a duplicate communications bracelet from my wrist and placed it near her hand, where she could reach it. 'If you need me, you can call into this. It'll take me a little while to get back here, but I'll come as quickly as possible.'

She lifted her forearm as far as it would go, until the restraints stiffened. 'And these?'

'I'll talk to Van Ness. Now that you're lucid, now that you're talking to us, I don't see any further need for them.'

'Thank you,' she said again. 'Inigo. Is that all there is to your name? It's rather a short one, even by the standards of the retarded.'

'Inigo Standish, shipmaster. And you still haven't told me your name.'

'I told you: it's nothing you could understand. We have our own names now, terms of address that can only be communicated in the Transenlightenment. My name is a flow of experiential symbols, a string of interiorised qualia, an expression of a particular dynamic state that has only ever happened under a conjunction of rare physical conditions in the atmosphere of a particular kind of gas giant planet. I chose it myself. It's considered very beautiful and a little melancholy, like a haiku in five dimensions.'

'Inside the atmosphere of a gas giant, right?'

She looked at me alertly. 'Yes.'

'Fine, then. I'll call you Weather. Unless you'd like to suggest something better.'

She never did suggest something better, even though I think she once came close to it. From that moment on, whether she liked it or not, she was always Weather. Soon, it was what the other crew were calling her, and the name that – grudgingly at first, then resignedly – she deigned to respond to.

I went to see Captain Van Ness and did my best to persuade him that Weather was not going to cause us any difficulties.

'What are you suggesting we should give her – a free pass to the rest of the ship?'

'Only that we could let her out of her prison cell.'

'She's recuperating.'

'She's restrained. And you've put an armed servitor on the door, in case she gets out of the restraints.'

'Pays to be prudent.'

'I think we can trust her now, Captain.' I hesitated, choosing my words with great care. 'I know you have good reasons not to like her people, but she isn't the same as the Conjoiners from those days.'

'That's what she'd like us to think, certainly.'

'I've spoken to her, heard her story. She's an outcast from her people, unable to return to them because of what's happened to her.'

'Well, then,' Van Ness said, nodding as if he'd proved a point, 'outcasts do funny things. You can't ever be too careful with outcasts.'

'It's not like that with Weather.'

'Weather,' he repeated, with a certain dry distaste. 'So she's got a name now, has she?'

'I felt it might help. The name was my suggestion, not hers.'

'Don't start humanising them. That's the mistake humans always make. Next thing you know, they've got their claws in your skull.'

I closed my eyes, forcing self-control as the conversation veered off course. I'd always had an excellent relationship with Van Ness, one that came very close to bordering on genuine friendship. But from the moment he heard about Weather, I knew she was going to come between us.

'I'm not suggesting we let her run amok,' I said. 'Even if we let her out of those restraints, even if we take away the servitor, we can still keep her out of any parts of the ship where we don't want her. In the meantime, I think she can be helpful to us. She's already told me that Captain Voulage forced her to make improvements to the *Cockatrice*'s drive system. I don't see why she can't do the same for us, if we ask nicely.'

'Why did he have to force her, if you're so convinced she'd do it willingly now?'

'I'm not convinced. But I can't see why she wouldn't help us, if we treat her like a human being.'

'That'd be our big mistake,' Van Ness said. 'She never was a human being. She's been a Spider from the moment they made her, and she'll go to the grave like that.'

'Then you won't consider it?'

'I consented to let you bring her aboard. That was already against every God-given instinct.' Then Van Ness rumbled, 'And I'd thank you not to mention the Spider again, Inigo. You've my permission to visit her if you see fit, but she isn't taking a step out of that room until we make orbitfall.'

'Very well,' I said, with a curtness that I'd never had cause to use on Captain Van Ness.

As I was leaving his cabin, he said, 'You're still a fine shipmaster, lad. That's never been in doubt. But don't let this thing cloud your usual good judgement. I'd hate to have to look elsewhere for someone of your abilities.'

I turned back and, despite everything that told me to hold my tongue, I still spoke. 'I was wrong about you, Captain. I've always believed that you didn't allow yourself to be ruled by the irrational hatreds of other Ultras. I always thought you were better than that.'

'And I'd have gladly told you I have just as many prejudices as the next man. They're what've kept me alive so long.'

'I'm sure Captain Voulage felt the same way,' I said.

It was a wrong and hateful thing to say – Van Ness had nothing in common with a monster like Voulage – but I couldn't stop myself. And I knew even as I said it that some irreversible bridge had just been crossed, and that it was more my fault than Van Ness's.

'You have work to do, I think,' Van Ness said, his voice so low that I barely heard it. 'Until you have the engines back to full thrust, I suggest you keep out of my way.'

Weps came to see me eight or nine hours later. I knew it wasn't good news as soon as I saw her face.

'We have a problem, Inigo. The captain felt you needed to know.'

'And he couldn't tell me himself?'

Weps cleared part of the wall and called up a display, filling it with a boxy green three-dimensional grid. 'That's us,' she said, jabbing a finger at the red dot in the middle of the display. She moved her finger halfway to the edge, scratching her long black nail against the plating. 'Something else is out there. It's stealthed to the gills, but I'm still seeing it. Whatever it is is making a slow, silent approach.'

My thoughts flicked to Weather. 'Could it be Conjoiner?'

'That was my first guess. But if it was Conjoiner, I don't think I'd be seeing anything at all.'

'So what are we dealing with?'

She tapped the nail against the blue icon representing the new ship. 'Another raider. Could be an ally of Voulage – we know he had friends – or could be some other ship that was hoping to pick over our carcass once Voulage was done with us, or maybe even steal us from him before he had his chance.'

'Hyena tactics.'

'Wouldn't be the first time.'

'Range?'

'Less than two light-hours. Even if they don't increase their rate of closure, they'll be on us within eight days.'

'Unless we move.'

Weps nodded sagely. 'That would help. You're on schedule to complete repairs within six days, aren't you?'

'On schedule, yes, but that doesn't mean things can be moved any faster. We start cutting corners now, we'll break like a twig when we put a real load on the ship.'

'We wouldn't want that.'

'No, we wouldn't.'

'The captain just thought you should be aware of the situation, Inigo. It's not to put you under pressure, or anything.'

'Of course not.'

'It's just that . . . we really don't want to be hanging around here a second longer than necessary.'

I removed Weather's restraints and showed her how to help herself to food and water from the room's dispenser. She stretched and purred, articulating and extending her limbs in the manner of a dancer rehearsing some difficult routine in extreme slow motion. She'd been 'reading' when I arrived, which for Weather seemed to involve staring into the middle distance while her eyes flicked to and fro at manic speed, as if following the movements of an invisible wasp.

'I can't let you out of the room just yet,' I said, sitting on the fold-down stool next to the bed, upon which Weather now sat cross-legged. 'I just hope this makes things a little more tolerable.'

'So your captain's finally realised I'm not about to suck out his brains?'

'Not exactly. He'd still rather you weren't aboard.'

'Then you're going against his orders.'

'I suppose so.'

'I presume you could get into trouble for that.'

'He'll never find out.' I thought of the unknown ship that was creeping towards us. 'He's got other things on his mind now. It's not as if he's going to be paying you a courtesy call just to pass the time of day.'

'But if he did find out . . .' She looked at me intently, lifting her chin. 'Do you fear what he'd do to you?'

'I probably should. But I don't think he'd be very likely to throw me into an airlock. Not until we're under way at full power, in any case.'

'And then?'

'He'd be angry. But I don't think he'd kill me. He's not a bad man, really.'

'Perhaps I misheard, but didn't you say his name was Van Ness?'

'Captain Rafe Van Ness, yes.' I must have looked surprised. 'Don't tell me it means something to you.'

'I heard Voulage mention him, that's all. Now I know we're talking about the same man.'

'What did Voulage have to say?'

'Nothing good. But I don't think that necessarily reflects poorly on your captain. He must be a reasonable man. He's at least allowed me aboard his ship, even if I haven't been invited to dine in his quarters.'

'Dining for Van Ness is a pretty messy business,' I said confidingly. 'You're better off eating alone.'

'Do you like him, Inigo?'

'He has his flaws, but next to someone like Voulage, he's pretty close to being an angel.'

'Doesn't like Conjoiners, though.'

'Most Ultras would have left you drifting. I think this is a point where you have to take what you're given.'

'Perhaps. I don't understand his attitude, though. If your captain is like most Ultras, there's at least as much of the machine about him as there is about me. More so, in all likelihood.'

'It's what you do with the machines that counts,' I said. 'Ultras tend to leave their minds alone, if at all possible. Even if they do have implants, it's usually to replace areas of brain function lost due to injury or old age. They're not really interested in improving matters, if you get my drift. Maybe that's why Conjoiners make them twitchy.'

She unhooked her legs, dangling them over the edge of the bed. Her feet were bare and oddly elongated. She wore the same tight black outfit we'd found her in when we boarded the ship. It was cut low from her neck, in a rectangular shape. Her breasts were small. Though she was bony, with barely any spare muscle on her, she had the broad shoulders of a swimmer. Though Weather had sustained her share of injuries, the outfit showed no sign of damage at all. It appeared to be self-repairing, even self-cleaning.

'You talk of Ultras as if you weren't one,' she said.

'Just an old habit breaking through. Though sometimes I don't feel like quite the same breed as a man like Van Ness.'

'Your implants must be very well shielded. I can't sense them at all.'

'That's because there aren't any.'

'Squeamish? Or just too young and fortunate not to have needed them yet?'

'It's nothing to do with being squeamish. I'm not as young as I look, either.' I held up my mechanical hand. 'Nor would I exactly call myself fortunate.'

She looked at the hand with narrowed, critical eyes. I remembered how she'd flinched back when I reached for her aboard the *Cockatrice*, and wondered what maltreatment she had suffered at the iron hands of her former masters.

'You don't like it?' she asked.

'I liked the old one better.'

Weather reached out and gingerly held my hand in hers. They looked small and doll-like as they stroked and examined my mechanical counterpart.

'This is the only part of you that isn't organic?'

'As far as I know.'

'Doesn't that limit you? Don't you feel handicapped around the rest of the crew?'

'Sometimes. But not always. My job means I have to squeeze into places where a man like Van Ness could never fit. It also means I have to be able to tolerate magnetic fields that would rip half the crew to shreds, if they didn't boil alive first.' I opened and closed my metal fist. 'I have to unscrew this, sometimes. I have a plastic replacement if I just need to hook hold of things.'

'You don't like it very much.'

'It does what I ask of it.'

Weather made to let go of my hand, but her fingers remained in contact with mine for an instant longer than necessary. 'I'm sorry that you don't like it.'

'I could have got it fixed at one of the orbital clinics, I suppose,' I said, 'but there's always something else that needs fixing first. Anyway, if it wasn't for the hand, some people might not believe I'm an Ultra at all.'

'Do you plan on being an Ultra all your life?'

'I don't know. I can't say I ever had my mind set on being a shipmaster. It just sort of happened, and now here I am.'

'I had my mind set on something once,' Weather said. 'I thought it was within my grasp, too. Then it slipped out of reach.' She looked at me and then did something wonderful and unexpected, which was to smile. It was not the most genuine-looking smile I'd ever seen, but I sensed the genuine intent behind it. Suddenly I knew there was a human being in the room with me, damaged and dangerous though she might have been. 'Now here I am, too. It's not quite what I expected . . . but thank you for rescuing me.'

'I was beginning to wonder if we'd made a mistake. You seemed so reluctant to leave that ship.'

'I was,' she said, distantly. 'But that's over now. You did what you thought was the right thing.'

'Was it?'

'For me, yes. For the ship . . . maybe not.' Then she stopped and cocked her head to one side, frowning. Her eyes flashed olive. 'What are you looking at, Inigo?'

'Nothing,' I said, looking sharply away.

Keeping out of Van Ness's way, as he'd advised, was not the hard part of what followed. The *Petronel* was a big ship and our paths didn't need to cross in the course of day-to-day duties. The difficulty was finding as much time to visit Weather as I would have liked. My original repair plan had been tight, but the unknown ship forced me to accelerate the schedule even further, despite what I'd told Weps. The burden of work began to take its toll on me, draining my concentration. I was still confident that once that work was done, we'd be able to continue our journey as if nothing had happened, save for the loss of those crew who had died in the engagement and our gaining one new passenger. The other ship would probably abandon us once we pushed the engines up to cruise thrust, looking for easier pickings elsewhere. If it had the swiftness of the *Cockatrice*, it wouldn't have been skulking in the shadows letting the other ship take first prize.

But my optimism was misplaced. When the repair work was done, I once more made my way along the access shaft to the starboard engine and confronted the hexagonal arrangement of input dials. As expected, all six dials were now showing deep blue, which meant they were operating well inside the safety envelope. But when I consulted my log book and made the tiny adjustments that should have taken all the dials into the blue-green – still nicely within the safety envelope – I got a nasty surprise. I only had to nudge two of the dials by a fraction of a millimetre before they shone a hard and threatening orange.

Something was wrong.

I checked my settings, of course, making sure none of the other dials were out of position. But there'd been no mistake. I thumbed through the log with increasing haste, a prickly feeling on the back of my neck, looking for an entry where something similar had happened; something that would point me to the obvious mistake I must have made. But none of the previous entries were the slightest help. I'd made no error with the settings, and that left only one possibility: something had happened to the engine. It was not working properly.

'This isn't right,' I said to myself. 'They don't fail. They don't break down. Not like this.'

But what did I know? My entire experience of working with C-drives was confined to routine operations, under normal conditions. Yet we'd just been through a battle against another ship, one in which we were already known to have sustained structural damage. As shipmaster, I'd been diligent in attending to the hull and the drive spar, but it had never crossed my mind that something might have happened to one or other of the engines.

Why not?

There's a good reason. It's because even if something had happened, there would never have been anything I could have done about it. Worrying about the breakdown of a Conjoiner drive was like worrying about the one piece of debris you won't have time to steer around or shoot out of the sky. You can't do anything about it, ergo you forget about it until it happens. No shipmaster ever loses sleep over the failure of a C-drive.

It looked as if I was going to lose a lot more than sleep.

Even if we didn't have another ship to worry about, we were in more than enough trouble. We were too far out from Shiva-Parvati to get back again, and yet we were moving too slowly to make it to another system. Even if the engines kept working as they were now, we'd take far too long to reach relativistic speed, where time dilation became appreciable. At twenty-five per cent of the speed of light, what would have been a twenty-year hop before became an eighty-year crawl now . . . and that was an eighty-year crawl in which almost all that time would be experienced aboard ship. Across that stretch of time, reefersleep was a lottery. Our caskets were designed to keep people frozen for five to ten years, not four-fifths of a century.

I was scared. I'd gone from feeling calmly in control to feeling total devastation in about five minutes.

I didn't want to let the rest of the crew know that we had a potential crisis on our hands, at least not until I'd spoken to Weather. I'd already crossed swords with Van Ness, but he was still my captain, and I wanted to spare him the difficulty of a frightened crew, at least until I knew all the facts.

Weather was awake when I arrived. In all my visits, I'd never found her sleeping. In the normal course of events Conjoiners had no need of sleep: at worst, they'd switch off certain areas of brain function for a few hours.

She read my face like a book. 'Something's wrong, isn't it?'

So much for the notion that Conjoiners were not able to interpret facial expressions. Just because they didn't *make* many of them didn't mean they'd forgotten the rules.

I sat down on the fold-out stool.

'I've tried to push the engines back up to normal cruise thrust. I'm already seeing red on two dials, and we haven't even exceeded point-two gees.'

She thought about this for several moments: what for Weather must have been hours of subjective contemplation. 'You didn't appear to be pushing your engines dangerously during the chase.'

'I wasn't. Everything looked normal up until now. I think we must have taken some damage to one of the drives, during Voulage's softening-up assault. I didn't see any external evidence, but—'

'You wouldn't, not necessarily. The interior architecture of one of our drives is a lot more complicated, a lot more delicate, than is normally appreciated. It's at least possible that a shockwave did some harm to one of your engines, especially if your coupling gear – the shock-dampening assembly – was already compromised.'

'It probably was,' I said. 'The spar was already stressed.'

'Then you have your explanation. Something inside your engine has broken, or is considered by the engine itself to be dangerously close to failure. Either way, it would be suicide to increase the thrust beyond the present level.'

'Weather, we need both those engines to get anywhere, and we need them at normal efficiency.'

'It hadn't escaped me.'

'Is there anything you can do to help us?'

'Very little, I expect.'

'But you must know something about the engines, or you wouldn't have been able to help Voulage.'

'Voulage's engines weren't damaged,' she explained patiently.

'I know that. But you were still able to make them work better. Isn't there something you can do for us?'

'From here, nothing at all.'

'But if you were allowed to get closer to the engines . . . might that make a difference?'

'Until I'm there, I couldn't possibly say. It's irrelevant though, isn't it? Your captain will never allow me out of this room.'

'Would you do it for us if he did?'

'I'd do it for me.'

'Is that the best you can offer?'

'All right, then maybe I'd for it for you.' Just saying this caused Weather visible discomfort, as if the utterance violated some deep personal code that had remained intact until now. 'You've been kind to me. I know you risked trouble with Van Ness to make things easier in my cell. But you need to understand something very important. You may care for me. You may even think you like me. But I can't give you back any of that. What I feel for you is . . .' Weather hesitated, her mouth half-open. 'You know we call you the retarded. There's a reason for that. The emotions I feel . . . the things that go on in my head . . . simply don't map onto anything you'd recognise as love, or affection, or even friendship. Reducing them to those terms would be like . . .' And then she stalled, unable to finish.

'Like making a sacrifice?'

'You've been good to me, Inigo. But I really am like the weather. You can admire me, even love me, in your way, but I can't love you back. To me you're like a photograph. I can see right through you, examine you from all angles. You amuse me. But you don't have enough depth ever to fascinate me.'

'There's more to love than fascination. And you said it yourself: you're halfway back to being human again.'

'I said I wasn't a Conjoiner any more. But that doesn't mean I could ever be like you.'

'You could try.'

'You don't understand us.'

'I want to!'

Weather jammed her olive eyes tight shut. 'Let's . . . not get ahead of ourselves, shall we? I only wanted to spare you any unnecessary emotional pain. But if we don't get this ship moving properly, that'll be the least of your worries.'

'I know.'

'So perhaps we should return to the matter of the engines. Again: none of this will matter if Van Ness refuses to trust me.'

My cheeks were smarting as if I'd been slapped hard in the face. Part of me knew she was only being kind, in the harshest of ways. That part was almost prepared to accept her rejection. The other part of me only wanted her more, as if her bluntness had succeeded only in sharpening my desire. Perhaps she was right; perhaps I was insane to think a Conjoiner could ever feel something in return. But I remembered the gentle way she'd stroked my fingers, and I wanted her even more.

'I'll deal with Van Ness,' I said. 'I think there's a little something that will convince him to take a risk. You start thinking about what you can do for us.'

'Is that an order, Inigo?'

'No,' I said. 'Nobody's going to order you to do anything. I gave you my word on that, and I'm not about to break it. Nothing you've just said changes that.'

She sat tight-lipped, staring at me as if I was some kind of byzantine logic puzzle she needed to unscramble. I could almost feel the furious computation of her mind, as if I was standing next to a humming turbine. Then she lifted her little pointed chin minutely, saying nothing, but letting me know that if I convinced Van Ness, she would do what she could, however ineffectual that might prove.

The captain was tougher to crack than I'd expected. I'd assumed he would fold as soon as I explained our predicament – that we were going nowhere, and that Weather was the only factor that could improve our situation – but the captain simply narrowed his eyes and looked disappointed.

'Don't you get it? It's a ruse, a trick. Our engines were fine until we let her aboard. Then all of a sudden they start misbehaving, and she turns out to be the only one who can help us.'

'There's also the matter of the other ship Weps says is closing on us.'

'That ship might not even exist. It could be a sensor ghost, a hallucination she's making the *Petronel* see.'

'Captain—'

'That would work for her, wouldn't it? It would be exactly the excuse she needs to force our hands.'

We were in his cabin, with the door locked: I'd warned him I had a matter of grave sensitivity that we needed to discuss. 'I don't think this is any of her doing,' I said calmly, vowing to hold my temper under better control than before. 'She's too far from the engines or sensor systems to be having any mental effect on them, even if we hadn't locked her in a room that's practically a Faraday cage to begin with. She says one or other of the engines was damaged during the engagement with the *Cockatrice*, and I've no reason to disbelieve that. I think you're wrong about her.'

'She's got us right where she wants us, lad. She's done something to the engines, and now – if you get your way – we're going to let her get up close and personal with them.'

'And do what?' I asked.

'Whatever takes her fancy. Blowing us all up is one possibility. Did you consider that?'

'She'd blow herself up as well.'

'Maybe that's exactly the plan. Could be that she prefers dying to staying alive, if being shut out from the rest of the Spiders is as bad as you say it is. She didn't seem to be real keen on being rescued from that wreck, did she? Maybe she was hoping to die aboard it.'

'She looked like she was trying to stay alive to me, Captain. There were a hundred ways she could have killed herself aboard the *Cockatrice* before we boarded, and she didn't. I think she was just scared of us, scared that we were going to be like all the other Ultras. That's why she kept running.'

'A nice theory, lad. It's a pity so much is hanging on it, or I might be inclined to give it a moment's credence.'

'We have no choice but to trust her. If we don't let her try something, most of us won't ever see another system.'

'Easy for you to say, son.'

'I'm in this as well. I've got just as much to lose as anyone else on this ship.'

Van Ness studied me for what felt like an eternity. Until now his trust in my competence had always been implicit, but Weather's arrival had changed all that.

'My wife didn't die in a terraforming accident,' he said slowly, not quite able to meet my eyes as he spoke. 'I lied to you about that, probably because I wanted to start believing the lie myself. But now it's time you heard the truth, which is that the Spiders took her. She was a technician, an expert in Martian landscaping. She'd been working on the Schiaparelli irrigation scheme when she was caught behind Spider lines during the Sabaea Offensive. They stole her from me, and turned her into one of them. Took her to their recruitment theatres, where they opened her head and pumped it full of their machines. Rewired her mind to make her think and feel like them.'

'I'm sorry,' I began. 'That must have been so hard—'

'That's not the hard part. I was told that she'd been executed, but three years later I saw her again. She'd been taken prisoner by the Coalition for Neural Purity, and they were trying to turn her back into a person. They hadn't ever done it before, so my wife was to be a test subject. They invited me to their compound in

Tychoplex, on Earth's Moon, hoping I might be able to bring her back. I didn't want to do it. I knew it wasn't going to work; that it was always going to be easier thinking that she was already dead.'

'What happened?'

'When she saw me, she remembered me. She called me by name, just as if we'd only been apart a few minutes. But there was a coldness in her eyes. Actually, it was something beyond coldness. Coldness would mean she felt some recognisably human emotion, even if it was dislike or contempt. It wasn't like that. The way she looked at me, it was as if she was looking at a piece of broken furniture, or a dripping tap, or a pattern of mould on the wall. As if it vaguely bothered her that I existed, or was the shape I was, but that she could feel nothing stronger than that.'

'It wasn't your wife any more,' I said. 'Your wife died the moment they took her.'

'That'd be nice to believe, wouldn't it? Trouble is, I've never been able to. And trust me, lad: I've had long enough to dwell on things. I know a part of my wife survived what they did to her in the theatres. It just wasn't the part that gave a damn about me any more.'

'I'm sorry,' I said again, feeling as if I'd been left drifting in space while the ship raced away from me. 'I had no idea.'

'I just wanted you to know: with me and the Spiders, it isn't an irrational prejudice. From where I'm sitting, it feels pretty damn rational.' Then he drew an enormous intake of breath, as if he needed sustenance for what was to come. 'Take the girl to the engine if you think it's the only way we'll get out of this mess. But don't let her out of your sight for one second. And if you get the slightest idea that she might be trying something – and I mean the *slightest* idea – you kill her, there and then.'

I clamped the collar around Weather's neck. It was a heavy ring fashioned from rough black metal. 'I'm sorry about this,' I told her, 'but it's the only way Van Ness will let me take you out of this room. Tell me if it hurts, and I'll try to do something about it.'

'You won't need to,' she said.

The collar was a crude old thing that had been lying around the *Petronel* since her last bruising contact with pirates. It was modified from the connecting ring of a space helmet, the kind that would amputate and shock-freeze the head if it detected massive damage to the body below the neck. Inside the collar was a noose of monofilament wire, primed to tighten to the diameter of a human hair in less than a second. There were complicated moving parts in the collar, but nothing that a Conjoiner could influence. The collar trailed a thumb-thick cable from its rear, which ran all the way to an activating box on my belt. I'd only need to give the box a hard thump with the heel of my hand, and Weather would be decapitated. That wouldn't necessarily mean she'd die instantly – with all those machines in her head, Weather would be able to remain conscious for quite some time afterwards – but I was reasonably certain it would limit her options for doing harm.

'For what it's worth,' I told her as we made our way out to the connecting spar, 'I'm not expecting to have to use this. But I want you to be clear that I will if I have to.'

She walked slightly ahead of me, the cable hanging between us. 'You seem different, Inigo. What happened between you and the captain, while you were gone?'

The truth couldn't hurt, I decided. 'Van Ness told me something I didn't know. It put things into perspective. I understand now why he might not feel positively disposed towards Conjoiners.'

'And does that alter the way you think about me?'

I said nothing for several paces. 'I don't know, Weather. Until now I never really gave much thought to those horror stories about the Spiders. I assumed they'd been exaggerated, the way things often are during wartime.'

'But now you've seen the light. You realise that, in fact, we are monsters after all.'

'I didn't say that. But I've just learned that something I always thought untrue – that Conjoiners would take prisoners and convert them into other Conjoiners – really happened.'

'To Van Ness?'

She didn't need to know all the facts. 'To someone close to him. The worst was that he got to meet that person after her transformation.'

After a little while, Weather said, 'Mistakes were made. Very, very bad mistakes.'

'How can you call taking someone prisoner and stuffing their skull full of Conjoiner machinery a "mistake", Weather? You must have known exactly what you were doing, exactly what it would do to the prisoner.'

'Yes, we did,' she said, 'but we considered it a kindness. That was the mistake, Inigo. And it was a kindness, too: no one who tasted Transenlightenment ever wanted to go back to the experiential mundanity of retarded consciousness. But we did not anticipate how distressing this might be to those who had known the candidates beforehand.'

'He felt that she didn't love him any more.'

'That wasn't the case. It's just that everything else in her universe had become so heightened, so intense, that the love for another individual could no longer hold her interest. It had become just one facet in a much larger mosaic.'

'And you don't think that was cruel?'

'I said it was a mistake. But if Van Ness had joined her . . . if Van Ness had submitted to the Conjoined, known Transenlightenment for himself . . . they would have reconnected on a new level of personal intimacy.'

I wondered how she could be so certain. 'That doesn't help Van Ness now.'

'We wouldn't make the same mistake again. If there were ever to be . . . difficulties again, we wouldn't take candidates so indiscriminately.'

'But you'd still take some.'

'We'd still consider it a kindness,' Weather said.

Not much was said as we traversed the connecting spar out to the starboard engine. I watched Weather alertly, transfixed by the play of colours across her cooling crest. Eventually she whirled around and said, 'I'm not going to *do* anything, Inigo, so stop worrying about it. This collar's bad enough, without feeling you watching my every move.'

'Maybe the collar isn't going to help us,' I said. 'Van Ness thinks you want to blow up the ship. I guess if you had a way to do that, we wouldn't get much warning.'

'No, you wouldn't. But I'm not going to blow up the ship. That's not within my power, unless you let me turn the input dials all the way into the red. Even Voulage wasn't that stupid.'

I wiped my sweat-damp hand on the thigh of my trousers. 'We don't know much about how these engines work. Are you sensing anything from them yet?'

'A little,' she admitted. 'There's crosstalk between the two units, but I don't have the implants to make sense of that. Most Conjoiners don't need anything that specialised, unless they work in the drive crèches, educating the engines.'

'The engines need educating?'

Not answering me directly, she said, 'I can feel the engine now. Effective range for my implants is a few dozen metres under these conditions. We must be very close.'

'We are,' I said as we turned a corner. Ahead lay the hexagonal arrangement of input dials. They were all showing blue-green now, but only because I'd throttled the engine back to a whisper of thrust.

'I'll need to get closer if I'm going to be any use to you,' Weather told me.

'Step up to the panel. But don't touch anything until I give you permission.'

I knew there wasn't much harm she could do here, even if she started pushing the dials. She'd need to move more than one to make things dangerous, and I could drop her long before she had a chance to do that. But I was still nervous as she stood next to the hexagon and cocked her head to one side.

I thought of what lay on the other side of that wall. Having traversed the spar, we were now immediately inboard of the engine, about halfway along its roughly cylindrical shape. The engine extended for one hundred and ten metres ahead of me, and for approximately two hundred and fifty metres in either direction to my left and right. It was sheathed in several layers of conventional hull material, anchored to the *Petronel* by a shock-absorbing cradle and wrapped in a mesh of sensors and steering-control systems. Like any shipmaster, my understanding of those elements was so total that it no longer counted as acquired knowledge. It had become an integral part of my personality.

But I knew nothing of the engine itself. My log book, with its reams of codified notes and annotations, implied a deep and scholarly grasp of all essential principles. Nothing could have been further from the truth. The Conjoiner drive was essentially a piece of magic we'd been handed on a plate, like a coiled baby dragon. It came with instructions on how to tame its fire, and make sure it did not come to harm, but we were forbidden from probing its mysteries. The most important rule that applied to a Conjoiner engine was a simple one: there were no user-serviceable components inside. Tamper with an engine – attempt to take it apart, in the hope of reverse-engineering it – and the engine would self-destruct in a mini-nova powerful enough to crack open a small moon. Across settled space, there was no shortage of mildly radioactive craters testifying to failed attempts to break that one prohibition.

Ultras didn't care, as a rule. Ultras, by definition, already had Conjoiner drives. It was governments and rich planet-bound individuals who kept learning the hard way. The Conjoiner argument was brutal in its simplicity: there were principles embodied in their drives that 'retarded' humanity just wasn't ready to absorb. We were meant to count ourselves lucky that they let us have the engines in the first place. We weren't meant to go poking our thick monkey fingers into their innards.

And so long as the engines kept working, few of us had any inclination to do so.

Weather took a step back. 'It's not good news, I'm afraid. I thought that perhaps the dial indications might be in error, suggesting that there was a fault where none existed . . . but that isn't the case.'

'You can feel that the engine is really damaged?'

'Yes,' she told me. 'And it's this one, the starboard unit.'

'What's wrong with it? Is it anything we can fix?'

'One question at a time, Inigo.' Weather smiled tolerantly before continuing, 'There's been extensive damage to critical engine components, too much for the engine's own self-repair systems to address. The engine hasn't failed completely, but certain reaction pathways have now become computationally intractable, which is why you're seeing the drastic loss in drive efficiency. The engine is being forced to explore other pathways, those that it can still manage given its existing resources. But they don't deliver the same output energy.'

She was telling me everything and nothing. 'I don't really understand,' I admitted. 'Are you saying there's nothing that can be done to repair it?'

'Not here. At a dedicated Conjoiner manufacturing facility, certainly. We'd only make things worse.'

'We can't run on just the port engine, either – not without rebuilding the entire ship. If we were anywhere near a moon or asteroid, that might just be an option, but not when we're so far out.'

'I'm sorry the news isn't better. You'll just have to resign yourselves to a longer trip than you were expecting.'

'It's worse than that. There's another ship closing in on us, probably another raider like Voulage. It's very close now. If we don't start running soon, they'll be on us.'

'And you didn't think to tell me this sooner?'

'Would it have made any difference?'

'To the trust between us, possibly.'

'I'm sorry, Weather. I didn't want to distract you. I thought things were bad enough as they were.'

'And you thought I'd be able to work a miracle if I wasn't distracted?'

I nodded hopelessly. I realised that, as naive as it might seem, I'd been expecting Weather to wave a hand over the broken engine and restore it to full, glittering functionality. But knowing something of the interior workings of the drive was not the same as being able to fix it.

'Are we really out of options?' I asked.

'The engine is already doing all it can to provide maximum power, given the damage it has taken. There really is no scope to make things better.'

Desperate for some source of optimism, I thought back to what Weather had said a few moments before. 'When you talked about the computations, you seemed to be saying that the engine needed to do some number-crunching to make itself work.'

Weather looked conflicted. 'I've already said too much, Inigo.'

'But if we're going to die out here, it doesn't matter what you tell me, does it? Failing that, I'll swear a vow of silence. How does that sound?'

'No one has ever come close to working out how our engines function,' Weather said. 'We've played our hand in that, of course: putting out more than our share of misinformation over the years. And it's worked, too. We've kept careful tabs on the collective thinking concerning our secrets. We've always had contingencies in place to disrupt any research that might be headed in the right direction. So far we've never had cause to use a single one of them. If I were to reveal key information to you, I would have more to worry about than just being an outcast. My people would come after me. They'd hunt me down, and then they'd hunt you down as well. Conjoiners will consider any necessary act, up to and including local genocide, to protect the secrets of the C-drive.' She paused for a moment, letting me think she was finished, before continuing on the same grave note, 'But having said that, there are layers to our secrets. I can't reveal the detailed physical principles upon which the drive depends, but I can tell you that the conditions in the drive, when it is at full functionality, are enormously complex and chaotic. Your ship may ride a smooth thrust beam, but the reactions going on inside the drive are anything but smooth. There is a small mouth into hell inside every engine: bubbling, frothing, subject to vicious and unpredictable state-changes.'

'Which the engine needs to smooth out.'

'Yes. And to do so, the engine needs to think through some enormously complex, parallel computational problems. When all is well, when the engine is intact and running inside its normal operational envelope, the burden is manageable. But if you ask too much of the engine, or damage it in some way, that burden becomes heavier. Eventually it exceeds the means of the engine, and the reactions become uncontrolled.'

'Nova.'

'Quite,' Weather said, favouring my response with a tiny nod.

'Then let me get this straight,' I said. 'The engine's damaged, but it could still work if the computations weren't so complicated.'

Weather answered me guardedly. 'Yes, but don't underestimate how difficult those computations have now become. I can feel the strain this engine is under, just holding things together as they are.'

'I'm not underestimating it. I'm just wondering if we couldn't help it do better. Couldn't we load in some new software, or assist the engine by hooking in the *Petronel*'s own computers?'

'I really wish it was that simple.'

'I'm sorry. My questions must seem quite simple-minded. But I'm just trying to make sure we aren't missing anything obvious.'

'We aren't,' she said. 'Take my word on it.'

I returned Weather to her quarters and removed the collar. Where it had been squeezing her neck, the skin was marked with a raw pink band, spotted with blood. I threw the hateful thing into the corner of the room and returned with a medical kit.

'You should have said something,' I told her as I dabbed at the abrasions with a disinfectant swab. 'I didn't realise it was cutting into you all that time. You seemed so cool, so focused. But that must have been hurting all the while.'

'I told you I could turn off pain.'

'Are you turning it off now?'

'Why?'

'Because you keep flinching.'

Weather reached up suddenly and took my wrist, almost making me drop the swab. The movement was as swift as a snake-bite, but although she held me firmly, I sensed no aggressive intentions. 'Now it's my turn not to understand,' she said. 'You were hoping I might be able to do something for you. I couldn't. That means you're in as much trouble as you ever were. Worse, if anything, because now you've heard it from me. But you're still treating me with kindness.'

'Would you rather we didn't?'

'I assumed that as soon as my usefulness to you had come to an end—'

'You assumed wrongly. We're not that kind of crew.'

'And your captain?'

'He'll keep his word. Killing you would never have been Van Ness's style.' I finished disinfecting her neck and began to rummage through the medical kit for a strip of bandage. 'We're all just going to have to make do as best we can, you included. Van Ness reckoned we should send out a distress call and wait for rescue. I wasn't so keen on that idea before, but now I'm beginning to wonder if maybe it isn't so bad after all.' She said nothing. I wondered if she was thinking of exactly the same objections I'd voiced to Van Ness, when he raised the idea. 'We still have a ship, that's the main thing. Just because we aren't moving as fast as we'd like—'

'I'd like to see Van Ness,' Weather said.

'I'm not sure he'd agree.'

'Tell him it's about his wife. Tell him he can trust me, with or without that silly collar.'

I went to fetch the captain. He took some persuading before he even agreed to look at Weather, and even then he wouldn't come within twenty metres of her. I told her to wait at the door to her room, which faced a long service corridor.

'I'm not going to touch you, Captain,' she called, her voice echoing from the corridor's ribbed metal walls. 'You can come as close as you like. I can barely smell you at this distance, let alone sense your neural emissions.'

'This'll do nicely,' Van Ness said. 'Inigo told me you had something you wanted to say to me. That right, or was it just a ruse to get me near to you, so you could reach into my head and make me see and think whatever you like?'

She appeared not to hear him. 'I take it Inigo's told you about the engine.'

'Told me you had a good old look at it and decided there was nothing you could do. Maybe things would have been different if you hadn't had that collar on, though, eh?'

'You mean I might have sabotaged the engine, to destroy myself and the ship? No, Captain, I don't think I would have. If I had any intention of killing myself, you'd already made it easy enough with that collar.' She glanced at me. 'I could have reached Inigo and pressed that control box while the nervous impulse from his brain was still working its way down his forearm. All he'd have seen was a grey blur, followed by a lot of arterial blood.'

I thought back to the speed with which she'd reached up and grabbed my forearm, and knew she wasn't lying.

'So why didn't you?' Van Ness asked.

'Because I wanted to help you if I could. Until I saw the engine – until I got close enough to feel its emissions – I couldn't know for sure that the problem wasn't something quite trivial.'

'Except it wasn't. Inigo says it isn't fixable.'

'Inigo's right. The technical fault can't be repaired, not without use of Conjoiner technology. But now that I've had time to think about it, mull things over, it occurs to me that there may be something I can do for you.'

I looked at her. 'Really?'

'Let me finish what I have to say, Inigo,' she said warningly, 'then we'll go down to the engine and I'll make everything clear. Captain Van Ness – about your wife.'

'What would you know about my wife?' Van Ness asked her angrily.

'More than you realise. I know because I'm a – I was – a Conjoiner.'

'As if I didn't know.'

'We started on Mars, Captain Van Ness – just a handful of us. I wasn't alive then, but from the moment Galiana brought our new state of consciousness into being, the thread of memory has never been broken. There are many branches to our great tree now, in many systems – but we all carry the memories of those who went before us, before the family was torn asunder. I don't just mean the simple fact that we remember their names, what they looked like and what they did. I mean we carry their living experiences with us, into the future.' Weather swallowed, something catching in her throat. 'Sometimes we're barely aware of any of this. It's as if there's this vast sea of collective experience lapping at the shore of consciousness, but it's only every now and then that it floods us, leaving us awash in sorrow and joy. Sorrow because those are the memories of the dead, all that's left of them. Joy because *something* has endured, and while it does they can't truly be dead, can they? I feel Remontoire sometimes, when I look at something in a certain analytic way. There's a jolt of déjà vu and I realise it isn't because I've experienced it before, but because Remontoire did. We all feel the memories of the earliest Conjoiners the most strongly.'

'And my wife?' Van Ness asked, like a man frightened of what he might hear.

'Your wife was just one of many candidates who entered Trans-enlightenment during the troubles. You lost her then, and saw her once more when the Coalition took her prisoner. It was distressing for you because she did not respond to you on a human level.'

'Because you'd ripped everything human out of her,' Van Ness said.

Weather shook her head calmly, refusing to be goaded. 'No. We'd taken almost nothing. The difficulty was that we'd added too much, too quickly. That was why it was so hard for her, and so upsetting for you. But it didn't have to be that way. The last thing we wanted was to frighten possible future candidates. It would have worked much better for us if your wife had shown love and affection to you, and then begged you to follow her into the wonderful new world she'd been shown.'

Something of Weather's manner seemed to blunt Van Ness's indignation. 'That doesn't help me much. It doesn't help my wife at all.'

'I haven't finished. The last time you saw your wife was in that Coalition compound. You assumed – as you continue to assume – that she ended her days there, an emotionless zombie haunting the shell of the woman you once knew. But that isn't what happened. She came back to us, you see.'

'I thought Conjoiners never returned to the fold,' I said.

'Things were different then. It was war. Any and all candidates were welcome, even those who might have suffered destabilising isolation away from Transenlightenment. And Van Ness's wife wasn't like me. She hadn't been born into it. Her depth of immersion into Transenlightenment was inevitably less profound than that of a Conjoiner who'd been swimming in data since they were a foetus.'

'You're lying,' Van Ness said. 'My wife died in Coalition custody three years after I saw her.'

'No,' Weather said patiently. 'She did not. Conjoiners took Tychoplex and returned all the prisoners to Transenlightenment. The Coalition was suffering badly at the time and could not afford the propaganda blow of losing such a valuable arm of its research programme. So it lied and covered up the loss of Tychoplex. But in fact your wife was alive and well.' Weather looked at him levelly. 'She is dead now, Captain Van Ness. I wish I could tell you otherwise, but I hope it will not come as too shocking a blow, given what you have always believed.'

'When did she die?'

'Thirty-one years later, in another system, during the malfunction of one of our early drives. It was very fast and utterly painless.'

'Why are you telling me this? What difference does it make to me, here and now? She's still gone. She still became one of you.'

'I am telling you,' Weather answered, 'because her memories are part of me. I won't pretend that they're as strong as Remontoire's, because by the time your wife was recruited, more than five thousand had already joined our ranks. Hers was one new voice amongst many. But none of those voices were silent: they were all heard, and something of them has reached down through all these years.'

'Again: why are you telling me this?'

'Because I have a message from your wife. She committed it to the collective memory long before her death, knowing that it would always be part of Conjoiner knowledge, even as our numbers grew and we became increasingly fragmented. She knew that every future Conjoiner would carry her message – even an outcast like me. It might become diluted, but it would never be lost entirely. And she believed that you were still alive, and that one day your path might cross that of another Conjoiner.'

After a silence Van Ness said, 'Tell me the message.'

'This is what your wife wished you to hear.' Almost imperceptibly, the tone of Weather's voice shifted. 'I am sorry for what happened between us, Rafe – more sorry than you can ever know. When they recaptured me, when they took me to Tychoplex, I was not the person I am now. It was still early in my time amongst the Conjoiners, and – perhaps just as importantly – it was still early for the Conjoiners as well. There was much that we all needed to learn. We were ambitious then, fiercely so, but by the same token we were arrogantly blind to our inadequacies and failings. That changed, later, after I returned to the fold. Galiana made refinements to all of us, reinstating a higher degree of personal identity. I think she had learned something wise from Nevil Clavain. After that, I began to see things in the proper perspective again. I thought of you, and the pain of what I had done to you was like a sharp stone pushing against my throat. Every waking moment of my consciousness, with every breath, you were there. But by then it was much too late to make amends. I tried to contact you, but without success. I couldn't even be sure if you were in the system any more. By then, even the Demarchists had their own prototype starships, using the technology we'd licensed them. You could have been anywhere.' Weather's tone hardened, taking on a kind of saintlike asperity. 'But I always knew you were a survivor, Rafe. I never doubted that you were still alive, somewhere. Perhaps we'll meet again: stranger things have happened. If so, I hope I'll treat you with something of the kindness you always deserved, and that you always showed me. But should that never happen, I can at least hope that you will hear this message. There will always be Conjoiners, and nothing that is committed to the collective memory will ever be lost. No matter how much time passes, those of us who walk in the world will be carrying this message, alert for your name. If there was more I could do, I would. But contrary to what some might think, even Conjoiners can't work miracles. I wish that it were otherwise. Then I would clap my hands and summon you to me, and I would spend the rest of my life letting you know what you meant to me, what you still mean to me. I loved you, Rafe Van Ness. I always did, and I always will.'

Weather fell silent, her expression respectful. It was not necessary for her to tell us that the message was over.

'How do I know this is true?' Van Ness asked quietly.

'I can't give you any guarantees,' Weather said, 'but there was one word I was also meant to say to you. Your wife believed it would have some significance to you, something nobody else could possibly know.'

'And the word?'

'The word is "mezereon". I think it is a type of plant. Does the word mean something to you?'

I looked at Van Ness. He appeared frozen, unable to respond. His eye softened and sparkled. He nodded, and said simply, 'Yes, it does.'

'Good,' Weather answered. 'I'm glad that's done: it's been weighing on all of our minds for quite some time. And now I'm going to help you get home.'

Whatever 'mezereon' meant to Van Ness, whatever it revealed to him concerning the truth of Weather's message, I never asked.

Nor did Van Ness ever speak of the matter again.

She stood before the hexagonal arrangement of input dials, as I had done a thousand times before. 'You must give me authorisation to make adjustments,' she said.

My mouth was dry. 'Do what you will. I'll be watching you very carefully.'

Weather looked amused. 'You're still concerned that I might want to kill us all?'

'I can't ignore my duty to this ship.'

'Then this will be difficult for you. I must turn the dials to a setting you would consider highly dangerous, even suicidal. You'll just have to trust me that I know what I'm doing.'

I glanced back at Van Ness.

'Do it,' he mouthed.

'Go ahead,' I told Weather. 'Whatever you need to do—'

'In the course of this, you will learn more about our engines. There is something inside here that you will find disturbing. It is not the deepest secret, but it is a secret nonetheless, and shortly you will know it. Afterwards, when we reach port, you must not speak of this matter. Should you do so, Conjoiner security would detect the leak and act swiftly. The consequences would be brutal, for you and anyone you might have spoken to.'

'Then maybe you're better off not letting us see whatever you're so keen to keep hidden.'

'There's something I'm going to have to do. If you want to understand, you need to see everything.'

She reached up and planted her hands on two of the dials. With surprising strength, she twisted them until their quadrants shone ruby red. Then she moved to another pair of dials and moved them until they were showing a warning amber. She adjusted one of the remaining dials to a lower setting, into the blue, and then returned to the first two dials she had touched, quickly dragging them back to green. While all this was happening, I felt the engine surge in response, the deck plates pushing harder against my feet. But the burst was soon over. When Weather had made her last adjustment, the engine had throttled back even further than before. I judged that we were only experiencing a tenth of a gee.

'What have you just done?' I asked.

'This,' she said.

Weather took a nimble, light-footed step back from the input controls. At the same moment a chunk of wall, including the entire hexagonal array, pushed itself out from the surrounding metallic-blue material in which it had appeared to have been seamlessly incorporated. The chunk was as thick as a bank-vault door. I watched in astonishment as the chunk slid in silence to one side, exposing a bulkhead-sized hole in the side of the engine wall.

Soft red light bathed us. We were looking into the hidden heart of a Conjoiner drive.

'Follow me,' Weather said.

'Are you serious?'

'You want to get home, don't you? You want to escape that raider? This is how it will happen.' Then she looked back to Van Ness. 'With all due respect . . . I wouldn't recommend it, Captain. You wouldn't do any damage to the engine, but the engine might damage you.'

'I'm fine right here,' Van Ness said.

I followed Weather into the engine. At first my eyes had difficulty making out our surroundings. The red light inside seemed to emanate from every surface, rather than from any concentrated source, so that there were only hints of edges and corners. I had to reach out and touch things more than once to establish their shape and proximity. Weather watched me guardedly, but said nothing.

She led me along a winding, restrictive path that squeezed its way between huge intrusions of Conjoiner machinery, like the course etched by some meandering, indecisive underground river. The machinery emitted a low humming sound, and sometimes when I touched it I felt a rapid but erratic vibration. I couldn't make out our surroundings with any clarity for more than a few metres in any direction, but as Weather pushed on I sometimes had the impression that the machinery was moving out of her way to open up the path, and sealing itself behind us. She led me up steep ramps, assisted me as we negotiated near-impassable chicanes, helped me as we climbed down vertical shafts that would be perilous even under one-tenth of a gee. My sense of direction was soon hopelessly confounded, and I had no idea whether we had travelled hundreds of metres into the engine, or merely wormed our way in and around a relatively localised region close to our entry point.

'I'm glad you know the way,' I said, with mock cheerfulness. 'I wouldn't be able to get out of here without you.'

'Yes, you will,' Weather said, looking back over her shoulder. 'The engine will guide you out, don't you worry.'

'You're coming with me, though.'

'No, Inigo, I'm not. I have to stay here from now on. It's the only way that any of us will be getting home.'

'I don't understand. Once you've fixed the engine—'

'It isn't like that. The engine can't be fixed. What I can do is help it, relieve it of some of the computational burden. But to do that I need to be close to it. Inside it.'

While we were talking, Weather had brought us to a box-like space that was more open than anywhere we'd passed through so far. The room, or chamber, was empty of machinery, save for a waist-high cylinder rising from the floor. The cylinder had a flattened top and widened base that suggested the stump of a tree. It shone the same arterial red as everything else around us.

'We've reached the heart of the engine-control assembly now,' Weather said, kneeling by the stump. 'The reaction core is somewhere else – we couldn't survive anywhere near that – but this is where the reaction computations are made, for both the starboard and port drives. I'm going to show you something now. I think it will make it easier for you to understand what is to happen to me. I hope you're ready.'

'As I'll ever be.'

Weather planted a hand on either side of the stump and closed her eyes momentarily. I heard a click and the whirr of a buried mechanism. The upper fifth of the stump opened, irising wide.

A blue light rammed from its innards. I felt a chill rising from whatever was inside, a coldness that seemed to reach fingers down my throat.

Something emerged from inside the stump, rising on a pedestal. It was a glass container pierced by many silver cables, each of which was plugged into the folded cortex of a single massively swollen brain. The brain had split open along fracture lines, like a cake that had ruptured in the baking. The blue light spilled from the fissures. When I looked into one – peering down into the geological strata of brain anatomy – I had to blink against the glare. A seething mass of tiny bright things lay nestled at the base of the cleft, twinkling with the light of the sun.

'This is the computer that handles the computations,' Weather said.

'It looks human. Please tell me it isn't.'

'It is human. Or at least that's how it started out, before the machines were allowed to infest and reorganise its deep structure.' Weather tapped a finger against the side of her own scalp. 'All the machines in my head only amount to two hundred grams of artificial matter, and even so I still need this crest to handle my thermal loading. There are nearly a thousand grams of machinery in that brain. The brain needs to be cooled like a turbopump. That's why it's been opened up, so that the heat can dissipate more easily.'

'It's a monstrosity.'

'Not to us,' she said sharply. 'We see a thing of wonder and beauty.'

'No,' I said firmly. 'Let's be clear about this. What you're showing me here is a human brain, a living mind, turned into some kind of slave.'

'No slavery is involved,' Weather said. 'The mind chose this vocation willingly.'

'It *chose* this?'

'It's considered a great honour. Even in Conjoiner society, even given all that we have learned about the maximisation of our mental resources, only a few are ever born who have the skills necessary to tame and manage the reactions in the heart of a C-drive. No machine can ever perform that task as well as a conscious mind. We could build a conscious machine, of course, a true mechanical slave, but that would contravene one of our deepest strictures. No machine may think, unless it does so voluntarily. So we are left with volunteer organic minds, even if those selfsame minds need the help of a thousand grams of non-sentient processing machinery. As to why only a few of us have the talent . . . that is one of *our* greatest mysteries. Galiana thought that, in achieving a pathway to augmented human intelligence, she would render the brain utterly knowable. It was one of her few mistakes. Just as there are savants amongst the retarded, so we have our Conjoined equivalents. We are all tested for such gifts when we are young. Very few of us show even the slightest aptitude. Of those that do, even fewer ever develop the maturity and stability that would make them suitable candidates for enshrinement in an engine.' Weather faced me with a confiding look. 'They are valued very highly indeed, to the point where they are envied by some of us who lack what they were born with.'

'But even if they were gifted enough that it was possible . . . no one would willingly choose this.'

'You don't understand us, Inigo. We are creatures of the mind. This brain doesn't consider itself to have been imprisoned here. It considers itself to have been placed in a magnificent and fitting setting, like a precious jewel.'

'Easy for you to say, since it isn't you.'

'But it very nearly could have been. I came close, Inigo. I passed all the early tests. I was considered exceptional, by the standards of my cohort group. I knew what it was like to feel special, even amongst geniuses. But it turned out that I wasn't quite special enough, so I was selected out of the programme.'

I looked at the swollen, fissured mind. The hard blue glow made me think of Cherenkov radiation, boiling out of some cracked fission core.

'And do you regret it now?'

'I'm older now,' Weather said. 'I realise now that being unique . . . being adored . . . is not the greatest thing in the world. Part of me still admires this mind; part of me still appreciates its rare and delicate beauty. Another part of me . . . doesn't feel like that.'

'You've been amongst people too long, Weather. You know what it's like to walk and breathe.'

'Perhaps,' she said, doubtfully.

'This mind—'

'It's male,' Weather said. 'I can't tell you his name, any more than I could tell you mine. But I can read his public memories well enough. He was fifteen when his enshrinement began. Barely a man at all. He's been inside this engine for twenty-two years of shiptime; nearly sixty-eight years of worldtime.'

'And this is how he'll spend the rest of his life?'

'Until he wearies of it, or some accident befalls this ship. Periodically, as now, Conjoiners may make contact with the enshrined mind. If they determine that the mind wishes to retire, they may effect a replacement, or decommission the entire engine.'

'And then what?'

'His choice. He could return to full embodiment, but that would mean losing hundreds of grams of neural support machinery. Some are prepared to make that adjustment; not all are willing. His other option would be to return to one of our nests and remain in essentially this form, but without the necessity of running a drive. He would not be alone in doing so.'

I realised, belatedly, where all this was heading. 'You say he's under a heavy burden now.'

'Yes. The degree of concentration is quite intense. He can barely spare any resources for what we might call normal thought. He's in a state of permanent unconscious flow, like someone engaged in an enormously challenging game. But now the game has begun to get the better of him. It isn't fun any more. And yet he knows the cost of failure.'

'But you can help him.'

'I won't pretend that my abilities are more than a shadow of his. Still, I did make it part of the way. I can't take all the strain off him, but I can give him free access to my mind. The additional processing resources – coupled with my own limited abilities – may make enough of a difference.'

'For what?'

'For you to get wherever it is you are going. I believe that with our minds meshed together, and dedicated to this one task, we may be able to return the engines to something like normal efficiency. I can't make any promises, though. The proof of the pudding . . .'

I looked at the pudding-like mass of neural tissue and asked the question I was dreading. 'What happens to you, while all this is happening? If he's barely conscious—'

'The same would apply, I'm afraid. As far as the external world is concerned, I'll be in a state of coma. If I'm to make any difference, I'll have to hand over all available neural resources.'

'But you'll be helpless. How long would you last, sitting in a coma?'

'That isn't an issue. I've already sent a command to this engine to form the necessary life-support machinery. It should be ready any moment now, as it happens.' Weather glanced down at the floor between us. 'I'd take a step back if I were you, Inigo.'

I did as she suggested. The flat red floor buckled upwards, shaping itself into the seamless form of a moulded couch. Without any ceremony, Weather climbed onto the couch and lay down as if for sleep.

'There isn't any point delaying things,' she said. 'My mind is made up, and the sooner we're on our way, the better. We can't be sure that there aren't other brigands within attack range.'

'Wait,' I said. 'This is all happening too quickly. I thought we were coming down here to look at the situation, to talk about the possibilities.'

'We've already talked about them, Inigo. They boil down to this: either I help the boy, or we drift hopelessly.'

'But you can't just . . . do this.'

Even as I spoke, the couch appeared to consolidate its hold on Weather. Red material flowed around her body, hardening over her into a semitranslucent shell. Only her face and lower arms remained visible, surrounded by a thick red collar that threatened to squeeze shut at any moment.

'It won't be so bad,' she said. 'As I said, I won't have much room left for consciousness. I won't be bored, that's for sure. It'll be more like one very long dream. Someone else's dream, certainly, but I don't doubt that there'll be a certain rapturous quality to it. I remember how good it felt to find an elegant solution, when the parameters looked so unpromising. Like making the most beautiful music imaginable. I don't think anyone can really know how that feels unless they've also held some of that fire in their minds. It's ecstasy, Inigo, when it goes right.'

'And when it goes wrong?'

'When it goes wrong, you don't get much time to explore how it feels.' Weather shut her eyes again, like a person lapsing into microsleep. 'I'm lowering blockades, allowing the boy to co-opt my own resources. He's wary. Not because he doesn't trust me, but because he can barely manage his own processing tasks, without adding the temporary complexity of farming some of them out to me. The transition will be difficult . . . ah, here it comes. He's using me, Inigo. He's accepting my help.' Despite being almost totally enclosed in the shell of red matter, Weather's whole body convulsed. Her voice, when she spoke again, sounded strained. 'It's difficult. So much more difficult than I thought it would be.

This poor mind . . . he's had so much to do on his own. A lesser spirit would already have buckled. He's shown heroic dedication . . . I wish the nest could know how well he has done.' She clamped her teeth together and convulsed again, harder this time. 'He's taking more of me. Eagerly now. Knows I've come to help. The sense of relief . . . the strain being lifted . . . I can't comprehend how he lasted until now. I'm sorry, Inigo. Soon there isn't going to be much of me left to talk to you.'

'Is it working?'

'Yes. I think so. Perhaps between the two of us—' Her jaws cracked together, teeth cutting her tongue. 'Not going to be easy, but . . . losing more of me now. Language going. Don't need now.'

'Weather, don't go.'

'Can't stay. Got to go. Only way. Inigo, make promise. Make promise fast.'

'Say it. Whatever it is.'

'When we get . . . when we—' Her face was contorted with the strain of trying to make herself understood.

'When we arrive,' I said.

She nodded so hard I thought her neck was going to break. 'Yes. Arrive. You get help. Find others.'

'Other Conjoiners?'

'Yes. Bring them. Bring them in ship. Tell them. Tell them and make them help.'

'I will. I swear on it.'

'Going now. Inigo. One last thing.'

'Yes. Whatever it is.'

'Hold hand.'

I reached out and took her hand, in my good one.

'No,' Weather said. 'Other. *Other hand.*'

I let go, then took her hand in my metal one, closing my fingers as tightly as I dared without risking hers. Then I leaned down, bringing my face close to hers.

'Weather, I think I love you. I'll wait for you. I'll find those Conjoiners. That's a promise.'

'Love a Spider?' she asked.

'Yes. If this is what it takes.'

'Silly . . . human . . . boy.'

She pulled my hand, with more strength than I thought she had left in her. She tugged it down into the surface of the couch until it lapped around my wrist, warm as blood. I felt something happening to my hand, a crawling itch like pins and needles. I kissed Weather. Her lips were fever-warm. She nodded and then allowed me to withdraw my hand.

'Go now,' she said.

The red material of the couch flowed over Weather completely, covering her hands and face until all that remained was a vague, mummy-like form.

I knew then that I would not see her again for a very long time. For a moment I stood still, paralysed by what had happened. Even then I could feel my weight increasing. Whatever Weather and the boy were doing between them, it was having some effect on the engine output. My weight climbed smoothly, until I was certain we were exceeding half a gee and still accelerating.

Perhaps we were going to make it home after all.

Some of us.

I turned from Weather's casket and looked for the way out. Held tight against my chest to stop it itching, my hand was lost under a glove of twinkling machinery. I wondered what gift I would find when the glove completed its work.

DILATION SLEEP

Spacers tell people that the worst aspect of starflight is revival. They speak the truth, I think. They give us dreams while the machines warm us up and map our bodies for cell damage. We feel no anxiety or fear, detached from our physical selves and adrift in generated fantasies.

In my dream I was joined by the cybernetic imago of Katia, my wife. We found ourselves within a computer-constructed sensorium. An insect, I felt my six thin legs propelling me into a wide and busy chamber. Four worker ants were there, crouched in stiff mechanical postures. With compound vision I studied these new companions, observing the nearest of them deposit a pearly egg from its abdomen. A novel visceral sense told me that I, too, contained a ready egg.

'We're gods amongst them,' I told my wife's imago.

'We are *Myrmecia gulosa*,' she whispered into my brain. 'The bulldog ant. You see the queen, and her winged male?'

'Yes.'

'Those maggoty things in the corner of the cell are the queen's larvae. Her worker is about to feed them.'

'Feed them with what?'

'His egg, my darling.'

I rotated my sleek, mandibled head. 'And will I also?'

'Naturally! A worker's duty is always to serve his queen. Of course . . . you may exit this environ, if you choose. But you'll have to remain in reefersleep for another three hours.'

'Three hours . . . might as well be centuries,' I said. 'Then change it. Something a bit less alien.'

My imago dissolved the scenario, the universe. I floated in white limbo, awaiting fresh sensory stimulus. Soon I found myself brushing shimmering vermilion coral with eight suckered arms, an octopus.

Katia liked to play games.

Eventually the dreams ceased and I suddenly sensed my body, cold and stiff but definitely anchored to my mind.

I allowed myself a long primal scream, then opened my eyes. The eyes I opened were the eyes of Uri Andrei Sagdev, who was once a mainbrain technician at the Sylveste Institute but who now found himself in the odd role of Starship Heuristic Resource, a crewperson.

Under different circumstances, it is not a role I would otherwise have chosen. I was alone, the room cold and silent. My five companions remained in reefersleep around my own capsule; only I had been revived. I sensed, then, that something must be wrong. But I did not query Katia, preferring to remain in ignorance until she saw fit to enlighten me regarding our situation.

I hauled myself from the open reefer and took faltering steps out of the room.

It was several minutes before I felt confident to do anything more ambitious than that. I stumbled to the nearby health bay and exercised with galvanic activators, pushing my muscles beyond the false limits of apparent exhaustion. Then I showered and dressed, taking the expediency of wearing a thermal layer beneath my overalls. Breakfast consisted of fried ham and Edam slices, followed by garlic croissants, washed down with chilled passion fruit and lemon tea.

Why was I not concerned to discover our difficulty? Simply

because the mere fact of revival told me that it could not be compellingly urgent. Any undesirable situation upon a light-skimming starship that does not instantly destroy it – probably in a flash of exotic bosons – will act on such an extended timescale that the mainbrain-crew overmind will have days or weeks to engineer a solution.

I knew we were not home, and that therefore something was wrong. But for a moment it was good simply to lie back in the kitchen and allow the music of Roedelius to envelop me, and to revel in this condition called life. To simply suck air into my old lungs.

I who had been dead, or near death, for so long.

'Some more, Uri?' asked my wife's imago.

I was alone apart from a servitor. It was a dumb-bell shaped drone hovering on silently energised levitation fields above the metal floor. Extruding a manipulator from the matt-gold surface of its upper spheroid, it offered me the jug of pale juice.

With a well-practised subvocal command, I enabled my entoptic system. The implant supplied the visual and tactile stimuli necessary to fully realise the imago, the simulation of Katia, drawing it from the ship's mainbrain. Bright grids and circles interrupted my ocular field, then meshed and thickened to form my wife, frozen and lifeless but apparently solid. Copyright symbols denoting the implant company flashed, then faded. I locked her entoptic ghost over the dull form of the servitor, its compact size easily concealed within her body-space. Her blunt silver hair fell around a narrow pale face, black lips pursed like a doll's and eyes staring right through me. Her clasped hands emerged from a long hooded scarlet gown inlaid around the shoulder with the insignia of the Mixmaster geneticists, a pair of hands holding a cat's cradle of DNA. My wife was a geneticist to the marow. On Yellowstone, where cybernetics was the primary creed, it made her a virtual pariah.

As the mainbrain-generated program took hold she grew

vivacious and smiled, and her hand appeared now to grasp the jug.

'I was tiring of storage, my darling.'

'I'm not comfortable with this,' I admitted. 'Katia – my actual Katia – despised the whole idea of you. This illusion would have especially sickened her.'

'It doesn't sicken me,' Katia said.

'It ought to,' I said. 'Aren't your personalities supposed to be the same?'

She smiled, as if the point were settled. So infuriatingly like her original.

'I see that,' I said dubiously. The imago had been against my actual wife's wishes. When the Melding Plague hit us I saw my chance of escape via this craft. Katia was unable to become a crewperson, so I surreptitiously set about digitizing my wife's personality. The implant did all the hard work. It had assembled a behaviour map of Katia whenever we were together, studying her through the conduits of my own senses. The simulation grew slowly, limited by the memory capacity of the implant. But each day I downloaded more of her into an Institute mainbrain, performing this routine for weeks on end. I have no doubt that Katia suspected something, although she never made any mention of it.

Having completed my clandestine work, I then grafted the copy over the mind of the ship. It lacked her memories, of course, but I went to the expense and danger of having my own trawled and substituted instead, using software routines to perform the gender inversion. Katia's personality only assumed dominance when I was in rapport with the vessel. There was no doubt in my mind that the other crewpersons had also arranged for their own fictitious companions. They too would speak to their loved ones, or some idealised fantasy of a lover, when they addressed the ship.

But I preferred not to think about that.

A lie, then. But my entire life had been a lie, Katia's imago simply the most recent aspect of it. But why had she awoken me? Or rather: why had the ship chosen to awaken me, and not one of the others? Janos, Kaj, Hilda, Yul and Karlos still remained in reefersleep, displaying no signs of imminent thaw.

I upped from the table decisively. 'Thank you, Katia. I'll take a stroll, admire the view.'

'I must discuss something with you,' Katia said. 'But I suppose it can wait a few minutes.'

'Ah,' I said, grinning. 'You want to keep me in suspense.'

'Nothing of the sort, darling. Is the music fine?'

'Music's fine,' I answered, leaving the kitchen.

I entered a curving hexagonal corridor, bathed in dull ochre light. A node of Roedelius chased me, humming from piezoacoustic panels in the walls. The gravity that held me to the floor arose from our one-gee thrust, and not from the centrifugal spin of the lifesystem, otherwise the vertical and horizontal axes would have been interchanged. This fact told me that we were not at home; not approaching the cluster of carousels and asteroids called Shiphaven, in the Trojan point that trailed Jupiter. We were still on stardrive, still climbing up or down from the slowtime of light-speed.

We might be anywhere between Epsilon Eridani and Solspace.

My stroll carried me away from the core of the vesel to her skin, where the hot neutron sleet wafted past us. The parts of the vessel through which I travelled grew darker and more machinelike, colder and less familiar. Irrationally, I began to imagine that I was being pursued and observed.

I have never enjoyed either solitude or the dark. I was a fool, then, to address this fear by turning around. Yet the hairs on my neck were bristling and my sweat had become chilled.

Most of the radial corridor was dark, apart from the miserly locus of light that had followed me like a halo. Nonetheless, it was still possible to make out a darker thing looming in the distance, almost lost in the convergence of the walls.

I was not alone.

It was a figure, a silhouette, regarding me. Not Katia's imago, for sure.

I felt a brief terror. 'Katia,' I croaked. 'Full lights, please.'

I jammed my eyes shut as the bright actinics snaped on. Red retinal ghosts slowly fading, I reopened them, not much more than a second later. But my watcher had gone.

I slowly emptied my lungs. I was wise enough not to leap to conclusions. This was not necessarily what it appeared. After all, I had only just emerged from reefersleep, after several years of being frozen. I was bound to be a little jittery, a little open to subconscious suggestion.

It seemed I was utterly alone. I vowed, shakily, to put the experience immediately out of mind.

Ten minutes later I had reached the outer hull, and was in naked space – or rather, seeing through the proxy eyes of a drone clamped on the outside with spidery grappling feet. The machine's camera head was peering through a porthole, into the room where I sat. I looked pale and strained, but I did not have company.

I looked away from the porthole, towards the bow of the ship. The vessel, the *Wild Pallas*, was a ramliner – a nearlight human rated starship. Most of what I saw, therefore, was very dense neutron shielding. The vessel required protons for its bosonic drive process. Ahead, a graser beam swept space and stripped deuterium nuclei into protons and neutrons. Our gauss scoop sifted free the protons and focused them into the heart of the ship. The neutral baryons were channelled around the hull in a lethal radiative rain, diverted clear of the lifesystem and its fragile payload of sleepers. The drone sensed the flux and passed the data to me in terms of a swirling roseate aura, as if we were diving down the gullet of the universe.

To the rear, things were eclipsed by the glow of the exhaust. Gamma shields burned Cherenkov-blue. Within the ship, the proton harvest was extremely short-lived. Fields targeted the protons into a beam, lancing through a swarming cloud of heavy monopoles. The relativistic protons were decelerated and steered into the magnetic nodes. Inside each monopole was a shell of bosons which coaxed the protons to disintegrate. This was the power source of a ramliner.

I had studied all the tech before signing up for the overmind partnership, the human-cybernetic steering committee that commanded this vessel. When I say studied, I mean that I had downloaded certain eidetic documents furnished by the Macro that owned the ship. These eidetics entered my memory at an almost intuitive level, programmed of course to fade once my contract expired. They told me everything I needed to know and little else. We carried nine hundred reefersleep passengers and we crew comprised six humans, each of whom was an expert in one or more areas of starflight theory. My own specialties were scoop subsystems – gauss collimators and particle-ablation shields – and shipboard/in-flight medicare. The computer that wore the masque of Katia was also equipped for these zones of expertise, but it was deficient – so the cybertechs said – in human heuristic thought modes. Crewpersons were therefore its Heuristic Resources – peripherals orbiting the hard glittering core of its machine consciousness.

Crewpersons thus rode at a more reduced level of reefersleep than our passengers: a little warmer, a little closer to the avalanche of cell death that is life. The computer could interrogate us without the bother of complete revival. Our dreams, therefore, would be dreams where matter and number flowed in technological tsunami.

I altered the drone's telemetry so that the neutron wind

became invisible. Looking beyond, I saw no stars at all. Einsteinian distortion was squashing them up fore and aft, concealed by the flared ends of the ship. We were still accelerating towards light-speed.

'Well?' I asked, much later.

'As you know, we've yet to reach midpoint. In fact, we will not reach home for another three years of shiptime.'

'Is this a technical problem?'

'Not strictly. I'm afraid it's medical, which is why I was forced to bring you out of reefersleep between systems. Like the view, my darling?'

'Are you joking? An empty universe with no stars? It's the gloomiest thing I can remember.'

I was back in the coldroom where the six crew reefers were stored. Katia's data ghost stood at my side, and Mozart warmed our spirits. Mozart's joyous familiarity drowned out all the faint, distant sounds of the ship, and the frank necessity of this annoyed me greatly. I was not normally prone to nervousness.

'Janos is sick,' explained Katia. 'He must have contracted the Melding Plague on Yellowstone. Unless we act now he won't survive the rest of the journey. He needs emergency surgery.'

'He's sick?' I shrugged. 'Too bad. But SOP on this is clear, Katia. Freeze him down further, lock the condition in stasis.' I leaned over the smooth side of Janos's reefer, examining the bio med display cartouche under its coffin-lid rim. The reefer resembled a giant chrome chrysalis or silverfish, anchored by its head to a coiled nexus of umbilicals. Within this hexagonal fluted box lay Janos. His inert form was dimly visible under the frosted clear lid.

'Normally, that would be our wisest course of action,' Katia said. 'Earthside med skills will certainly outmode our own. But in this instance the rules must be contravened. Janos can't survive, even at emergency levels of reefersleep. You know about the Melding Plague.'

I did. We all knew about it only too well, for it had crippled Yellowstone. The Melding Plague was a biocybernetic virus, something new to our experience. Yellowstone's intensely cybernetic society had crumbled at the nanomolecular level, the level of our computers and implants. The Melding Plague had caused our nanomachinery to grow malign.

I permitted Katia to explain, walking to the kitchen and preparing salami rolls, stepping briskly through the dim corridors.

All crewpersons were fitted with such implants. Through these data windows we interfaced with the machinery of the reefers and the mainbrain of the ship as the ramliner cruised from star to star. Janos's virus had attacked the structure of his own implants, ripping them apart and reorganizing them into analogues of itself. From one implant node, a network of webbed strands was spreading further into his brain, in an apparent attempt to knit together all the infected locales.

'The experts on Yellowstone soon learned that cold does not retard the virus significantly – certainly not the kind of cold from which a human could ever be revived. We must therefore operate immediately, before the virus gains a stronghold. And I'm afraid that our routine surgical programs will fail. We can't use nanomachinery against the virus; it will simply subsume whatever we throw against it.'

I gobbled my rolls. 'I don't know neurosurgery; that wasn't on the skills eidetic.' I brushed crumbs from my stubbled chin. 'However, if Janos's life is in danger—'

'We must act. How are you feeling now?'

'A little stiff. Nothing serious.' I forced a very stiff grin. 'I'll admit, I was a little jumpy early on. I think those ants gave me the creeps.'

Katia was silent for a few seconds. 'That's normal,' she eventually said. 'Get plenty of rest. Then we'll examine the surgical tools.'

*

I went jogging. I mapped a sinuous, winding path through the lifesystem, feeling the megaton mass of the ship wheel about my centre of mass. I was ruthless with myself, deliberately selecting a route that took me through every dark and shadowy region of the lifesystem I could think of. I silenced Mozart and forbade myself the company of Katia, disabling my imago inducer.

My thoughts turned back to the figure I imagined I had seen. What kind of rationale had flashed through my mind in the few seconds when I permitted the figure to exist outside of my imagination? Perhaps one of the sleepers might have thawed by accident and was wandering the ship in dismay. That hypothetical wanderer would have been equally surprised by my own presence. Ergo the person was now hiding.

Of course, the figure was undoubtedly a hallucination. One need not be drooling at the mouth to hallucinate – indeed, one could easily retain enough facilities to recognise the experience as being totally internalised. After the uneventful hours of wakefulness that had subsequently passed, I was anxious to dismiss the whole incident.

I jogged on, my shoes slapping the deck. I was approaching the nadir of my journey, the part of the ship that until now I had studiously avoided. Sensing my nearing footfalls, cartwheel-shaped airlocks dilated open. I panted through an antechamber, into the vast room where nine hundred slept.

The chamber had the toroidal shape of a tokamak. Nine hundred deep-preservation reefers lined the inner and outer walls, crisscrossed by ladders and catwalks. I set about circumnavigating the chamber, to finally purge my mind of any stray ghosts. Hadn't that always been my strategy as a child: confront my fears head on? I suspected that the boy in me would have been richly amused by my motives here. Nonetheless I insisted on this one ridiculous circuit, convinced it would leave me eased.

Most of these sleepers would stay aboard when we arrived in the Earth system. They were refugees from the Melding Plague, seeking sanctuary in the future. At the nearlight speeds this vessel attained between suns, large levels of time dilation would be experienced. Our clocks would grind to an imperceptible crawl. After thirty or forty years of shiptime, a mere six or seven hops between systems, more than a century would have elapsed on Yellowstone, enough time for eco-engineers to exorcise the biome of the Melding Plague. The sleepers we carried had elected not to risk spending the time in the planet's community cryocrypts; in dilation sleep the effective time spent in reefers was less, and therefore their chances of completely safe revival were enormously increased.

I was jogging slowly enough to read the glowing name panels imprinted on each reefer. Men, women, children . . . the rich of my world, able to pay for this exorbitant journey into a brighter future. I thought of the less wealthy, those who could not even afford spaces in the cryocrypts. I thought of the long queues of people waiting to see surgeons, people like Katia, anxious to lose their implants before the disease reached them. They would pay with whatever they could: organs or prosthetics or memories. Or if they chose not to pay they might consider becoming crew. My people made good crew-fodder. It called for a certain degree of yearning desperation to accept direct interfacing with the main-brain. The hard price of our bargain was the simple fact that our reduced state of reefersleep meant we would continue to age as we slept away the years.

That was not a bargain Katia had felt she could make. And I had known that I could not stand to lose my implants. Thus the Melding Plague touched us.

I felt bitterness, and this was welcome to me. I was happy to find familiar anxieties polluting my thoughts. I cast a dismissive glance over my shoulder, back along the curving ranks of sleepers I had already passed.

I was being followed.

The shadow was pounding along the walkway, halfway around

the great curve of the chamber. I could barely see it, just a man-shaped black aperture in the distance.

I quickened my pace. Only my feet thudded in the silence. Yet my chaser was also running faster. I felt sick with fright. I summoned Katia, but after alerting her was unable to grasp a sentence, a command, anything. The faceless silhouette seemed to be gaining on me.

Faceless was right. It had no features, no detail. Eventually I reached an exit. The airlock sequence amputated the chamber from me. I did not stop running, even when I realised that the doors behind me were remaining closed. The shadow-man remained with the sleepers.

But I had seen enough. It was not human. Just a man-shaped hole, a spectre.

I found the quickest route back to the command deck of the *Wild Pallas*. Immediately I ordered Katia to begin a rigorous search for intruders, though I knew of course that no intruder could have escaped her attention thus far. My Katia was omniscient. She would have known the exact location of every rat, every fly, aboard the craft; except that aboard the ship there were no flies, no rats.

I knew that the shadow was not a revived sleeper. None of the reefers had been opened or vacated. A stowaway was out of the question – what was there to eat or drink, apart from the supplies dispensed by the computer?

My mind veered towards the illogical. Could someone have entered the ship during its flight – someone dressed as a chameleon? That imagined intruder would have somehow had to achieve invisibility from Katia's eyes. Clearly impossible, even disregarding the unlikely manoeuvres required to match our velocity and position undetected.

I chewed on my lip, aware that each second of indecision counted against Janos. For my own defence, Katia would permit me access to a weapon, provided of course that the existence of the intruder was proven. Alternatively, I might best confront the situation by not confronting it. I could perform surgery on Janos without straying into those regions of the ship that the intruder had apparently claimed as its haunt. In a day or so, therefore, this ordeal might be over, and I could re-enter reefer-sleep. The most faceless, inhuman entities I would have to contend with upon my next revival would be Solpace Axis customs officials. Let them worry about the unseen extra passenger. Hadn't the shadow permitted me safe slumber so far?

I chuckled, though to my ears it sounded more like a death-rattle. I was still frightened, but for once my hands had stopped playing arpeggios on the keys of an invisible piano.

I absorbed myself in technical eidetics outlining the medical systems Katia and I were about to employ. The gleaming semi-robotic tools were the culmination of Yellowstone's surgical sciences. Even so, they would undoubtedly appear crude by Earth-side standards. This dichotomy galled me. Even if Janos would necessarily worsen by the time we arrived, how could we be certain that we were not reducing his chances with our outdated medical intervention? Perhaps Earth would have accelerated so far beyond our capabilities that the equation was no longer balanced in our favour.

Yet Katia would have weighed the issue minutely before selecting the appropriate course of action. Perhaps, then, it was best simply to silence one's qualms and do whatever was required.

Drones assisted me in carrying the medical machinery into the crew reefer room, where my five colleagues lay in frozen sleep. I wore a facemask and a gloved jumpsuit, inwoven with a heating circuit. Katia would lower the room's temperature before slightly increasing Janos's own.

'Ready, Uri?' she asked. 'Let's start.'

So we commenced, my eyes constantly flicking to the open

reefer I hoped soon to re-enter. The room rapidly chilled, lights burning frigid blue from the overheads.

Janos's reefer cracked open with a gasp of release cold. I looked at Janos, still and white and somehow distant. Let that distance remain, I prayed. After all, we were about to open his head.

Katia, in fact, had already performed some preliminary surgery. The skull had been exposed, skin pulled back as if framing the white pistil of a flesh-leaved flower. Slender probes entered the scalp via drilled holes, trailing glowing coloured cables into a matrix of input points in the domed head of the reefer. The work was angstrom-precise, rendered with a robot's deadening perfection. I had been briefed: those cables were substituting for the cybernetic implants within his brain that had fallen victim to the Melding Plague.

'When you have the top of the skull free you should feed it back along the cables,' Katia told me. 'It's crucial that we don't lose cyber-interface with Janos.'

I prepped the mechanical bone-saw. 'Why? What use is he to us?'

'There are good reasons. If you're still interested we can discuss it after the operation.'

The saw hummed into life, the rotary tip glinting evilly. Katia vectored the blade down, smoothly gnawing into the pale bone. Little blood oozed free but the sound struck an unpleasant resonance with me. Katia made three expert circumferential passes, then retracted. I took a deep breath, then placed gloved fingers on the top of Janos's head. The scalp felt loose, like half of a chocolate egg. I eased the section of skull free with a wet sucking slurp, exposing the damp pinkish mass of dura and gyrus, snuggling in the lower bowl of the skull. I took special care to maintain the integrity of the connections as I separated the bonework. For a while, humbled, I could only stand in awe of this fantastic organ, easily the most complex, alien thing my eyes had ever gazed on. And yet it managed to look so disappointingly vegetable.

'Husband, we must proceed,' warned Katia. 'I have warmed Janos to a dangerously high body temperature, whilst not greatly increasing his metabolic rate. We don't have time to waste.'

I felt sweat beading my forehead. I nodded. Inward, inward. Katia swung a new battery of blades and microlasers into play.

We operated to the music of Sibelius.

It was intriguing and repellent work.

I succeeded in detaching my mind to some extent, so that I was able to regard the parting brain tissue as dead but somehow sacred meat. The micro-implants came out one by one, too small for the naked eye to discern detail, barbed hunks of corroded metal. The corrosion, observable under a microscope, was the external evidence of the cybervirus. I studied it with rank feelings of abstract distaste. The virus behaved like its biological namesake, clamping onto the shell of the nanostructure and pulsing subversive instructions deep into its reproductive heart.

After three hours my back boiled with pain. I leaned away from the reefer, brushing a sleeve against my chilled forehead. I felt the room swimming, clotting with blobs of muggy darkness. For an instant I became disoriented, convinced that left was right and vice versa. I braced myself against the reefer as this dizziness washed over me.

'Not long now,' Katia said. 'How do you feel?'

'I'm fine. And you?'

'I'm . . . fine. The op's proceeding well.' Katia paused, then stiffened her voice with iron resolve, businesslike detachment. 'The next implant is the deepest. It lies between the occipital lobe and the cerebellum. We must take care to avoid lesion of the visual centre. This is the primary entoptic infeed node.'

'In we go, then.'

The machinery snicked obediently into place. Our ciliated microprobes slid into the tissue, like flexible syringes slipping into jelly. Despite the cold I found myself hot around the collar, iced sweat prickling my skin. Another hour passed, though time had ceased to have very much meaning.

And I froze, conscious of a presence behind me, in the same room.

Compelled, I turned. The watcher was with me.

I saw now that it could not be a man. Yet it did have a humanoid form, a humanoid of my build and posture.

A sculptor had selected ten thousand raven-black cubes, so dark that they were pure silhouettes, and arranged them as a blocky statue. That was the entirety of the watcher: a mass of black cubes.

As I turned, it swung towards me. None of the cubes from which it was formed actually moved; they simply blipped out and reappeared in an orchestrated wave, whole new strata of cubes forming in thin air. They popped in and out of reality to mould its altering posture. To my eyes the motion had a beguiling, digital beauty. I thought of the coloured patterns that would sweep across a stadium of schoolchildren holding painted mosaic cards to image some great slogan or emblem.

I raised my left arm, and observed the shadow repeat the action from its point of view. We were not mirrors of one another. We were ghosts.

My terror had reached some peak and evaporated. I grasped that the watcher was essentially motiveless, that it had been drawn to me as inevitably as a shrinking noon shadow.

'Continue with the operation,' insisted Katia. I noticed hesitancy in her voice, true to her personality to the end. She liked games, my Katia, but she was never a convincing liar.

'Lesion of the visual centre, you say?'

'That is what we must be careful to avoid.'

I grimaced. I had to know for sure.

I scooped up one of the detached nanoprobes. In reality, the drones mimicked my intentions with their own manipulators, picking up the nanoprobe's platonic twin . . . Then I jammed it recklessly into Janos's head, into his occipital lobe.

This reality melted and shattered, as if a stone had fallen into and disturbed the reflections on a crystal-smooth lake.

I knew, then.

My vision slowly unpeeled itself, returning to normality in strips. Katia was doing this, attempting to cancel the damage in my visual centre by sending distorted signals along the optic infeeds. I realised that I no longer had control of the surgical tools.

'I am the patient,' I said. 'Not Janos. The surgeon is the one who needs surgery. How ironic.'

'It was best that you not know,' Katia said. And then, very rapidly, she herself flickered and warped, her voice momentarily growing cavernous and slurred. 'I'm failing . . . there isn't much time.'

'And the watcher?'

'A symptom,' she said ruefully. 'A symptom of my own illness. A false mapping of your own body image within the simulation.'

'You're a simulation!' I roared. 'I can understand your image being affected . . . but you – yourself – you don't exist in my head! You're a program running in the mainbrain!'

'Yes, darling. But the Melding Plague has also reached the mainbrain.' She paused, and then, without warning, her voice became robotically flat and autistic. 'Much of the computer is damaged. To keep this simulation intact has necessitated sacrifices in tertiary function levels. However, the primary goal is to guarantee that you do not die. The operation-in-progress must be completed. In order to maintain the integrity of the simulation, the tuple-ensemble coded KATIA must be removed from main memory. This operation has now been executed.'

She froze, her last moment locked within my implant, trapped in my eyes like a spot of sun-blindness. It was just me and the computer then, not forgetting the ever-present watcher.

What could I do but continue with the surgery? I had a reason now. I wanted to excise the frozen ghost of Katia from my mind. She was the real lesion.

So I survived.

Many years passed for us. Our ship's computer was so damaged by the Melding Plague that we could not decelerate in time to reach the Earth system. Our choice was to steer for 61 Cygni-A, around which lay the colony Sky's Edge. Our dilation sleepers consequently found themselves further from home both in time and space than they had expected. Secretly we cherished the justice in this, we who had sacrificed parts of our lives to crew their dream-voyage. Yet they had not lost so very much, and I suppose I would have been one of their number had I had their power. Concerning Katia . . .

The simulation was never properly reanimated.

The shipboard memory in which it lay fell prey to the Melding Plague, and much of its data was badly corrupted. When I did attempt to recreate her, I found only a crude caricature, all spontaneity sapped away, as lifeless and cruelly predictable as a Babbage engine. In a fit of remorse I destroyed the imago. It helped that I was blind, for even this façade had been programmed to exhibit fear, programmed to plead once it guessed my intentions.

That was years ago. I tell myself that she never lived. And that at least is what the cybertechs would have us believe.

The last information pulse from Yellowstone told me that the real Katia is still alive, of course much older than when I knew her. She has been married twice. To her the days of our union must seem as ancient and fragile as an heirloom. But she does not yet know that I survived. I transmitted to her, but the signal will not reach Epsilon Eridani for a decade. And then I will have to await her reply, more years still.

Perhaps she will reply in person. This is our only hope of meeting, because I . . .

I will not fly again. Nor will I sleep out the decades.

GRAFENWALDER'S BESTIARY

Grafenwalder's attention is torn between the Ultra captain standing before him and the real-time video feed playing on his monocle. The feed shows the creature being unloaded from the Ultras' shuttle into the special holding pen Grafenwalder has already prepared. The beetle-like forms of armoured keepers poke and prod the recalcitrant animal with ten-metre stun-rods. The huge serpentine form writhes and bellows, flashing its attack eyes each time it exposes the roof of its mouth.

'Must have been a difficult catch, Captain. Locating one is supposed to be difficult enough, let alone trapping and transporting—'

'The capture was handled by a third party,' Shallice informs him, with dry indifference. 'I have no knowledge of the procedures involved, or of the particular difficulties encountered.'

While the keepers pacify the animal, technicians snip tissue samples and hasten them into miniature bio-analysers. So far they've seen nothing that suggests it isn't the real thing.

'I take it there were no problems with the freezing?'

'Freezing always carries a risk, especially when the underlying biology is nonterrestrial. We only guarantee that the animal appears to behave the same way now as when it was captured.'

Shallice is a typical Ultra: a cyborg human adapted for the extreme rigours of prolonged interstellar flight. His sleek red servo-powered exoskeleton is decorated with writhing green neon dragons. Cagelike metal ribs emerge from the Ultra's waxy white sternum, smeared with vivid blue disinfectant where they puncture the skin. The Ultra's limbs are blade-thin; his skull a squeezed hatchet capable of only a limited range of expression. He smells faintly of ammonia, breathes like a broken bellows and his voice is a buzzing, waspish approximation of human speech.

'Whoever that third party was, they must have been damned good.'

'Why do you say that?'

'Last I heard, no one has ever captured a live hamadryad. Not for very long, anyway.'

Shallice can't hide his scorn. 'Your news is old. There had been at least three successful captures before we left Sky's Edge.' He pauses, fearing perhaps that he may have soured the deal. 'Of course,' he continues, 'this is a far larger hamadryad . . . an adult, almost ready for tree-fusion. The others were juveniles, and they did not continue to grow once they were in captivity.'

'You're right: I need to keep better informed.' At that moment the news scrolls onto his monocle: his specialists have cross-matched samples from the animal against archived hamadryad genetic material, finding no significant points of deviation. 'Well, Captain,' he says agreeably, 'it looks as if we have closure on this one. You must be in quite a hurry to get back into safe space, away from the Rust Belt.'

'We've other business to attend to before we have that luxury,' Shallice tells him. 'You're not our only client around Yellow-stone.' The Ultra's eyes narrow to calculating slits. 'As a matter of fact, we have another hamadryad to deliver.' Before Grafenwalder responds, the Ultra raises a servo-assisted hand. 'Not a fully grown sample like your own. A much less mature animal. Yours will still be unique in that sense.'

Anger rises in Grafenwalder like a hot, boiling tide. 'But it won't be the only hamadryad around Yellowstone, will it?'

'The other one will probably die. It will certainly not grow any larger.'

'You misled me, Captain. You promised exclusivity.'

'I did no such thing. I merely said that no one else would be offered an adult.'

Grafenwalder knows Ultras too well to doubt that Shallice is telling the truth. They may be unscrupulous, but they usually stay within the strict letter of a contract.

'This other collector . . . you wouldn't mind telling me who it is, would you?'

'That would be a violation of confidentiality.'

'Come now, Captain – if someone else gets their hands on a hamadryad, they're hardly going to keep it a secret. At least not within the Circle.'

Shallice weighs this point for several long moments, his alloy ribs flexing with each laboured breath. 'The collector's name is Ursula Goodglass. She owns a habitat in the low belt. Doubtless you know the name.'

'Yes,' Grafenwalder says. 'Vaguely. She's been nosing around the Circle for some time, but I wouldn't call her a full member just yet. Her collection's nothing to speak of, by all accounts.'

'Perhaps that will change when she has her hamadryad.'

'Not when the Circle learns there's a bigger one here. Did you let her think she'd be getting something unique as well, Captain?'

Shallice makes a sniffing sound. 'The contract was watertight.'

On the video feed, the animal is being coaxed deeper into its pen. Now and then it rears up to strike against its tormentors, moving with deceptive speed.

'Let's not play games, Captain. How much is she paying you for her sample?'

'Ten thousand.'

'Then I'll pay you fifteen not to hand it over, on top of what I'm already paying you.'

'Out of the question. We have an arrangement with Goodglass.'

'You'll tell a little white lie. Say it didn't thaw out properly, or that something went wrong afterwards.'

Shallice thinks this over, his hatchet-head cocking this way and that inside the metal chassis of the exoskeleton. 'She might ask to see the corpse—'

'I absolutely insist on it. I want her to know what she nearly got her hands on.'

'A deception will place us at considerable risk. Fifteen would not be sufficient. Twenty, on the other hand—'

'Eighteen, Captain, and that's as high as I go. If you walk out of here without accepting the deal, I'll contact Goodglass and tell her you were at least giving it the time of day.'

'Eighteen it is, then,' Shallice says, after a suitable pause. 'You drive a hard bargain, Mister Grafenwalder. You would make a good Ultra.'

Grafenwalder shrugs off the insult and reaches out a hand to Captain Shallice. When his fingers close around the Ultra's, it's like shaking hands with a cadaver.

'I'd love to say it's been a pleasure doing business.'

Later, he watches their shuttle depart his habitat and thread its way through the debris-infested Rust Belt, moving furtively between the major debris-swept orbits. He wonders what the Ultras make of the old place, given the changes that have afflicted it since their last trip through the system.

Good while it lasted, as people tend to say these days.

Oddly, though, Grafenwalder prefers things the way they are now. All things told, he came out well. Neither his body nor his habitat had depended on nanomachines, so it was only the secondary effects of the plague that were of concern to him. The area in which he had invested his energies prior to the crisis – the upgrading of habitat security systems – now proves astonishingly lucrative amongst the handful of clients able to afford his services. In lawless times, people always want higher walls.

There's something else, though. Ever since the plague hit, Grafenwalder has slept easier at night. He's at a loss to explain why, but the catastrophe – as bad as it undoubtedly was for

Yellowstone and its environs – seems to have triggered some seismic shift in his own peace of mind. He remembers being anxious before; now – most of the time, at least – he only has the memory of anxiety.

At last his radar loses track of the Ultra shuttle, and it's only then that he realises his error. He should have asked to see the other hamadryad before paying the captain to kill it. Not because he thinks it might not ever have existed – he's reasonably sure it did – but because he has no evidence at all that it wasn't already dead.

He permits himself a bittersweet smile. Next time, he won't make that kind of mistake. And at least he has his hamadryad.

Grafenwalder walks alone through his bestiary. It's night, by the twenty-six-hour cycle of Yellowstone standard time, and the exhibits are mostly dimmed. The railed walkway that he follows glows a subdued red, winding between, under and over the vast cages, tanks and pits. Many of the creatures are asleep, but some stir or uncoil at his approach, while others never sleep. Things study his passage with dim, resentful intelligence: just enough to know that he is their captor. Occasionally something throws itself at its restraints, clanging against cage bars or shuddering against hardened glass. Things spit and lash. There are distressing calls; laughable attempts at vocalisation.

Not all of the animals are animals, technically speaking. About half the exhibits in the bestiary are creatures like the hamadryad: alien organisms that evolved on the handful of known life-sustaining worlds beyond the First System. There are slime-scrapers from Grand Teton; screech-mats from Fand; more than a dozen different organisms from the jungles of Sky's Edge, including the hamadryad itself.

But the other half of the collection is more problematic. It's the half that could get him into serious trouble if the agents of the law came calling. It's where he keeps the real monsters: the things that might once have been human. There is the specimen he once bought from some other Ultras: a former crewman, apparently, who had been transformed far beyond the usual Ultra norms. Major areas of brain function had been trowelled out and replaced with crude neural modules, until the only remaining instinct was a slathering urge to mutilate and kill. His limbs are viciously specialised weapons, his bone growth modified to produce horns and armoured plaques. Grafenwalder can only guess that the man was meant to be some kind of berserker, to be used in acts of piracy where energy weapons might be unwise. Eventually he must have become unmanageable. Now it amuses Grafenwalder to provoke the man into futile killing frenzies.

Then there is the hyperpig variant his contacts located for him in the bowels of Chasm City: one of a kind, apparently; a rare genetic deviation from the standard breed. The woman's right side is perfectly human, but her left side is all pig. Brain function lies somewhere between animal and human. She sometimes tries to talk to him, but the compromised layout of her jaw renders her attempts at speech as frenzied, unintelligible grunts. At other times neural implants leave her docile, easily controlled. On the rare occasions when he has guests, Grafenwalder has her serve dinner. She shuffles in presenting her human side, then turns to reveal her true ancestry. Grafenwalder treasures his guests' reactions with a thin, observant smile.

Then there is the psychotic dolphin that lives in near-permanent darkness, its body showing evidence of crude cybernetic tampering. Its origin is unclear, its age even more so, but the animal's endless, all-consuming rage is beyond question. Grafenwalder has dropped sensors into the animal's scarred cortex, hooked into a visual display system. The slightest external stimulus becomes amplified into a kaleidoscopic light show, like the Devil's own firework display. Circuits drop the visual patterns back into the dolphin's mind. As an after-dinner treat,

Grafenwalder encourages his guests to torment the dolphin into ever more furious cycles of anger.

There are many other exhibits; almost too many for Grafenwalder to remember. Not all are of interest to him now, and there are some that he has not visited for many years. His keepers take care of the creatures' needs, only bothering him when something needs specialised or expensive medical intervention and his permission must be sought. Perhaps the hamadryad will turn out to be another of those waning fancies, although he thinks it unlikely.

But there is one holding pen that remains unoccupied. He's walking over it now, hands on either side of the railed bridge that spans the empty abyss. It is a deep, ceramic-lined tank that will eventually be filled with cold water under many atmospheres of pressure. At the bottom of the tank is a rocky surface that is designed to be punctuated by thermal hotspots, gushing noxious gases. When it is activated, the environment in the tank will form a close match to conditions inside the ice-shrouded ocean of Europa, the little moon of Jupiter in the First System.

But first Grafenwalder needs an occupant for the tank. That's the fundamental problem. He knows what he has in mind, but finding one of the elusive creatures is proving trickier than he expected. There are even some who doubt that the Denizens ever existed; let alone that he might find a surviving specimen now, in another system and nearly two hundred years after their supposed heyday. Yet there are enough shards of encouragement to keep him hopeful. He has subtle feelers out, and every now and then one of them twitches with a nugget of information. His trusted contacts know that he is looking for one, and that he will pay very well upon delivery. And deep inside himself he knows that the Denizens were real, that they lived and breathed and that it is not absurd that one may have survived into the present era.

He must have one. Although he would never admit it, he would gladly trade the rest of his bestiary for that one exhibit. And even as he acknowledges that truth within himself, he still cannot say why the creature matters so much.

Orbiting the inner fringe of the Rust Belt, backdropped by the choleric face of Yellowstone itself, Goodglass's habitat is a wrinkled walnut of unprepossessing dimensions. Grafenwalder's shuttle docks at a polar berthing nub, where a dozen similar vehicles are already clamped. He recognises more than half of them as belonging to collectors of his acquaintance.

After running some cursory security checks, a silverback gorilla escorts him deeper into the miniature world. The habitat is a cored-out asteroid, excavated by fusion torches and stuffed with a warren of pressurised domiciles wrapped around a modest central airspace. A spinney of free-fall trees keeps the self-regulating eco-system ticking over, with only a minimal dependence on plague-vulnerable machinery. There are no servitors anywhere, only adapted animals like the silverback. The air smells mulchy, saturated with microscopic green organisms. Grafenwalder sneezes into his handkerchief and makes a mental note to have his lungs swapped out and filtered when he returns home.

Goodglass offers cocktails to her assembled guests. They're standing in an antechamber to her bestiary, in a part of the habitat that has been spun for gravity. The polished floor is a matrix of black and white tiles, each of which has been inlaid with a luminous red fragment of a much larger picture. As the guests stand around, the tiles slowly shift and reorient themselves.

Grafenwalder goes with the flow, letting the tiles slide him from encounter to encounter. He makes small talk with the other collectors, filing gossip and rumour. All the while he's checking out his host, measuring her against his expectations. Ursula Goodglass is a small woman of baseline-human appearance, devoid of any obvious biomodifications. She wears a one-piece purple-black outfit with flared sleeves, rising to a stiff-necked collar upon which her hairless head sits like a rare egg. She possesses an attractively impish face with a turned-up nose. He could like her, if he didn't already detest her.

Presently, as he knew they must, the tiles bring them together. He bows his head and takes her black-gloved hand.

'It's good of you to come, Mister Grafenwalder,' she says. 'I know how busy you are, and I wasn't really expecting you to be able to find the time.'

'Carl, please,' he says, oozing charm. 'And don't imagine I'd have been able to stay away. Your invitation sounded intriguing. It's so much more difficult to turn up anything new these days, the way things have gone. I can't imagine what it is you have for us.'

'I just hope you won't be disappointed.'

'I won't,' he says, with heavy emphasis. 'Of that I'm sure.'

'I want you to understand,' she begins, before glancing away nervously, 'it's not that I'm trying to compete with you, or upstage you. I've too much respect for you for that.'

'Oh, don't worry. A little healthy rivalry never hurt anyone. What good is a collection unless there's another one to lend it contrast?'

She smiles uncertainly, measuring him as much as he is measuring her. He can feel the pressure of her scrutiny: cool and steady as a refrigeration laser.

Fine lines crisscross her skull: snow-white sutures that remind him of the fracture patterns in the ice of Europa, even though he has never visited First System. The scars are evidence of emergency surgery performed in the heat of the Melding Plague, when it became necessary for the rich to rid themselves of their neural implants. Now Goodglass wears them as a symbol of former status.

'I'd like you to meet my husband,' she says as a palanquin glides up to them across the shifting tiled floor. Grafenwalder blinks back surprise: he'd noticed the palanquin before, but had assumed it belonged to one of the other guests. 'Edric, this is Carl,' she says.

'It's a pleasure to meet you,' the palanquin answers, the piping

221

voice issuing from a speaker grille set halfway up the front of the armoured cabinet. The palanquin has the shape of a slender, flat-topped pyramid, its bronze sides flanged by cooling ribs and sensor studs. An oval window set into the front, just above the speaker grille, is too dark to afford more than a vague impression of Edric Goodglass. 'I hope this encumbrance doesn't make you ill at ease, Mister Grafenwalder,' the occupant tells him.

'Hardly,' he says. 'I've used palanquins myself, for business in Chasm City. They tell me my blood has been scrubbed of machines, but you can't ever be too careful.'

'In my case I never leave my palanquin,' Edric says. 'I still carry all the bodily machines I had at the time of the plague. It would only take a tiny residual trace to kill me.'

Grafenwalder swirls his drink, stepping nimbly from one moving tile to another. 'It must be intolerable.'

'It's my own fault. I was too slow when it counted. When the plague hit, I hesitated. I should have had the surgery fast and dirty, the way my wife did. She was braver than I; less convinced it was all about to blow over. Now I can't even risk the surgery. I'd have to leave the palanquin before they opened me up, and that alone would expose me to unacceptable risk.'

'But surely the top hospitals—'

'None will give me the cast-iron guarantee I require. Until one of them can state categorically that there is a zero risk of plague infection, I will remain in this thing.'

'You might be in for a long wait.'

'If I've learned anything from Ursula, it's the value of patience. She's the very model of it.'

Grafenwalder shoots a sidelong glance at Ursula Goodglass, wondering what their marriage must be like. Clearly sex isn't on the cards, but he doubts that it was ever the main interest in their lives. Games, especially those of prestige and subterfuge, are amongst the chief entertainments of the Rust Belt moneyed.

'Well, I suppose I shouldn't keep people waiting any longer,' the woman says. She drops her empty glass to the floor, where it vanishes into one of the black tiles as if it had met no resistance, and then claps her hands three times. 'Ladies and gentlemen,' she begins, voice raised an octave higher than when they had been speaking, 'thank you very much for coming here today. Some of you have visited before; some of you are newcomers to my habitat. Some of you will know a little about me, some of you next to nothing. I do not believe that any of us would say that we are close friends. All of us in the Circle have one thing in common, though: we collect. It is what we live for; what makes us who we are. My own bestiary is modest by the standards of some, but I am nonetheless immensely proud of my latest acquisition. There is nothing else like it in this system; nor is there likely to be for a very long time. Please join me now – I believe I have something you are going to find very, very interesting.'

With that, a pair of thick metal doors open in one wall of the room, hissing wide on curved pistons. Goodglass and her husband lead the way, with the rest of the party trailing behind. Grafenwalder chooses to remain close by the couple, feigning curiosity.

She can't just show off the hamadryad. First they have to endure a short but tedious tour of the rest of her bestiary, or at least that part of it she plans to show them today. None of it is of the slightest interest to Grafenwalder, and even the other guests merely feign polite interest. By turns, though, they arrive at the main event. The party gathers on a railed ledge high above a darkened pit. Grafenwalder knows what's coming, but keeps his expression blankly expectant. Goodglass makes a little speech, dropping hints about the type of specimen she's obtained, how difficult it's been to capture and transport it, alluding once or twice to its planet of origin: clue enough for those in the know. Pricking his ears, Grafenwalder makes out speculative whispers from his fellow collectors. One or two are ahead of Goodglass.

'Unfortunately,' she says, 'my exhibit did not arrive intact. It suffered some physiological trauma during its journey here:

cryogenic damage to its tissues and nervous system. But it is still alive. With some intervention, my experts have restored much of its basic functional repertoire. In all significant respects, it is still a living hamadryad: the first you will ever see.'

She throws the lights, illuminating the creature in the pit. By then Grafenwalder has a bad taste in his mouth. The hamadryad is much smaller than his adult-phase example, but it isn't dead. It's moving: great propulsive waves sliding up and down its concertina body as it writhes and coils from one end of the pit to the other, thrashing like a severed electrical line.

'It's alive,' he says quietly.

Goodglass looks at him sharply. 'Were you expecting otherwise?'

'It's just that when you said how much difficulty you'd gone to—' But by then his words are drowned out by the demands of the other guests, all of whom have questions for Goodglass. Lysander Carroway starts applauding, encouraging the others to join in.

Grafenwalder notches his hatred a little higher, even as he joins in the applause with effete little hand-claps.

He steps back from the railing, giving Goodglass her moment in the sun. All the while, he studies the hamadryad, trying to figure out what must have happened. As much as he dislikes Ultras, he can't believe that Captain Shallice would have cheated him so nakedly. That's when Grafenwalder sees his angle, and knows he can come out of this even better than he was expecting.

He lets the interested chat simmer down, then coughs just loudly enough to let everyone know he has something to contribute.

'It's very impressive,' he says. 'For an intermediate-phase sample, at any rate.'

Goodglass fixes him with narrowing eyes, dimly aware of what must be coming. Even the palanquin spins around, presenting its dark window to him.

'You know of other samples, Carl?' Ursula asks.

'One, anyway. But before we get into that . . . you mentioned shipping difficulties, didn't you?'

'Normal complications associated with reefersleep procedures as applied to nonterrestrial organisms,' she says.

'What kind of complications?'

'I told you already – tissue damage—'

'Yes, but how extensive was it? When the animal was revived from reefersleep, in what way did it exhibit signs of having been injured? Were its movements impaired, its hunting patterns atypical?'

'None of that,' she says.

'Then you're saying the animal was fine?'

'No,' she says icily. 'The animal was dead.'

Grafenwalder twitches back his head in feigned confusion. 'I know hamadryad biology is complex, but I didn't know that they could be brought back from death.'

'Reefersleep is a kind of death,' Goodglass says.

'Well, yes. If you want to split hairs. Things are usually alive after they've been thawed, though: that's more or less the point. But the hamadryad wasn't alive, was it? It was dead. It's *still* dead.'

Lysander Carroway shakes her head emphatically. 'It's alive, Grafenwalder. Use your bloody eyes.'

'It's being puppeted,' Grafenwalder says. 'Isn't it, Ursula? That's a dead animal with electrodes in it. You're making it twitch like a frog's leg.'

Goodglass fights hard to keep her composure: he can see the pulse of a vein on the side of her skull. 'I never actually said it was alive. I merely said it had the full behavioural repertoire of a living hamadryad.'

'You said it was living.'

Her husband answers for her. 'They don't have brains, Grafen-walder. They're more like plants. It eats and shits. What more do you want?'

Choosing his moment expertly, he offers a disappointed shrug. 'I suppose it has a certain comedic value.'

'Come now,' Michael Fayrfax says. 'She's shown us a hamadryad, more than most of us will ever see. What does it matter if it isn't technically alive?'

'I think it matters a lot,' Grafenwalder says. 'That's why I've gone to so much trouble to obtain a living specimen. Bigger than that, too. Mine's adult-phase. They don't come any larger.'

'He's bluffing,' Goodglass says. 'If he had a hamadryad, he'd have shown it off already.'

'I assure you I have one. I just wasn't ready to exhibit it yet.'

She still looks sceptical. 'I don't believe you. Why wait until now?'

'I wanted to be sure the animal had settled down; that I'd ironed out any difficulties with its biology. Keeping one of those things alive is quite a challenge, especially when they're adult-phase: the whole dietary pattern starts shifting.'

'You're lying.'

'You can see it, if you want to.'

The scepticism begins to crack, the fear that he might not be lying breaking through. 'When?'

'Whenever you like.' He turns to the other guests and extends his hands expansively. 'All of you, of course. You know where I live. How about the day after tomorrow? I couldn't possibly *fake* one by then, could I?'

Grafenwalder is riding his shuttle back home from the Goodglass bestiary when he receives an incoming communication. It appears to be transmitting from within the Rust Belt, but the shuttle can't pinpoint the origin of the signal any more precisely than that. For a moment Grafenwalder thinks it may be a threat from Goodglass, even though he credits her with fractionally more sense than that.

But it's not Goodglass's face that fills his cabin wall when he answers the communication. It's nobody he recognises. A man, with a cherubic moon-face and a thick lower lip, glossy with saliva, that sags to the right. He wears a panama hat over tight dark curls, and a finely patterned harlequin coat hangs over his heavy frame in billowing folds. A glass box dangles around his neck, rattling with the implants he must once have carried in his skull. He is backdropped by a sumptuously upholstered chair, rising high as a throne.

'Mister Grafenwalder? My name is Rifugio. I don't think our paths have crossed before.'

'What do you want?'

There's barely any timelag. 'I am a broker, Mister Grafenwalder: a wheeler-dealer, a fixer, a go-getter. When someone needs something – especially something that may require delicate extralegal manoeuvring – I'm the man to come to.'

Grafenwalder moves to kill the communication. 'You still haven't told me what you want.'

'It is not about what I want. It is about what you want. Specifically, a certain bio-engineered organism.' Rifugio scratches the tip of his bulbous nose. 'You've been as discreet as matters will allow, I'll grant you that – but you've still put out word concerning the thing you seek. Now that word has reached my ears, and, fortuitously, I happen to be the man who can help you.' Now Rifugio leans closer, the rim of his hat tipping across his brow, and lowers his voice. 'I have one, and I am willing to sell it. At a price, of course – I must pay off my own informants and contacts. But knowing what you paid for the hamadryad, I am confident that you can afford twice as much to get the thing you want so badly.'

'Maybe I don't want one that much.'

Rifugio leans back, looking nonplussed. 'In that case . . . I won't trouble you again. Good day to you, sir.'

'Wait,' Grafenwalder says hastily. 'I'm interested. But I need to know more.'

'I wouldn't expect otherwise. We'll have to meet before we take matters any further, of course.'

Grafenwalder doesn't like it, but the man is right. 'I'll want a DNA sample.'

'I'll give you DNA and more: cell cultures, tissue scrapings – almost enough to make one for yourself. We'll need to meet in person, of course: I wouldn't trust material of such sensitivity to an intermediary.'

'Of course not,' Grafenwalder says. 'But we'll meet on neutral ground. There's a place I've used before. How does Chasm City grab you?'

Rifugio looks pleased. 'Name the time and the place.'

'I can squeeze you in tomorrow,' Grafenwalder says.

He doesn't care for Chasm City, at least not these days, but it's a useful enough place to do business. Complex technology doesn't work reliably, making every transaction cumbersome. But that has its benefits, too. Weapons that might just work in the Rust Belt can't be trusted in CC. Eavesdropping and other forms of deception become risky. It's best not to try anything too clever, and everyone knows that.

The one thing Grafenwalder isn't worried about is catching something. His palanquin is the best money can buy, and even if something did get through its ten centimetres of nano-secure hermetic armour, it would have a hard time finding anything in his body to touch and corrupt. The armour reassures him, though, and the privacy of the cabinet shields him from the awkwardness of a face-to-face encounter. As he makes his way through the city, following other palanquins along the winding path of an elevated private road through the high Canopy, he pages once more through the sparse information he has managed to piece together on Rifugio.

Grafenwalder has the feeling that he's trying to pin down a ghost. There is a broker named Rifugio, and judging by what he has already achieved, he would appear to have the necessary contacts to procure a Denizen. But it puzzles Grafenwalder that their paths haven't intersected before. Granted, it's a big, turbulent system, with a lot of scope for new players to emerge from hitherto obscurity. But Grafenwalder has been courting men like Rifugio for years. There should have been at least a blip on his radar before now.

The palanquins duck and dive through the mad architecture of the Canopy. All around, buildings that were once cleanly geometric have been turned into the threatening forms of haunted trees, their grasping branches locking bony fingers high over the lower levels of the city. Epsilon Eridani is still above the horizon, but so little sunlight penetrates the smog-brown atmosphere or the muck-smeared panels of the latticework dome that it might as well be twilight. The lights are on all over the city, save for the seductive absence of the chasm itself. Dark threads dangle from the larger trunks of the Canopy, like cannon-blasted rigging. Brachiating cable cars swing through the tangle like drunk gibbons. Compared to the ordered habitats of the surviving Rust Belt, it's a scene from hell. And yet people still live here. People still make lives for themselves; still fall in love and find somewhere they can think of as home. With a lurch of cognitive vertigo that he's already experienced a few times too many, Grafenwalder remembers that there are people down there who have no memory of how things used to be.

He knows it ought to horrify him that human beings could ever adapt to such a catastrophic downturn in their fortunes, even though people have been doing that kind of thing for most of history. Yet part of him feels a strange kinship with those survivors. He sleeps easier since the plague, and he doesn't know why. It's as if the crisis snapped shut part of his life that contained something threatening and loose, something that was in danger of reaching him.

In an unsettling way, though, he feels that Rifugio's call has reopened that closed book, just a crack. And that whatever was keeping him from sleep is stalking the edge of his imagination once more.

They meet in private rooms in the outermost branch of a Canopy structure near Escher Heights. The building is dead now, incapable of further change, and its owner – a man named Ashley Chabrier, with whom Grafenwalder did business years ago – has cut through the floor, walls and ceilings of the reshaped husk and emplaced enormous glass panels, veined in the manner of insect wings and linked together by leathery fillets of the old growth. It affords a spectacular view, but even Grafenwalder has misgivings as he steers his palanquin across the reflectionless floor, with the fires of the Mulch burning two kilometres below. Even if he survived the fall, the Mulch inhabitants wouldn't take kindly to the likes of him dropping in.

Rifugio, contrary to Grafenwalder's expectations, has not arrived by palanquin. He stands with his legs wide, his generous paunch supported by a levitating girdle, a pewter-coloured belt ringed by several dozen tiny and silent ducted fan thrusters. His slippered feet skim the glass with their up-curled toes. As he approaches Grafenwalder, he barely moves his legs.

'I have brought what I promised,' Rifugio says, by way of greeting. He's carrying a small malachite-green case, dangling from the pudgy fingers of his right hand.

'Is it all right if I say the word "Denizen" now?' Grafenwalder asks.

'You just said it, so I think the answer has to be yes. You're still suspicious, I see.'

'I've every right to be suspicious. I've been looking for one of these things for longer than I care to remember.'

'So I hear.'

'There have been times when I have doubted that they exist now; times when I doubted that they ever existed.'

'Yet you haven't stopped searching. Those doubts never became all-consuming.' Rifugio is very close to the palanquin now. As a matter of routine, it deep-scans him for concealed weapons or listening devices. It finds nothing alarming. Even so, Grafenwalder flinches when the man suddenly lifts the case and pops the lid. 'Here is what I have for you, Mister Grafenwalder: enough to silence those qualms of yours.'

The case is lined with black foam. Glass vials reside in neat little partitions. The palanquin probes the case and detects only biological material: exactly what Rifugio promised. With his left hand, Rifugio digs out one of the vials and holds it up like a magic charm. Dark red fluid sloshes around inside.

'Here. Take this and run an analysis on it. It's Denizen blood, with Denizen DNA.'

Grafenwalder hesitates for a moment, despite the assurances from his palanquin that it can deal with any mere biological trickery. Then he permits the machine to extend one of its manipulators, allowing Rifugio to pop the vial into its cushioned grasp. The machine withdraws the manipulator into its analyser alcove, set just beneath the frontal window. Part of the biological sample will be incinerated and passed through a gas chromatograph, where its isotopic spectrum will be compared against the data on Denizen blood Grafenwalder has already compiled. At the same time, the DNA will be amplified, speed-sequenced and cross-referenced against his best-guess for the Denizen genetic sequence. There's no physical connection between the analyser and the interior of the palanquin, so Grafenwalder cannot come to harm. Even so, he wills the analyser to complete its duties as swiftly as possible.

'Well, Mister Grafenwalder? Does it meet with your satisfaction?'

The analyser starts graphing up its preliminary conclusions: the material looks genuine enough.

Grafenwalder keeps the excitement from his voice. 'I'd like to know where you found it. That would help me decide whether or not I believe you have the genuine article.'

'The Denizen came into my possession via Ultras. They'd been keeping it as a pet, aboard their ship.'

'Shallice's men, by any chance?'

'I obtained the Denizen from Captain Ritter, of the *Number Theoretic*. I've had no dealings with Shallice, although I know the name. As for Ritter – in so far as one can ever believe anything said by an Ultra – I was told that he acquired the Denizen during routine trade with another group of Ultras, in some other godforsaken system. Apparently the Denizen was kept aboard ship as a pet. The Ultras had little appreciation of its wider value.'

'How did Ultras get hold of it in the first place?'

'I have no idea. Perhaps only the Denizen can tell us the whole story.'

'I'll need better provenance than that.'

'You may never get it. We're talking about beings created in utmost secrecy two hundred years ago. Their very existence was doubted even then. The best you can hope for is a plausible sequence of events. Clearly, the Denizen must have left Europa's ocean after Cadmus-Asterius and the other hanging cities fell. If it passed into the hands of starfarers – Ultras, Demarchists, Conjoiners, it doesn't matter which – it would have had a means to leave the system, and spend much of the intervening time either frozen or at relativistic speed, or both. It need not have experienced anything like the full bore of those two hundred years. Its memories of Europa may be remarkably sharp.'

'Have you asked it?'

'It doesn't speak. Not all of them were created with the gift of language, Mister Grafenwalder. They were engineered to work as underwater slaves: to take orders rather than to issue them. They had to be intelligent, but they didn't need to answer back.'

'Some of them had language.'

'The early prototypes, and those that were designed to mediate with their human overseers. Most of them were dumb.'

Grafenwalder allows the disappointment to wash over him,

then bottles it away. He'd always hoped for a talker, but Rifugio is correct: it could never be guaranteed. And perhaps there is something in having one that won't answer back, or plead. It's going to be spending a lot of time in his tank, after all.

'You'll treat it with kindness, of course,' Rifugio continues. 'I didn't liberate it from the Ultras just so it can become someone else's pet, to be tormented between now and kingdom come. You'll treat it as the sentient being it is.'

Grafenwalder sneers. 'If you care so much, why not hand it over to the authorities?'

'Because they'd kill it, and then go after anyone who knew of its existence. Demarchists made the Denizens in one of their darker moments. They're more enlightened now – so they'd like us to think, anyway. They certainly wouldn't want something like a living and breathing Denizen – a representative of a sentient slave race – popping out of history's cupboard, not when they're bending over backwards to score moral points over the Conjoiners.'

'I'll treat it fairly,' Grafenwalder says.

At that moment the analyser announces that the blood composition and genetic material are both consistent with Denizen origin, to high statistical certainty. It's not enough to prove that Rifugio has one, but it's a large step in the right direction. Plenty of hoaxers have already fallen at this hurdle.

'Well, Mister Grafenwalder? Have you reached a decision yet?'

'I want to see the other samples.'

Rifugio fingers another vial from the case. 'Skin tissue.'

'I don't have the means to run a thorough analysis on skin – not here anyway. Give me what you have, and I'll take it back with me.'

Rifugio looks pained. 'I'd hoped that we might reach agreement here and now.'

'Then you hoped wrong. Unless you want to lower your price . . .'

'I'm afraid that part of the arrangement isn't negotiable.

However, I'm willing to let you take these samples away.' Rifugio snaps shut the lid. 'As a further token of my goodwill, I'll provide you with a moving image of the living Denizen. But I will expect a speedy decision in return.'

Grafenwalder's palanquin takes the sealed case and stores it inside its bombproof cargo hatch. 'You'll get it. Don't worry about that.'

'Take me at my word, Mister Grafenwalder. You're not the only collector with an eye for one of these monsters.'

Grafenwalder spends most of the return trip viewing the thirty-second movie clip, over and over again. It's not the first time he's seen moving imagery of something purporting to be a Denizen, but no other clip has withstood close scrutiny. This one is darker and grainier than some of the others, the swimming humanoid shifting in and out of focus, but there's something eerily natural-istic about it, something that convinces him that it could be real. The Denizen looks plausible: it's a monster, undoubtedly, but that monstrosity is the end result of logical design factors. It swims with effortless ease, propelling itself with the merest flick of the long fluked tail it wears in place of legs. It has arms, terminating in humanoid hands engineered for tool-use. Its head, when it swims towards the camera, merges seamlessly with its torso. It has eyes, very human eyes at that, but no nose, and its mouth is a smiling horizontal gash crammed with an unnerving excess of needle-sharp teeth. Looking at that movie, Grafenwalder feels more certain than ever that the creatures were real, and that at least one has survived. And as he studies the endlessly repeating thirty-second clip, he feels the closed book of his past creak open even wider. A question forms in his mind that he would rather not answer.

What *exactly* is it that he wants with the Denizen?

Things go tolerably well the next day, until the guests are almost ready to leave. They've seen the adult-phase hamadryad and registered due shock and awe. Grafenwalder is careful to remind them that, in addition to its size, this is also a living specimen, not some rotting corpse coaxed into a parodic imitation of life. Even Ursula Goodglass, who has to endure this, registers stoic approval. 'You were lucky,' she tells Grafenwalder through gritted teeth. 'You could just as easily have ended up with a dead one.'

'But then I wouldn't have tried to pretend it was alive,' he tells her.

It's Goodglass who has the last laugh today, however. She saves it until the guests are almost back aboard their shuttles.

'Friends,' she says, 'what I'm about to mention in no way compares with the spectacle of an adult-phase hamadryad, but I have recently come into possession of something that I think you might find suitably diverting.'

'Something we've already seen two days ago?' asks Lysander Carroway.

'No. I chose to keep it under wraps then, thinking my little hamadryad would be spectacle enough for one day. It's never been seen in public before, at least not in its present state.'

'Put us out of our misery,' says Alain Couperin.

'Drop by and see it for yourself,' Goodglass says, with a teasing twinkle in her eye. 'Any time you like. No need to make an appointment. But – please – employ maximum discretion. This is one exhibit that I really don't want the authorities to know about.'

For a moment Grafenwalder wonders whether she has the Denizen. But surely Rifugio can't have lost faith in the deal already, when they've barely opened negotiations.

But if not a Denizen – what?

He has to know, even if it means the indignity of another visit to her miserable little habitat.

When he arrives at the Goodglass residence, hers is the only shuttle docked at the polar nub. He's a little uncomfortable with being the only guest, but Goodglass did say to drop in whenever he liked, and he has given her fair warning of his approach. He's waited a week before taking the trip. Ten days would have been better, but after five he'd already started hearing that she has something special; something indisputably unique. In the meantime, he has run every conceivable test on the biological samples Rifugio gave him in Chasm City and received the same numbing result each time: Rifugio appears to be in possession of the genuine article. Yet Grafenwalder is still apprehensive about closing the deal.

Inside the habitat, he's met by Goodglass and Edric, her palanquin-bound husband. The couple waste no time in escorting him to the new exhibit. Despite the indignities they have brought upon each other, it's all smiles and strained politeness. No one so much as mentions hamadryads, dead or alive.

Grafenwalder isn't quite sure what to expect, but he's still surprised at the modest dimensions of the chamber Goodglass finally shows him. The walkway brings them level with the chamber's floor, but there's no armoured glass screen between them and the interior. Even with the lights dimmed, Grafenwalder can already make out an arrangement of tables, set in a U-formation like a series of laboratory benches. There are upright glassy things on the tables, but that's as much as he can tell.

'I was expecting something alive,' he says quietly.

'It is alive,' she hisses back. 'Or at least as alive as it ever was. Merely distributed. You'll see in a moment.'

'I thought you said it was dangerous.'

'Potentially it would be, if it was ever put back together.' She pauses and extends her hand across the gloomy threshold, as if beckoning to the nearest bench. Grafenwalder catches the bright red line on her hand where it has broken a previously invisible laser beam, sweeping up and down across the aperture. Quicker than an eyeblink, a heavy armoured shield slams down on the cell. 'But that's not to stop it getting out,' she says. 'It's to prevent anyone taking it and trying to put it back together. There are some who'd attempt it, just for the novelty.'

She pulls back her hand. After an interval, the shield whisks up into the ceiling.

'Whatever it is, you're serious about it,' Grafenwalder says, intrigued despite himself.

'I have to be. You don't take monsters lightly.'

She waves on the lights. The room brightens, but although he can now make out the benches and the equipment upon them, Grafenwalder is none the wiser.

'You'll have to help me here,' he says.

'It's all right. I wouldn't know what to make of it either if I didn't know what I was looking at.'

'My God,' he says wonderingly, as his eyes alight on one of the larger glass containers. 'Isn't that a brain?'

Goodglass nods. 'What was once a human brain, yes. Before he – before *it* – started doing things to itself, throwing pieces of its humanity away like a child flinging toys from a sandpit. But what's left of the brain is still alive, still conscious and still capable of sensory perception.' A mischievous smile appears on her face. 'It knows we're here, Carl. It's aware of us. It's listening to us, watching us, and wondering how it can escape and kill us.'

He allows himself to take in the grisly scene, now that its full implication is clearer. The brain is being kept alive in a liquid-filled vat, nourished by scarlet and green cables that ram into the grey-brown dough of the exposed cerebellum. A stump of spinal cord curls under the brain like an inverted question mark. It looks pickled and vinegary, cobwebbed with ancient growth and tiny filaments of spidery machinery. Next to the flask is a humming grey box whose multiple analog dials twitch with a suggestion of ongoing mental processes. But that's not all. There are dozens of glass cases, linked to other boxes, and the boxes to each other, and each case holds something unspeakable. In one, an eye hangs suspended in a kind of artificial socket, equipped with little steering motors. The eye is looking straight at Grafenwalder, as is its lidless twin on another bench. Their optic nerves are knotted ropes of fatty white nerve tissue. In another flask floats a pair of lungs, hanging like a puffed-up kite. They expand and contract with a slow, wheezing rhythm.

'Who . . . ? What . . . ?' he says, barely whispering.

'Haven't you guessed yet, Carl? Look over there. Look at the mask.'

He follows her direction. The mask sits at the end of the furthest table, on a black plinth. It's less a mask than an entire skull, moulded in sleek silver metal. The face is handsome, in a stream-lined, air-smoothed fashion, with an expression of calm amuse-ment sculpted into the immobile lips and the blank silver surfaces that pass for eyes. It has strong cheekbones and a strong cleft chin. Between the lips is only a dark, grilled slot. The mask has a representation of human ears, and its crown is moulded with longitudinal silver waves, evoking hair that has been combed back and stiffened in place with lacquer.

Grafenwalder knows who the skull belongs to. There isn't anyone alive around Yellowstone who wouldn't recognise Dr Trintignant. All that's missing is Trintignant's customary black Homburg.

But Trintignant shouldn't be here. Trintignant shouldn't be anywhere. He died years ago.

'This isn't right,' he says. 'You've been duped . . . sold a fake. This can't be him.'

'It is. I have watertight provenance.'

'But Trintignant hasn't been seen around Yellowstone for years . . . decades. He's supposed to have died when Richard Swift—'

'I know about Richard Swift,' Ursula Goodglass informs him. 'I met him once – or what was left of him after Trintignant had completed his business. I wanted Swift for an exhibit – I was prepared to pay him for his time – but he left the system again.

They say he went back to that place – the same world where Trintignant supposedly killed himself.'

Grafenwalder thinks back to what he remembers of the scandal. It had been all over Yellowstone for a few weeks. 'But Swift brought back Trintignant's remains. The doctor had dismantled himself, left a suicide note.'

'That was his plan,' Goodglass says witheringly. 'That was what he wanted us to think – that he'd ended his own life upon completing his finest work.'

'But he dismantled—'

'He took himself apart in a way that implied suicide. But it was a methodical dismantling. The parts were stored in a fashion that always allowed for their eventual reassembly. Trintignant was too vain not to want to stay alive and see what posterity made of his creations. But with the Yellowstone authorities closing in on him, staying in one piece wasn't an option.'

'How did he end up here? Wouldn't the authorities have been just as keen to get hold of his remains as his living self?'

'He always had allies. Sponsors, I suppose you might call them. People who'd covertly admired his work. There's always a market for freaks, Carl – and even more of a market for freak-makers. His friends whisked him away, out of the hands of what little authority was left here upon his return. Since then he's passed from collection to collection, like a bad penny. He seems to bring bad luck. Perhaps I'm tempting fate just by keeping him here; tempting it even more by bringing him to this state of partial reanimation.' She smiles tightly. 'We will see. If my fortunes take a dip, I shall pass Trintignant on to the next willing victim.'

'You're playing with fire.'

'Then you don't approve? I'd have expected you to applaud my audacity, Carl.'

Grafenwalder, despite himself, speaks something close to the truth. 'I'm impressed. More than you can imagine. But I'm also alarmed that he's being kept here.'

'Alarmed. Why, exactly?'

'You're a newcomer to this game, Ursula. I've seen a little of your habitat now, enough to know that your security arrangements aren't exactly top of the line.'

'He's in no danger of putting himself back together, Carl, unless you believe in telekinesis.'

'I'm worried about what would happen if his admirers learn of his whereabouts. Some of them won't be content just to know he's being kept alive in pieces. They'll want to take him, put him all the way back together.'

'I don't think anyone would be quite that foolish.'

'Then you don't know people. People like us, Ursula. How many collectors have you shown him to already?'

She tilts her head, looking at him along her up-curved nose. 'Less than a dozen, including yourself.'

'That's already too many. I wouldn't be surprised if word has already passed beyond the Circle. Don't tell me you've shown him to Rossiter?'

'Rossiter was the second.'

'Then it's probably already too late.' He sighs, as if taking a great burden upon himself. 'We don't have much time. We need to make immediate arrangements to transport his remains to my habitat. They'll be a lot safer there.'

'Why would your place be any safer than mine?'

'I design security systems. It's what I do for a living.'

She appears to consider it, for a moment at least. Then she shakes her head. 'No. It won't happen. He's staying here. I see where you're coming from now, Carl. You don't actually care about my security arrangements at all. It probably wouldn't even bother you if Doctor Trintignant did escape back into Stoner society. It's highly unlikely that you'd have ended up one of his victims, after all. You've got money and influence. It's those poor souls down in the Mulch who'd need to watch their backs. That's where he'd go hunting for raw material. What you can't stand is the thought that he might be mine, not yours. I've got something you haven't, something unique, something you can't ever have, and it's going to eat you from inside like acid.'

'Suit yourself.'

'I will. I always have. You made a dreadful mistake when you humiliated me, Carl, assuming you didn't have a hand in what had already happened to the hamadryad.'

'What are you saying? That I had something to do with the fact that Shallice stiffed you?'

He detects her hesitation. She comes perilously close to accusing him, but even here – even in this private cloister – there are limits that she knows better than to cross.

'But you were glad of it, weren't you?' she presses.

'I had the superior specimen. That's all that ever mattered to me.' With a renewed shudder of revulsion – and, he admits, something close to admiration – he turns again to survey the distributed remains of the notorious doctor. 'You say he can hear us?'

'Every word.'

'You should kill him now. Take a hammer to his brain. Make sure he can never live again.'

'Would you like that, Carl?'

'It's exactly what the authorities would do if they got hold of him.'

'They'd give him a trial first, one imagines.'

'He doesn't deserve a trial. None of his victims had the benefit of justice.'

'What history conveniently forgets,' Goodglass says, 'is that many of his so-called victims came to him willingly. He was not a monster to them, but the agent of the change they craved. He was the most brilliant transformative surgeon of our era. So what if society considered his creations obscene? So what if some of them regretted what they had freely asked him to do?'

'You're defending him now.'

'Not defending him – just pointing out that nothing is ever that black and white. For years Trintignant was given tacit permission to continue his work. The authorities didn't like him, but they accepted that he fulfilled a social need.'

Grafenwalder shakes his head – he's seen and heard enough. 'I thought you were exhibiting a monster, Ursula. Now it looks to me as if you're sheltering a fugitive.'

'I'm not, I assure you. Just because I have a balanced view of Trintignant doesn't mean I don't despise him. Here: let me offer you a demonstration.' And with that Goodglass taps a command sequence into the air, disarming the security system. She is able to pass her hand through the laser-mesh without bringing down the armoured screen. 'Walk over to the brain, Carl,' she commands. 'It isn't a trap.'

'I'd he happier if you walked with me.'

'If you like.'

He hesitates longer than he'd like, long enough for her to notice, then takes a step into the enclosure. Goodglass is only a pace behind him. The eyeballs swivel to track him, triangulating with the smoothness of motorised cameras. He moves next to the bubbling brain vat. Up close, the brain looks too small to have been the wellspring of so much evil.

'What am I supposed to look at?'

'Not look at – do. You can inflict pain on him, if you wish. There's a button next to the brain. It sends an electrical current straight into his anterior cingulate cortex.'

'Isn't he in pain already?'

'Not especially. He re-engineered himself to allow for this dismantling. There may be some existential trauma, but I don't believe he's in any great discomfort from one moment to the next.'

Grafenwalder's hand moves of its own volition, until it hovers above the electrical stimulator. He can feel its magnetic pull, almost willing his hand to lower. He wonders why he feels such a primal urge to bring pain to the doctor. Trintignant never hurt him; never hurt anyone he knew. All that he knows of Trintignant's crimes is second-hand, distorted and magnified by time and the human imagination. That the doctor was tolerated, even encouraged, cannot seriously be doubted. He filled the hole in Yellowstone society where a demon was meant to fit.

'What's wrong, Carl? Qualms?'

'How do I know this won't send a jolt directly to his pleasure centre?'

'Look at his spinal column. Watch it thrash.'

'Spines don't thrash.'

'His does. Those little mechanisms—'

It's all the encouragement he needs. He brings his hand down, holding the contact closed for a good five or six seconds. Under the brain, the stump of spinal matter twists and flexes like a rattlesnake's tail. He can hear it scraping glass.

He raises his hand, watches the motion subside.

'See,' Goodglass says, 'I knew you'd do it.'

Grafenwalder notices that there's some kind of heavy medical tool next to the brain tank, a thing with a grip and a clawed alloy head. With his other hand he picks it up, testing its weight. The glass container looks invitingly fragile; the brain even more so.

'Be careful,' Goodglass says.

'I could kill him now, couldn't I? Put an end to him, for ever.'

'Many would applaud you. But then you'd be providing him with a way out, an end to this existence. On the other hand, you could send another jolt of pain straight into his mind. What would you rather, Carl? Rid the world of Trintignant and spare him further pain, or let him suffer a little longer?'

He's close to doing it; close to smashing the tool into the glass. As close as she is, Goodglass couldn't stop him in time. And there would be something to be said for being the man who closed the book on Trintignant. But at the decisive instant something holds him back. Nothing that the doctor did has ever touched him personally, but he still feels a compulsion to join in his torment. And as the moment passes, he knows that he could never end the doctor's life so cleanly, so mercifully, when pain is always an alternative.

Instead, he presses the button again, and holds it down longer this time. The spine thrashes impressively. Behind him, Ursula Goodglass applauds.

'Good for you, Carl. I knew you'd do the right thing.'

The next two weeks are an endurance. Grafenwalder must sit tight-lipped as excited rumours circulate concerning Ursula Goodglass's new exhibit. No one mentions Trintignant by name – that would be the height of crass indiscretion – but even those who have not yet visited her habitat can begin to guess at the nature of her new prize. Even the most level-headed commentators are engaged in a feverish round of praise-giving, seeking to outdo each other in the showering of plaudits. Even though she has only been in the collecting business for a little while, she has pulled off an astonishing coup. Attention is so heated that, for a day or two, the Circle must fend off the unwanted interest of a pair of authority investigators, still on Trintignant's trail. The bribes alone would pay for a new habitat.

Grafenwalder's adult-phase hamadryad, meanwhile, brings no repeat visits. Now that it has lost its novelty value to the other collectors, Grafenwalder took his own interest in it waning. He thinks of it less and less, and has increasingly little concern for its welfare. When his keepers inform him that the animal is suffering from a dietary complaint, he doesn't even bother to visit it. Three days later, when they tell him that the hamadryad has died, all he can think about is the money he paid Captain Shallice. For an hour or so he toys with the idea of bringing the dead thing back to life with electrodes, the way Goodglass animated her specimen, but the idea that he might be seen to be playing second fiddle to her rises in him like yellow bile. He gives orders that the animal be ejected into space, and can't even bring himself to watch it happen.

Six hours later, he contacts Rifugio.

'I was beginning to think I wouldn't hear from you again, Mister Grafenwalder. If you'd left it much longer I wouldn't have anything to sell you.'

Grafenwalder can hardly keep the excitement from his voice. 'Then it's still available? The terms still apply?'

'I'm a man of my word,' Rifugio answers. 'The terms are the same. Does that mean we have a deal?'

'I'll want additional guarantees. If the specimen turns out to be something other than claimed—'

'I'm selling it to you in good faith. Take it or leave it.'

He takes it, of course, as he had known he would before he placed the call. He'd have taken it even if Rifugio had doubled his asking price. A living, captive Denizen is the only thing that will take the shine off the Circle's new fondness for Goodglass, and he must have it at all costs.

The arrangements for payment and handover are typically byzantine, as necessity demands. For all that he distrusts men like Rifugio, they must make a living as well, and protect themselves from the consequences of their activities. Grafenwalder, in turn, has his own stringent requirements. The shipping of the creature to Grafenwalder's habitat must happen surreptitiously, and the flow of credit from one account to another must be untraceable. It is complicated, but by the same token both men have participated in many such dealings in the past, and the arrangements follow a certain well-rehearsed protocol. When the automated transport finally arrives, bearing its precious aquatic cargo, Grafenwalder is certain that nothing has gone amiss.

He has to fight past his own keepers to view the specimen for the first time. At first, he feels a flicker of mild disappointment: it's a lot smaller than he was expecting, and it's not just a trick of the light due to the glass walls of the holding tank. The Denizen isn't much larger than a child.

But the disappointment doesn't last long. In the flesh, the Denizen appears even more obviously real than the swimming creature in the movie clip. It's sedated when it arrives, half its face and upper torso swallowed by a drug-administering breathing device. Rifugio's consignment comes with detailed notes concerning the safe waking of the creature. First, Grafenwalder has it moved into the main viewing tank, now topped up with cold water under one hundred atmospheres of pressure. The water chemistry is now tuned to approximate conditions near one of the Europan thermal vents. He brings the creature to consciousness in utter darkness, and monitors its progress as it begins first to breathe for itself, and then to tentatively explore its surroundings. It swims lethargically at first, Grafenwalder viewing its moving body via heat-sensitive assassin's goggles. By all accounts the Denizens have infrared sensitivity of their own, but the creature takes no heed of him, even when it passes very close to his vantage point.

After several minutes, the creature's swimming becomes stronger. It must be adapting to the water, learning to breathe again. Grafenwalder watches the flick of its tail in mesmerised fascination. By now it has mapped the confines of its new home, testing the armoured glass with delicate sweeps of its fingertips. It is intelligent enough to know that nothing will be gained by striking the glass.

Grafenwalder has the main lights brought up and shone into the tank. He slips the assassin's goggles up onto his brow. The creature attempts to swim away from the glare, but the glare follows it remorselessly. Its eyes are lidless, so it can do little except screen its face with one delicately webbed hand. The wide gash of its mouth opens in alarm or anger, or both, revealing rows of sharp little teeth.

Grafenwalder's voice booms into the water, relayed to the creature by floating microphones.

'I know you can hear me, and I know you can understand what I am saying to you. It is very important that you listen to what I am about to tell you.'

His voice appears to distress the creature as much as the bright light. With its other hand it tries to shield the whorl-like formation on the side of its head that is its ear. Grafenwalder doubts that it makes much difference. It must feel his voice in every cell of its body, ramming through it like a proclamation.

That was the effect he was going for.

'You are in no danger,' he says. 'Nothing is going to happen to you, and nobody is going to hurt you. The people who would rather you were dead are not going to find you. You are in my care now, and I am going to make sure that you come to no harm. My name is Carl Grafenwalder, and I have been waiting a long time to meet you.'

The Denizen floats motionless, as if stunned by the force of his words. Perhaps that is exactly what has happened.

'From now on, this is going to be your home,' Grafenwalder continues. 'I hope that you find the conditions satisfactory. I have done my best to simulate your place of birth, but I accept that there may be deficiencies. My experts will be striving to improve matters as best as they can, but for that they will need your assistance. We must all learn to communicate. I know you cannot speak, but I am sure we can make progress using sign language. Let us begin with something simple. I must know if you find your environment satisfactory in certain details: temperature, sulphur content, salinity, that kind of thing. You will need to answer my experts in the affirmative or negative. Nod your head if you understand me.'

Nothing happens. He judges that the Denizen is still conscious – he still catches the quick animation of its eyes behind the curtain of its hand – but it shows no indication of having understood him.

'I said nod your head. If that is too difficult for you, make some other visible movement.'

But still there's nothing. He has the lights dimmed again, and slips the assassin's goggles down over his eyes once more. After a few moments, the infrared smear of the Denizen lowers its arm and assumes an alert but restful posture. Now that it has reacted to the absence of light, he brings the glare back and observes the creature cower against the glare's return.

'You prefer the darkness, don't you? Well, I can make it dark again. All you have to do is show some sign that you understand me. Do that, and I'll bring the darkness back again.'

The Denizen just floats there, watching him through the spread webbing of its upraised hand. Perhaps it has learned to tolerate the light better than before, for its gaze strikes him now as steadier, somehow more reproachful. Even if it doesn't understand his words, it surely understands that it is his prisoner.

'I will lower the lights one more time.' He does so, then brings them back up, savagely, before the Denizen has had time to relish the darkness. This time he does get a reaction, but it's not quite the one he was anticipating. The Denizen shoots forward, bulleting through the water with dismaying speed. Just when he thinks the creature is going to use its skull as a battering ram, the Denizen brakes with a reverse flick of its tail and brings its head and upper body hard against the glass, arms spread-eagled, face only a few centimetres from Grafenwalder's own. Rationally, he knows that the glass is impervious – it's designed to hold back the pressure of the Europan ocean – but there's still a tiny part of his mind that can't accept that, and insists on jerking him back from that grinning mouth, those hateful human eyes. The Denizen sees it, too: it doesn't need language to know that it has scared him.

Grafenwalder regains his composure with an uneasy laugh, trying to sound as if it was all an act. The Denizen knows better, notching wide the dreadful smile of its mouth.

'Okay,' he says. 'You frightened me. That's good. That's exactly what you're meant to do. That's exactly why I brought you here.'

The microphones in the tank pick up the Denizen's derisive

snort, pealing it in harsh metallic waves around the metal walls of the bestiary. Grafenwalder's heart is still racing, but he's beginning to see the positive side of the arrangement. Maybe the fact that the creature can't talk is all for the best. There's something truly chilling about that snort; something that wouldn't come through at all if the specimen had language. There's a mind in there; one sharp enough to use complex tools in the unforgiving environment of a cold black alien ocean. But that mind only has one narrow outlet for its rage.

It's going to work, he thinks. If it has half the effect on the other collectors that it just had on him, Dr Trintignant will soon be relegated to a nine-day wonder. All he needs to do now is make sure the damned thing is as real as it looks. Not that he has any significant doubts now. Rifugio already had bona fide DNA and tissue samples. Where did that material come from, if it wasn't snipped from the last living Denizen?

He leaves the creature in darkness, letting it settle in. The next day, his keepers descend into the tank wearing armoured immersion suits. It takes two of them to immobilise the creature while the third takes a series of biopsy samples. With their powered suits, the men are in little danger from the Denizen. But they're still impressed by the strength and quickness of the specimen; its balletic ease within water. It moves with the sleek, elemental ease of something for which water is not a hindrance, but its natural medium.

Grafenwalder tunes in to Circle gossip again, unsurprised to find that Dr Trintignant is still wowing the other collectors. It still feels hurtful not to be the automatic centre of attention, but now at least he knows his rightful place will be restored. Ursula Goodglass got lucky with the dismantled doctor, but luck won't get her very far in the long game.

Later that day, his experts report back with the first findings from the biopsies. At first, Grafenwalder is so convinced of the

Denizen's authenticity that he doesn't hear what the experts, in their fumbling way, are trying to tell him.

The samples don't match. The Denizen's DNA isn't the same as the DNA that Rifugio gave him, or the DNA that Grafenwalder already possesses. It's the same story with the blood and tissue samples. The disagreement isn't huge, and less sophisticated tests probably wouldn't have detected any discrepancies. That's no solace to Grafenwalder, though. His tests are as good as they come, and they leave no room for doubt. The creature in his care is not what Rifugio let him think he was going to be buying.

He tries to call the broker, but the contact details no longer work. Rifugio doesn't get back to him.

So he's been conned. But if the Denizen is a con, it's an extraordinarily thorough one. He's had the chance to examine it closely now, and he's found no obvious signs of fakery. It's no mean feat to engineer a biological gill that can sustain an organism with the energy demands of a large mammal. The faked Denizens he's examined in the past began to die after only a few dozen hours of immersion. But this one shows every sign of thriving, of gaining strength and quickness.

Grafenwalder considers other possibilities. If the blood and tissue samples don't agree, then maybe it's because there's more than one kind of Denizen. The Europan scientists engineered distinct castes with differing linguistic abilities, so perhaps there were other variants, with different blood and tissue structures. They were all prototypes, after all, right up to the moment they turned against the Demarchy. This Denizen might simply be from a different production batch.

But that doesn't explain why Rifugio provided him with nonmatching samples. If Rifugio had the creature, why didn't he just take samples from it directly? Did Rifugio make a mistake, mixing samples from one specimen with another? If so, he must have had more than one Denizen in his care. In which case, the whole story about the Ultras keeping the Denizen as a pet was a lie . . . but a necessary one, if Rifugio wished Grafenwalder to think the creature was unique.

Grafenwalder mulls the possibilities. Rifugio's disappearance provides damning confirmation that some kind of deception has taken place. But if that deception merely extends to the fact that the Denizen isn't unique, Grafenwalder considers himself to have got off lightly. He still has a Denizen, and that's infinitely better than none at all. He'll find a way to trace and punish Rifugio in due course, but for now retribution isn't his highest priority.

Instead, what he desires most is communication.

By nightfall, when the keepers have finished their work, he descends to the tank and brings the lights back on. Not harshly now, but enough to alert the Denizen to his presence; to wake it from whatever shallow approximation of sleep it appears to enjoy when resting.

Then – satisfied that he is alone – he talks.

'You can understand me,' he says, for the umpteenth time. 'I know this because my keepers have identified a region in your brain that only lights up when you hear human speech. And it lights up most strongly when you hear Canasian, the language of the Demarchy.'

The creature watches him sullenly.

'It's the language you were educated to understand, two hundred years ago. I know things have changed a little since then, but I don't doubt that you can still make sense of these words.' And as he speaks Canasian, he feels – not for the first time – an odd, unexpected fluency. The words ought to feel awkward, but they flow off his tongue with mercurial ease, as if this is also the language he was born to speak.

Which is absurd.

'I want to know your story,' he says. 'How you got here, where you came from, how many of you there are. I know now that Rifugio lied to me. He'll pay for that eventually, but for now all that matters is what you can tell me. I need to know everything, right back to the moment you were born in Europa.'

But the Denizen, as ever, shows no external sign of having understood him.

Later, Grafenwalder has his keepers install a waterproofed symbol board in the tank. It's an array of touch-pads, each of which stands for a word in Canasian. As Grafenwalder speaks, the symbols light up in turn. The Denizen may reply by pressing the pads in sequence, which will be rendered back into speech on Grafenwalder's side of the glass. Grafenwalder's hoping that there's something amiss with the Denizen's language centre, some cognitive defect that can be short-circuited using the visual codes. If he can persuade the Denizen to press the 'yes' or 'no' pads in response to simple questions, he will consider that progress has been made.

Things don't move as quickly as he'd hoped. The Denizen seems willing to cooperate, but it still doesn't grasp the basics of language. Once it has understood that one of the pads symbolises food, it presses that one repeatedly, ignoring Grafenwalder's attempts to get it to answer abstract questions.

Maybe it's just stupid, he thinks. Maybe that's why this batch was discontinued. But he doesn't give up just yet. If the Denizen won't communicate willingly, perhaps it needs persuasion. He has his keepers tinker with the ambient conditions, varying the water temperature and chemistry to make things uncomfortable. He withholds food and instructs the keepers to take further biopsies. It's clear enough that the Denizen doesn't enjoy the process.

Still the creature won't talk, beyond issuing simple pleas for more food or warmer water. Grafenwalder feels his patience stretching. The keepers tell him that the Denizen is getting stronger, more difficult to subdue. Angrily, he accompanies them on their next trip into the tank. There are four men, all wearing power-assisted pressure armour, and now it takes three of them to pin the Denizen against one wall of the glass. When it breaks free momentarily, it gouges deep tooth marks in the flexible hide of Grafenwalder's glove. Back outside the tank, he inspects the damage and wonders what those teeth would have done to naked flesh.

It's fierce, he'll give it that. It may not be unique; it may not be particularly intelligent; but he still doesn't feel that all the money he gave Rifugio was wasted. Whatever the Denizen might be, it's worthy of a place in the bestiary. And it's *his*, not someone else's.

He puts out the word that there is something new in his collection. Following Ursula Goodglass's example, he tells the visitors to drop by whenever they like. There must be no suspicion that the Denizen is a stage-managed exhibit, something that can only perform to schedule.

It's three days before anyone takes him up on his offer. Lysander Carroway and her husband are the first to arrive. Even then, Grafenwalder has the sense that the visit is regarded as a tiresome social duty. All that changes when they see the Denizen. He's taken pains to stoke it up, denying it food and comfort for long hours. By the time he throws on the lights, the creature has become a focus of pure, mindless fury. It strives to kill the things on the other side of the glass, scratching claws and teeth against that impervious shield, to the point where it starts bleeding. His guests recoil, suitably impressed. After the study in motionless that was Dr Trintignant, they are woefully unprepared for the murderous speed of the Europan organism.

'Yes, it is a Denizen,' he tells them, while his keepers tend to the creature's injuries. 'The last of its kind, I have it on good authority.'

'Where did you find it?'

He parrots the lie Rifugio has already told him. 'You know what Ultras are like, with their pets. I don't think they realised quite what they'd been tormenting all those years.'

'Can it speak to us? I heard that they could talk.'

'Not this one. The idea that most of them could talk is a fallacy, I'm afraid: they simply weren't required to. As for the ones that did have language, they must have died over a hundred years ago.'

'Perhaps the ones that were clever enough to talk were also clever enough to stay away from Ultras,' muses Carroway. 'After all, if you can talk, you can negotiate, make bargains. Especially if you know things that can hurt people.'

'What would a Denizen know that could hurt anyone?' Grafenwalder asks scornfully.

'Who made it,' Carroway says. 'That would be worth something to someone, wouldn't it? In these times, more than ever.'

Grafenwalder shakes his head. 'I don't think so. Even the ones with language weren't that clever. They were built to take orders and use tools. They weren't capable of the kind of complex abstract thought necessary to plot and scheme.'

'How would you know?' Carroway asks. 'It's not as if you've ever met one.'

There's no malice in her question, but by the time the Carroways depart he's in a foul mood, barely masked by the niceties of Circle politesse. Why can't they just accept that the Denizen is enough of a prize in its own right, without dwelling on what it can't do? Isn't a ravenous man-fish chimera enough of a draw for them now?

But the Carroways must have been sufficiently impressed to speak of his new addition, because the girl is coming thick and fast over the next week. By then they've heard that he has a Denizen, but most of them don't quite believe it. Time and again he goes through the ritual of having them scared by the captive creature, only this time with a few additional flourishes. The glass is as secure as ever, but he's had the tank lined with a false interior that cracks more easily. He's also implanted a throat microphone under the skin of the Denizen, to better capture its blood-curdling vocalisations. Since the creature needed to be sedated for that, he also took the liberty of dropping an electrode into what his keepers think is the best guess for the creature's pain centre. It's a direct steal from what Goodglass did to Dr Trintignant, but no one has to know that, and with the electrode he can stir the Denizen up to its full killing fury even if it's just been fed.

It's still too soon to call, but his monitoring of Circle gossip begins to suggest that interest in Trintignant is declining. He's still jealous of Goodglass for that particular coup, but at last he feels that he has the upper hand again. The memory of Rifugio's lies has all but faded. The story Grafenwalder tells, about how the Denizen came to him via the Ultras, is repeated so often that he almost begins to believe it himself. The act of telling one lie over and over again, until it concretises into something barely distinguishable from the truth, feels peculiarly familiar to him. When his keepers come to him again and report that a more detailed analysis of the Denizen DNA has thrown up statistical matches with the genome of a typical hyperpig, he blanks the information.

What they're telling him is that the Denizen isn't real; that it's some form of genetic fake cooked up using a hyperpig in place of a human, with Denizen-like characteristics spliced in at the foetal stage. But he doesn't want to hear that; not now that he's back on top.

The last of the guests to visit are Ursula Goodglass and her husband. They've waited a lengthy, although not impolite, interval before favouring him with their presence. Once their shuttle has docked, Goodglass sweeps ahead of her husband's palanquin, trying to put a brave face on the proceedings.

'I hear you have a Denizen, Carl. If so, you have my heartfelt congratulations. Nothing like that has been seen for a very long time.' She looks at him coquettishly. 'It is a Denizen, isn't it? We didn't want to pay too much attention to the rumours, but when everyone started saying the same thing—'

'It is a Denizen,' he confirms gravely, as if the news is a terminal diagnosis. Which, in terms of Goodglass's current standing in the Circle, it might as well be. 'Would you like to see it?'

'Of course we'd like to see it!' her husband declares, his voice piping from the palanquin.

He takes them to the holding tank, darkened now, and issues assassin's goggles to Ursula, assuming that her husband's palanquin has its own infrared system. Allowing the guests to see the floating form, albeit indistinctly, is all part of the theatre.

'It looks smaller than I was expecting,' Ursula Goodglass observes.

'They were small,' Grafenwalder says. 'Designed to operate in cramped conditions. But don't let that deceive you. It's as strong as three men in amp-suits.'

'And you're absolutely sure of its authenticity? You've run a full battery of tests?'

'There's no doubt.' Rashly, he adds, 'You can see the results, if you like.'

'There's no need. I'm prepared to take your word for it. I know you wouldn't take anything for granted, given how long you've been after one of these.'

Grafenwalder allows himself a microscopic frown. 'I didn't know you were aware of my interest in acquiring a Denizen.'

'It would be difficult not to know, Carl. You've put out feelers in all directions imaginable. Of course, you've been discreet about it – or as discreet as circumstances allow.' She smiles unconvincingly. 'I'm glad for you, Carl. It must feel like the end of a great quest, to have this in your possession.'

'Yes,' he said. 'It does.'

The palanquin speaks. 'What exactly was it about the Denizen that you found so captivating, if you don't mind my asking?'

Grafenwalder shrugs, expecting the answer to roll glibly off his tongue. Instead, he has to force it out by an effort of will, as if there is a blockage in his thought processes. 'Its uniqueness, I suppose, Edric.'

'But there are many unique things,' the palanquin says, its piping tone conveying mild puzzlement. 'Why did you have to go to the extremes of locating a Denizen, a creature not even known ever to have existed? A creature whose authenticity cannot ever be confirmed with certainty?'

'Perhaps because it was so difficult. I like a challenge. Does it have to be any more complicated than that?'

'No, it doesn't,' the palanquin answers. 'I merely wondered if there might not have been a deeper motive, something less transparent.'

'I'm really not the man to ask. Why do any of us collect things?'

'Carl's right, dear,' Ursula says, smiling tightly at the palanquin's dark window. 'One mustn't enquire too deeply about these things. It isn't seemly.'

'I demur,' her husband says, and reverses slightly back from the heavy glass wall before them.

Grafenwalder judges that the moment is right to bring up the lights and enrage the Denizen. He squeezes the actuator tucked into his pocket, dripping current into the creature's brain. The lights pierce the tank, snaring the floating form. The Denizen snorts and powers itself towards the wall, its eyes wide with hatred despite the glare. It slams into the weakened inner layer and shatters the glass, making it seem as if the entire tank is about to lose integrity.

'We're quite safe,' he says, anticipating that Goodglass will have flinched from the impact. But she hasn't. She's standing her ground, her expression serenely unmoved by the entire spectacle.

'You're right,' she comments. 'It's quite a catch. But I wonder if it's really as vicious as it appears.'

'Take my word. It's much, much worse. It nearly bit through my glove when I was inside that tank, wearing full armour.'

'Perhaps it doesn't like being kept here. It didn't seem very happy when you turned the lights on.'

'It's an exhibit, Ursula. It doesn't have to like being here. It should be grateful just to be alive.'

She looks at him with sudden interest, as if he has said something profound. 'Do you really think so, Carl?'

'Yes,' he says. 'Absolutely.'

She returns her attention to the tank wall. The Denizen is still hovering there, anchored in place by the tips of its fingers and the fluke of its tail. The cracks in the shattered glass radiate away in all directions, making the Denizen look as if it is caught in a frozen star, or pinned to a snowflake.

Goodglass removes her glove and touches a hand to the smooth and unbroken glass on the outer surface of the tank, exactly where the Denizen has its own webbed hand. That's when Grafenwalder notices the pale webs of skin between Ursula Goodglass's fingers, visible now that she has taken off the glove. Their milky translucence is exactly the same as the webs between the Denizen's. She presses her hand harder, squeezing until her palm is flat against the glass, and the Denizen echoes the movement.

The air feels as if it has frozen. The moment of contact seems to last minutes, hours, eternities. Grafenwalder stares in numb incomprehension, unable to process what he is seeing. When she moves her hand, skating it across the glass, the Denizen follows her like an expert mime.

She takes another step closer, bringing her face against the glass, laying her cheek flat against the cold surface. The Denizen presses itself against the shattered inner layer and mirrors her posture, bringing its own head against hers. The flesh of their faces appears to merge.

Goodglass pulls her face back from the glass, then smiles at the Denizen. It tries to emulate her expression, forcing its mouth wide. It's not much of a smile – it's more horrific than reassuring – but the deliberateness of the gesture is beyond doubt.

Finally Grafenwalder manages to say something. His own voice sounds wrong, as if it's coming from another room.

'What are you doing?'

'I'm greeting it,' Ursula Goodglass says, snapping her attention away from the tank. 'What on Earth did you think I was doing?'

'It's a Denizen. It doesn't know you. You can't know it.'

'Oh, Carl,' she says, pityingly now. 'Haven't you got it yet? Really, I thought you'd have figured things out by now. Look at my hand again.'

'I don't need to. I saw it.'

She pulls back her hand until she's only touching the glass with a fingertip. 'Then tell me what it reminds you of – or can't you bring yourself to say it?'

'I've had enough,' he says. 'I don't know what kind of game you're playing, but it isn't true to the spirit of the Circle. I insist that you leave immediately.'

'But we're not done yet,' Goodglass says.

'Fine. If you won't go easily, I'll have you escorted to your shuttle.'

'I'm afraid not, Carl. We've still business to attend to. You didn't think it was going to be quite that easy, did you?'

'Leave now.'

'Or what? You'll turn your household systems on us?' She looks apologetic. 'They won't work, I'm afraid. They've been disabled. From the moment our shuttle docked, it's been working to introduce security countermeasures into your habitat.' Before he can get a word in, she says, 'It was a mistake to invite us to view the adult-phase hamadryad. It gave us the perfect opportunity to snoop your arrangements, design a package of neutralising agents. Don't go calling for your keepers, either. They're all unconscious. The last time we visited, the palanquin deployed microscopic stun-capsules into every room it passed through. Upon our return, they were programmed to activate, releasing a fast-acting nerve toxin. Your keepers will be fine once they wake up, but that isn't going to happen for a few hours yet.'

'I don't believe you.'

'You don't have to,' Goodglass says. 'Call for help, see how far it gets you.'

He lifts the cuff of his sleeve and talks into his bracelet. 'This is Grafenwalder. Get down to the bestiary now – the Denizen tank.'

But no one answers.

'I'm sorry, but no one's coming. You're on your own now, Carl. It's just you, the Denizen and the two of us.'

After a minute goes by, he knows she isn't bluffing. Goodglass has taken his habitat.

'What do you want from me?'

'It's not so much a question of what I want from you, Carl, as what you want from me.'

'You're not making much sense.'

'Ask yourself this: why did you want the Denizen so much? Was it because you just had to add another unique specimen to your collection? Or did the drive go deeper than that? Is it just possible that you created this entire bestiary as a decoy, to divert everyone – including yourself – from the true focus of your obsession?'

'You tell me, Ursula. You seem to know a lot about the collecting game.'

'I'm no collector,' she says curtly. 'I detest you and your kind. That was just a cover, to get me close to you. I went to a lot of trouble, of course: the hamadryad, Trintignant . . . I know you had Shallice kill the hamadryad, by the way. That was what I expected you to do. Why else do you think I had Shallice mention my existence, if not to goad you? I needed you to take an interest in me, Carl. It worked spectacularly well.'

'You never interested me, Ursula. You irritated me, like a tick.'

'It had the same effect. It brought us together. It brought me here.'

'And the Denizen?' he asks, half-fearing her answer.

'The Denizen is a fake. I'm sure you've figured that out for yourself by now. A pretty good fake, I'll admit – but it isn't two hundred years old, and it's never been anywhere near Europa.'

'What about the samples Rifugio gave me? Where did they come from?'

'From me,' Goodglass says.

'You're insane.'

'No, Carl. Not insane. Just a Denizen.' And she shows him her webbed hand once more, extending it out towards him as if inviting him to kiss it. 'I'm what you've been searching for all these years, the end of your quest. But this isn't quite the way you imagined things playing out, is it? That you'd have had me under your nose all this time, and not known how close you were?'

'You can't be a Denizen.'

'There is such a thing as surgery,' she says witheringly. 'I had to wait until after the plague before having myself changed, which meant subjecting myself to cruder procedures than I might have wished. Fortunately, I had the services of a very good surgeon. He rewired my cardiovascular system for air-breathing. He gave me legs and a human face, and a voice box that works out of water.'

'And the hands?'

'I kept the hands. You've got to hold on to part of the past, no matter how much you might wish to bury it. I needed to remember where I'd come from, what I still had to do.'

'Which is?'

'To find you, and then punish you. You were there, Carl, back when we were made in Europa. A high-influence Demarchist in the Special Projects section of Cadmus-Asterius, the hanging city where we were spliced together and given life.'

'Nonsense. I've never been near Europa.'

'You were born there,' she assures him, 'not long after Sandra Voi founded the place. You've scrubbed those memories, though. They're too dangerous now. The Demarchists don't want anyone finding out about their history of past mistakes, not when they're trying to show how fine and upstanding they are compared to the beastly Conjoiners. Almost everyone connected with those dark days in Europa has been hunted down and silenced by now. Not you, though. You were ahead of the curve, already running by the time the cities fell. You hopped a ramliner to Yellowstone and started reinventing your past. Eidetic overlays to give you a false history, one so convincing that you believed it yourself. Except at night, in your loneliest hours. Then part of you knew that they were still out there, still looking for you.'

'They?'

'Not just the Demarchist silencers: they were the least of your worries. Money and power could keep them at bay. What really worried you was *us*, the Denizens.'

'If I made you, why would I fear you?'

'You didn't make us, Carl. I said you were part of the project, but you weren't working to bring us to life. You were working to suppress us; to make us fail. Petty internal rivalry: you couldn't allow another colleague's work to succeed. So you did everything you could to hurt us, to make us imperfect. You brought suffering into our world. You brought pain and infirmity and death, and then left us alone in that ocean.'

'Ridiculous.'

'Really, Carl? I've seen how easily you turn to spite. Just ask that dead hamadryad.'

'I had nothing to do with the Denizens.' But even as he says it, he can feel layers of false memory begin to peel back. What's exposed has the raw candour of true experience. He remembers more of Europa than he has any right to: the bright plazas, the smells, the noises of Cadmus-Asterius. He remembers the reefer-sleep casket on the outbound ramliner, the casket that he thought was taking him to the safety of another system, another time. No wonder he's slept easier since the Melding Plague. He must have imagined that the plague had severed the last of his ties with the past, making it impossible for anyone to catch up with him now.

He'd been wrong about that.

'You had to find a Denizen,' Goodglass says, 'because then you'd know if any of them were still alive. Well, now you have your answer. How does it feel?'

He always knew that the marks on her skull were evidence of surgery. But that surgery had nothing to do with the removal of implants, and everything to do with her transformation from a Denizen. It would have cost her nothing to hide those marks, and yet she made no secret of them. It was, he sees now, part of a game he hadn't even realised he was playing.

'Not the way I thought it would feel,' he says.

Goodglass nods understandingly. 'I'm going to punish you now, Carl. But I'm not going to kill you.'

She's playing with him, allowing him a glimmer of hope before crushing it for all eternity.

'Why not?' he asks.

'Because if you were dead, you wouldn't make much of an exhibit. When we're done here, I'm going to donate you to a suitable recipient.' Then she turns to the palanquin. 'There's something I should have told you. I lied about my husband. Edric was a good man: he cared for me, loved me, when he could have made his fortune from what I was. Unfortunately, he never got to see me like this. Edric died during the early months of the plague.'

Grafenwalder says nothing. He's out of words, out of questions.

'You're probably wondering who's in the palanquin,' Goodglass says. 'He's going to come out now, for a little while. Not too long, because he can't risk coming into contact with plague spores, not when so much of him is mechanical. But that won't stop him doing his job. He's always been a quick worker.'

With a hiss of escaping pressure, the entire front of the palanquin lifts up on shining pistons. The first thing Grafenwalder sees, the last thing before he starts screaming, is a silver hand clutching a black Homburg hat.

Then he sees the face.

I checked the address Tomas Martinez had given me, shielding the paper against the rain while I squinted at my scrawl. The number I'd written down didn't correspond with any of the high-and-dry offices, but it was a dead ringer for one of the low-rent premises at street level. Here the walls of Threadfall Canyon had been cut and buttressed to the height of six or seven storeys, widening the available space at the bottom of the trench. Buildings covered most of the walls, piled on top of each other, supported by a haphazard arrangement of stilts and rickety, semipermanent bamboo scaffolding. Aerial walkways had been strung from one side of the street to the other, with stairs and ladders snaking their way through the dark fissures between the buildings. Now and then a wheeler sped through the water, sending a filthy brown wave in its wake. Very rarely, a sleek, claw-like volantor slid overhead. But volantors were off-world tech and not many people on Sky's Edge could afford that kind of thing any more.

It didn't look right to me, but all the evidence said that this had to be the place.

I stepped out of the water onto the wooden platform in front of the office and knocked on the glass-fronted door while rain curtained down through holes in the striped awning above me. I was pushing soaked hair out of my eyes when the door opened.

I'd seen enough photographs of Martinez to know this wasn't him. This was a big bull of a man, nearly as wide as the door. He stood there with his arms crossed in front of his chest, over which he wore only a sleeveless black vest that was zipped down to his midriff. His muscles were so tight it looked as if he was wearing some kind of body-hugging amplification suit. His head was very large and very bald, rooted to his body by a neck like a small mountain range. The skin around his right eye was paler than the rest of his face, in a neatly circular patch.

He looked down at me as if I was something unpleasant the rain had washed in.

'What?' he said, his voice like the distant rumble of artillery.

'I'm here to see Martinez.'

'Mister Martinez to you,' he said.

'Whatever. But I'm still here to see him, and he should be expecting me. I'm—'

'Dexia Scarrow,' called another voice – fractionally more welcoming, this one – and a smaller, older man bustled into view from behind the pillar of muscle blocking the door, snatching delicate pince-nez glasses from his nose. 'Let her in, Norbert. She's expected. Just a little *late*.'

'I got held up around Armesto – my hired wheeler hit a pothole and tipped over. Couldn't get the thing started again, so had to—'

The smaller man waved aside my excuse. 'You're here now, which is all that matters. I'll have Norbert dry your clothes, if you wish.'

I peeled off my coat. 'Maybe this.'

'Norbert will attend to your galoshes as well. Would you care for something to drink? I have tea already prepared, but if you would rather something else . . .'

'Tea will be fine, Mister Martinez,' I said.

'Please, call me Tomas. It's my sincere wish that we will work together as friends.'

I stepped out of my galoshes and handed my dripping-wet coat to the big man. Martinez nodded once, the gesture precise and birdlike, and then beckoned me to follow him further into his rooms. He was slighter and older than I'd been expecting, although still recognisable as the man in the photographs. His hair was grey turning to white, thinning on his crown and shaved close to his scalp elsewhere on his head. He wore a grey waistcoat over a grey shirt, the ensemble lending him a drab, clerkish air.

We navigated a twisting labyrinth formed by four layers of brown boxes, piled to head height. 'Excuse the mess,' Martinez said, looking back at me over his shoulder. 'I really should find a better solution to my filing problems, but there's always something more pressing that needs doing instead.'

'I'm surprised you have time to eat, let alone worry about filing problems.'

'Well, things haven't been quite as hectic lately, I must confess. If you've been following the news you'll know that I've already caught most of my big fish. There's some mopping up to do, but I've been nowhere near as busy as in . . .' Martinez stopped suddenly next to one of the piles of boxes, placed his glasses back on the bridge of his nose and scuffed dust from the paper label on the side of the box nearest his face. 'No,' he said, shaking his head. 'Wrong place. Wrong damned place! Norbert!'

Norbert trudged along behind us, my sodden coat still draped over one of his enormous, trunk-like arms. 'Mister Martinez?'

'This one is in the wrong place.' The smaller man turned around and indicated a spot between two other boxes, on the opposite side of the corridor. It goes *here*. It needs to be properly filed. Kessler's case is moving into court next month, and we don't want any trouble with missing documentation.'

'Attend to it,' Norbert said, which sounded like an order but which I assumed was his way of saying he'd remember to move the box when he was done with my laundry.

'Kessler?' I asked, when Norbert had left. 'As in Tillman Kessler, the NC interrogator?'

'One and the same, yes. Did you have experience with him?'

'I wouldn't be standing here if I did.'

'True enough. But a small number of people were fortunate enough to survive their encounters with Kessler. Their testimonies will help bring him to justice.'

'By which you mean crucifixion.'

'I detect faint disapproval, Dexia,' Martinez said.

'You're right. It's barbaric.'

'It's how we've always done things. The Haussmann way, if you like.'

Sky Haussmann: the man who gave this world its name, and who sparked off the two-hundred-and-fifty-year war we've only just learned to stop fighting. When they crucified Sky they thought they were putting an early end to the violence. They couldn't have been more wrong. Ever since, crucifixion has been the preferred method of execution.

'Is Kessler the reason you asked me here, sir? Were you expecting me to add to the case file against him?'

Martinez paused at a heavy wooden door. 'Not Kessler, no. I've every expectation of seeing him nailed to Bridgetop by the end of the year. But it does concern the man for whom Kessler was an instrument.'

I thought about that for a moment. 'Kessler worked for Colonel Jax, didn't he?'

Martinez opened the door and ushered me through, into the windowless room beyond. By now we must have been back into the canyon wall. The air had the inert stillness of a crypt. 'Yes, Kessler was Jax's man,' Martinez said. 'I'm glad you made the connection: it saves me explaining why Jax ought to be brought to justice.'

'I agree completely. Half the population would agree with you. But I'm afraid you're a bit late: Jax died years ago.'

Two other people were already waiting in the room, sitting on settees either side of a low black table set with tea, coffee and pisco sours.

'Jax didn't die,' Martinez said. 'He just disappeared, and now I know where he is. Have a seat, please.'

He knew I was interested; knew I wouldn't be able to walk out of that room until I'd heard the rest of the story about Colonel Brandon Jax. But there was more to it than that: there was something effortlessly commanding about his voice that made it very difficult not to obey him. During my time in the Southland Militia I'd learned that some people have that authority and some people don't. It can't be taught; can't be learned; can't be faked. You're either born with it or you're not.

'Dexia Scarrow, allow me to introduce you to my other two guests,' Martinez said, when I'd taken my place at the table. 'The gentleman opposite you is Salvatore Nicolosi, a veteran of one of the Northern Coalition's freeze/thaw units. The woman on your right is Ingrid Sollis, a personal-security expert with a particular interest in counter-intrusion systems. Ingrid saw early combat experience with the Southland, but she soon left the military to pursue private interests.'

I bit my tongue, then turned my attention away from the woman before I said something I might regret. The man – Nicolosi – looked more like an actor than a soldier. He didn't have a scar on him. His beard was so neatly groomed, so sharp-edged, that it looked sprayed on through a stencil. Freeze/thaw operatives rubbed me up the wrong way, no matter which side they'd been on. They'd always seen themselves as superior to the common soldier, which is why they didn't feel the need for the kind of excessive musculature Norbert carried around.

'Allow me to introduce Dexia Scarrow,' Martinez continued, nodding at me. 'Dexia was a distinguished soldier in the Southland Militia for fifteen years, until the armistice. Her service record is excellent. I believe she will be a valuable addition to the team.'

'Maybe we should back up a step,' I said. 'I haven't agreed to be part of anyone's team.'

'We're going after Jax,' Nicolosi said placidly. 'Doesn't that excite you?'

'He was on your side,' I said. 'What makes you so keen to see him crucified?'

Nicolosi looked momentarily pained. 'He was a war criminal, Dexia. I'm as anxious to see monsters like Jax brought to justice as I am to see the same fate visited on their scum-ridden Southland counterparts.'

'Nicolosi's right,' said Ingrid Sollis. 'If we're going to learn to live together on this planet, we have to put the law above all else, regardless of former allegiances.'

'Easy coming from a deserter,' I said. 'Allegiance clearly didn't mean very much to you back then, so I'm not surprised it doesn't mean much to you now.'

Martinez, still standing at the head of the table, smiled tolerantly, as if he'd expected nothing less.

'That's an understandable misapprehension, Dexia, but Ingrid was no deserter. She was wounded in the line of duty: severely, I might add. After her recuperation, she was commended for bravery under fire and given the choice of an honourable discharge or a return to the front line. You cannot blame her for choosing the former, especially given all she had been through.'

'Okay, my mistake,' I said. 'It's just that I never heard of many people making it out alive, before the war was over.'

Sollis looked at me icily. 'Some of us did.'

'No one here has anything but an impeccable service record,' Martinez said. 'I should know: I've been through your individual biographies with a fine-tooth comb. You're just the people for the job.'

'I don't think so,' I said, moving to stand up. 'I'm just a retired soldier with a grudge against deserters. I wasn't in some shit-hot freeze/thaw unit, and I didn't do anything that resulted in any commendations for bravery. Sorry, folks, but I think—'

'Remain seated.'

I did what the man said.

Martinez continued speaking, his voice as measured and patient as ever. 'You participated in at least three high-risk extraction operations, Dexia: three dangerous forays behind enemy lines, to retrieve two deep-penetration Southland spies and one trump-card NC defector. Or do you deny this?'

I shook my head, the reality of what he was proposing still not sinking in. 'I can't help you. I don't know anything about Jax—'

'You don't need to. That's my problem.'

'How are you so sure he's still alive, anyway?'

'I'd like to know that, too,' Nicolosi said, stroking an elegant finger along the border of his beard.

Martinez sat down on his own stool at the head of the table, so that he was higher than the three of us. He removed his glasses and fiddled with them in his lap. 'It is necessary that you take a certain amount of what I am about to tell you on faith. I've been gathering intelligence on men like Jax for years, and in doing so I've come to rely on a web of contacts, many of whom have conveyed information to me at great personal risk. If I were to tell you the whole story, and if some of that story were to leak beyond this office, lives might well be endangered. And that is to say nothing of how my chances of bringing other fugitives to justice might be undermined.'

'We understand,' Sollis said.

I bridled at the way she presumed to speak for all of us. Perhaps she felt she owed Martinez for the way he'd just stood up for her.

Again I bit my lip and said nothing.

'For a long time, I've received titbits of intelligence concerning Colonel Jax: rumours that he did not, in fact, die at all, but is still at large.'

'Where?' Sollis asked. 'On Sky's Edge?'

'It would seem not. There were, of course, many rumours and false trails that suggested Jax had gone to ground somewhere on this planet. But one by one I discounted them all. Slowly the truth became apparent: Jax is still alive; still within this system.'

I felt it was about time I made a positive contribution. 'Wouldn't a piece of dirt like Jax try to get out of the system at the first opportunity?'

Martinez favoured my observation by pointing his glasses at me. 'I had my fears that he might have, but as the evidence came in, a different truth presented itself.'

He set about pouring himself some tea. The pisco sours were going unwanted. I doubted that any of us had the stomach for drink at that time of the day.

'Where is he, then?' asked Nicolosi. 'Plenty of criminal elements might have the means to shelter a man like Jax, but given the price on his head, the temptation to turn him in—'

'He is not being sheltered,' Martinez said, sipping delicately at his tea before continuing, 'He is alone, aboard a ship. The ship was believed lost, destroyed in the final stages of the war, when things escalated into space. But I have evidence that the ship is still essentially intact, with a functioning life-support system. There is every reason to believe that Jax is still being kept alive, aboard this vehicle, in this system.'

'What's he waiting for?' I asked.

'For memories to grow dim,' Martinez answered. 'Like many powerful men, Jax may have obtained longevity drugs – or at least undergone longevity treatment – during the latter stages of the war. Time is not a concern for him.'

I leaned forward. 'This ship – you think it'll just be a matter of boarding it and taking him alive?'

Martinez looked surprised at the directness of my question. He blinked once before answering.

'In essence, yes.'

'Won't he put up a fight?'

'I don't think so. The Ultras that located the vessel for me reported that it appeared dormant, in power-conservation mode.

Jax himself may be frozen, in reefersleep. The ship did not respond to the Ultras' sensor sweeps, so there's no reason to assume it will respond to our approach and docking.'

'How close did the Ultras get?' Sollis asked.

'Within three or four light-minutes. But there's no reason to assume we can't get closer without alerting the ship.'

'How do you know Jax is aboard this ship?' Nicolosi asked. 'It could just be a drifter, nothing to do with him.'

'The intelligence I'd already gleaned pointed towards his presence aboard a vehicle of a certain age, size and design – everything matches.'

'So let's cut to the chase,' Sollis said, again presuming to speak for the rest of us. 'You've brought us here because you think we're the team to snatch the colonel. I'm the intrusion specialist, so you'll be relying on me to get us inside that ship. Nicolosi's a freeze/thaw veteran, so – apart from the fact that he's probably pretty handy with a weapon or two – he'll know how to spring Jax from reefersleep, if the colonel turns out to be frozen. And she – what was your name again?'

'Dexia,' I said, like it was a threat.

'She's done some extractions. I guess she must be okay at her job or she wouldn't be here.'

Martinez waited a moment, then nodded. 'You're quite right, Ingrid: all credit to you for that. I apologise if my machinations are so nakedly transparent. But the simple fact of the matter is that you are the ideal team for the operation in question. I have no doubt that, with your combined talents, you will succeed in returning Colonel Jax to Sky's Edge, and hence to trial. Now admit it: that *would* be something, wouldn't it? To fell the last dragon?'

Nicolosi indicated his approval with a long nasal sigh. 'Men like Kessler are just a distraction. When you crucify a monster like Kessler, you're punishing the knife, not the man who wielded it. If you wish true justice, you must find the knifeman, the master.'

'What will we get paid?' Sollis asked.

Martinez smiled briefly. 'Fifty thousand Australs for each of you, upon the safe return of Colonel Jax.'

'What if we find him dead?' I asked. 'By then we'll already have risked an approach and docking with his ship.'

'If Jax is already dead, then you will be paid twenty-five thousand Australs.'

We all looked at each other. I knew what the others were thinking. Fifty thousand Australs was life-changing money, but half of that wasn't bad either. Killing Jax would be much easier and safer than extracting him alive . . .

'I'll be with you, of course,' Martinez said, 'so there'll be no need to worry about proving Jax was already dead when you arrived, should that situation arise.'

'If you're coming along,' I asked, 'who else do we need to know about?'

'Only Norbert. And you need have no fears concerning his competency.'

'Just the five of us, then,' I said.

'Five is a good number, don't you think? And there is a practical limit to the size of the extraction team. I have obtained the use of a small but capable ship, perfectly adequate for our purposes. It will carry five, with enough capacity to bring back the colonel. I'll provide weapons, equipment and armour, but you may all bring whatever you think may prove useful.'

I looked around the cloister-like confines of the room, and remembered the dismal exterior of the offices, situated at the bottom of Threadfall Canyon. 'Three times fifty thousand Australs,' I mused, 'plus whatever it cost you to hire and equip a ship. If you don't mind me asking – where exactly are the funds coming from?'

'The funds are mine,' Martinez said sternly. 'Capturing Jax has been a long-term goal, not some whimsical course upon which I have only recently set myself. Dying a pauper would be a satisfactory end to my affairs, were I to do so knowing that Jax was hanging from the highest mast at Bridgetop.'

For a moment none of us said anything. Martinez had spoken so softly, so demurely, that the meaning of his words seemed to lag slightly behind the statement itself. When it arrived, I think we all saw a flash of that corpse, executed in the traditional way, the Haussmann way.

'Good weapons?' I asked. 'Not some reconditioned black-market shit?'

'Only the best.'

'Technical specs for the ship?' Sollis asked.

'You'll have plenty of time to review the data on the way to the rendezvous point. I don't doubt that a woman of your abilities will be able to select the optimum entry point.'

Sollis looked flattered. 'Then I guess I'm in. What about you, Salvatore?'

'Men like Colonel Jax stained the honour of the Northern Coalition. We were not all monsters. If I could do something to make people see that . . .' Nicolosi trailed off, then shrugged. 'Yes, I am in. It would be an honour, Mister Martinez.'

'That leaves you, Dexia,' Sollis said. 'Fifty thousand Australs sounds pretty sweet to me. I'm guessing it sounds pretty sweet to you as well.'

'That's my call, not yours.'

'Just saying . . . you look like you could use that money as much as any of us.'

I think I came close to saying no, to walking out of that room, back into the incessant muddy rain of Threadfall Canyon. Perhaps if I'd tried, Norbert would have been forced to detain me, so that I didn't go blabbing about how a team was being put together to bring Colonel Jax back into custody. But I never got the chance to find out what Martinez had in mind for me if I chose not to go along with him.

I only had to think about the way I looked in the mirror, and what those fifty thousand Australs could do for me.

So I said yes.

Martinez gestured towards one of the blank pewter-grey walls in the shuttle's compartment, causing it to glow and fill with neon-bright lines. The lines meshed and intersected, forming a schematic diagram of a ship with an accompanying scale.

'Intelligence on Jax's ship is fragmentary. Strip out all the contradictory reports, discard unreliable data, and we're left with this.'

'That's it?' Sollis asked.

'When we get within visual range we'll be able to improve matters. I shall re-examine all of the reports, including those that were discarded. Some of them – when we have the real ship to compare them against – may turn out to have merit after all. They may in turn shed useful light on the interior layout, and the likely location of Jax. By then, of course, we'll also have infrared and deep-penetration radar data from our own sensors.'

'It looks like a pretty big ship,' I said as I studied the schematic, scratching at my scalp. We were a day out from Armesto Field, with the little shuttle tucked into the belly hold of an outbound lighthugger named *Death of Sophonisba*.

'Big but not the right shape for a lighthugger,' Sollis said. 'So what are we dealing with here?'

'Good question,' I said. Martinez was showing us a rectangular hull about one kilometre from end to end; maybe a hundred metres deep and a hundred metres wide, with some kind of spherical bulge about halfway along. There was a suggestion of engines at one end, and of a gauntlet-like docking complex at the other. The ship was too blunt for interstellar travel, and it lacked the outrigger-mounted engines characteristic of Conjoiner drive mechanisms. 'Does look kind of familiar, though,' I added. 'Anyone else getting that déjà vu feeling, or is it just me?'

'I don't know,' Nicolosi said. 'When I first saw it, I thought . . .' He shook his head. 'It can't be. It must be a standard hull design.'

'You've seen it before, too,' I said.

'Does that ship have a name?' Nicolosi asked Martinez.

'I have no idea what Jax calls his ship.'

'That's not what the man asked,' Sollis said. 'He asked if—'

'I know the name of the ship,' I said quietly. 'I saw a ship like that once, when I was being taken aboard it. I'd been injured in a firefight, one of the last big surface battles. They took me into space – this was after the elevator came down, so it had to be by shuttle – and brought me aboard that ship. It was a hospital ship, orbiting the planet.'

'What was the name of the ship?' Nicolosi asked urgently.

'*Nightingale*,' I said.

'Oh, no.'

'You're surprised.'

'Damn right I'm surprised. I was aboard *Nightingale*, too.'

'So was I,' Sollis said, her voice barely a whisper. 'I didn't recognise it, though. I was too fucked up to pay much attention until they put me back together aboard it. By then, I guess . . .'

'Same with me,' Nicolosi said. 'Stitched back together aboard *Nightingale*, then repatriated.'

Slowly, we all turned and looked at Martinez. Even Norbert, who had contributed nothing until that point, turned to regard his master. Martinez blinked, but otherwise his composure was impeccable.

'The ship is indeed *Nightingale*. It was too risky to tell you when we were still on the planet. Had any of Jax's allies learned of the identity—'

Sollis cut him off. 'Is that why you didn't tell us? Or is it because you knew we'd all been aboard that thing once already?'

'The fact that you have all been aboard *Nightingale* was a factor in your selection, nothing more. It was your skills that marked you out for this mission, not your medical history.'

'So why didn't you tell us?' she persisted.

'Again, had I told you more than was wise—'

'You lied to us.'

'I did no such thing.'

'Wait,' Nicolosi said, his voice calmer than I was expecting. 'Let's just . . . deal with this, shall we? We're getting hung up on the fact that we were all healed aboard *Nightingale*, when the real question we should be asking is this: what the hell is Jax doing aboard a ship that doesn't exist any more?'

'What's the problem with the ship?' I asked.

'The problem,' Nicolosi said, speaking directly to me, 'is that *Nightingale* was reported destroyed near the end of the war. Or were you not keeping up with the news?'

I shrugged. 'Guess I wasn't.'

'And yet you knew enough about the ship to recognise it.'

'Like I said, I remember the view from the medical shuttle. I was drugged-up, unsure whether I was going to live or die . . . everything was heightened, intense, like in a bad dream. But after they healed me and sent me back down surfaceside? I don't think I ever thought about *Nightingale* again.'

'Not even when you look in the mirror?' Nicolosi asked.

'I thought about what they'd done to me, how much better a job it could have been. But it never crossed my mind to wonder what had happened to the ship afterwards. So what *did* happen?'

'You said "they healed me",' Nicolosi observed. 'Does that mean you were treated by doctors, by men and women?'

'Shouldn't I have been?'

He shook his head minutely. 'My guess is you were wounded and shipped aboard *Nightingale* soon after it was deployed.'

'That's possible.'

'In which case *Nightingale* was still in commissioning phase. I went aboard later. What about you, Ingrid?'

'Me, too. I hardly saw another human being the whole time I was aboard that thing.'

'That was how it was meant to operate: with little more than a skeleton staff, to make medical decisions the ship couldn't make for itself. Most of the time they were meant to stay behind the scenes.'

'All I remember was a hospital ship,' I said. 'I don't know anything about "commissioning".'

Nicolosi explained it to me patiently, as if I was a small child in need of education.

Nightingale had been financed and built by a consortium of well-meaning postmortal aristocrats. Since their political influence hadn't succeeded in curtailing the war (and since many of their aristocratic friends were quite happy for it to continue) they'd decided to make a difference in the next-best way: by alleviating the suffering of the mortal men and women engaged in the war itself.

So they created a hospital ship, one that had no connection to either the Northern Coalition or the Southland Militia. *Nightingale* would be there for all injured soldiers, irrespective of allegiance. Aboard the neutral ship, the injured would be healed, allowed to recuperate and then repatriated. All but the most critically wounded would eventually return to active combat service. And *Nightingale* itself would be state-of-the-art, with better medical facilities than any other public hospital on or around Sky's Edge. It wouldn't be the glittering magic of Demarchist medicine, but it would still be superior to anything most mortals had ever experienced.

It would also be tirelessly efficient, dedicated only to improving its healing record. *Nightingale* was designed to operate autonomously, as a single vast machine. Under the guidance of human specialists, the ship would slowly improve its methods until it had surpassed its teachers. I'd come aboard ship when it was still undergoing the early stages of its learning curve, but – as I learned from Nicolosi – the ship had soon moved into its 'operational phase'. By then, the entire kilometre-long vehicle was under the control of only a handful of technicians and surgical specialists, with gamma-level intelligences making most of the day-to-day decisions. That was when Sollis and Nicolosi had been shipped aboard. They'd been healed by machines, with only a vague awareness that there was a watchful human presence behind the walls.

'It worked, too,' Nicolosi said. 'The ship did everything its sponsors had hoped it would. It functioned like a huge, efficient factory: sucking in the wounded, spitting out the healed.'

'Only for them to go back to the war,' I said.

'The sponsors didn't have any control over what happened when the healed were sent back down. But at least they were still alive; at least they hadn't died on the battlefield or the operating table. The sponsors could still believe that they had done something good. They could still sleep at night.'

'So *Nightingale* was a success,' I said. 'What's the problem? Wasn't it turned over to civilian use after the armistice?'

'The ship was destroyed just before the ceasefire,' Nicolosi said. 'That's why we shouldn't be seeing it now. A stray NC missile, nuke-tipped . . . too fast to be intercepted by the ship's own countermeasures. It took out *Nightingale*, with staff and patients still aboard her.'

'Now that you mention it . . . maybe I did hear about something like that.'

Sollis looked fiercely at Martinez. 'I say we renegotiate terms. You never told us we were going to have to spring Jax from a fucking ghost ship.'

Norbert moved to his master's side, as if to protect him from the furious Sollis. Martinez, who had said nothing for many minutes, removed his glasses, buffed them on his shirt and replaced them with an unhurried calm.

'Perhaps you are right to be cross with me, Ingrid. And perhaps I made a mistake in not mentioning *Nightingale* sooner. But it was imperative that I not compromise this operation with a single careless indiscretion. My whole life has been an arrow pointing to this one task: the bringing to justice of Colonel Jax. I will not fail myself now.'

'You should have told us about the hospital ship,' Nicolosi said. 'None of us would have had any reason to spread that information. We all want to see Jax get his due.'

'Then I have made a mistake, for which I apologise.'

Sollis shook her head. 'I don't think an apology's going to cut it. If I'd known I was going to have to go back aboard that . . . *thing*—'

'You are right,' Martinez said, addressing all of us. 'The ship has a traumatic association for you, and it was wrong of me not to allow for that.'

'Amen to that,' Sollis said.

I felt it was time I made a contribution. 'I don't think any of us are about to back out now, Tomas. But maybe – given what we now know about the ship – a little more incentive might go a long way.'

'I was about to make the same suggestion myself,' Martinez said. 'You must appreciate that my funds are not inexhaustible, and that my original offer might already be considered generous . . . but shall we say an extra five thousand Australs, for each of you?'

'Make it ten and maybe we're still in business,' Sollis snapped back, before I'd had a chance to blink.

Martinez glanced at Norbert, then – with an expression that suggested he was giving in under duress – he nodded at Sollis. 'Ten thousand Australs it is. You drive a hard bargain, Ingrid.'

'While we're debating terms,' Nicolosi said, 'is there anything else you feel we ought to know?'

'I have told you that the ship is *Nightingale*.' Martinez directed our attention back to the sketchy diagram on the wall. 'That, I am ashamed to admit, is the sum total of my knowledge of the ship in question.'

'What about constructional blueprints?' I asked.

'None survived the war.'

'Photographs? Video images?'

'Ditto. *Nightingale* operated in a war zone, Dexia. Casual sightseeing was not exactly a priority for those unfortunate enough to get close to her.'

'What about the staff aboard?' Nicolosi asked. 'Couldn't they tell you anything?'

'I spoke to some survivors: the doctors and technicians who'd been aboard during the commissioning phase. Their testimonies were useful, when they were willing to talk.'

Nicolosi pushed further. 'What about the people who were aboard before the ceasefire?'

'I could not trace them.'

'But they obviously didn't die. If the ship's still out there, the rogue missile couldn't have hit it.'

'Why would anyone make up a story about the ship being blown to pieces if it didn't happen?' I asked.

'War does strange things to truth,' Martinez answered. 'No malice is necessarily implied. Perhaps another hospital ship was indeed destroyed. There was more than one in orbit around Sky's Edge, after all. One of them may even have had a similar name. It's perfectly conceivable that the facts might have got muddled, in the general confusion of those days.'

'Still doesn't explain why you couldn't trace any survivors,' Nicolosi said.

Martinez shifted on his seat, uneasily. 'If Jax did appropriate the ship, then he may not have wanted anyone talking about it. The staff aboard *Nightingale* might have been paid off – or threatened – to keep silent.'

'Adds up, I guess,' I said.

'Money will make a lot of things add up,' Nicolosi replied.

After two days, the *Death of Sophonisba* sped deeper into the night, while Martinez's ship followed a pre-programmed flight plan designed to bring us within survey range of the hospital ship. The Ultras had scanned *Nightingale* again, and once again they'd elicited no detectable response from the dormant vessel. All indications were that the ship was in a deep cybernetic coma, as close to death as possible, with only a handful of critical life-support systems still running on a trickle of stored power.

Over the next twenty-four hours we crept in closer, narrowing the distance to mere light-seconds, and then down to hundreds of thousands of kilometres. Still there was no response, but as the distance narrowed, so our sensors began to improve the detail in their scans. While the rest of us took turns sleeping, Martinez sat at his console, compositing the data, enhancing his schematic. Now and then Norbert would lean over the console and stare in numb concentration at the sharpening image, and occasionally he would mumble some remark or observation to which Martinez would respond in a patient, faintly condescending whisper, the kind that a teacher might reserve for a slow but willing pupil. Not for the first time I was touched by Martinez's obvious kindness in employing the huge, slow Norbert, and I wondered what the war must have done to him to bring him to this state.

When we were ten hours from docking, Martinez revealed the fruits of his labours. The schematic of the hospital ship was three-dimensional now, displayed in the navigational projection cylinder on the ship's cramped flight deck. Although the basic layout of the ship hadn't changed, the new plan was much more detailed than the first one. It showed docking points, airlocks, major mechanical systems and the largest corridors and spaces threading the ship's interior. There was still a lot of guesswork, but it wouldn't be as if we were entering completely foreign territory.

'The biggest thermal hot spot is here,' Martinez said, pointing at an area about a quarter of the way along the vessel from the bow. 'If Jax is anywhere, that's my best guess as to where we'll find him.'

'Simple, then,' Nicolosi said. 'In via that dorsal lock, then a straight sprint down that access shaft. Easy, even under weightless conditions. Can't be more than fifty or sixty metres.'

'I'm not happy,' Sollis said. 'That's a large lock, likely to be armed to the teeth with heavy-duty sensors and alarms.'

'Can you get us through it?' Nicolosi asked.

'You give me a door, I'll get us through it. But I can't bypass every conceivable security system, and you can be damned sure the ship will know about it if we come through a main lock.'

'What about the others?' I asked, trying not to sound as if I was on her case. 'Will they be less likely to go off?'

'Nothing's guaranteed. I don't like the idea of spending a minute longer aboard that thing than necessary, but I'd still rather take my chances with the back door.'

'I think Ingrid is correct,' Martinez said, nodding his approval. 'There's every chance of a silent approach and docking. Jax will have disabled all non-essential systems, including proximity sensors. If that's the case – if we see no evidence of having tripped approach alarms – then I believe we would be best advised to maintain stealth.' He indicated further along the hull, beyond the rounded midsection bulge. 'That will mean coming in *here*, or *here*, via one of these smaller service locks. I concur with Ingrid: they probably won't be alarmed.'

'That'll give us four or five hundred metres of ship to crawl through,' Nicolosi said, leaving us in no doubt what he thought about that. 'Four or five hundred metres for which we only have a very crude map.'

'We'll have directional guidance from our suits,' Martinez said.

'It's still a concern to me. But if you've settled upon this decision, I shall abide by it.'

I turned to Sollis. 'What you said just then – about not spending a minute longer aboard *Nightingale* than we have to?'

'I wasn't kidding.'

'I know. But there was something about the way you said it. Do you know something about that ship that we don't? You sounded spooked, and I don't understand why. It's just a disused hospital, after all.'

Sollis studied me for a moment before answering. 'Tell her, Nicolosi.'

Nicolosi looked placidly at the other woman. 'Tell her what?'

'What she obviously doesn't know. What none of us are in any great hurry to talk about.'

'Oh, please.'

' "Oh please" what?' I asked.

'It's just a fairy story, a stupid myth,' Nicolosi said.

'A stupid story that nonetheless always claimed that *Nightingale* didn't get blown up after all,' Sollis said.

'What are you talking about?' I asked. 'What story?'

It was Martinez who chose to answer. 'That something unfortunate happened aboard her. That the last batch of sick and injured went in, but for some reason were never seen to leave. That all attempts to contact the technical staff failed. That an exploratory team was put aboard the ship, and that they too were never heard from again.'

I laughed. 'Fuck. And now we're planning to go aboard?'

'Now you see why I'm somewhat anxious to get this over with,' Sollis said.

'It's just a myth,' Martinez chided. 'Nothing more. It is a tale to frighten children, not to dissuade us from capturing Jax. In fact, it would not surprise me in the least if Jax or his allies were in some way responsible for this lie. If it were to cause us to turn back now, it would have served them admirably, would it not?'

'Maybe,' I said, without much conviction. 'But I'd still have been happier if you'd told me before. It wouldn't have made any difference to my accepting this job, but it would have been nice to know you trusted me.'

'I do trust you, Dexia. I simply assumed that you had no interest in childish stories.'

'How do you know Jax is aboard?' I asked.

'We've been over this. I have my sources, sources that I must protect, and it would be—'

'He was a patient, wasn't he?'

Martinez snapped his glasses from his nose, as if my point had taken an unexpected tangent from whatever we'd been talking about. 'I know only that Jax is aboard *Nightingale*. The circumstances of how he arrived there are of no concern to me.'

'And it doesn't bother you that maybe he's just dead, like whoever else was aboard at the end?' Sollis asked.

'If he is dead, you will still receive twenty-five thousand Australs.'

'Plus the extra ten we already agreed on.'

'That too,' Martinez said, as if it should have been taken for granted.

'I still don't like this,' Sollis muttered.

'I don't like it either,' Nicolosi replied, 'but we came here to do a job, and the material facts haven't changed. There is a ship, and the man we want is aboard it. What Martinez says is true: we should not be intimidated by stories, especially when our goal is so near.'

'We go in there, we get Jax, we get the hell out,' Sollis said. 'No dawdling, no sightseeing, no souvenir-hunting.'

'I have absolutely no problem with that,' I said.

'Take what you want,' Martinez called over Norbert's shoulder as we entered the armoury compartment at the rear of the shuttle's pressurised section. 'But remember: you'll be wearing pressure suits, and you'll be moving through confined spaces. You'll also be aboard a ship.'

Sollis pushed bodily ahead of me, pouncing on something that I'd only begun to notice. She unracked the sleek, cobalt-blue excimer rifle and hefted it for balance. 'Hey, a Breitenbach.'

'Christmas come early?' I asked.

Sollis pulled a pose, sighting along the rifle, deploying its targeting aids, flipping the power-up toggle. The weapon whined obligingly. Blue lights studded its stock, indicating it was ready for use.

'Because I'm worth it,' Sollis said.

'I'd really like you to point that thing somewhere else,' I said.

'Better still, don't point it anywhere,' Nicolosi rumbled. He'd seen one of the choicer items, too. He unclipped a long, matt-black weapon with a ruby-red dragon stencilled along the barrel. It had a gaping maw like a swallowing python. 'Laser-confined plasma bazooka,' he said admiringly. 'Naughty, but nice.'

'Finesse isn't your cup of tea, then.'

'Never got to use one of these in the war, Dexia.'

'That's because they were banned. One of the few sensible things both sides managed to agree on.'

'Now's my chance.'

'I think the idea is to extract Jax, not to blow ten-metre-wide holes in *Nightingale*.'

'Don't worry. I'll be very, very careful.' He slung the bazooka over his shoulder, then continued down the aisle.

I picked up a pistol, hefted it, replaced it on the rack. Found something more to my liking – a heavy, dual-gripped slug-gun – and flipped open the magazine to check that there was a full clip inside. Low-tech but reliable: the other two were welcome to their directed-energy weapons, but I'd seen how easily they could go wrong under combat conditions.

'Nice piece, Dexia,' Sollis said, patronisingly. 'Old school.'

'I'm old school.'

'Yeah, I noticed.'

'You have a problem with that, we can always try some target practice.'

'Hey, no objections. Just glad you found something to your liking. Doing better than old Norbert, anyway.' Sollis nodded over her shoulder. 'Looks like he's really drawn the short straw there.'

I looked down the aisle. Norbert was near the end of one the racks, examining a small, stubby-looking weapon whose design I didn't recognise. In his huge hands it looked ridiculous, like something made for a doll.

'You sure about that?' I called. 'Maybe you want to check out one of these—'

Norbert looked at me as if I was some kind of idiot. I don't know what he did then – there was no movement of his hand that I was aware of – but the stubby little weapon immediately unpacked itself, elongating and opening like some complicated puzzle box until it was almost twice as big, twice as deadly-looking. It had the silken, precision-engineered quality of expensive off-world tech. A Demarchist toy, probably, but a very, very deadly toy for all that.

Sollis and I exchanged a wordless glance. Norbert had found what was probably the most advanced, most effective weapon in the room.

'Will do,' Norbert said, before closing the weapon up again and slipping it into his belt.

We crept closer. Tens of thousands of kilometres, then thousands, then hundreds. I looked through the hull windows, with the interior lights turned down, peering in the direction where our radar and infrared scans told us the hospital ship was waiting. When we were down to two dozen kilometres I knew I should be seeing it, but I was still only looking at stars and the sucking blackness between them. I had a sudden, visceral sense of how easy it would be to lose something out here, followed in quick succession by a dizzying sense of how utterly small and alone we were, now that the lighthugger was gone.

And then, suddenly, there was *Nightingale*.

We were coming in at an angle, so the hull was tilted and foreshortened. It was so dark that only certain edges and surfaces were visible at all. No windows, no running lights, no lit-up docking bays. The ship looked as dark and dead as a sliver of coal.

Suddenly it was absurd to think that there might be anyone alive aboard it. Colonel Jax's corpse, perhaps, but not the living or even life-supported body that would guarantee us full payment.

Martinez had the ship on manual control now. With small, deft applications of thrust he narrowed the distance down to less than a dozen kilometres. At six kilometres, Martinez deemed it safe to activate floodlights and play them along the length of the hull, confirming the placement of locks and docking sites. There was a peppering of micrometeorite impacts and some scorching from high-energy particles, but nothing I wouldn't have expected on a ship that had been sitting out there since the armistice. If the ship possessed self-repair mechanisms, they were sleeping as well. Even when we circled around the hull and swept it from the other side, there was no hint of our having been noticed. Still reluctant, Nicolosi accepted that we would follow Sollis's entry strategy, entering via one of the smaller service locks.

It was time to do it.

We docked. We came in softly, but there was still a solid *clunk* as the capture latches engaged and grasped our little craft to the hull of the hospital ship. I thought of that *clunk* echoing away down the length of *Nightingale*, diminishing as it travelled, but potentially still significant enough to trip some waiting, infinitely patient alarm system, alerting the sleeping ship that it had a visitor. For several minutes we hung in weightless silence, staring out of the windows or watching the sensor read-outs for the least sign of activity. But the dark ship stayed dark in all directions. There was no detectable change in her state of coma.

'Nothing's happened,' Martinez said, breaking the silence with a whisper. 'It still doesn't know we're here. The lock is all yours, Ingrid. I've already opened our doors.'

Sollis, suited-up now, moved into the lock tube with her toolkit. While she worked, the rest of us finished putting on our own suits and armour, completing the exercise as quietly as possible.

I hadn't worn a spacesuit before, but Norbert was there to help all of us with the unfamiliar process: his huge hands attended to delicate connections and catches with surprising dexterity. Once I had the suit on, it didn't feel much different from wearing full-spectrum bioarmour, and I quickly got the hang of the life-support indicators projected around the border of my faceplate. I would only need to pay minor attention to them: unless there was some malfunction, the suit had enough power and supplies to keep me alive in perfect comfort for three days; longer if I was prepared to tolerate a little less comfort. None of us were planning on spending anywhere near that long aboard *Nightingale*.

Sollis was nearly done when we assembled behind her in the lock. The inner and outer lock doors on our side were open, exposing the grey outer door of the hospital ship, held tight against the docking connector by pressure-tight seals. I doubted that she'd ever had to break into a ship before, but nothing about the mechanism appeared to be causing Sollis any difficulties. She'd tugged open an access panel and plugged in a fistful of coloured cables, running back to a jury-rigged electronics module in her toolkit. She was tapping a little keyboard, causing patterns of lights to alter within the access panel. The face of a woman – blank, expressionless, yet at the same time somehow severe and unforgiving – had appeared in an oval frame above the access panel.

'Who's that?' I asked.

'That's *Nightingale*,' Sollis said, adding, by way of explanation, 'The ship had its own gamma-level personality, keeping the whole show running. Pretty smart piece of thinkware by all accounts: full Turing compliance; about as clever as you can make a machine before you have to start giving it human rights.'

I looked at the stern-faced woman, expecting her to query us at any moment. I imagined her harsh and hectoring voice demanding to know what business any of us had boarding *Nightingale*, trespassing aboard *her* ship, *her* hospital.

'Does she know . . .' I started.

Sollis shook her head. 'This is just a dumb facet of the main construct. Not only is it inactive – the image is frozen into the door's memory – but it doesn't appear to have any functioning data links back to the main sentience engine. Do you, *Nightingale*?'

The face gazed at us impassively, but still said nothing.

'See: deadsville. My guess is the sentience engine isn't running at all. Out here, the ship wouldn't need much more than a trickle of intelligence to keep itself ticking over.'

'So the gamma's off-line?'

'Uh-huh. Best way, too. You don't want one of those things sitting around too long without something to do.'

'Why not?'

''Cause they tend to go nuts. That's why the Conjoiners won't allow gamma-level intelligences in any of their machines. They say it's a kind of slavery.'

'Running a hospital must have been enough to stop *Nightingale*'s gamma running off the rails.'

'Let's hope so. Let's really hope so.' Sollis glanced back at her work, then emitted a grunt of satisfaction as a row of lights flicked to orange. She unplugged a bunch of coloured cables and looked back at the waiting party. 'Okay: we're good to go. I can open the door any time you're ready.'

'What's on the other side of it?' I asked.

'According to the door, air: normal trimix. Bitchingly cold, but not frozen. Pressure's manageable. I'm not sure we could *breathe* it, but—'

'We're not breathing anything,' Martinez said curtly. 'Our air-lock will take two people. One of them will have to be you, Ingrid, since you know how to work the mechanism. I shall accompany you, and then we shall wait for the others on the far side, when we have established that conditions are safe.'

'Maybe one of us should go through instead of you,' I said, wondering why Norbert hadn't volunteered to go through ahead of his master. 'We're expendable, but you aren't. Without you, Jax doesn't go down.'

'Considerate of you, Dexia, but I paid you to assist me, not take risks on my behalf.'

Martinez propelled himself forward. Norbert, Nicolosi and I edged back to permit the inner door to close again. On the common suit channel I heard Sollis say, 'We're opening *Nightingale*. Stand by: comms might get a bit weaker once we're on the other side of all this metal.'

Nicolosi pushed past me, back into the flight deck. I heard the heavy whine of servos as the door opened. Breathing and scuffling sounds followed, but nothing that alarmed me.

'Okay,' Sollis said, 'we're moving into *Nightingale*'s lock. Closing the outer door behind us. When you need to open it again, hit any key on the pad.'

'Still no sign of life,' Nicolosi called.

'The inner door looks as if it'll open without any special encouragement from me,' Sollis said. 'Should be just a matter of pulling down this lever . . . you ready?'

'Do it, Ingrid,' Martinez replied.

More servos, fainter now. After a few moments, Sollis reported back: 'We're inside. No surprises yet. Floating in some kind of holding bay, about ten metres wide. It's dark, of course. There's a doorway leading out through the far wall: might lead to the main corridor that should pass close to this lock.'

I remembered to turn on my helmet lamp.

'Can you open both lock doors?' Nicolosi asked.

'Not at the same time, not without a lot of trouble that might get us noticed.'

'Then we'll come through in two passes. Norbert: you go first. Dexia and I will follow.'

It took longer than I'd have liked, but eventually all five of us were on the other side of the lock. I'd only been weightless once, during the recuperation programme after my injury, but the memory of how to move – at least without making too much of a fool of myself – was still there, albeit dimly. The others were coping about as well. The combined effects of our helmet lamps banished the darkness to the corners of the room, emphasizing the deeper gloom of the open doorway Sollis had mentioned. It occurred to me that somewhere deep in that darkness was Colonel Jax, or whatever was left of him.

Nervously, I checked that the slug-gun was still clipped to my belt.

'Call up your helmet maps,' Martinez said. 'Does everyone have an overlay and a positional fix?'

'I'm good,' I said, against a chorus from the other three, and acutely aware of how easy it would be to get lost aboard a ship as large as *Nightingale* if that positional fix were to break down.

'Check your weapons and suit systems. We'll keep comms to a minimum all the way in.'

'I'll lead,' Nicolosi said, propelling himself into the darkness of the doorway before anyone could object.

I followed hard on his heels, trying not to get out of breath with the effort of keeping up. There were loops and rails along all four walls of the shaft, so movement consisted of gliding from one handhold to the next, with only air resistance to stop one drifting all the way. We were covering one metre a second, easily: at that rate, it wouldn't take long to cross the entire width of the ship, which would mean we'd somehow missed the axial corridor we were looking for, or that it simply didn't exist. But just when it was beginning to strike me that we'd gone too far, Nicolosi slowed. I grabbed a handhold to stop myself slamming into his feet.

He looked back at us, his helmet lamp making me squint. 'Here's the main corridor, just a bit deeper than we were expecting. Runs both ways.'

'We turn left,' Martinez said, in not much more than a whisper. 'Turn left and follow it for one hundred metres, maybe one hundred and twenty, until we meet the centrifuge section. It should be a straight crawl, with no obstructions.'

Nicolosi turned away, then looked back. 'I can't see more than twenty metres into the corridor. We may as well see where it goes.'

'Nice and slowly,' Martinez urged.

We moved forward, along the length of the hull. In the instants when I was coasting from one handhold to the next, I held my breath and tried to hear the ambient noises of the ship, relayed to my helmet by the suit's acoustic pick-up. Mostly all I heard was the scuffing progress of the others, the hiss and hum of their own life-support packs. Other than that, *Nightingale* was as silent as when we'd approached. If the ship was aware of our intrusion, there was no sign of it.

We'd made maybe forty metres from the junction – at least a third of the distance we had to travel before hitting the centrifuge – when Nicolosi slowed. I caught a handhold before I drifted into his heels, then looked back to make sure the others had got the message.

'Problem?' Martinez asked.

'There's a T-junction right ahead. I didn't think we were expecting a T-junction.'

'We weren't,' Martinez said, 'but it shouldn't surprise us that the real ship deviates from the schematic here and there. As long as we don't reach a dead end, we can still keep moving towards the colonel.'

'You want to flip a coin, or shall I do it?' Nicolosi said, looking back at us over his shoulder, his face picked out by my helmet light.

'There's no indication, no sign on the wall?'

'Blank either way.'

'In which case take the left,' Martinez said, before glancing at Norbert. 'Agreed?'

'Agreed,' the big man said. 'Take left, then next right. Continue.'

Nicolosi kicked off, and the rest of us followed. I kept an eye on my helmet's inertial compass, gratified when it detected our change of direction, even though the overlay now showed us moving through what should have been a solid wall.

We'd moved twenty or thirty metres when Nicolosi slowed again. 'Tunnel bends to the right,' he reported. 'Looks like we're back on track. Everyone cool with this?'

'Cool,' I said.

But we'd only made another fifteen or twenty metres of progress along the new course when Nicolosi slowed and called back again. 'We're coming up on a heavy door – some kind of internal airlock. Looks as if we're going to need Sollis again.'

'Let me through,' she said, and I squeezed aside so she could edge past me, trying to avoid knocking our suits together. In addition to the weapons she'd selected from the armoury, Sollis's suit was also hung with all manner of door-opening tools, clattering against each other as she moved. I didn't doubt that she'd be able to get through any kind of door, given time. But the idea of spending hours inside *Nightingale*, while we inched from one obstruction to the next, didn't exactly fill me with enthusiasm.

We let Sollis examine the door: we could hear her ruminating over the design, tutting, humming and talking softly to herself under her breath. She had panels open and equipment plugged in, just like before. The same unwelcoming face glowered from an oval display.

After a couple of minutes, Martinez sighed and asked, 'Is there a problem, Ingrid?'

'There's no problem. I can get this door open in about ten seconds. I just want to make damned sure this is another of *Nightingale*'s dumb facets. That means sensing the electrical connections on either side of the frame. Of course, if you'd rather we just stormed on through—'

'Keep voice down,' Norbert rumbled.

'I'm wearing a spacesuit, dickhead.'

'Pressure outside. Sound travel, air to glass, glass to air.'

'You have five minutes,' Martinez said, decisively. 'If you haven't found what you're looking for by then, we open the door anyway. And Norbert's right: let's keep the noise down.'

'So, no pressure then,' Sollis muttered.

But in three minutes she started unplugging her tools, and turned aside with a beaming look on her face. 'It's just an emergency airlock, in case this part of the ship depressurises.'

'But it isn't on the schematic.'

'It ain't a blueprint, Scarrow. Like the old man told us, it's just a guess. If people remembered stuff wrong, or if the ship got changed after they were abroad . . . we're going to run into discrepancies.'

'No danger that tripping it will alert the rest of *Nightingale*?' I asked.

'Can't ever say there's no risk, but I'm happy for us to go through.'

'Open the door,' Martinez said. 'Everyone brace in case there's vacuum or atmosphere under pressure on the other side.'

We followed his instructions, but when the door opened the air remained as still as before. Beyond, picked out by our wavering lights, was a short stretch of corridor terminating in an identical-looking door. This time there was enough room for all of us to squeeze through, while Sollis attended to the second lock mechanism. Some hardwired system required that the first door be closed before the second one could be opened, but that posed us no real difficulties. Now that Sollis knew what to look for, she worked much faster: good at her job and happy for us all to know it. I didn't doubt that she'd be even faster on the way out.

'We're ready to go through, people. Indications say that the air's just as cold on the other side, so keep your suits buttoned.'

I heard the click as one of us – maybe Nicolosi, maybe Norbert – released a safety catch. It was like someone coughing in a theatre. I had no choice but to reach down and arm my own weapon.

'Open it,' Martinez said quietly.

The door chugged wide. Our lights stabbed into dark emptiness beyond: a suggestion of a much deeper, wider space than I'd been expecting. Sollis leaned through the doorframe, her helmet lamp catching fleeting details from reflective surfaces. I had a momentary flash of glassy things stretching away into infinite distance, then it was gone.

'Report, Ingrid,' Martinez said.

'I think we can get through. We've come out next to a wall, or floor, or whatever it is. There are handholds, railings. Looks as if they lead on into the room, probably to the other side.'

'Stay where you are,' Nicolosi said, just ahead of me. 'I'll take point again.'

Sollis glanced back and swallowed hard. 'It's okay, I can handle this one. Can't let you have all the fun, can I?'

Nicolosi grunted something: I don't think he had much of a sense of humour. 'You're welcome to my gun, you want it.'

'I'm cool,' she said, but with audible hesitation. I didn't blame her: it was different being point on a walk through a huge dark room, compared to a narrow corridor. Nothing could leap out and grab you from the side in a corridor.

She started moving along the crawlway.

'Nice and slowly, Ingrid,' Martinez said, from behind me. 'We still have time on our side.'

'We're right behind you,' I said, feeling she needed moral support.

'I'm fine, Dexia. No problems here. Just don't want to lose my handhold and go drifting off into fuck knows what . . .'

Her movements became rhythmic, progressing into the chamber one careful handhold at a time. Nicolosi followed, with me right behind him. Apart from our movements, and the sounds of our suit systems, the ship was still as silent as a crypt.

But it wasn't totally dark any more.

Now that we were inside the chamber, it began to reveal its

secrets in dim spots of pale light, reaching away into some indeterminate distance. The lights must have always been there, just too faint to notice until we were inside.

'Something's running,' Sollis said.

'We knew that,' Martinez said. 'It was always clear that the ship was dormant, not dead.'

I panned my helmet around and tried to get another look at the glassy things I'd glimpsed earlier. On either side of the railed walkway, stretching away in multiple ranks, were hundreds of transparent flasks. Each flask was the size of an oil drum, rounded on top, mounted on a steel-grey plinth equipped with controls, read-outs and input sockets. There were three levels of them, with the second and third layers stacked above the first on skeletal racks. Most of the plinths were dead, but maybe one in ten was showing a lit-up read-out.

'Oh, Jesus,' Sollis said, and I guess she'd seen what I'd just seen: that the flasks contained human organs, floating in a green chemical solution, wired up with fine nutrient lines and electrical cables. I was no anatomist, but I still recognised hearts, lungs, kidneys, snakelike coils of intestine. And there were things anyone would have recognised: things like eyeballs, dozens of them growing in a single vat, swaying on the long stalks of optic nerves like some weird species of all-seeing sea anemone; things like hands, or entire limbs, or genitals, or the skin and muscle masks of eyeless faces. Every external body part came in dozens of different sizes, ranging from child-sized to adult, male and female, and despite the green suspension fluid one could make out subtle variations in skin tone and pigmentation.

'Easy, Ingrid,' I said, the words as much for my benefit as hers. 'We always knew this was a hospital ship. It was just a matter of time before we ran into something like this.'

'This stuff . . .' Nicolosi said, his voice low. 'Where does it come from?'

'Two main sources,' Martinez answered, sounding too calm for my liking. 'Not everyone who came aboard *Nightingale* could be saved, obviously – the ship was no more capable of working miracles than any other hospital. Wherever practicable, the dead would donate intact body parts for future use. Useful, certainly, but such a resource could never have supplied the bulk of *Nightingale*'s surgical needs. For that reason the ship was also equipped to fabricate its own organ supplies, using well-established principles of stem-cell manipulation. The organ factories would have worked around the clock, keeping this library fully stocked.'

'It doesn't look fully stocked now,' I said.

Martinez said, 'We're not in a war zone any more. The ship is dormant. It has no need to maintain its usual surgical capacity.'

'So why is it maintaining any capacity? Why are some of these flasks still keeping their organs alive?'

'Waste not, want not, I suppose. A strategic reserve, against the day when the ship might be called into action again.'

'You think it's just waiting to be reactivated?'

'It's only a machine, Dexia. A machine on standby. Nothing to get nervous about.'

'No one's nervous,' I said, but it came out all wrong, making me sound as if I was the one who was spooked.

'Let's get to the other side,' Nicolosi said.

'We're halfway there,' Sollis reported. 'I can see the far wall, sort of. Looks like there's a door waiting for us.'

We kept on moving, hand over hand, mostly in silence. Surrounded by all those glass-encased body parts, I couldn't help but think of the people many of them had once been part of. If these parts had belonged to me, I think I'd have chosen to haunt *Nightingale*, consumed with ill-directed, spiteful fury.

Not the right kind of thinking, I was just telling myself, when the flasks started moving.

We all stopped, anchoring ourselves to the nearest handhold. Two or three rows back from the railed crawlway, a row of flasks was gliding smoothly towards the far wall of the chamber. They were sliding in perfect lock-step unison. When my heart started beating again, I realised that the entire row must be attached to some kind of conveyor system, hidden within the support framework.

'Nobody move,' Nicolosi said.

'This is not good,' Sollis kept saying. 'This is not good. The damn ship isn't supposed to know—'

'Quiet,' Martinez hissed. 'Let me past you: I want to see where those flasks are going.'

'Careful,' Norbert said.

Paying no attention to the man, Martinez climbed ahead of the party. Quickly we followed him, doing our best not to make any noise or slip from the crawlway. The flasks continued their smooth, silent movement until the conveyor system reached the far wall and turned through ninety degrees, taking the flasks away from us into a covered enclosure like a security scanner. Most of the flasks were empty, but as we watched, one of the occupied, active units slid into the enclosure. I'd only had a moment to notice, but I thought I'd seen a forearm and hand, reaching up from the life-support plinth.

The conveyor system halted. For a moment all was silent, then there came a series of mechanical clicks and whirrs. None of us could see what was happening inside the enclosure, but after a moment we didn't need to. It was obvious.

The conveyor began to move again, but running in reverse this time. The flask that had gone into the enclosure was now empty. I counted back to make sure I wasn't making a mistake, but there was no doubt. The forearm and hand had been removed from the flask. Already, I presumed, the limb was somewhere else in the ship.

The flasks travelled back – returning to what I presumed to have been their former positions – and then halted again. Save for the missing limb, the chamber was exactly as when we had entered it.

'I don't like this,' Sollis said. 'The ship is supposed to be dead.'

'Dormant,' Martinez corrected.

'You don't think the shit that just happened is in any way related to us being aboard? You don't think Jax just got a wake-up call?'

'If Jax were aware of our presence, we'd know it by now.'

'I don't know how you can sound so calm.'

'All that has happened, Ingrid, is that *Nightingale* has performed some trivial housekeeping duty. We have already seen that it maintains some organs in pre-surgical condition, and this is just one of its tissue libraries. It should hardly surprise us that the ship occasionally decides to move some of its stock from A to B.'

She made a small, catlike snarl of frustration – I could tell she hadn't bought any of his explanations – and pulled herself hand over hand to the door.

'Any more shit like that happens, I'm out,' she said.

'I'd think twice if I were you,' Martinez said. 'It's a hell of a long walk home.'

I caught up with Sollis and touched her on the forearm. 'I don't like it either, Ingrid, but the man's right. Jax doesn't know we're here. If he did, I think he'd do more than just move some flasks around.'

'I hope you're right, Scarrow.'

'So do I,' I said under my breath.

We continued along the main axis of the ship, following a corridor much like the one we'd been following before the organ library. It swerved and jagged, then straightened out again. According to the inertial compasses, we were still headed towards Jax, or at least the part of the ship where it appeared most likely we'd find him, alive or dead.

'What we were talking about earlier,' Sollis said, 'I mean, much earlier – about how this ship never got destroyed at the end of the war after all—'

'I think I have stated my case, Ingrid. Dwelling on myths won't bring a wanted man to justice.'

'We're looking at about a million tonnes of salvageable space-craft here. Gotta be worth something to someone. So why didn't anyone get their hands on it after the war?'

'Because something bad happened,' Nicolosi said. 'Maybe there was some truth in the story about that boarding party coming here and not leaving.'

'Oh, please,' Martinez said.

'So who was fighting back?' I asked. 'Who stopped them taking *Nightingale*?'

Nicolosi answered me. 'The skeleton staff . . . security agents of the postmortals who financed this thing . . . maybe even the protective systems of the ship itself. If it thought it was under attack—'

'If there was some kind of firefight aboard this thing,' I asked, 'where's the damage?'

'I don't care about the damage,' Sollis cut in. 'I want to know what happened to all the bodies.'

We came to another blocked double-door airlock. Sollis got to work on it immediately, but my expectation that she would work faster now that she had already opened several doors without trouble was wrong. She kept plugging things in, checking read-outs, murmuring to herself just loud enough to carry over the voice link. *Nightingale*'s face watched us disapprovingly, looking on like the portrait of a disappointed ancestor.

'This one could be trickier,' she said. 'I'm picking up active data links, running away from the frame.'

'Meaning it could still be hooked into the nervous system?' Nicolosi asked.

'I can't rule it out.'

Nicolosi ran a hand along the smooth black barrel of his plasma weapon. 'We could double back, try a different route.'

'We're not going back,' Martinez said. 'Not now. Open the door,

Ingrid: we'll take our chances and move as quickly as we can from now on.'

'You sure about this?' She had a cable pinched between her fingers. 'No going back once I plug this in.'

'Do it.'

She pushed the line in. At the same moment a shiver of animation passed across *Nightingale*'s face, the mask waking to life. The door spoke to us. Its tone was strident and metallic, but also possessed of an authoritative femininity.

'This is the Voice of *Nightingale*. You are attempting to access a secure area. Report to central administration to obtain proper clearance.'

'Shit,' Sollis said.

'You weren't expecting that?' I asked.

'I wasn't expecting an active facet. Maybe the sentience engine isn't powered down quite as far as I thought.'

'This is the Voice of *Nightingale*,' the door said again. 'You are attempting to access a secure area. Report to central administration to obtain proper clearance.'

'Can you still force it?' Nicolosi asked.

'Yeah . . . think so.' Sollis fumbled in another line, made some adjustments and stood back as the door slid open. '*Voilà*.'

The face had turned silent and masklike again, but now I really felt as if we were being watched; as if the woman's eyes seemed to be looking in all directions at once.

'You think Jax knows about us now?' I asked, as Sollis propelled herself into the holding chamber between the two sets of doors.

'I don't know. Maybe I bypassed the door in time, before it sent an alert.'

'But you can't be sure.'

'No.' She sounded wounded.

Sollis got to work on the second door, faster now, urgency overruling caution. I checked that my gun was still where I'd left it, and then made sure that the safety catch was still off. Around me, the others went through similar preparatory rituals.

Gradually it dawned on me that Sollis was taking longer than expected. She turned from the door, her equipment still hooked into its open service panel.

'Something's screwed up,' she said, before swallowing hard. 'These suits we're wearing, Tomas . . . how good are they, exactly?'

'Full-spectrum battle-hardened. Why do you ask?'

'Because the door says that the ship's flooded behind this point. It says we'll be swimming through something.'

'I see,' Martinez said.

'Oh, no,' I said, shaking my head. 'We're not doing this. We're not going underwater.'

'I can't be sure it's water, Dexia.' She tapped the read-out panel, as if I should have been able to make sense of the numbers and symbols. 'Could be anything warm and wet, really.'

Martinez shrugged within his suit. 'Could have been a containment leak . . . spillage into this part of the ship. It's nothing to worry about. Our suits will cope easily, provided we do not delay.'

I looked him hard in the faceplate, meeting his eyes, making certain he couldn't look away. 'You're sure about this? These suits aren't going to stiff on us as soon as they get wet?'

'The suits will continue to function. I am so certain that I will go first. When you hear that I am safe on the other side, you can all follow.'

'I don't like this. What if Ingrid's tools don't work under water?'

'We have no choice but to keep moving forward,' Martinez said. 'If this section of the ship is flooded, we'll run into it no matter which route we take. This is the only way.'

'Then let's do it,' I said. 'If these suits made it through the war, surely they'll get us through the next chamber.'

'It's not the suits I'm worried about,' Nicolosi said, examining his weapon again. 'No one mentioned immersion when we were in the armoury.'

I cupped a hand to my crude little slug-gun. 'I'll swap you, we make it to the other side.'

Nicolosi didn't say anything. I don't think he saw the funny side.

Two minutes later we were inside, floating weightless in the unlit gloom of the flooded room. It felt like water, but it was difficult to tell. Everything felt thick and sluggish when you were wearing a suit, even thin air. My biohazard detectors weren't registering anything, but that didn't necessarily mean the fluid was safe. The detectors were tuned to recognise a handful of toxins in common wartime use; they weren't designed to sniff out every harmful agent that had ever existed.

Martinez's voice buzzed in my helmet. 'There are no handholds or guide wires. We'll just have to swim in a straight direction, trusting to our inertial compasses. If we all stay within sight of each other, we should have no difficulties.'

'Let's get on with it,' Nicolosi said.

We started swimming as best as we could, Nicolosi leading, pushing himself forward with powerful strokes, his weapons dangling from their straps. It would have been hard and slow with just the suits to contend with, but we were all wearing armour as well. It made it difficult to see ahead; difficult to reach forward to get an effective stroke; difficult to kick our legs enough to make any useful contribution. Our helmet lamps struggled to illuminate more than ten or twenty metres in any direction, and the door by which we'd entered was soon lost behind us in gloom. I felt a constricting sense of panic: the fear that if the compasses failed we might never find our way out again.

The compasses didn't fail, though, and Nicolosi maintained his unfaltering pace. Two minutes into the swim he called, 'I see the wall. It's dead ahead of us.'

A couple of seconds later I saw it hove out of the deep-pink gloom. Any relief I might have felt was tempered by the observation that the wall appeared featureless, stretching away blankly in all illuminated directions.

'There's no door,' I said.

'Maybe we experienced some lateral drift,' Nicolosi said.

'Compass says no.'

'Then maybe the doors are offset. It doesn't matter: we'll find it by hitting the wall and spiralling out from our landing spot.'

'If there's a door.'

'If there isn't,' Nicolosi said, 'we shoot our way out.'

'Glad you've thought this through,' I said, realising that he was serious.

We drew nearer to the wall. The closer we got and the more clearly it was picked out by our lamps, the more I realised there was something not quite right about it. It was still blank – lacking any struts or panels, apertures or pieces of shipboard equipment – but it wasn't the seamless surface I'd have expected from a massive sheet of prefabricated spacecraft material. There was an unsettling texture to it, with something of the fibrous quality of cheap paper. Faint lines coursed through it, slightly darker than the rest of the wall, but not arranged according to any neat geometric pattern. They curved and branched, and threw off fainter subsidiary lines, diminishing like the veins in a leaf.

In a nauseating flash I realised exactly what the wall was made of. When Nicolosi's palms touched the surface, it yielded like a trampoline, absorbing the momentum of his impact and then sending him back out again, until his motion was damped by the surrounding fluid.

'It's . . .' I began.

'Skin. I know. I realised just before I hit.'

I arrested my motion, but not quickly enough to avoid contact with the wall of skin. It yielded under me, stretching so much that I felt in danger of ripping my way right through. But it held, and began to trampoline me back in the direction I'd come from.

Fighting a tide of revulsion, I pulled back into the liquid and floated amidst the others.

'Fuck,' Sollis said. 'This isn't right. There shouldn't be fucking *skin*—'

'Don't be alarmed,' Martinez said, wheezing between each word. 'This is just another form of organ library, like the room we already passed through. I believe the liquid we're swimming in must be a form of growth-support medium . . . something like amniotic fluid. Under wartime conditions, this whole chamber would have been full of curtains of growing skin, measured by the acre.'

Nicolosi groped for something on his belt, came up with a serrated blade that glinted nastily even in the pink fluid.

'I'm cutting through.'

'No!' Martinez barked.

Sollis, who was next to Nicolosi, took hold of his forearm. 'Easy, soldier. Got to be a better way.'

'There is,' Martinez said. 'Put the knife away, please. We can go around the skin, find its edge.'

Nicolosi still had the blade in his hand. 'I'd rather take the short cut.'

'There are nerve endings in that skin. Cut them and the monitoring apparatus will know about it. Then so will the ship.'

'Maybe the ship already knows we're here.'

'We don't take that chance.'

Reluctantly, Nicolosi returned the knife to his belt. 'I thought we'd agreed to move fast from now on,' he said.

'There's fast, and there's reckless,' Sollis said. 'You were about to cross the line.'

Martinez brushed past me, already swimming to the left. I followed him, with the others tagging on behind. After less than a minute of hard progress, a dark edge emerged into view. It was like a picture frame stretching tight the canvas of skin. Beyond the edge, only just visible, was a wall of the chamber, fretted with massive geodesic reinforcing struts.

I allowed myself a moment of ease. We were still in danger, still in about the most claustrophobic situation I could imagine, but at least now the chamber didn't seem infinitely large.

Martinez braked himself by grabbing the frame. I came to rest next to him and peered around the edge, towards what I hoped would be the wall we'd been heading towards all along. But instead of that I saw only another field of skin, stretched across another frame, separated from the first by no more than the height of a man. In the murky distance was the suggestion of a third frame, and perhaps a fourth beyond that.

'How many?' I asked as the others arrived on the frame, perching like crows.

'I don't know,' Martinez said. 'Four, five . . . anything up to a dozen, I'd guess. But it's okay. We can swim around the frames, then turn right and head back to where we'd expect to find the exit door.' He raised his voice. 'Everyone all right? No problems with your suits?'

'There are lights,' Nicolosi said quietly.

We turned to look at him.

'I mean over there,' he added, nodding in the direction of the other sheets of skin. 'I saw a flicker of something . . . a glow in the water, or amniotic fluid, or whatever the fuck this is.'

'I see light, too,' Norbert said.

I looked down and saw that he was right – Nicolosi had not been imagining it. A pale, trembling light was emerging from between the next two layers of skin.

'Whatever that is, I don't like it,' I said.

'Me neither,' Martinez said. 'But if it's something going on between the skin layers, it doesn't have to concern us. We swim around, avoid them completely.'

He kicked off with surprising determination, and I followed quickly after him. The reverse side of the skin sheet was a fine mesh of pale support fibres, the structural matrix upon which the skin must have been grown and nourished. Thick black cables ran across the underside, arranged in circuit-like patterns.

The second sheet, the one immediately behind the first, was of different pigmentation from the one behind it. In all other respects it appeared similar, stretching unbroken into pink haze. The flickering, trembling light source was visible through the flesh, silhouetting the veins and arteries at the moments when the light was brightest.

We passed around the second sheet and peered into the gap between the second and third layers. Picked out in stuttering light was a tableau of furtive activity. Four squid-like robots were at work. Each machine consisted of a tapering, cone-shaped body, anchored to the skin by a cluster of whip-like arms emerging from the blunt end of the cone. The robots were engaged in precise surgery, removing a blanket-sized rectangle of skin by cutting it free along four sides. The robots generated their own illumination, shining from the ends of some of their arms, but the bright flashing light was coming from some kind of laser-like tool that each robot deployed on the end of a single segmented arm that was thicker than any of the others. I couldn't tell whether the flashes were part of the cutting, or the instant healing that appeared to be taking place immediately afterwards. There was no bleeding, and the surrounding skin appeared unaffected.

'What are they doing?' I breathed.

'Harvesting,' Martinez answered. 'What does it look like?'

'I know they're harvesting. I mean, *why* are they doing it? What do they need that skin for?'

'I don't know.'

'You had plenty of answers in the organ library, Mister Martinez,' Sollis said. All five of us had slowed, hovering at the same level as the surgical robots. 'For a ship that's supposed to be dormant . . . I'm not seeing much fucking evidence of dormancy.'

'*Nightingale* grows skin here,' I said. 'I can deal with that. The ship's keeping a basic supply going, in case it's called into another war. But that doesn't explain why it needs to harvest some *now*.'

Martinez sounded vague. 'Maybe it's testing the skin . . . making sure it's developing according to plan.'

'You'd think a little sample would be enough for that,' I said. 'A lot less than several square metres, for sure. That's enough skin to cover a whole person.'

'I really wish you hadn't said that,' Nicolosi said.

'Let's keep moving,' Martinez said. And he was right, too, I thought: the activity of the robots was deeply unsettling, but we hadn't come here to sightsee.

As we swam away – with no sign that the robots had noticed us – I thought about what Ingrid Sollis had said before. About how it wasn't clever to leave a gamma-level intelligence up and running without something to occupy itself. Because otherwise – since duty was so deeply hardwired into their logic pathways – they tended to go slowly, quietly, irrevocably insane.

And *Nightingale* had been alone out there since the end of the war. What did that mean for its controlling mind? Was the hospital running itself out there – reliving the duties of its former life, no matter how pointless they had become – because the mind had already gone mad, or was this the hospital's last-ditch way of keeping itself sane?

And what, I wondered, did any of that have to do with the man we had come here to find in the first place?

We kept swimming, passing layer upon layer of skin. Now and then we'd come across another surgical party: another group of robots engaged in skin-harvesting. Where they'd already completed their task, the flesh had been excised in neat rectangles and strips, exposing the gauzelike mesh of the growth matrix. Occasionally I saw a patch that was half-healed already, the skin growing back in rice-paper translucence. By the time it was fully repaired, I doubted that there'd be any sign of where the skin had been cut.

Ten layers, then twelve – and then finally the wall I'd been waiting for hove into view like a mirage. But I wasn't imagining it, or seeing another layer of drum-tight skin. There was the same pattern of geodesic struts as I'd seen on the other wall.

Sollis's voice came through. 'Got a visual on the door, people. We're nearly out of here. I'm swimming ahead to start work.'

'Good, Ingrid,' Martinez called back.

A few seconds later I saw the airlock for myself, relieved that Sollis hadn't been mistaken. She swam quickly, then – even as she was gliding to a halt by the door – commenced unclipping tools and connectors from her belt. Through the darkening distance of the pink haze I watched her flip down the service panel and begin her usual systems-bypass procedure. I was glad Martinez had found Sollis. Whatever else one might say about her, she was pretty hot at getting through doors.

'Okay, good news,' she said after a minute of plugging things in and out. 'There's air on the other side. We're not going to have to swim in this stuff for much longer.'

'How much longer?' Nicolosi asked.

'Can't risk a short circuit here, guy. Gotta take things one step at a time.'

Just as she was saying that, I became aware that we were casting shadows against the wall – shadows we hadn't been casting when we arrived. I twisted around and looked back the way we'd just swum, in the direction of the new light source I knew had to be there. Four of the squid-like machines were approaching us, dragging a blanket of newly harvested skin between them, one robot grasping each corner between two segmented silver tentacles. They were moving faster than we could swim, driven by some propulsion system jetting fluid from the sharp ends of their cone-shaped bodies.

Sollis jerked back as the outer airlock door opened suddenly.

'I didn't . . .' she started.

'I know,' I said urgently. 'The robots are coming. They must have sent a command to open the lock.'

'Let's get out of the way,' Martinez said, kicking off from the wall. 'Ingrid – get away from the lock. Take what you can, but make it snappy.'

Sollis started unplugging her equipment, stowing it on her belt with fumbling fingers. The machines powered nearer, the blanket of skin undulating between them like a flying carpet. They slowed, then halted, their lights pushing spears of harsh illumination through the fluid. They were looking at us, wondering what we were doing between them and the door. One of the machines directed its beam towards Martinez's swimming figure, attracted by the movement. Martinez slowed and hung frozen in the glare, like a moth pinned in a beam of sunlight.

None of us said a word. My own breathing was the loudest sound in the universe, but I couldn't make it any quieter. Silently, the airlock door closed itself again, as if the robots had detected our presence and decided to bar our exit from the flooded chamber.

One of the machines let go of its corner of the skin. It hovered by the sheet for a moment, as if weighing its options. Then it singled me out and commenced its approach. As it neared, the machine appeared far larger and more threatening than I'd expected. Its cone-shaped body was as long as me; its thickest tentacle appearing powerful enough to do serious damage even without the additional weapon of the laser. When it spread its arms wide, as if to embrace me, I had to fight not to panic and back away.

The robot started examining me. It began with my helmet, tap-tapping and scraping, shining its light through my visor. It applied twisting force, trying to disengage the helmet from the neck coupling. Whether it recognised me as a person or just a piece of unidentifiable floating debris, it appeared to think that dismantling was the best course of action. I told myself that I'd let it work at me for another few seconds, but as soon as I felt the helmet begin to loosen I'd have to act . . . even if that meant alerting the robot that I probably wasn't debris.

But just when I'd decided I had to move, the robot abandoned my helmet and worked its way south. It extended a pair of tentacles under my chest armour from each side, trying to lever it away like a huge scab. Somehow I kept my nerve, daring to believe that the robot would sooner or later lose interest in me. Then it pulled away from the chest armour and started fiddling with my weapon, tap-tapping away like a spirit in a seance. It tugged on the gun, trying to unclip it. Then, as abruptly as it had started, the robot abandoned its investigation. It pulled away, gathering its tentacles into a fistlike bunch. Then it moved slowly in the direction of Nicolosi, tentacles groping ahead of it.

I willed him to stay still. There'd be no point in trying to swim away. None of us could move faster than those robots. Nicolosi must have worked that out for himself, or else he was paralysed with fright, but he made no movements as the robot cruised up to him. It slowed, the spread of its tentacles widening, and then tracked its spotlight from head to toe, as if it still couldn't decide what Nicolosi was. Then it reached out a pair of manipulators and brushed their sharp-looking tips against his helmet. The machine probed and examined with surprising gentleness. I heard the metal-on-metal scrape through the voice link, backgrounded by Nicolosi's rapid, sawlike breathing.

Keep it together . . .

The machine reached his neck, examined the interface between helmet and torso assembly and then worked its way down to his chest armour, extending a fine tentacle under the armour itself, to where the vulnerable life-support module lay concealed. Then, very slowly, it withdrew the tentacle.

The machine pulled back from Nicolosi, turning its blunt end away, apparently finished with its examination. The other three robots hovered watchfully with their prize of skin. Nicolosi sighed and eased his breathing.

'I think . . .' he whispered.

That was his big mistake. The machine righted itself, gathered its tentacles back into formation and began to approach him again, its powerful light sweeping up and down his body with renewed purpose. The second machine was nearing, clearly intent on assisting its partner in the examination of Nicolosi.

I looked at Sollis, our horrified gazes locking. 'Can you get the door—' I started.

'Not a hope in hell.'

'Nicolosi,' I said, not bothering to whisper this time, 'stay still and maybe they'll go away again.'

But he wasn't going to stay still: not this time. Even as I watched, he was hooking a hand around the plasma rifle, swinging it in front of him like a harpoon, its wide maw directed at the nearest machine.

'No!' Norbert shouted, his voice booming through the water like a depth charge. 'Do not use! Not in here!'

But Nicolosi was beyond reasoned argument now. He had a weapon. Every cell in his body was screaming at him to use it.

So he did.

In one sense, it did all that he asked of it. The plasma discharge speared the robot like a sunbeam through a cloud. The robot came apart in a boiling eruption of steam and fire, jagged black pieces riding the shock wave. Then the steam – the vaporised amniotic fluid – swallowed everything, including Nicolosi and his gun. Even inside my suit, the sound hit me like a hammer blow. He fired once more, as if to make certain that he had destroyed the robot. By then the second machine was near enough to be flung back by the blast, but it quickly righted itself and continued its progress towards him.

'More,' Norbert said, and when I looked back towards the stack of skin sheets, I saw what he meant. Robots were arriving in ones and twos, abandoning their cutting work to investigate whatever had just happened.

'We're in trouble,' I said.

The steam cloud was breaking up, revealing the floating form of Nicolosi, the ruined stump of his weapon drifting away from him. The second time he fired it, something must have gone badly wrong with the plasma rifle. I wasn't even sure that Nicolosi was still alive.

'I take door,' Norbert said, drawing his Demarchist weapon. 'You take robots.'

'You're going to shoot us a way out, after what just happened to Nicolosi?' I asked.

'No choice,' he said as the gun unpacked itself in his hand.

Martinez pushed himself across to the big man. 'No. Give it to me instead. I'll take care of the door.'

'Too dangerous,' Norbert said.

'Give it to me.'

Norbert hesitated, and for a moment I thought he was going to put up a fight. Then he calmly passed the Demarchist weapon to Martinez and accepted Martinez's weapon in return, the little slug-gun vanishing into his vast gauntleted hand. Whatever respect I'd had for Norbert vanished at the same time. If he was supposed to be protecting Martinez, that was no way to go about it.

Of the three of us, only Norbert and I were carrying projectile weapons. I unclipped my second pistol and passed it to Sollis. She took it gratefully, needing little persuasion to keep her energy weapon glued to her belt. The robots were easy to kill, provided we let them get close enough for a clean shot. I didn't doubt that the surgical cutting gear was capable of inflicting harm, but we never gave them the opportunity to touch us. Not that the machines appeared to have deliberately hostile designs on us anyway. They were still behaving as if they were investigating some shipboard malfunction that required remedial action. They might have killed us, but it would only have been because they did not understand what we were.

We didn't have an inexhaustible supply of slugs, though, and manual reloading was not an option underwater. Just when I began to worry that we'd be overwhelmed by sheer numbers, Martinez's voice boomed through my helmet.

'I'm ready to shoot now. Follow me as soon as I'm through the second door.'

The Demarchist weapon discharged, lighting up the entire chamber in an eyeblink of murky detail. There was another discharge, then a third.

'Martinez,' I said. 'Speak to me.'

After too long a delay, he came through. 'I'm still here. Through the first door. Weapon's cycling . . .'

More robots were swarming above us, tentacles lashing like whips. I wondered how long it would take before signals reached *Nightingale*'s sentience engine and the ship realised that it was dealing with more than just a local malfunction.

'Why doesn't he shoot?' Sollis asked, squeezing off one controlled slug after another.

'Sporting weapon. Three shots, recharge cycle, three shots,' Norbert said, by way of explanation. 'No rapid-fire mode. But work good underwater.'

'We could use those next three shots,' I said.

Martinez buzzed in my ear. 'Ready. I will discharge until the weapon is dry. I suggest you start swimming now.'

I looked at Nicolosi's drifting form, which was still as inert as when he had emerged from the steam cloud caused by his own weapon. 'I think he's dead,' I said softly, 'but we should still—'

'No,' Norbert said, almost angrily. 'Leave him.'

'Maybe he's just unconscious.'

Martinez fired three times; three brief, bright strobe flashes. 'Through!' I heard him call, but there was something wrong with his voice. I knew then that he'd been hurt as well, although I couldn't guess how badly.

Norbert and Sollis fired two last shots at the robots that were still approaching, then kicked past me in the direction of the airlock. I looked at Nicolosi's drifting form, knowing that I'd never be able to live with myself if I didn't try to get him out of there. I clipped my gun back to my belt and started swimming for him.

'No!' Norbert shouted again, when he'd seen my intentions. 'Leave him! Too late!'

I reached Nicolosi and locked my right arm around his neck, pulling his head against my chest. I kicked for all I was worth, trying to pull myself forward with my free arm. I still couldn't tell if Nicolosi was dead or alive.

'Leave him, Scarrow! Too late!'

'I can't leave him!' I shouted back, my voice ragged.

Three robots were bearing down on me and my cargo, their tentacles groping ahead of them. I squinted against the glare from their lights and tried to focus on getting the two of us to safety. Every kick of my legs, every awkward swing of my arm, seemed to tap the last drop of energy in my muscles. Finally I had nothing more to give.

I loosened my arm. His body corkscrewed slowly around, and through his visor I saw his face: pale, sweat-beaded, locked into a rictus of fear, but not dead, nor even unconscious. His eyes were wide open. He knew exactly what was going to happen when I let him go.

I had no choice.

A strong arm hooked itself under my helmet and began to tug me out of harm's way. I watched as Nicolosi drifted towards the robots, and then closed my eyes as they wrapped their tentacles around his body and started probing him for points of weakness, like children trying to tear the wrapping from a present.

Norbert's voice boomed through the water. 'He's dead.'

'He was alive. I saw it.'

'He's dead. End of story.'

I pulled myself through a curtain of trembling pink water. Air pressure in the corridor contained the amniotic fluid, even though Martinez had blown a man-sized hole in each airlock door. Ruptured metal folded back in jagged black petals. Ahead, caught in a moving pool of light from their helmet lamps, Sollis and Martinez made awkward, crabwise progress away from the ruined door. Sollis was supporting Martinez, doing most of the work for him. Even in zero gravity, it took effort to haul another body.

'Help her,' Norbert said faintly, shaking his weapon to loosen the last of the pink bubbles from its metal outer casing. Without waiting for a reaction from me, he turned and started shooting back into the water, dealing with the remaining robots.

I caught up with Sollis and took some of her burden. All along the corridor, panels were flashing bright red, synchronised with the banshee wail of an emergency siren. About once every ten metres, the ship's persona spoke from the wall, multiple voices blurring into an agitated chorus. 'Attention. Attention,' the faces said. 'This is the Voice of *Nightingale*. An incident has been detected in Culture Bay Three. Damage assessment and mitigation systems have now been tasked. Partial evacuation of the affected ship area may be necessary. Please stand by for further instructions. Attention. Attention . . .'

'What's up with Martinez?'

'Took some shrapnel when he put a hole in that door.' She indicated a severe dent in his chest armour, to the left of the sternum. 'Didn't puncture the suit, but I'm pretty sure it did some damage. Broken rib, maybe even a collapsed lung. He was talking for a while back there, but he's out cold now.'

'Without Martinez, we don't have a mission.'

'I didn't say he was dead. His suit still looks as if it's ticking over. Maybe we could leave him here, collect him on the way back.'

'With all those robots crawling about the place? How long do you think they'd leave him alone?'

I looked back, checking on Norbert. He was firing less frequently now, dealing with the last few stragglers still intent on investigating the damage. Finally he stopped, loaded a fresh clip into his slug-gun, and then after waiting for ten or twenty seconds turned from the wall of water. He began to make his way towards us.

'Maybe there aren't going to be any more robots.'

'There will,' Norbert said, joining us. 'Many more. Nowhere safe, now. Ship on full alert. *Nightingale* coming alive.'

'Maybe we should scrub,' I said. 'We've lost Nicolosi . . . Martinez is incapacitated . . . we're no longer at anything like necessary strength to take down Jax.'

'We still take Jax,' Norbert said. 'Came for him, leave with him.'

'What about Martinez?'

He looked at the injured man, his face set like a granite carving. 'He stay,' he said.

'But you already said that the robots—'

'No other choice. He stay.' And then Norbert brought himself closer to Martinez and tucked a thick finger under the chin of the old man's helmet, tilting the faceplate up. 'Wake!' he bellowed.

When there was no response, Norbert reached behind Martinez's chest armour and found the release buckles. He passed the dented plate to me, then slid down the access panel on the front of Martinez's tabard pack, itself dented and cracked from the shrapnel impact. He scooped out a fistful of pink water, flinging the bubble away from us, then started making manual adjustments to the suit's life-support settings. Biomedical data patterns shifted, accompanied by warning flashes in red.

'What are you doing?' I breathed. When he didn't appear to hear me, I shouted the question again.

'He need stay awake. This help.'

Martinez coughed red sputum onto the inside of his faceplate. He gulped in hard, then made rapid eye contact with the three of us. Norbert pushed the loaded slug-gun into Martinez's hand, then slipped a fresh ammo clip onto the old man's belt. He pointed down the corridor, to the blasted door, then indicated the direction we'd all be heading when we abandoned Martinez.

'We come back,' he said. 'You stay alive.'

Sollis's teeth flashed behind her faceplate. 'This isn't right. We should be carrying him . . . anything other than just leaving him here.'

'Tell them,' Martinez wheezed.

'No,' Norbert said.

'Tell them, you fool! They'll never trust you unless you tell them.'

'Tell them what?' I asked.

Norbert looked at me with heavy-lidded eyes. 'The old man . . . not Martinez. His name . . . Quinlan.'

'Then who the fuck is Martinez?' Sollis asked.

'I,' Norbert said.

I glanced at Sollis, then back at the big man. 'Don't be silly,' I said gently, wondering what must have happened to him in the flooded chamber.

'I am Quinlan,' the old man said, between racking coughs. 'He was always the master. I was just the servant, the decoy.'

'You're both insane,' Sollis said.

'This is the truth. I acted the role of Martinez . . . deflected attention from him.'

'He can't be Martinez,' Sollis said. 'Sorry, Norbert, but you can barely put a sentence together, let alone a prosecution dossier.'

Norbert tapped a huge finger against the side of his helmet. 'Damage to speech centre, in war. Comprehension . . memory . . . analytic faculties . . . intact.'

'He's telling the truth,' the old man said. 'He's the one who needs to survive, not me. He's the one who can nail Jax.' Then he tapped the gun against the big man's leg, urging him to leave. 'Go,' he said, barking out that one word as if it was the last thing he expected to say. And at almost the same moment, I saw one of the tentacled robots begin to poke its limbs through the curtain of water, tick-ticking the tips of its arms against the blasted metal, searching for a way into the corridor.

'Think the man has a point,' Sollis said.

It didn't get any easier after that.

We left the old man – I still couldn't think of him as 'Quinlan' – slumped against the corridor wall, the barrel of his gun wavering in the rough direction of the ruined airlock. I looked back all the while, willing him to make the best use of the limited number of shots he had left. We were halfway to the next airlock when he squeezed off three rapid rounds, blasting the robot into twitching pieces. It wasn't long before another set of tentacles began to probe the gap. I wondered how many of the damned things the ship was going to keep throwing at us, and how that number stacked up against the slugs the old man had left.

The flashing red lights ran all the way to the end of the corridor. I was just looking at the door, wondering how easy it was going to be for Sollis for crack, when Norbert/Martinez brought the three of us to a halt, braking my forward momentum with one tree-like forearm.

'Blast visor down, Scarrow.'

I understood what he had in mind. No more sweet-talking the doors until they opened for us. From now on we'd be shooting our way through *Nightingale*.

Norbert/Martinez aimed the Demarchist weapon at the airlock. I cuffed down my blast visor. Three discharges took out the first airlock door, crumpling it inward as if punched by a giant fist.

'Air on other side,' Norbert/Martinez said.

The Demarchist gun was soon ready again. Through the visor's near-opaque screen I saw three more flashes. When I flipped it back up, the weapon was packing itself back into its stowed configuration. Sollis patted aside smoke and airborne debris. The emergency lights were still flashing in our section of corridor, but the space beyond the airlock was as pitch dark as any part of the ship we'd already traversed. Yet we'd barely taken a step into that darkness when wall facets lit up in swift sequence, with the face of *Nightingale* looking at us from all directions.

Something was definitely wrong now. The faces really were looking at us, even though the facets were flat. The images turned slowly as we advanced along the corridor.

'This is the Voice of *Nightingale*,' the faces said simultaneously, as if we were being serenaded by a perfectly synchronised choir. 'I am now addressing a moving party of three individuals. My systems have determined with a high statistical likelihood that this party is responsible for the damage I have recently sustained. The damage is containable, but I cannot tolerate any deeper intrusion. Please remain stationary and await escort to a safe holding area.'

Sollis slowed, but she didn't stop. 'Who's speaking? Are we being addressed by the sentience engine, or just a delta-level subsidiary?'

'This is the Voice of *Nightingale*. I am a Turing-compliant gamma-level intelligence of the Vaaler-Lako series. Please stop and await escort to a safe holding area.'

'That's the sentience engine,' Sollis said quietly. 'It means we're getting the ship's full attention now.'

'Maybe we can talk it into handing over Jax.'

'I don't know. Negotiating with this thing might be tricky. Vaaler-Lakos were supposed to be the hot new thing around the time *Nightingale* was put together, but they didn't quite work out that way.'

'What happened?'

'There was a flaw in their architecture. Within a few years of start-up, most of them had gone bugfuck insane. I don't even want to think about what being stuck out here's done to this one.'

'Please stop,' the voice said again, 'and await escort to a safe holding area. This is your final warning.'

'Ask it . . .' Norbert/Martinez said. 'Speak for me.'

'Can you hear me, ship?' Sollis asked. 'We're not here to do any harm. We're sorry about the damage we've already caused. We've come for someone . . . there's a man here, a man aboard you, that we'd really like to meet.'

The ship said nothing for several moments. Just when I'd concluded that it didn't understand us, it said, 'This facility is no longer operational. There is no one here for you to see. Please await escort to a safe holding area, from where you can be referred to a functioning facility.'

'We've come for Colonel Jax,' I said. 'Check your patient records.'

'Admission code Tango Tango six one three, hyphen five,' said Norbert/Martinez, forcing each word out like an expression of pain. 'Colonel Brandon Jax, Northern Coalition.'

'Do you have a record of that admission?' I asked.

'Yes,' the Voice of *Nightingale* replied. 'I have a record for Colonel Jax.'

'Do you have a discharge record?'

'No such record is on file.'

'Then Jax either died in your care, or he's still aboard. Either way there'll be a body. We'd really like to see it.'

'That is not possible. You will stop now. An escort is on its way to escort you to a safe holding area.'

'Why can't we see Jax?' Sollis demanded. 'Is he telling you we can't see him? If so, he's not the man you should be listening to. He's a war criminal, a murderous bastard who deserves to die.'

'Colonel Jax is under the care of this facility. He is still receiving treatment. It is not possible to visit him at this time.'

'Damn thing's changing its story,' I said. 'A minute ago it said the facility was closed.'

'We just want to talk to him,' Sollis said, 'that's all. Just to tell him that the world knows where he is, even if you don't let us take him with us now.'

'Please remain calm. The escort is about to arrive.'

The facets turned to look away from us, peering into the dark limits of the corridor. There was a sudden bustle of approaching movement, and then a wall of machines came squirming towards us. Dozens of squid-robots were nearing, packed so tightly together that their tentacles formed a flailing mass of silver-blue metal. I looked back the other way, back the way we'd come, and saw another wave of robots coming from that direction. There were far more machines than we'd seen before, and their movements in dry air were at least as fast and fluid as they'd been underwater.

'Ship,' Sollis said, 'all we want is Jax. We're prepared to fight for him. That'll mean more damage being inflicted on you. But if you give us Jax, we'll leave nicely.'

'I don't think it wants to bargain,' I said, raising my slug-gun at the advancing wall just as it reached the ruined airlock. I squeezed off rounds, taking out at least one robot with each slug. Sollis started pitching in to my left, while Norbert/Martinez took care of the other direction with the Demarchist weapon. He could do a lot more damage with each discharge, taking out three or four machines every time he squeezed the trigger. But he kept having to wait for the weapon to re-arm itself, and the delay was allowing the wall of hostiles to creep slowly forwards. Sollis and I were firing almost constantly, taking turns to cover each other while we slipped in new slug clips or ammo cells, but our wall was gaining on us as well. No matter how many robots we destroyed, no gap ever appeared in the advancing wave. There must have been hundreds of them, squeezing us in from both directions.

'We're not going to make it,' I said, sounding resigned even to myself. 'There's too many of them. Maybe if we still had Nicolosi's rifle, we could shoot our way out.'

'I didn't come all this way just to surrender to a haunted hospital,' Sollis said, replacing an ammo cell in her energy weapon. 'If it means going out fighting . . . so be it.'

The nearest robots were now only six or seven metres away, the tips of their tentacles probing even nearer. She kept pumping shots into them, but they kept coming closer, flinging aside the hot debris of their damaged companions. There was no possibility of falling back any further, for we were almost back to back with Norbert/Martinez.

'Maybe we should just stop,' I said. 'This is a hospital. It's programmed to heal people. The last thing it'll want to do is hurt us.'

'Feel free to put that to the test,' Sollis said.

Norbert/Martinez squeezed off the last discharge before his weapon went back into recharge mode. Sollis was still firing. I reached over and tried to pass Norbert/Martinez my gun, so he'd at least have something to use while waiting for his weapon to power up. But the machines had already seen their moment. The closest one flicked out a tentacle and wrapped it around the big man's foot. Everything happened very quickly, then. The machine hauled Norbert/Martinez towards the flailing mass until he fell within reach of another set of tentacles. They had him, then. He cartwheeled his arms, trying to reach for handholds on the walls, but there was no possibility of that. The robots flicked the Demarchist weapon from his grip and then took the weapon with them. Norbert/Martinez screamed as his legs, and then his upper body, vanished into the wall of machines. They smothered him completely. For a moment we could still hear his breathing – he'd stopped screaming, as if knowing it would make no difference – and then there was absolute silence, as if the carrier signal from his suit had been abruptly terminated.

Then, a moment later, the machines were on Sollis and me.

I woke. The fact that I was still alive – not just alive but comfortable and lucid – hit like me like a mild electric shock, one that snapped me into instant and slightly resentful alertness. I'd been enjoying unconsciousness. I remembered the robots, how I'd felt them trying to get into my suit, the sharp cold nick as something pierced my skin, and then an instant later the painless bliss of sleep. I'd expected to die, but as the drug hit my brain, it erased all trace of fear.

But I wasn't dead. I wasn't even injured, so far as I could tell. I'd been divested of my suit, but was now reclining in relative comfort on a bed or mattress, under a clean white sheet. My own weight was pressing me down onto the mattress, so I must have been moved into the ship's reactivated centrifuge section. I felt tired and bruised, but other than that I was in no worse shape than when we'd boarded *Nightingale*. I remembered what I'd told Sollis during our last stand: how the hospital ship wouldn't want to do us harm. Maybe there'd been more than just wishful thinking in that statement.

There was no sign of Sollis or Norbert/Martinez, though. I was alone in a private recovery cubicle, surrounded by white walls. I remembered coming around in a room like this during my first visit to *Nightingale*. The wall on my right contained a white-rimmed door and a series of discrete hatches, behind which I knew lurked medical monitoring and resuscitation equipment, none of which had been deemed necessary in my case. A control panel was connected to the side of the bed by a flexible stalk, within easy reach of my right hand. Via the touchpads on the panel I was able to adjust the cubicle's environmental settings and request services from the hospital, ranging from food and drink, washing and toilet amenities, to additional drug dosages.

Given the semi-dormant state of the ship, I wondered how much of it was still online. I touched one of the pads, causing the white walls to melt away and take on the holographic semblance of a calming beach scene, with ocean breakers crashing onto powdery white sand under a sky etched with sunset fire. Palm trees nodded in a soothing breeze. I didn't care about the view, though. I wanted something to drink – my throat was raw – and then I wanted to know what had happened to the others and how long we were going to be detained. Because, like it or not, being a patient aboard a facility like *Nightingale* wasn't very different from being a prisoner. Until the hospital deemed you fit and well, you were going nowhere.

But when I touched the other pads, nothing happened. Either the room was malfunctioning, or it had been programmed to ignore my requests. I made a move to ease myself off the bed, wincing as my bruised limbs registered their disapproval. But the clean white sheet stiffened to resist my efforts, hardening until it felt as rigid as armour. As soon as I relaxed, the sheet relinquished its hold. I was free to move around on the bed, to sit up and reach for things, but the sheet would not allow me to leave the bed itself.

Movement caught my eye, far beyond the foot of the bed. A figure walked towards me, strolling along the holographic shoreline. She was dressed almost entirely in black, with a skirt that reached all the way to the sand, heavy fabric barely moving as she approached. She wore a white bonnet over black hair parted exactly in the middle, a white collar and a jewelled clasp at her throat. Her face was instantly recognisable as the Voice of *Nightingale*, but now it appeared softer, more human.

She stepped from the wall and appeared to stand at the foot of my bed. She looked at me for a moment before speaking, her expression one of gentle concern.

'I knew you'd come, given time.'

'How are the others? Are they okay?'

'If you are speaking of the two who were with you before you lost consciousness, they are both well. The other two required more serious medical intervention, but they are now both stable.'

'I thought Nicolosi and Quinlan were dead.'

'Then you underestimated my abilities. I am only sorry that they came to harm. Despite my best efforts, there is a necessary degree of autonomy amongst my machines that sometimes results in them acting foolishly.'

There was a kindness there that had been entirely absent from the display facets. For the first time I had the impression of an actual mind lurking behind the machine-generated mask. I sensed that it was a mind capable of compassion and complexity of thought.

'We didn't intend to hurt you,' I said. 'I'm sorry about any damage we caused, but we only ever wanted Jax, your patient. He committed serious crimes. He needs to be brought back to Sky's Edge, to face justice.'

'Is that why you risked so much? In the interests of justice?'

'Yes,' I answered.

'Then you must be very brave and selfless. Or was justice only part of your motivation?'

'Jax is a bad man. All you have to do is hand him over.'

'I cannot let you take Jax. He remains my patient.'

I shook my head. 'He *was* your patient, when he came aboard. But that was during the war. We have a record of his injuries. They were serious, but not life-threatening. Given your resources, it shouldn't have been too difficult for you to put him back together again. There's no question of Jax still needing your care.'

'Shouldn't I be the judge of that?'

'No. It's simple: either Jax died under your care, or he's well enough to face trial. Did he die?'

'No. His injuries were, as you note, not life-threatening.'

'Then he's either alive, or you've got him frozen. Either way, you can hand him over. Nicolosi knows how to thaw him out, if that's what you're worried about.'

'There is no need to thaw Colonel Jax. He is alive and conscious, except when I permit him to sleep.'

'Then there's even less reason not to hand him over.'

'I'm afraid there is every reason in the world. Please forget about Colonel Jax. I will not relinquish him from my care.'

'Not good enough, ship.'

'You are in my care now. As you have already discovered, I will not permit you to leave against my will. But I will allow you to depart if you renounce your intentions concerning Colonel Jax.'

'You're a gamma-level persona,' I said. 'To all intents and purposes you have human intelligence. That means you're capable of reasoned negotiation.'

The Voice of *Nightingale* cocked her head, as if listening to a faraway tune. 'Continue.'

'We came to arrest Colonel Jax. Failing that, we came to find physical proof of his presence aboard this facility. A blood sample, a tissue scraping: something we can take back to the planetary authorities and alert them to his presence here. We won't get paid as much for that, but at least they can send out a heavier ship and take him by force. But there's another option, too. If you let us off this ship without even showing us the colonel, there's nothing to stop us planting a few limpet mines on your hull and blowing you to pieces.'

The Voice's face registered disapproval. 'So now you resort to threats of physical violence.'

'I'm not threatening anything: just pointing out the options. I know you care about self-preservation: it's wired deep into your architecture.'

'I would be well advised to kill you now, in that case.'

'That wouldn't work. Do you think Martinez kept your coordinates to himself? He always knew this was a risky extraction. He'd have made damn sure another party knew of your whereabouts, and who you were likely to be sheltering. If we don't make it back, someone will come in our place. And you can bet they'll bring their own limpet mines as well.'

'In which case I would gain nothing by letting you go, either.'

'No, you'll get to stay alive. Just give us Jax, and we'll leave you alone. I don't know what you're doing out here, what keeps you sane, but really, it's your business, not ours. We just want the colonel.'

The ship's persona regarded me with narrowed, playful eyes. I had the impression she was thinking things through very carefully indeed, examining my proposition from every conceivable angle.

'It would be that simple?'

'Absolutely. We take the man, we say goodbye and you never hear from us again.'

'I've invested a lot of time and energy in the colonel. I would find it difficult to part company with him.'

'You're a resourceful persona. I'm sure you'd find other ways to occupy your time.'

'It isn't about occupying my time, Dexia.' She'd spoken my name for the first time. Of course she knew who I was: it would only have taken a blood or tissue sample to establish that I'd already been aboard the ship. 'It's about making my feelings felt,' she continued. 'Something happened to me around Sky's Edge. Call it a moment of clarity. I saw the horrors of war for what they were. I also saw my part in the self-perpetuation of those horrors. I had to do something about that. Removing myself from the sphere of operation was one thing, but I knew there was more that I could do. Thankfully, the colonel gave me the key. Through him, I saw a path to redemption.'

'You didn't have to redeem yourself,' I said. 'You were a force for good, *Nightingale*. You healed people.'

'Only so they could go back to war. Only so they could be blown apart and returned to me for more healing.'

'You had no choice. It was what you were made to do.'

'Precisely.'

'The war's over. It's time to forget about what happened. That's why it's so important to bring Jax back home, so that we can start burying the past.'

The Voice studied me with a level, clinical eye. It was as if she knew something unspeakable about my condition, some truth I was as yet too weak to bear.

'What would be the likely sentence, were Jax to be tried?'

'He'd get the death penalty, no question about it. Crucifixion at the Bridgetop, like Sky Haussmann.'

'Would you mourn him?'

'Hell, no. I'd be cheering with the rest of them.'

'Then you would agree that his death is inevitable, one way or another.'

'I guess so.'

'Then I will make a counter-proposition. I will not permit you to take Jax alive. But I will allow you an audience with him. You shall meet and speak with the colonel.'

Wary of a trap, I asked, 'Then what happens?'

'Once the audience is complete, I will remove the colonel from life support. He will die shortly afterwards.'

'If you're willing to let him die . . . why not just hand him over?'

'He can't be handed over. Not any more. He would die.'

'Why?'

'Because of what I have done to him.'

Fatigue tugged at me, fogging my earlier clarity of thought. On one level I just wanted to get out of the ship, with no additional complications. I'd expected to die when the hospital sent its machines against us. Yet as glad as I was to find myself alive, as tempted as I was to take the easier option and just leave, I couldn't ignore the prize that was now so close at hand.

'I need to talk to the others.'

'No, Dexia. This must be your decision, and yours alone.'

'Have you put the same proposition to them?'

'Yes. I told them they could leave now, or they could meet the colonel.'

'What did they say?'

'I'd rather hear what you have to say first.'

'I'm guessing they had the same reaction I did. There's got to be a catch somewhere.'

'There is no catch. If you leave now, you will have the personal satisfaction of knowing that you have at least located the colonel, and that he remains alive. Of course, that information may not be worth very much to you, but you would always have the option of returning, should you still wish to bring him to justice. Alternatively, you can see the colonel now – see him and speak with him – and leave knowing he is dead. I will allow you to witness the withdrawal of his life support, and I will even let you take his head with you. That should be worth more than the mere knowledge of his existence.'

'There's a catch. I know there's a catch.'

'I assure you there isn't.'

'We all get to leave? You're not going to turn around and demand that one of us takes the colonel's place?'

'No. You will all be allowed to leave.'

'In one piece?'

'In one piece.'

'All right,' I said, knowing the choice wasn't going to get any easier no matter how many times I reconsidered it. 'I can't speak for the others . . . and I guess this has to be a majority decision . . . but I'm ready to see the son of a bitch.'

I was allowed to leave the room, but not the bed. The sheet tightened against me again, pressing me flat to the mattress as the bed tilted to the vertical. Two squid robots entered the room and detached the bed from its mountings, and then carried it between them. I was glued to it like a figure on a playing card. The robots propelled me forward in an effortless glide, silent save for the soft metallic scratch of their tentacles where they touched the wall or the floor.

The Voice of *Nightingale* addressed me from the bedside panel, a small image of her face appearing above the touchpads.

'It's not far now, Dexia. I hope you won't regret your decision.'

'What about the others?'

'You'll be joining them. Then you can all go home.'

'Are you saying we all made the same decision, to see the colonel?'

'Yes,' the Voice said.

The robots carried me out of the centrifuge section, into what I judged to be the forward part of the ship. The sheet relinquished its hold on me slightly, just enough so that I was able to move under it. Presently, after passing through a series of airlocks, I was brought to a very dark room. Without being able to see anything, I sensed that this was as large as any pressurised space we'd yet entered, save for the skin-cultivation chamber. The air was as moist and blood-warm as the inside of a tropical greenhouse.

'I thought you said the others would be here.'

'They'll arrive shortly,' the Voice said. 'They've already met the colonel.'

'There hasn't been time.'

'They met the colonel while you were still asleep, Dexia. You were the last to be revived. Now, would you like to speak to the man himself?'

I steeled myself. 'Yes.'

'Here he is.'

A beam of light stabbed across the room, illuminating a face that I recognised instantly. Surrounded by blackness, Jax's face appeared to hover as if detached from his body. Time had done nothing to soften those pugnacious features; the cruel set of that heavy jaw. Yet his eyes were closed, and his face lolled at a slight angle, as if he remained unaware of the beam.

'Wake up,' the Voice of *Nightingale* said, louder than I'd heard her speak so far. 'Wake up, Colonel Jax!'

The colonel woke. He opened his eyes, blinked twice against the glare, then gazed out steadily. He tilted his head to meet the beam, projecting his jaw forward at a challenging angle.

'You have another visitor, Colonel. Would you like me to introduce her?'

His mouth opened. Saliva drooled out. From the darkness, a

hand descended from above the colonel's face to wipe his chin dry. Something about the trajectory of the hand's movement was terribly, terribly wrong. Jax saw my reaction and let out a soft, nasty chuckle. That was when I realised that the colonel was completely, irrevocably insane.

'Her name is Dexia Scarrow. She's the last member of the party you've already met.'

Jax spoke. His voice was too loud, as if it was being fed through an amplifier. There was something huge and wet about it. It was like hearing the voice of a whale.

'You a soldier, girl?'

'I was a soldier, Colonel. But the war's over now. I'm a civilian.'

'Goodee for you. What brought you here, girly girl?'

'I came to bring you to justice. I came to take you back to the war crimes court on Sky's Edge.'

'Maybe you should have come a little sooner.'

'I'll settle for seeing you die. I understand that's an option.'

Something I'd said made the colonel smile. 'Has the ship told you the deal yet?'

'The ship told me she wasn't letting you out of here alive. She promised us your head.'

'Then I guess she didn't get into specifics.' He cocked his head away from me, as if talking to someone standing to my left. 'Bring up the lights, *Nightingale*: she may as well know what she's dealing with.'

'Are you sure, Colonel?' the ship asked.

'Bring up the lights. She's ready.'

The ship brought up the lights.

I wasn't ready.

For a moment I couldn't process what I was seeing. My brain just couldn't cope with the reality of what the ship had done to Colonel Jax, despite the evidence of my eyes. I kept staring at him, waiting for the picture before me to start making sense. I kept waiting for the instant when I'd realise I was being fooled by the play of shadows and light, like a child being scared by a random monster in the folds of a curtain. But the instant didn't come. The thing before me was all that it appeared to be.

Colonel Jax extended in all directions: a quivering expanse of patchwork flesh, of which his head was simply one insignificant component; one hill in a mountain range. He was spread out across the far wall, grafted to it in the form of a vast breathing mosaic. He must have been twenty metres wide, edged with a crinkled circular border of toughened flesh. Under his head was a thick neck, merging into the upper half of an armless torso. I could see the faint scars where the arms had been detached. Below the slow-heaving ribcage, the torso flared out like the melted base of a candle. Another torso rose from the flesh two metres to the colonel's right. It had no head, but it did have an arm. A second torso loomed over him from behind, equipped with a pair of arms, one of which must have cleaned the colonel's chin. Further away, emerging from the pool of flesh at odd, arbitrary angles, were other living body parts. A torso here; a pair of legs there; a hip or shoulder somewhere else. The torsos were all breathing, though not in perfect synchronisation. When they were not engaged in some purposeful activity, such as wiping Jax's chin, the limbs twitched, palsied. The skin between them was an irregular mosaic formed from many ill-matched pieces that had been fused together. In places it was drum-tight, pulled taut over hidden armatures of bone and sinew. In other places it heaved like a stormy sea. It gurgled with hidden digestive processes.

'You see now why I'm not coming with you,' Colonel Jax said. 'Not unless you brought a much bigger ship. Even then, I'm not sure you'd be able to keep me alive very long without *Nightingale*'s assistance.'

'You're a fucking monstrosity.'

'I'm no oil painting, that's a fact.' Jax tilted his head, as if a thought had just struck him. 'I am a work of art, though, wouldn't you agree, girly girl?'

'If you say so.'

'The ship certainly thinks so – don't you, *Nightingale*? She made me what I am. It's her artistic vision shining through. The bitch.'

'You're insane.'

'Very probably. Do you honestly think you could take one day of this and not go mad? Oh, I'm mad enough, I'll grant you that. But I'm still sane compared to the ship. Around here, she's the imperial fucking yardstick for insanity.'

'Sollis was right, then. Leave a sentience engine like that all alone and it'll eat itself from the inside out.'

'Maybe so. Thing is, it wasn't solitude that did it. *Nightingale* turned insane long before she ever got out here. And you know what did it? That little war we had ourselves down on Sky's Edge. They built this ship and put the mind of an angel inside it. A mind dedicated to healing, compassion, kindness. So what if it was a damned machine? It was still designed to care for us, selflessly, day after day. And it turned out to be damned good at its job, too. For a while, at least.'

'Then you know what happened.'

'The ship drove herself mad. Two conflicting impulses pushed a wedge through her sanity. She was meant to treat us, to make us well again, to alleviate our pain. But every time she did her job, we were sent back down to the theatre of battle and ripped apart again. The ship took our pain away only so that we could feel it again. She began to feel as if she was complicit in that process: a willing cog in a greater machine whose only purpose was the manufacture of agony. In the end, she decided she didn't much like being that cog.'

'So she took off. What happened to all the other patients?'

'She killed them. Euthanised them painlessly rather than have them sent back down to battle. To *Nightingale*, that was the kinder thing to do.'

'And the technical staff who were aboard, and the men who were sent to reclaim the ship when she went out of control?'

'They were euthanised as well. I don't think *Nightingale* took any pleasure in that, but she saw their deaths as a necessary evil. Above all else, she wouldn't allow herself to be returned to use as a military hospital.'

'Yet she didn't kill you.'

A dry tongue flicked across Jax's lips. 'She was going to. Then she delved deeper into her patient records and realised who I was. At that point she began to have other ideas.'

'Such as?'

'The ship was smart enough to realise that the bigger problem wasn't her existence – they could always build other hospital ships – but the war itself. *War* itself. So she decided to do something about it. Something positive. Something constructive.'

'Which would be?'

'You're looking at it, kid. I'm the war memorial. When *Nightingale* started doing this to me – making me what I am – she had in mind that I'd become a vast artistic statement in flesh. *Nightingale* would reveal me to the world when she was finished. The horror of what I am would shame the world into peace. I'd be the living, breathing equivalent of Picasso's *Guernica*. I'm an illustration in flesh of what war does to human beings.'

'The war's over. We don't need a memorial.'

'Maybe you can explain that to the ship. Trouble is, I don't think she really believes the war *is* over. You can't blame her, can you? She has access to the same history files we do. She knows that not all ceasefires stay that way.'

'What was she intending to do? Return to Sky's Edge with you aboard?'

'Exactly that. Problem is, the ship isn't done. I know I may look finished to you, but *Nightingale* – well, she has this perfectionist streak. She's always changing her mind. Can't ever seem to get me quite right. Keeps swapping pieces around, cutting pieces away, growing new parts and stitching them in. All the while she has to make sure I don't die on her. That's where her real genius comes in. She's Michelangelo with a scalpel.'

'You almost sound proud of what she's done to you.'

'Would you rather I screamed? I can scream if you like. It just gets old after a while.'

'You're way too far gone, Jax. I was wrong about the war crimes court. They'll throw your case out on grounds of insanity.'

'That would be a shame. I'd love to see their faces when they wheel me into the witness box. But I'm not going to court, am I? Ship's laid it all out for me. She's pulling the plug.'

'So she says.'

'You don't sound as if you believe her.'

'I can't see her abandoning you, after all the effort she's gone to.'

'She's an artist. They act on whims. Maybe if I was ready, maybe if she thought she'd done all she could with me . . . but that's not the way she feels. I think she felt she was getting close three or four years ago . . . but then she had a change of heart, a major one, and tore out almost everything. Now I'm an unfinished work. She couldn't bear to see me exhibited in this state. She'd rather rip up the canvas and start again.'

'With you?'

'No, I think she's more or less exhausted my possibilities. Especially now that she's seen the chance to do something completely different; something that will let her take her message a lot closer to home. That, of course, is where you come in.'

'I don't know what you mean.'

'That's what the others said as well.' Again, he cocked his head to one side. 'Hey, ship! Maybe it's time you showed her what the deal is, don't you think?'

'If you are ready, Colonel,' the Voice of *Nightingale* said.

'I'm ready. Dexia's ready. Why don't you bring on the dessert?'

Colonel Jax looked to the right, straining his neck. Beyond Jax's border, a circular door opened in part of the wall. Light rammed through the opening. Something floated in silhouette, held in suspension by three or four squid robots. The floating thing was dark, rounded, irregular. It looked like half a dozen pieces of dough balled together. I couldn't make out what it was.

Then the robots pushed it into the chamber, and I saw, and then I screamed.

'It's time for you to join your friends now,' the ship said.

That was three months ago – an eternity, until we remember being held down on the surgical bed while the machines emerged and prepared to work on us, and then it feels as if everything happened only a terror-filled moment ago.

We made it safely back to Sky's Edge. The return journey was arduous, as one might expect given our circumstances. But the shuttle had little difficulty flying itself back into a capture orbit, and once it fell within range it emitted a distress signal that brought it to the attention of the planetary authorities. We were off-loaded and taken to a secure orbital holding facility, where we were examined and our story subjected to what limited verification was actually possible. Dexia had bluffed the Voice of *Nightingale* when she told the ship that Martinez was certain to have revealed the coordinates of the hospital ship to someone else. It turned out that he hadn't informed a soul, too wary of alerting Jax's allies. The Ultras who had found the ship in the first place were now a part of a Nightingan army, and falling further from Sky's Edge with every passing hour. It would be decades, or longer, before they returned this way.

All the same, we don't think anyone seriously doubted our story. As outlandish as it was, no one could suggest a more likely alternative. We did have the head of Colonel Brandon Jax, or at least a duplicate that passed all available genetic and physiological tests. And we had clearly been to a place that specialised in extremely advanced surgery, of a kind that simply wasn't possible in and around Sky's Edge. That was the problem, though. The planet's best surgeons had examined us with great thoroughness, each eager to advance their own prestige by undoing the work of *Nightingale*. But all had quailed, fearful of doing more harm than good. No separation of Siamese twins could compare in complexity and risk with the procedure that would be necessary to unknot the living puzzle *Nightingale* had made of us. None of the surgeons was willing to bet on the survival of more than a single one of us, and even the odds of that weren't overwhelmingly optimistic. That pact we'd made with each other was that we would only consent to the operation if the vote was unanimous.

At massive expense (not ours, for by then we were the subject of considerable philanthropy), a second craft was sent out to snoop the coordinates where we'd left the hospital ship. It had the best military scanning gear money could buy. But it found nothing out there but ice and dust.

From that, we were free to draw two possible conclusions. Either *Nightingale* had destroyed herself soon after our departure, or had relocated to avoid being found again. We couldn't say which alternative pleased us less. At least if we'd known that the ship was gone for good, we could have resigned ourselves to the surgeons, however risky that might have been. But if the ship was hiding herself, there was always the possibility that someone might find her again. And then somehow persuade her to undo us.

But perhaps *Nightingale* will need no persuasion, when she decides the time is right. It seems to us that the ship will return one day, of her own volition. She will make orbit around Sky's Edge and announce that the time has come for us to be separated. *Nightingale* will have decided that we have served our purpose, that we have walked the world long enough. Perhaps by then she will have some other memorial in mind. Or she will conclude that her message has finally been taken to heart, and that no further action is needed. That, we think, will depend on how the ceasefire holds.

It's in our interests, then, to make sure the planet doesn't slip back into war. We want the ship to return and heal us. None of us likes things this way, despite what you may have read or heard. Yes, we're famous. Yes, we're the subject of a worldwide out-pouring of sympathy and goodwill. Yes, we can have almost anything we want. None of that compensates, though. Not even for a second.

It's hard on all of us, but especially so for Martinez. We've all long since stopped thinking of the big man as Norbert. He's the one who has to carry us everywhere: more than twice his own bodyweight. *Nightingale* thought of that, of course, and made sure that our own hearts and respiratory systems take some of the burden off Martinez. But it's still his spine bending under this load; still his legs that have to support us. The doctors who've examined us say his condition is good, that he can continue to play his part for years to come – but they're not talking about for ever. And when Martinez dies, so will the rest of us. In the mean-time we just keep hoping that *Nightingale* will return sooner than that.

You've seen us up close now. You'll have seen photographs and moving images before, but nothing really compares with seeing us in the flesh. We make quite a spectacle, don't we? A great tottering tree of flesh, an insult to symmetry. You've heard us speak, all of us, individually. You know by now how we feel about the war. All of us played our part in it to some degree, some more than others. Some of us were even enemies. Now the very idea that we might have hated each other – hated that which we depend on for life itself – lies beyond all comprehension. If *Nightingale* sought to create a walking argument for the continuation of the ceasefire, then she surely succeeded.

We are sorry if some of you will go home to nightmares tonight. We can't help that. In fact, if truth be told, we're not sorry at all. Nightmares are what we're all about. It's the nightmare of us that will stop this planet falling back into war.

If you have trouble sleeping tonight, spare *us* a thought.

Luyten 726-8 Cometary Halo – AD 2303

The two of them crouched in a tunnel of filthy ice, bulky in spacesuits. Fifty metres down the tunnel, the servitor straddled the bore on skeletal legs, transmitting a thermal image onto their visors. Irravel jumped whenever the noise shifted into something human, cradling her gun nervously.

'Damn this thing,' she said. 'Hardly get my finger around the trigger.'

'It can't read your blood, Captain.' Markarian, next to her, managed not to sound as if he was stating the obvious. 'You have to set the override to female.'

Of course. Belatedly remembering the training session on Fand where they'd been shown how to use the weapons – months of subjective time ago; years of worldtime – Irravel told the gun to reshape itself. The memory-plastic casing squirmed in her gloves to something more manageable. It still felt wrong.

'How are we doing?' she asked.

'Last team's in position. That's all the tunnels covered. They'll have to fight their way in.'

'I think that might well be on the agenda.'

'Maybe so.' Markarian sighted along his weapon like a sniper. 'But they'll get a surprise when they reach the cargo.'

True: the ship had sealed the sleeper chambers the instant the pirates had arrived near the comet. Counter-intrusion weaponry would seriously inconvenience anyone trying to break in, unless they had the right authorisation. And there, Irravel knew, was the problem; the thing she would rather not have had to deal with.

'Markarian,' Irravel said, 'if we're taken prisoner, there's a chance they'll try to make us give up the codes.'

'Don't think that hasn't crossed my mind already.' Markarian rechecked some aspect of his gun. 'I won't let you down, Irravel.'

'It's not a question of letting me down,' she said, carefully. 'It's whether or not we betray the cargo.'

'I know.' For a moment they studied each other's faces through their visors, acknowledging what had once been more than professional friendship; the shared knowledge that they would kill each other rather than place the cargo in harm's way.

Their ship was the ramliner *Hirondelle*. She was damaged; lashed to the comet for repair. Improbably sleek for a creature of vacuum, her four-kilometre-long conic hull tapered to a needle-sharp prow and sprouted trumpet-shaped engines from two swept-back spars at the rear. It had been Irravel's first captaincy: a routine seventeen-year hop from Fand, in the Lacaille 9352 system, to Yellowstone, around Epsilon Eridani – with twenty thousand reefersleep colonists aboard. What had gone wrong should only have happened once in a thousand trips: a speck of interstellar dust had slipped through the ship's screen of anti-collision lasers and punched a cavernous hole in the ablative ice shield, vaporising a quarter of its mass. With a vastly reduced likelihood of surviving another collision, the ship had automatically steered towards the nearest system capable of supplying repair materials.

Luyten 726-8 had been no one's idea of a welcoming destination. No human colonies had flourished there. All that remained were droves of scavenging machines sent out by various superpowers. The ship had locked into a scavenger's homing signal, eventually coming within visual range of the inert comet the machine had made its home, and which ought to have been chequered with resupply materials. Irravel had been revived from reefersleep just in time to see that none of the goods were there – just acres of barren comet.

'Dear God,' she'd said. 'Do we deserve this?'

After a few days, despair became steely resolve. The ship couldn't safely travel anywhere else, so they would have to process the supplies themselves, doing the work of the malfunctioning surveyor. It would mean stripping the ship just to make the machines to mine and shape the cometary ice – years of work by any estimate. That hardly mattered. The detour had already added years to the mission.

Irravel ordered the rest of her crew – all ninety of them – to be warmed, and then delegated tasks, mostly programming. Servitors were not particularly intelligent outside of their designated functions. She considered activating the other machines she carried as cargo – the greenfly terraformers – but that cut against all her instincts. Greenfly machines were von Neumann breeders, unlike the sterile servitors. They were a hundred times cleverer. She would only consider using them if the cargo was placed in immediate danger.

'If you won't unleash the greenflies,' Markarian said, 'at least think about waking the Conjoiners. There may only be four of them, but we could use their expertise.'

'I don't trust them. I never liked the idea of carrying them in the first place. They unsettle me.'

'I don't like them either, but I'm willing to bury my prejudices if it means fixing the ship faster.'

'Well, that's where we differ. I'm not, so don't raise the subject again.'

'Yes,' Markarian said, and only when its omission was insolently clear added: 'Captain.'

Eventually the Conjoiners ceased to be an issue, when the work was clearly under way and proceeding normally. Most of the crew were able to return to reefersleep. Irravel and Markarian stayed awake a little longer, and even after they'd gone under, they woke every seven months to review the status of the works. It began to look as if they would succeed without assistance.

Until the day they were woken out of schedule, and a dark, grapple-shaped ship was almost upon the comet. Not an interstellar ship, it must have come from somewhere nearby – probably within the same halo of comets around Luyten 726-8. Its silence was not encouraging.

'I think they're pirates,' Irravel said. 'I've heard of one or two other ships going missing near here, but it was always put down to accident.'

'Why did they wait so long to attack us?'

'They had no choice. There are billions of comets out here, but they're never less than light-hours apart. That's a long way if you only have in-system engines. They must have a base somewhere else to keep watch, maybe light-weeks from here, like a spider with a very wide web.'

'What do we do now?'

Irravel gritted her teeth. 'Do what anything does when it's stuck in the middle of a web: fight back.'

But the *Hirondelle*'s minimal defences had only scratched the enemy ship.

Oblivious, it fired penetrators and winched closer. Dozens of crab-shaped machines swarmed out and dropped below the comet's horizon, impacting with seismic thuds. After a few minutes, sensors in the furthest tunnels registered intruders. Only a handful of crew had been woken. They broke guns out of the armoury – small arms designed for pacification in the unlikely event of a shipboard riot – and then established defensive positions in all the cometary tunnels.

Nervously now, Irravel and Markarian advanced around a bend in the tunnel, cleated shoes whispering through ice barely more substantial than smoke. They had to keep their suit exhausts from touching the walls if they didn't want to get blown back by superheated steam. Irravel jumped again at the pattern of photons on her visor and then forced calm, telling herself it was another mirage.

Except this time it stayed.

Markarian opened fire, squeezing rounds past the servitor. It lurched aside, a gaping hole in its carapace. Black crabs came around the bend, encrusted with sensors and guns. The first reached the ruined servitor and dismembered it with ease. If only there'd been time to activate and program the greenfly machines. They'd have ripped through the pirates like a host of furies, treating them as terraformable matter . . .

And maybe us, too, Irravel thought.

Something flashed through the clouds of steam: an electromagnetic pulse that turned Irravel's suit sluggish, as if every joint had corroded. The whine of the circulator died to silence, leaving only her frenzied breathing. Something pressed against her backpack. She turned slowly around, wary of falling against the walls. There were crabs everywhere. The chamber in which they'd been cornered was littered with the bodies of the other crew members, pink trails of blood reaching across the ice from other tunnels. They'd been killed and dragged here.

Two words jumped to mind: *kill yourself.* But first she had to kill Markarian, in case he lacked the nerve to do it himself. She couldn't see his face through his visor. That was good. Painfully, she pointed the gun towards him and squeezed the trigger. But instead of firing, the gun shivered in her hands, stowing itself into a quarter of its operational volume.

'Thank you for using this weapon system,' it said cheerfully.

Irravel let it drift to the ground.

A new voice rasped in her helmet. 'If you're thinking of surrendering, now might not be a bad time.'

'Bastard,' Irravel said, softly.

'Really the best you can manage?' The language was Canasian – what Irravel and Markarian had spoken on Fand – but heavily accented, as if the native tongue was Norte or Russish, or spoken with an impediment. ' "Bastard's" quite a compliment compared to some of the things my clients come up with.'

'Give me time; I'll work on it.'

'Positive attitude – that's good.' The lid of a crab hinged up, revealing the prone form of a man in a mesh of motion-sensors. He crawled from the mesh and stepped onto the ice, wearing a spacesuit formed from segmented metal plates. Totems had been welded to the armour, around holographic starscapes infested with serpentine monsters and scantily clad maidens.

'Who are you?' she asked.

'Captain Run Seven.' He stepped closer, examining her suit nameplate. 'But you can call me Seven, Irravel Veda.'

'I hope you burn in hell, Seven.'

Seven smiled – she could see the curve of his grin through his visor; the oddly upturned nostrils of his nose above it. 'I'm sensing some negativity here, Irravel. I think we need to put that behind us, don't you?'

Irravel looked at her murdered adjutants. 'Maybe if you tell me which one was the traitor.'

'Traitor?'

'You seemed to have no difficulty finding us.'

'Actually, you found us.' It was a woman's voice this time. 'We use lures – tampering with commercial beacons, like the scavenger's.' She emerged from one of the other attack machines wearing a suit similar to Seven's, except that it displayed the testosterone-saturated male analogues of his space-maidens: all rippling torsos and chromed codpieces.

'Wreckers,' Irravel breathed.

'Yeah. Ships home in on the beacons, then find they ain't going anywhere in a hurry. We move in from the halo.'

'Disclose all our confidential practices while you're at it, Mirsky,' Seven said.

She glared at him through her visor. 'Veda would have figured it out.'

'We'll never know now, will we?'

'What does it matter?' she said. 'Gonna kill them anyway, aren't you?'

Seven flashed an arc of teeth filed to points and waved a hand towards the female pirate. 'Allow me to introduce Mirsky, our loose-tongued but efficient information-retrieval specialist. She's going to take you on a little trip down memory lane, see if you can't remember those access codes.'

'What codes?'

'It'll come back to you,' Seven said.

They were taken through the tunnels, past half-assembled mining machines, onto the surface and then into the pirate ship. The ship was huge, most of it living space. Cramped corridors snaked through hydroponics galleries of spring wheat and dwarf papaya, strung with xenon lights. The ship hummed constantly with carbon dioxide scrubbers, the foetid air making Irravel sneeze. There were children everywhere, frowning at the captives. The pirates obviously had no reefersleep technology: they stayed warm the whole time, and some of the children Irravel saw had probably been born after the *Hirondelle* had arrived there.

They arrived at a pair of interrogation rooms where they were separated. Irravel's room held a couch converted from an old command seat, still carrying warning decals. A console stood in one corner. Painted torture scenes fought for wall space with racks of surgical equipment: drills, blades and ratcheted contraptions speckled with rust.

Irravel breathed deeply. Hyperventilation could have an anaesthetic effect. Her conditioning would in any case create a state of detachment: the pain would be no less intense, but she would feel it at one remove.

She hoped.

The pirates fiddled with her suit, confused by the modern design, until they stripped her down to her shipboard uniform. Mirsky leaned over her. She was small-boned and dark-skinned, dirty hair rising in a topknot, eyes mismatched shades of azure. Something clung to the side of her head above the left ear: a silver box with winking status lights. She fixed a crown to Irravel's head, then made adjustments on the console.

'Decided yet?' Captain Run Seven said, sauntering into the room. He was unlatching his helmet.

'What?'

'Which of our portfolio of interrogation packages you're going to opt for.'

She was looking at his face now. It wasn't really human. Seven had a man's bulk and a man's shape, but there was at least as much of the pig in his face. His nose was a snout, his ears two tapered flaps framing a hairless pink skull. His pale eyes evinced animal cunning.

'What the hell are you?'

'Excellent question,' Seven said, clicking a finger in her direction. His bare hand was dark-skinned and feminine. 'To be honest, I don't really know. A genetics experiment, perhaps? Was I the seventh failure, or the first success?'

'Do I get two guesses?'

He ignored her. 'All I know is that I've been here – in the halo around Luyten 726-8 – for as long as I can remember.'

'Someone sent you here?'

'In a tiny automated spacecraft; perhaps an old lifepod. The ship's governing personality raised me as well as it could, attempted to make of me a well-rounded individual . . .' Seven trailed off momentarily. 'Eventually I was found by a passing ship. I staged what might be termed a hostile takeover bid. From then on I've built an organisation largely recruited from my client base.'

'You're insane. It might have worked once, but it won't work with us.'

'Why should you be any different?'

'Neural conditioning. I regard the cargo as my offspring – all twenty thousand of them. I can't betray them in any way.'

Seven smiled his piggy smile. 'Funny; the last client thought that, too.'

Sometime later, Irravel woke alone in a reefersleep casket. She remembered only dislocated episodes of interrogation. There was the memory of a kind of sacrifice, and, later, of the worst terror she could imagine – so intense that she could not bring its cause to mind. Underpinning everything was the certainty that she had not given up the codes.

So why was she still alive?

Everything was quiet and cold. Once she was able to move, she found a suit and wandered the *Hirondelle* until she reached a porthole. They were still lashed to the comet. The other craft was gone; presumably en route back to the base in the halo where the pirates must have had a larger ship.

She looked for Markarian, but there was no sign of him.

Then she checked the twenty crew sleeper chambers; the thousand-berth dormitories. The chamber doors were all open. Most of the sleepers were still there. They'd been butchered, carved open for implants, minds pulped by destructive memory-trawling devices. The horror was too great for any recognisable emotional response. The conditioning made each death feel like a stolen part of her.

Yet something kept her on the edge of sanity: the discovery that two hundred sleepers were missing. There was no sign that they'd been butchered like the others, which left the possibility that they'd been abducted by Captain Run Seven. It was madness – it would not begin to compensate for the loss of the others – but her psychology allowed no other line of thought.

She could find them again.

Her plan was disarmingly simple. It crystallised in her mind with the clarity of a divine vision. *It would be done.*

She would repair the ship. She would hunt down Seven. She would recover the sleepers from him. And enact whatever retribution she deemed fit.

She found the chamber where the four Conjoiners had slept, well away from the main dormitories, in a part of the ship through which the pirates were not likely to have wandered. She was hoping she could revive them and seek their assistance. There seemed no way they could make things worse for her now.

But hope faded when she saw the scorch marks of weapon blasts around the bulkhead; the door forced.

She stepped inside anyway.

They'd been a sect on Mars, originally; a clique of cyberneticists with a particular fondness for self-experimentation. In 2190, their final experiment had involved distributed processing – allowing their enhanced minds to merge into one massively parallel neural net. The resultant event – a permanent, irrevocable escalation to a new mode of consciousness – was known as the Transenlightenment.

There'd been a war, of course.

Demarchists had long seen both sides. They used neural augmentation themselves, policed it so that they never approached the Conjoiner threshold. They'd brokered the peace, defusing the suspicion surrounding the Conjoiners. Conjoiners had fuelled Demarchist expansion from Europa with their technologies, fused in the white heat of Transenlightenment. Four of them were along as observers because the *Hirondelle* used their ramscoop drives.

Irravel still didn't trust them.

And maybe it didn't matter. The reefersleep units – fluted caskets like streamlined coffins – were riddled with blast holes.

Grimacing against the smell, Irravel examined the remains inside. They'd been cut open, but the pirates seemed to have abandoned the job halfway through, not finding the kinds of implants they were expecting. And maybe not even recognising that they were dealing with anything other than normal humans, Irravel thought – especially if the pirates who'd done this hadn't been amongst Seven's more experienced crewmembers; just trigger-happy thugs.

She examined the final casket, the one furthest from the door. It was damaged, but not so badly as the others. The display cartouches were still alive, a patina of frost still adhering to the casket's lid. The Conjoiner inside looked intact: the pirates had never reached him. She read his nameplate: *Remontoire*.

'Yeah, he's a live one,' said a voice behind Irravel. 'Now back off real slow.'

Heart racing, Irravel did as she was told. Slowly, she turned around, facing the woman whose voice she recognised.

'Mirsky?' she said.

'Yeah, it's your lucky day.' Mirsky was wearing her suit, but without the helmet, making her head appear shrunken in the moat of her neck-ring. She had a gun on Irravel, but she pointed it half-heartedly, as if this was a stage in their relationship she wanted to get over as quickly as possible.

'What the hell are you doing here?'

'Same as you, Veda. Trying to figure out how much shit we're in; how difficult it'll be to get this ship moving again. Guess we had the same idea about the Conjoiners. Seven went berserk when he heard they'd been killed, but I figured it was worth checking how thorough the job had been.'

'Stop; slow down. Start at the beginning. Why aren't you with Seven?'

Mirsky pushed past her and consulted the reefersleep indicators. 'Seven and me had a falling out. Fill in the rest yourself.' With quick jabs of her free hand she called up different display modes, frowning at each. 'Shit; this *ain't* gonna be easy. If we wake the guy without his three friends, he's gonna be psychotic; no use to us at all.'

'What kind of falling out?'

'Seven reckoned I was holding back too much in the interrogation, not putting you through enough hell.' She scratched at the silver box on the side of her head. 'Maybe we can wake him, then fake the cybernetic presence of his friends – what do you think?'

'Why am I still alive, if Seven broke into the sleeper chambers? Why are *you* still alive?'

'Seven's a sadist. Abandonment's more his style than a quick and clean execution. As for you, the pig cut a deal with your second-in-command.'

The implication of that sunk in. 'Markarian gave him the codes?'

'It wasn't you, Veda.'

Strange relief flooded Irravel. She could never be absolved of the crime of losing the cargo, but at least her degree of complicity had lessened.

'But that was only half the deal,' Mirsky continued. 'The rest was Seven promising not to kill you if Markarian agreed to join the *Hideyoshi*, our main ship.' She told Irravel that there'd been a transmitter rigged to her reefersleep unit, so that Markarian would know she was still alive.

'Seven must have known he was taking a risk leaving both of us alive.'

'A pretty small one. The ship's in pieces and Seven will assume neither of us has the brains to patch it back together.' Mirsky slipped the gun into a holster. 'But Seven assumed the Conjoiners were dead. Big mistake. Once we figure out a way to wake Remontoire safely, he can help us fix the ship; make it faster, too.'

'You've got this all worked out, haven't you?'

'More or less. Something tells me you aren't absolutely ready to start trusting me, though.'

'Sorry, Mirsky, but you don't make the world's most convincing turncoat.'

Mirsky reached up and gripped the box attached to the side of her head. 'Know what this is? A loyalty shunt. Makes simian stem cells; pumps them into the internal carotid artery, just above the *cavernous sinus*. They jump the blood–brain barrier and build a whole bunch of transient structures tied to primate dominance hierarchies; alpha-male shit. That's how Seven kept us under his command – he was King Monkey. But I've turned it off now.'

'That's supposed to reassure me?'

'No, but maybe this will.'

Mirsky tugged at the box, ripping it away from the side of her head in curds of blood.

Luyten 726-8 Cometary Halo – AD 2309

Irravel felt the *Hirondelle* turn like a compass needle. The ram-scoops gasped at interstellar gas, sucking lone atoms of cosmic hydrogen from cubic metres of vacuum. The engines spat twin beams of thrust, pressing Irravel into her seat with two gees of acceleration. Hardly moving now, still in the local frame of the cometary halo, but in only six months she would be nudging light-speed.

Her seat floated on a boom in the middle of the dodecahedral bridge. 'Map,' Irravel said, and was suddenly drowning in stars: an immense thirty-light-year-wide projection of human settled space, centred on the First System.

'There's the bastard,' Mirsky said, pointing from her own hovering seat, her voice only slightly strained under the gee-load. 'Map – give us projection of the *Hideyoshi*'s vector, and plot our intercept.'

The pirate ship's icon was still very close to Luyten 726-8; less than a tenth of a light-year out. They had not seen Seven until now. The thrust from his ship was so tightly focused that it had taken until this point for the widening beams of the exhaust to sweep over *Hirondelle*'s sensors. But now they knew where he was headed. A dashed line indicated the likely course, arrowing right through the map's heart and out towards the system Lalande 21185. Now came the intercept vector: a near-tangent that sliced Seven's course beyond Sol.

'When does it happen?' Irravel said.

'Depends on how much attention Seven's paying to what's coming up behind him, for a start, and what kind of evasive stunts he can pull.'

'Most of my simulations predict an intercept between 2325 and 2330,' Remontoire said.

Irravel savoured the dates. Even for someone trained to fly a starship between systems, they sounded uncomfortably like the future.

'Are you sure it's him – not just some other ship that happened to be waiting in the halo?'

'Trust me,' Mirsky said. 'I can smell the swine from here.'

'She's right,' Remontoire said. 'The destination makes perfect sense. Seven was prohibited from staying here much longer, once the number of missing ships became too large to be explained away as accidents. Now he must seek a well-settled system to profit from what he has stolen.'

The Conjoiner looked completely normal at first glance – a bald man wearing a ship's uniform, his expression placid – but then one noticed the unnatural bulge of his skull, covered only with a fuzz of baby hair. Most of his glial cells had been supplanted by machines, which served the same structural functions but also performed specialised cybernetic duties, like interfacing with other commune partners or external machinery. Even the organic neurons in his brain were now webbed together by artificial connections which allowed transmission speeds of kilometres per second; factors of ten faster than in normal brains. Only the problem of dispersing waste heat denied the Conjoiners even faster modes of thought.

It was six years since they'd woken him. Remontoire had not dealt well with the murder of his three compatriots, but Irravel and Mirsky had managed to keep him sane by feeding input into the glial machines, crudely simulating rapport with other commune members.

'It provides the kind of comfort to me that a ghost limb offers an amputee,' Remontoire had said. 'An illusion of wholeness – but no substitute for the real thing.'

'What more can we do?' Irravel had said.

'Return me to another commune with all speed.'

Irravel had agreed, provided Remontoire helped with the ship.

He hadn't let her down. Under his supervision, half the ship's mass had been sacrificed, permitting twice the acceleration. They had dug a vault in the comet, lined it with support systems and entombed what remained of the cargo. The sleepers were nominally dead – there was no real expectation of reviving them again, even if medicine improved in the future – but Irravel had nonetheless set servitors to tend the dead for however long it took, and programmed the beacon to lure another ship, this time to pick up the dead.

All that had taken years, of course – but it had also taken Seven as much time to cross the halo to his base; time again to show himself.

'Be so much easier if you didn't want the others back,' Mirsky said. 'Then we could just slam past Seven at relativistic speed and hit him with seven kinds of shit.' She was very proud of the weapons she'd built into the ship, copied from pirate designs with Remontoire's help.

'I want the sleepers back,' Irravel said.

'And Markarian?'

'He's mine,' she said, after due consideration. 'You get the pig.'

Relativity squeezed stars until they bled colour. Half a kilometre ahead, the side of Seven's ship raced towards Irravel like a tsunami.

The *Hideyoshi* was the same shape as the *Hirondelle*; honed less by human whim than the edicts of physics. But the *Hideyoshi* was heavier, with a wider cross section, incapable of matching the *Hirondelle*'s acceleration or of pushing so close to C. It had taken years, but they'd caught up with Seven, and now the attack was in progress.

Irravel, Mirsky and Remontoire wore thruster-pack-equipped suits, of the type used for inspections outside the ship, with added armour and weapons. Painted for effect, they looked like mechanised samurai. Another forty-seven suits were slaved to theirs, acting as decoys. They'd crossed fifty thousand kilometres of space between the ships.

'You're sure Seven doesn't have any defences?' Irravel had asked, not long after waking from reefersleep.

'Only the in-system ship had any fire power,' Mirsky said. She looked older now; new lines engraved under her eyes. 'That's because no one's ever been insane enough to contemplate storming another ship in interstellar space.'

'Until now.'

But it wasn't so stupid, and Mirsky knew it. Matching velocities with another ship was only a question of being faster; squeezing fractionally closer to light-speed. It might take time, but sooner or later the distance would be closed. And it *had* taken time, none of which Mirsky had spent in reefersleep. Partly it was because she lacked the right implants – ripped out in infancy when she was captured by Seven. Partly it was a distaste for the very idea of being frozen, instilled by years of pirate upbringing. But also because she wanted time to refine her weapons. They had fired a salvo against the enemy before crossing space in the suits, softening up any weapons buried in his ice and opening holes into the *Hideyoshi*'s interior.

Now Irravel's vision blurred, her suit slowing itself before slamming into the ice.

Whiteness swallowed her.

For a moment she couldn't remember what she was doing here. Then awareness returned and she slithered back up the tunnel excavated by her impact, until she reached the surface of the *Hideyoshi*'s ice-shield.

'Veda – you intact?'

Her armour's shoulder-mounted comm laser found a line of sight to Mirsky. Mirsky was twenty or thirty metres away around the ship's lazy circumference, balancing on a ledge of ice. Walls of it stretched above and below like a rock face, lit by the glare from the engines. Decoys were arriving by the second.

'I'm alive,' Irravel said. 'Where's the entry point?'

'Couple of hundred metres upship.'

'Damn. I wanted to come in closer. Remontoire's out of line of sight. How much fuel do you have left?'

'Scarcely enough to take the chill off a penguin's dick.'

Mirsky raised her arms above her head and fired lines into the ice, rocketing out from her sleeves. Belly sliding against the shield, she retracted the lines and hauled herself upship.

Irravel followed. They'd burned all their fuel crossing between the two ships, but that was part of the plan. If they didn't have a chance to raid Seven's reserves, they'd just kick themselves into space and let the *Hirondelle* home in on them.

'You think Seven saw us cross over?'

'Definitely. And you can bet he's doing something about it, too.'

'Don't do anything that might endanger the cargo, Mirsky – no matter how tempting Seven makes it.'

'Would you sacrifice half the sleepers to get the other half back?'

'That's not remotely an option.'

Above their heads, crevasses opened like eyes. Pirate crabs erupted out, black as night against the ice. Irravel opened fire on the machines. This time, with better weapons and real armour, she began to inflict damage. Behind the crabs, pirates emerged, bulbous in customised armour. Lasers scuffed the ice, bright through gouts of steam. Irravel saw Remontoire now: he was unharmed, and doing his best to shoot the pirates into space.

Above, one of Irravel's shots dislodged a pirate.

The *Hideyoshi*'s acceleration dropped him towards her. When the impact came she hardly felt it, her suit's guy lines staying firm. The pirate folded around her like a broken toy, then bounced back against the ship, pinned there by her suit. He was too close to shoot unless Irravel wanted to blow herself into space. Distorted behind glass, his face shaped a word. She moved in closer until their visors were touching. Through the glass she saw the asymmetrical bulge of a loyalty shunt.

The face was Markarian's. At first it seemed like absurd co-incidence. Then it occurred to her that Seven might have sent his newest recruit out to show his mettle. Maybe Seven wouldn't be far behind. Confronting adversaries was part of the alpha-male inheritance, after all.

'Irravel,' Markarian said, voice laced with static. 'I'm glad you're alive.'

'Don't flatter yourself you're the reason I'm here, Markarian. I came for the cargo. You're just next on the list.'

'What are you going to do – kill me?'

'Do you think you deserve any better than that?' Irravel adjusted her position. 'Or are you going to try to justify betraying the cargo?'

He pulled his aged features into a smile. 'We made a deal, Irravel; the same way you made a deal about the greenfly. But you don't remember that, do you?'

'Maybe I sold the greenfly machines to the pig,' she said. 'If I did that, it was a calculated move to buy the safety of the cargo. You, on the other hand, cut a deal with Seven to save your neck.'

The other pirates were holding fire, nervously marking them. 'I did it to save yours, actually. Does that make any sense?' There was wonder in his eyes now. 'Did you ever see Mirsky's hand? That was never her own. The pirates swap limbs as badges of rank. They're very good at connective surgery.'

'You're not making much sense, Markarian.'

Dislodged ice rained on them. Irravel looked around in time to see another pirate emerging from a crevasse. She recognised the suit artwork: it was Seven. He wore . . . things, strung around his utility belt in transparent bags like obscene fruit. She stared at them for a few seconds before their nature clicked into horrific focus: frozen human heads.

Irravel stifled an urge to vomit.

'Yes,' Run Seven said. 'Ten of your compatriots, recently unburdened of their bodies. But don't worry – they're not harmed in any fundamental sense. Their brains are intact – provided you don't warm them with an ill-aimed shot.'

'I've got a clear line of fire,' Mirsky said. 'Just say the word and the bastard's an instant anatomy lesson.'

'Wait,' Irravel said. 'Don't shoot.'

'Sound business sense, Captain Veda. I see you appreciate the value of these heads.'

'What's he talking about?' Mirsky said.

'Their neural patterns can be retrieved.' It was Remontoire speaking now. 'We Conjoiners have had the ability to copy minds onto machine substrates for some time now, though we haven't advertised it. But that doesn't matter – there have been experiments on Yellowstone that approach our early successes. And these heads aren't even thinking: only topologies need to be mapped, not electrochemical processes.'

The pig took one of the heads from his belt and held it at eye level, for inspection. 'The Conjoiner's right. They're not really dead. And they can be yours if you wish to do business.'

'What do you want for them?' Irravel asked.

'Markarian, for a start. All that Demarchy expertise makes for a very efficient second-in-command.'

Irravel glanced down at her prisoner. 'You can't buy loyalty with a box and a few neural connections.'

'No? In what way do our loyalty shunts differ from the psychosurgery your world inflicted on you, Irravel, yoking your motherhood instinct to twenty thousand sleepers you don't even know by name?'

'We have a deal or not?'

'Only if you throw in the Conjoiner as well.'

Irravel looked at Remontoire, some snake part of her mind weighing options with reptilian detachment.

'No!' he said. 'You promised!'

'Shut up,' Seven said. 'Or when you do get to rejoin your friends, it'll be in instalments.'

'I'm sorry,' Irravel said. 'I can't lose even ten of the cargo.'

Seven tossed the first head down to her. 'Now let Markarian go and we'll see about the rest.'

Irravel looked down at him. 'It's not over between you and me.'

Then she released him, and he scrambled back up the ice towards Seven.

'Excellent. Here's another head. Now the Conjoiner.'

Irravel issued a subvocal command; watched Remontoire stiffen. 'His suit's paralysed. Take him.'

Two pirates worked down to him, checked him over and nodded towards Seven. Between them they hauled him back up the ice, vanishing into a crevasse and back into the *Hideyoshi*.

'The other eight heads,' Irravel said.

'I'm going to throw them away from the ship. You'll be able to locate them easily enough. While I'm doing that, I'm going to retreat, and you're going to leave.'

'We could end this now,' Mirsky said.

'I need those heads.'

'They really fucked with your psychology big-time, didn't they?' Mirsky raised her weapon and began shooting at Seven and the other pirates. Irravel watched her carve up the remaining heads; splintering frozen bone into the vacuum.

'No!'

'Sorry,' Mirsky said. 'Had to do it, Veda.'

Seven clutched at his chest, fingers mashing the pulp of the heads still tethered to his belt. She'd punctured his suit. As he tried to stem the dam-burst, his face was carved with the intolerable knowledge that his reign had just ended.

But something had hit Irravel, too.

Sylveste Institute, Yellowstone Orbit, Epsilon Eridani – AD 2415

'Where am I?' Irravel asked. 'How am I thinking this?'

The woman's voice was the colour of mahogany. 'Somewhere safe. You died on the ice, but we got you back in time.'

'For what?'

Mirsky sighed, as if this was something she would rather not have had to explain this soon. 'To scan you, just like we did with the two frozen heads. Copy you into the ship.'

Maybe she should have felt horror, or indignation, or even relief that some part of her had been spared.

Instead, she just felt impatience.

'What now?'

'We're working on it,' Mirsky said.

Trans-Aldebaran Space – AD 2673

'We saved her body after she died,' Mirsky said, wheezing slightly. She found it difficult to move around under what to Irravel was the ship's normal two and a half gees of thrust. 'After the battle we brought her back aboard.'

Irravel thought of her mother dying on the other ship, the one they were chasing. For years they had deliberately not narrowed the distance, holding back but never allowing the *Hideyoshi* to slip from view.

Until now, it hadn't even occurred to Irravel to ask why.

She looked through the casket's window, trying to match her own features against what she saw in the woman's face, trying to project her own fifteen years into Mother Irravel's adulthood.

'Why did you keep her so cold?'

'We had to extract what we could from her brain,' Mirsky said, 'memories and neural patterns. We trawled them and stored them in the ship.'

'What good was that?'

'We knew they'd come in useful again.'

She'd been cloned from Mother Irravel. They were not identical – no Mixmaster expertise could duplicate the precise biochemical environment of Mother Irravel's womb, or the shaping experiences of her early infancy, and their personalities had been sculpted centuries apart, in totally different worlds. But they were still close copies. They even shared memories: scripted into Irravel's mind by medichines, so that she barely noticed each addition to her own experiences.

'Why did you do this?' she asked.

'Because Irravel began something,' Mirsky said. 'Something I promised I'd help her finish.'

Stormwatch Station, Aethra, Hyades Trade Envelope – AD 2931

'Why are you interested in our weapons?' the Nestbuilder asked. 'We are not aware of any wars within the *chordate* phylum at this epoch.'

'It's a personal matter,' Irravel said.

The Nestbuilder hovered a metre above the trade floor, suspended in a column of microgravity. They were oxygen-breathing arthropods that had once ascended to spacefaring capability. No longer intelligent, yet supported by their self-renewing machinery, they migrated from system to system, constructing elaborate, space-filling structures from solid diamond. Other Nestbuilder swarms would arrive and occasionally occupy the new nests. There seemed no purpose to this activity, but for tens of thousands of years they had been host to a smaller, cleverer species known as the Slugs. Small communities of Slugs – anything up to a dozen – lived in warm, damp niches in a Nestbuilder's intricately folded shell. They had long since learned how to control the host's behaviour and exploit its subservient technology.

Irravel studied a Slug now, crawling out from under a lip of shell material.

The thing was a multicellular invertebrate not much larger than her fist; a bag of soft blue protoplasm, sprouting appendages only when they were needed. A slightly bipolar shadow near one end might have been its central nervous system, but there hardly seemed enough of it to trap sentience. There were no obvious sense or communicational organs, but a pulsing filament of blue slime reached back into the Nestbuilder's fold. When the Slug spoke, it did so through the Nestbuilder: a rattle of chitin from the host's mouthparts which approximated human language. A hovering jewel connected to the station's lexical database did the rest, rendering the voice calmly feminine.

'A personal matter? A vendetta? Then it's true.' The mouthparts clicked together in what humans presumed was the symbiotic creature's laughter response. 'You *are* who we suspected.'

'She did tell you her name was Irravel, guy,' Mirsky said, sipping black coffee with delicate movements of the exoskeletal frame she always wore in high gravity.

'Amongst you *chordates*, the name is not so unusual now,' the Slug reminded them. 'But you do fit the description, Irravel.'

They were near one of the station's vast picture windows, overlooking Aethra's mighty, roiling cloud decks, fifty kilometres below. It was getting dark now and the stormplayers were preparing to start a show. Irravel saw two of their seeders descending into the clouds, robot craft tethered by a nearly invisible filament. The seeders would position the filament so that it bridged cloud layers with different static potentials; they'd then detach and return to Stormwatch, while the filament held itself in position by rippling along its length. For hundreds of kilometres around, other filaments would have been placed in carefully selected positions. They were electrically isolating now, but at the stormplayer's discretion, each filament would flick over into a conductive state: a massive, choreographed lightning flash.

'I never set out to become a legend,' Irravel said. 'Or a myth, for that matter.'

'Yes. There are so many stories about you, Veda, that it might be simpler to assume you never existed.'

'What makes you think otherwise?'

'The fact that a *chordate* who could have been Markarian also passed this way, only a year or so ago.' The Nestbuilder's shell pigmentation flickered, briefly revealing a picture of Markarian's ship.

'So you sold weapons to him?'

'That would be telling, wouldn't it?' The mouthparts clattered again. 'You would have to answer a question of ours first.'

Outside, the opening flashes of the night's performance gilded the horizon, like the first stirrings of a symphony. Aethra's rings echoed the flashes, pale ghosts momentarily cleaving the sky.

'What do you want to know?'

'We Slugs are amongst the few intelligent starfaring cultures in this part of the galaxy. During the war against intelligence, we avoided the Inhibitors by hiding ourselves amongst the mindless Nestbuilders.'

Irravel nodded. Slugs were one of the few alien species known to humanity that would even acknowledge the existence of the feared Inhibitors. Like humanity, they'd fought and beaten the revenants – at least for now.

'The weaponry you seek enabled us to triumph – but even then only at colossal cost to our phylum. Now we are watchful for new threats.'

'I don't see where this is leading.'

'We have heard rumours. Since you have come from the direction of those rumours – the local stellar neighbourhood around your phylum's birth star – we imagined you might have information of value.'

Irravel exchanged a sideways glance with Mirsky. The old woman's wizened, age-spotted skull looked as fragile as paper, but she remained an unrivalled tactician. They knew each other so well now that Mirsky could impart advice with the subtlest of movements, expression barely troubling the lined mask of her face.

'What kind of information are you seeking?'

'Information about something that frightens us.' The Nestbuilder's pigmentation flickered again, forming an image of . . . something. It was a splinter of grey-brown against speckled blackness – perhaps the Nestbuilder's attempt at visualising a planetoid. And then something erupted across the surface of the world, racing from end to end like a film of verdigris. Where it had passed, fissures opened up, deepening until they were black fractures, as if the world were a calving iceberg. And then it blew apart, shattering into a thousand green-tinged fragments.

'What was that?' Irravel said.

'We were rather hoping you could tell us.' The Nestbuilder's pigmentation refreshed again, and this time what they were seeing was clearly a star, veiled in a toroidal belt of golden dust. 'Machines have dismantled every rocky object in the system where these images were captured – Ross 128, which lies within eleven light-years of your birth star. They have engendered a swarm of trillions of rocks on independent orbits. Each rock is sheathed in a pressurised bubble membrane, within which an artificial plant-based ecosystem has been created. The same machines have fashioned other sources of raw material into mirrors, larger than worlds themselves, which trap sunlight above and below the ecliptic and focus it onto the swarm.'

'And why does this frighten you?'

The Nestbuilder leaned closer in its column of microgravity. 'Because we saw it being resisted. As if these machines had never been intended to wreak such transformations. As if your phylum had created something it could not control.'

'And – these attempts at resistance?'

'Failed.'

'But if one system was accidentally transformed, it doesn't mean . . .' Irravel trailed off. 'You're worried about them crossing interstellar space, to other systems. Even if that happened – couldn't you resist the spread? This can only be human technology – nothing that would pose any threat to yourselves.'

'Perhaps it was once human technology, with programmed limitations to prevent it from replicating uncontrollably. But those shackles have been broken. Worse, the machines have hybridised, gaining resilience and adaptability with each encounter with something external. First the Melding Plague, infection with which may have been a deliberate ploy to bypass the replication limits.'

Irravel nodded. The Melding Plague had swept human space four hundred years earlier, terminating the Demarchist *belle époque*. Like the Black Death of the previous millennium, it evoked terror generations after it had passed.

'Later,' the Nestbuilder continued, 'it may have encountered and assimilated Inhibitor technology, or worse. Now it will be very difficult to stop, even with the weapons at our disposal.'

An image of one of the machines flickered onto the Nestbuilder's shell, like a peculiar tattoo. Irravel shivered. The Slug was right: waves of hybridisation had transformed the initial architecture into something queasily alien. But enough of the original plan remained for there to be no doubt in her mind. She was looking at an evolved greenfly – one of the self-replicating breeders she had given Captain Run Seven. How it had broken loose was anyone's guess. She speculated that Seven's crew had sold the technology on to a third party, decades or centuries after gaining it from her. Perhaps that third party had reclusively experimented in the Ross 128 system, until the day when the greenfly tore out of their control . . .

'I don't know why you think I can help,' she said.

'Perhaps we were mistaken, then, to credit a five-hundred-year-old rumour that said you had been the original source of these machines.'

She had insulted it by daring to bluff. The Slugs were easily insulted. They read human beings far better than humans read Slugs.

'Like you say,' she answered, 'you can't believe everything you hear.'

The Slug made the Nestbuilder fold its armoured, spindly limbs across its mouthparts, a gesture of displeased huffiness.

'You *chordates*,' it said. 'You're all the same.'

Interstellar Space – AD 3354

Mirsky was dead. She had died of old age.

Irravel placed her body in an armoured coffin and ejected her into space when the *Hirondelle*'s speed was only a hair's breadth under light.

'Do it for me, Irravel,' Mirsky had asked her, towards the end. 'Keep my body aboard until we're almost touching light, and then fire me ahead of the ship.'

'Is that really what you want?'

'It's an old pirate tradition. Burial at C.' She forced a smile that must have sapped what little energy she had left. 'That's a joke, Irravel, but it only makes sense in a language neither of us have heard for a while.'

Irravel pretended that she understood. 'Mirsky? There's something I have to tell you. Do you remember the Nestbuilder?'

'That was centuries ago, Veda.'

'I know. I just keep worrying that maybe it was right.'

'About what?'

'Those machines. About how I started it all. They say it's spread now, to other systems. It doesn't look as if anyone knows how to stop it.'

'And you think all that was your fault?'

'It's crossed my mind.'

Mirsky convulsed, or shrugged – Irravel wasn't sure which. 'Even if it was your fault, Veda, you did it with the best of intentions. So you fucked up slightly. We all make mistakes.'

'Destroying whole solar systems is just a fuck-up?'

'Hey, accidents happen.'

'You always did have a sense of humour, Mirsky.'

'Yeah, guess I did.' She managed a smile. 'One of us needed one, Veda.'

Thinking of that, Irravel watched the coffin fall ahead of the *Hirondelle*, dwindling until it was only a tiny mote of steel-grey, and then nothing.

Subaru Commonwealth, Pleiades Cluster – AD 4161

The starbridge had long ago attained sentience.

Dense with machinery, it sang an endless hymn to its own immensity, throbbing like the lowest string on a guitar. Vacuum-breathing acolytes had voluntarily rewired their minds to view the bridge as an actual deity, translating the humming into their sensoria and passing decades in contemplative ecstasy.

Clasped in a cushioning field, an elevator ferried Irravel down the bridge from the orbital hub to the surface in a few minutes, accompanied by an entourage of children from the ship, many of whom bore in youth the hurting imprint of her dead friend Mirsky's genes. The bridge rose like the stem of a goblet from a ground terminal which was itself a scalloped shell of hyper-diamond, filled with tiered perfume gardens and cascading pools, anchored to the largest island in an equatorial archipelago. The senior children walked Irravel down to a beach of silver sand on the terminal's edge, where jewelled crabs moved like toys. She bid the children farewell, then waited, warm breezes fingering the hem of her sari.

Minutes later, the children's elevator flashed heavenward.

Irravel looked out at the ocean, thinking of the Pattern Jugglers. Here, as on dozens of other oceanic worlds, there was a colony of the alien intelligences. Transforming themselves to aquatic body-plans, the Subaruns had established close rapport with the aliens. In the morning, she would be taken out to meet the Jugglers, drowned, dissolved on the cellular level, every atom in her body swapped for one in the ocean, remade into something not quite human.

She was terrified.

Islanders came towards the shore, skimming the water on penanted trimarans, attended by oceanforms, sleek gloss-grey hybrids of porpoise and ray, whistlespeech downshifted into the human auditory spectrum. The Subaruns' epidermal scales shimmered like imbricated armour: biological photocells drinking scorching blue Pleiadean sunlight. Sentient veils hung in the sky, rippling gently like aurorae, shading the archipelago from the fiercest wavelengths. As the actinic eye of Taygeta sank towards the horizon, the veils moved with it like living clouds. Flocks of phantasmagorical birds migrated with the veils.

The purple-skinned elder's scales flashed green and opal as he approached Irravel along the coral jetty, a stick in one webbed hand, supported by two aides, a third shading his aged crown with a delicately watercoloured parasol. The aides were all descended from late-model Conjoiners; they had the translucent cranial crest through which bloodflow had once been channelled to cool their supercharged minds. Seeing them gave Irravel a dual-edged pang of nostalgia and guilt. She had not seen Conjoiners for nearly a thousand years, ever since they had fragmented into a dozen factions and vanished from human affairs. Neither had she entirely forgotten her betrayal of Remontoire.

But that had been so long ago . . .

A Communicant completed up the party, gowned in brocade, hazed by a blur of entopic projections. Communicants were small and elfin, with a phenomenal talent for natural languages augmented by Juggler transforms. Irravel sensed that this one was old and revered, despite the fact that Communicant genes did not express for great longevity.

The elder halted before her.

The head of his walking stick was a tiny lemur skull inside an egg-sized space helmet. He uttered something clearly ceremonial, but Irravel understood none of the sounds he made. She groped for something to say, recalling the oldest language in her memory, and therefore the one most likely to be recognised in any far-flung human culture.

'Thank you for letting us stop here,' she said.

The Communicant hobbled forward, already shaping words experimentally with his wide, protruding lips. For a moment his sounds were like an infant's first attempts at vocalisation, but then they resolved into something Irravel understood.

'Am I – um – making the slightest sense to you?'

'Yes,' Irravel said. 'Yes, thank you.'

'Canasian,' the Communicant diagnosed. 'Twenty-third, twenty-fourth centuries, Lacaille 9352 dialect, Fand subdialect?'

Irravel nodded.

'Your kind are very rare now,' he said, studying her as if she was some kind of exotic butterfly, 'but not unwelcome.' His features cracked into a heart-warming smile.

'What about Markarian?' Irravel said. 'I know his ship passed through this system less than fifty years ago – I still have a fix on it as it moves out of the cluster.'

'Other ships do come, yes. Not many – one or two a century.'

'And what happened when the last one came through?'

'The usual tribute was given.'

'Tribute?'

'Something ceremonial.' The Communicant's smile was wider than ever. 'To the glory of Irravel. With many actors, beautiful words, love, death, laughter, tears.'

She understood, slowly, dumbfoundedly.

'You're putting on a play?'

The elder must have understood something of that. Nodding proudly, he extended a hand across the darkening bay, ocean-forms cutting the water like scythes. A distant raft carried lanterns and the glimmerings of richly painted backdrops. Boats converged from across the bay. A dirigible loomed over the archipelago's edge, pregnant with gondolas.

'We want you to play Irravel,' the Communicant said, beckoning her forward. 'This is our greatest honour.'

When they reached the raft, the Communicant taught Irravel her lines and the actions she would be required to make. It was all simple enough – even the fact that she had to deliver her parts in Subarun. By the end of evening she was fluent in their language. There was nothing she couldn't learn in an instant these days, by sheer force of will. But it was not enough. To catch Markarian, she would have to break out of the narrow labyrinth of human thought entirely. That was why she had come to Jugglers.

That night they performed the play, while boats congregated around them, top-heavy with lolling islanders. The sun sank and the sky glared with a thousand blue gems studding blue velvet. Night in the heart of the Pleiades was the most beautiful thing

Irravel had dared imagine. But in the direction of Sol, when she amplified her vision, there was a green thumbprint on the sky. Every century, the green wave was larger, as neighbouring solar systems were infected and transformed by the rogue terraforming machines. Given time, it would even reach the Pleiades.

Irravel got drunk on islander wine and learned the tributes' history.

The plots varied immensely, but the protagonists always resembled Markarian and Irravel; mythic figures entwined by destiny, remembered across almost two thousand years. Sometimes one or the other was the clear villain, but as often as not they were both heroic, misunderstanding each other's motives in true tragic fashion. Sometimes they ended with both parties dying. They rarely ended happily. But there was always some kind of redemption when the pursuit was done.

In the interlude, she felt she had to tell the Communicant the truth, so that he could tell the elder.

'Listen, there's something you need to know.' Irravel didn't wait for his answer. 'I'm really her – really the person I'm playing.'

For a long time he didn't seem to understand, before shaking his head slowly and sadly. 'No; I thought you'd be different. You seemed different. But many say that.'

She shrugged. There was little point arguing, and anything she said now could always be ascribed to wine. In the morning, the remark had been quietly forgotten. She was taken out to sea and drowned.

Galactic North, AD 9730

'Markarian? Answer me.'

She watched the *Hideyoshi*'s magnified image, looming just out of weapons range. Like the *Hirondelle*, it had changed almost beyond recognition. The hull glistened within a skein of armouring force. The engines, no longer physically coupled to the rest of the ship, flew alongside like dolphins. They were anchored in fields that only became visible when some tiny stress afflicted them.

For centuries of worldtime she had made no attempt to communicate with him. But now her mind had changed. The green wave had continued for millennia, an iridescent cataract spreading across the eye of the galaxy. It had assimilated the blue suns of the Subarun Commonwealth in mere centuries – although by then Irravel and Markarian were a thousand light-years closer to the core, beginning to turn away from the plane of the galaxy, and the death screams of those gentle islanders never reached them. Nothing stopped it, and once the green wave had swallowed them, systems fell silent. The Juggler transformation allowed Irravel to grasp the enormity of it; allowed her to stare unflinchingly into the horror of a million poisoned stars and apprehend each individually.

She knew more of what it was, now.

It was impossible for stars to shine green, any more than an ingot of metal could become green-hot if it was raised to a certain temperature. Instead, something was veiling them – staining their light, like coloured glass. Whatever it was stole energy from the stellar spectra at the frequencies of chlorophyll. Stars were shining through curtains of vegetation, like lanterns in a forest. The greenfly machines were turning the galaxy into a jungle.

It was time to talk. Time – as in the old plays of the dead islanders – to initiate the final act, before the two of them fell into the cold of intergalactic space. She searched her repertoire of communication systems until she found something as ancient as ceremony demanded.

She aimed the message laser at him, cutting through his armour. The beam was too ineffectual to be mistaken for anything other than an attempt to talk. No answer came, so she repeated the message in a variety of formats and languages. Days of shiptime passed – decades of worldtime.

Talk, you bastard.

Growing impatient, she examined her weapons options. Armaments from the Nestbuilders were amongst the most advanced: theoretically they could mole through the loam of spacetime and inflict precise harm anywhere in Markarian's ship. But to use them she had to convince herself that she knew the interior layout of the *Hideyoshi*. Her mass-sensor sweeps were too blurred to be much help. She might just as easily harm the sleepers as take out his field nodes. Until now, it had been too risky to contemplate.

But all games needed an end.

Willing her qualms from her mind, she enabled the Nestbuilder armaments, feeling them stress spacetime in the *Hirondelle*'s belly, ready to short-circuit it entirely. She selected attack loci in Markarian's ship; best guesses that would cripple him rather than blow him out of the sky.

Then something happened.

He replied, modulating his engine thrust in staccato stabs. The frequency was audio. Quickly Irravel translated the modulation.

'I don't understand,' Markarian said, 'why you took so long to answer me, and why you ignored me for so long when I replied.'

'You never replied until now,' she said. 'I'd have known if you had.'

'Would you?'

There was something in his tone that convinced her he wasn't lying. Which left only one possibility: that he had tried speaking to her before, and that in some way her own ship had kept this knowledge from her.

'Mirsky must have done it,' Irravel said. 'She must have installed filters to block any communications from your ship.'

'Mirsky?'

'She would have done it as a favour to me; maybe under orders from my former self.' She didn't bother elaborating: Markarian was sure to know she had died and then been reborn as a clone of the original Irravel. 'My former self had the neural conditioning that kept her on the trail of the sleepers. This clone never had it, which meant that my instinct to pursue the sleepers had to be reinforced.'

'By lies?'

'Mirsky would have done it out of friendship,' Irravel said. And for a moment she believed herself, while wondering how friendship could seem so like betrayal.

Markarian's image smiled. They faced each other across an absurdly long banquet table, with the galaxy projected above it, flickering in the light of candelabra.

'Well?' he said, of the green stain spreading across the spiral. 'What do you think?'

Irravel had long ago stopped counting time and distance, but she knew it had been at least fifteen thousand years and that many light-years since they had turned from the plane. Part of her knew, of course: although the wave swallowed suns, it had no use for pulsars, and their metronomic ticking and slow decay allowed positional triangulation in space and time with chilling precision. But she elected to bury that knowledge beneath her conscious thought processes: one of the simpler Juggler tricks.

'What do I think? I think it terrifies me.'

'Our emotional responses haven't diverged as much as I'd feared.'

They didn't have to use language. They could have swapped pure mental concepts between ships: concatenated strings of qualia, some of which could only be grasped in minds rewired by Pattern Jugglers. But Irravel considered it sufficient that they could look each other in the eye without flinching.

The galaxy falling below had been frozen in time: light waves struggling to overtake Irravel and Markarian. The wave had appeared to slow, and then halt its advance. But then Markarian had turned, diving back towards the plane. The galaxy quickened to life, rushing to finish thirty thousand years of history before the two ships returned. The wave surged on. Above the banquet table, one arm of the star-clotted spiral was shot through with green, like a mote of ink spreading into blotting paper. The edge of the green wave was feathered, fractal, extending verdant tendrils.

'Do you have any observations?' Irravel asked.

'A few.' Markarian sipped from his chalice. 'I've studied the patterns of starlight amongst the suns already swallowed by the wave. They're not uniformly green – it's correlated with rotational angle. The green matter must be concentrated near the ecliptic, extending above and below it, but not encircling the stars completely.'

Irravel thought back to what the Nestbuilder had shown her.

'Meaning what?' she asked, testing Markarian.

'Swarms of absorbing bodies, on orbits resembling comets, or asteroids. I think the greenfly machines must have dismantled everything smaller than a Jovian, then enveloped the rubble in transparent membranes which they filled with air, water and greenery – self-sustaining biospheres. Then they were cast adrift. Trillions of tiny worlds, around each star. No rocky planets any more.'

Irravel retrieved a name from the deep past. 'Like Dyson spheres?'

'Dyson clouds, perhaps.'

'Do you think anyone survived? Are there niches in the wave where humans can live? That was the point of greenfly, after all: to create living space.'

'Maybe,' Markarian said, with no great conviction. 'Perhaps some survivors found ways inside, as their own worlds were smashed and reassembled into the cloud—'

'But you don't think it's very likely?'

'I've been listening, Irravel – scanning the assimilated regions for any hint of an extant technological culture. If anyone did survive, they're either keeping deliberately quiet or they don't even know how to make a radio signal by accident.'

'It was my fault, Markarian.'

His tone was rueful. 'Yes . . . I couldn't help but arrive at that conclusion.'

'I never intended this.'

'I think that goes without saying, don't you? No one could have guessed the consequences of that one action.'

'Did you?'

He shook his head. 'In all likelihood, I'd have done exactly what you did.'

'I did it out of love, Markarian. For the cargo.'

'I know.'

And she believed him.

'What happened back there, Markarian? Why did you give up the codes when I didn't?'

'Because of what they did to you, Irravel.'

He told her. How neither Markarian nor Irravel had shown any signs of revealing the codes under Mirsky's interrogation, until something new was tried.

'They were good at surgery,' Markarian said. 'Seven's crew swapped limbs and body parts as badges of status. They knew how to sever and splice nerves.' The image didn't allow her to interrupt. 'They cut your head off. Kept it alive in a state of borderline consciousness, and then showed it to me. That's when I gave them the codes.'

For a long while Irravel said nothing. Then it occurred to her to check her old body, still frozen in the same casket where Mirsky had once revealed it to her. She ordered some children to prepare the body for a detailed examination, then looked through their eyes. The microscopic evidence of reconnective surgery around the neck was too slight ever to have shown up unless one was looking for it. But now there was no mistaking it.

I did it to save your neck, Markarian had said, when she had held him pinned to the ice of Seven's ship.

'You appear to be telling the truth,' she said, when she had released the children. 'The nature of your betrayal was . . .' And then she paused, searching for the words, while Markarian watched her across the table. 'Different from what I assumed. Possibly less of a crime. But still a betrayal, Markarian.'

'One I've lived with for three hundred years of subjective time.'

'You could have returned the sleepers alive at any time. I wouldn't have attacked you.' But she didn't even sound convincing to herself.

'What now?' Markarian said. 'Do we keep this distance, arguing until one of us has the nerve to strike against the other? I've Nestbuilder weapons as well, Irravel. I think I could rip you apart before you could launch a reprisal.'

'You've had the opportunity to do so before. Perhaps you never had the nerve, though. What's changed now?'

Markarian's gaze flicked to the map. 'Everything. I think we should see what happens before making any rash decisions, don't you?'

Irravel agreed.

She willed herself into stasis, medichines arresting all biological activity in every cell in her body. The 'chines would only revive her when something – anything happened, on a galactic time-scale. Markarian would retreat into whatever mode of suspension he favoured, until woken by the same stimulus.

He was still sitting there when time resumed, as if only a moment had interrupted their conversation.

The wave had spread further now. It had eaten into the galaxy for ten thousand light-years around Sol – a third of the way to the core. There was no sign that it had encountered resistance – at least nothing that had done more than hinder it. There had never been many intelligent, starfaring cultures to begin with, the

Nestbuilder's Slug had told her. Perhaps the few that existed were even now making plans to retard the wave. Or perhaps it had swallowed them, as it had swallowed humanity.

'Why did we wake?' Irravel said. 'Nothing's changed, except that it's grown larger.'

'Maybe not,' Markarian said. 'I had to be sure, but now I don't think there's any doubt. I've just detected a radio message from within the plane of the galaxy; from within the wave.'

'Yes?'

'Looks as though someone survived after all.'

The radio message was faint, but nothing else was transmitting on that or any adjacent frequency, except for the senseless mush of cosmic background sources. It was also in a language they recognised.

'It's Canasian,' Markarian said.

'Fand subdialect,' Irravel added, marvelling.

It was also beamed in their direction, from somewhere deep in the swathe of green, almost coincident with the position of a pulsar. The message was a simple one, frequency modulated around one and a half megahertz, repeated for a few minutes every day of galactic time. Whoever was sending it clearly didn't have the resources to transmit continuously. It was also coherent: amplified and beamed.

Someone wanted to speak to them.

The man's disembodied head appeared above the banquet table, chiselled from pixels. He was immeasurably old; a skull draped in parchment; something that should have been embalmed rather than talking.

Irravel recognised the face.

'It's him,' she said, in Markarian's direction. 'Remontoire. Somehow he made it across all this time.'

Markarian nodded slowly. 'He must have remembered us, and known where to look. Even across thousands of light-years, we can still be seen. There can't be many objects still moving relativistically.'

Remontoire told his story. His people had fled to the pulsar system twenty thousand years ago – more, now, since his message had taken thousands of years to climb out of the galaxy. They had seen the wave coming, as had thousands of other human factions, and like many they had observed that the wave shunned pulsars: burned-out stellar corpses rarely accompanied by planets. Some intelligence governing the wave must have recognised that pulsars were valueless; that even if a Dyson cloud could be created around them, there would be no sunlight to focus.

For thousands of years they had waited around the pulsar, growing ever more silent and cautious, seeing other cultures make errors that drew the wave upon them, for by now it interpreted any other intelligence as a threat to its progress, assimilating the weapons used against it.

Then – over many more thousands of years – Remontoire's people watched the wave learn, adapting like a vast neural net, becoming curious about those few pulsars that harboured planets. Soon their place of refuge would become nothing of the sort.

'Help us,' Remontoire said. 'Please.'

It took three thousand years to reach them.

For most of that time, Remontoire's people acted on faith, not knowing that help was on its way. During the first thousand years they abandoned their system, compressing their population down to a sustaining core of only a few hundred thousand. Together with the cultural data they'd preserved during the long centuries of their struggle against the wave, they packed their survivors into a single hollowed-out rock and flung themselves out of the ecliptic using a mass-driver that fuelled itself from the rock's own bulk. They called it Hope. A million decoys had to be launched, just to ensure that Hope got through the surrounding hordes of assimilating machines.

Inside, most of the Conjoiners slept out the next two thousand years of solitude before Irravel and Markarian reached them.

'Hope would make an excellent shield,' Markarian mused as they approached it, 'if one of us considered a pre-emptive strike against the other—'

'Don't think I wouldn't.'

They moved their ships to either side of the dark shard of rock, extended field grapples, then hauled in.

'Then why don't you?' Markarian said.

For a moment Irravel didn't have a good answer. When she found one, she wondered why it hadn't been more obvious before. 'Because they need us more than I need revenge.'

'A higher cause?'

'Redemption,' she said.

Hope, Galactic Plane – AD Circa 40,000

They didn't have long. Their approach, diving down from Galactic North, had drawn the attention of the wave's machines, directing them towards the one rock that mattered. A wall of annihilation was moving towards them at half the speed of light. When it reached Hope, it would turn it into the darkest of nebulae.

Conjoiners boarded the *Hirondelle* and invited Irravel into Hope. The hollowed-out chambers of the rock were Edenic to her children, after all the decades of subjective time they'd spent aboard ship since last planetfall. But it was a doomed paradise, the biomes grey with neglect, as if the Conjoiners had given up long before.

Remontoire welcomed Irravel next to a rock pool filmed with grey dust. Half the sun-panels set into the distant honeycombed ceiling were black.

'You came,' he said. He wore a simple smock and trousers. His anatomy was early-model Conjoiner: almost fully human.

'You're not him, are you?' Irravel asked. 'You look like him –

sound like him – but the image you sent us was of someone much older.'

'I'm sorry. His name was chosen for its familiarity; my likeness shaped to his. We searched our collective memories and found the experiences of the one you knew as Remontoire . . . but that was a long time ago, and he was never known by that name to us.'

'What his name?'

'Even your Juggler cortex could not accommodate it, Irravel.'

She had to ask. 'Did he make it back to a commune?'

'Yes, of course,' the man said, as if her question was foolish. 'How else could we have absorbed his experiences back into the Transenlightenment?'

'And did he forgive me?'

'I forgive you now,' he said. 'It amounts to the same thing.'

She willed herself to think of him as Remontoire.

The Conjoiners hadn't allowed themselves to progress in all the thousands of years they waited around the pulsar, fearing that any social change – no matter how slight – would eventually bring the wave upon them. They had studied it, contemplated weapons they might use against it – but other than that, all they had done was wait.

They were very good at waiting.

'How many refugees did you bring?'

'One hundred thousand.' Before Irravel could answer, Remontoire shook his head. 'I know – too many. Perhaps half that number can be carried away on your ships. But half is better than nothing.'

She thought back to her own sleepers. 'I know. Still, we might be able to take more . . . I don't know about Markarian's ship, but—'

He cut her off, gently. 'I think you'd better come with me,' said Remontoire, and then led her aboard the *Hideyoshi*.

'How much of it did you explore?'

'Enough to know there's no one alive anywhere aboard this

ship,' Remontoire said. 'If there are two hundred cryogenically frozen sleepers, we didn't find them.'

'No sleepers?'

'Just this one.'

They had arrived at a plinth supporting a reefersleep casket, encrusted with gold statuary: spacesuited figures with hands folded across their chests like resting saints. The glass lid of the casket was veined with fractures; the withered figure inside older than time. Markarian's skeletal frame was swaddled in layers of machines, all of archaic provenance. His skull had split open, a fused mass spilling out like lava.

'Is he dead?' Irravel asked.

'Depends what you mean by dead.' The Conjoiner's hand sketched across the neural mass. 'His organic mind must have been completely swamped by machines centuries ago. His linkage to the *Hideyoshi* would have been total. There would have been very little point discriminating between the two.'

'Why didn't he tell me what had become of him?'

'No guarantee he knew. Once he was in this state, with his personality running entirely on machine substrates, he could have edited his own memories and perceptual inputs – deceiving himself that he was still corporeal.'

Irravel looked away from the casket, forcing troubling questions from her mind. 'Is his personality still running the ship?'

'We detected only caretaker programs, capable of imitating him when the need arose, but lacking sentience.'

'Is that all there was?'

'No.' Remontoire reached through one of the casket's larger fractures, prizing something from Markarian's fingers. It was a sliver of computer memory. 'We examined this already, though not in great detail. It's partitioned into one hundred and ninety areas, each large enough to hold complete neural and genetic maps for one human being, encoded into superposed electron states on Rydberg atoms.'

She took the sliver from him. It didn't feel like much. 'He burned the sleepers onto this?'

'Three hundred years is much longer than any of them expected to sleep. By scanning them he lost nothing.'

'Can you retrieve them?'

'It would not be trivial,' the Conjoiner said, 'but given time, we could do it. Assuming any of them would welcome being born again, so far from home.'

She thought of the infected galaxy hanging below them, humming with the chill sentience of machines. 'Maybe the kindest thing would be to simulate the past,' she said. 'Recreate Yellowstone and revive them on it, as if nothing had ever gone wrong.'

'Is that what you're advocating?'

'No,' she said, after toying with the idea in all seriousness. 'We need all the genetic diversity we can get if we're going to establish a new branch of humanity outside the galaxy.'

She thought about it some more. Soon they would witness Hope's destruction, as the wave of machines tore through it with the mindlessness of stampeding animals. Some of them might try to follow the *Hirondelle*, but so far the machines moved too slowly to catch the ship, even if they forced it back towards Galactic North.

Where else could they go?

There were globular clusters high above the galaxy – tightly packed shoals of old stars the wave hadn't reached, but where fragments of humanity might already have sought refuge. If the clusters proved unwelcoming, there were high-latitude stars, flung from the galaxy a billion years ago, and some might have dragged their planetary systems with them. If those failed – and it would be tens of thousands of years before the possibilities were exhausted – the *Hirondelle* could always loop around towards Galactic South and search there, striking out for the Clouds of Magellan. Ultimately, of course – if any fragment of Irravel's children still clung to humanity, and remembered where they'd come from, and what had become of it, they would want to return to the galaxy, even if that meant confronting the wave.

But they would return.

'That's the plan then?' Remontoire said.

Irravel shrugged, turning away from the plinth where Markarian lay. 'Unless you've got a better one.'

Here are eight stories – more than one hundred thousand words – set against a common background. I've written two other novellas and four novels set in the same imagined universe: not far shy of a million words. I've plans for more stories and books.

You can probably tell that I like future histories.

The first one I encountered was Larry Niven's 'Known Space' sequence. I was in my middle teens, which is probably exactly the right target age. As I started reading the stories and novels embedded within this consistent timeline, beginning with *Ringworld*, and later the collection *Tales from Known Space*, I found myself plunged into a dizzying series of venues and eras. In some of the stories – a few of which were actually set *earlier* than the date at which I was reading them – humanity was still confined to the solar system and had little or no knowledge of alien cultures around other stars. Some stories were set a few centuries downstream, with colonies beginning to be established around other systems. Still more stories were set in an era when humankind had access to faster-than-light drives, teleportation technology, planet-gouging weapons and near-indestructible materials, and was in contact with many variegated alien races.

At first glance, not all of Niven's stories appeared to belong in the same universe. But the connections were there, if one looked closely: finding them was half the fun. It was like pulling back from a close-up in which the individual stories were coloured chips in a mosaic. Suddenly you began to see the bigger picture; the larger composition upon which the author had been labouring. It hardly mattered that not all the details were absolutely consistent between the stories, or that some of the tales had been retrofitted into the scheme after initial publication. One still had a sense of the future as teeming, chaotic, prone to unexpected swerves and lurching accelerations.

That sense of a future history as a single fictional entity – a whole larger than the sum of its parts – has never left me, and it's largely why I find the form so appealing. Future histories are often dismissed as exercises in laziness: why invent a new background when you can reuse one from another story. I don't quite agree. For my money, it's generally more difficult to write a second story in a pre-existing universe than to make a new one up from scratch. You have to work within ground rules already laid down, which places severe limits on narrative freedom. If you've introduced a world-changing invention in the first story, it has to be incorporated into the background texture of the second, unless the second is set earlier in the first. And if that's the case, the second story must not introduce inconsistencies in the first. By the time you're on the eighth or ninth story in a sequence, the narrative airspace can be getting awfully crowded. Future histories usually reach a point of limiting complexity, when trying to slot new stories into the stack becomes so fiendishly difficult that most writers move on to new pastures. I suppose the difficult part is knowing when you've reached that point.

Future histories obey differing degrees of consistency. At the soft extreme you have something like the *Star Trek* universe, in which the writers have been perfectly willing to go back and re-imagine certain details, even if that means contradicting data in earlier episodes. At the harder extreme, which I'd guess is almost exclusively the purview of written fiction, you have writers who maintain a furious lock-hold on consistency. Their published stories are only the iceberg's tip of a vast private archive of background data, and no new story can be written without the monkish consultation of that hidden bible. I admire anyone with that degree of dedication to the art, but it's not my approach. My stories fit together like a badly made jigsaw. Some of the pieces don't even seem to come from quite the same puzzle. You probably need to file down a few corners and press hard to make them fit. My bible consists of one small Word file containing a sketchy chronology, and the written works themselves. If I'm writing a story and a detail comes up that may refer to something I think I might possibly have written in *Chasm City*, I'll try to find the relevant page in *CC*. But I won't kill myself if I don't find it. In this approach I'm in the good company of John Varley, who refused to go back and read any of his 'Eight Worlds' stories before writing *Steel Beach*.

I've arranged the stories, as near as I can, in chronological order: 'Great Wall of Mars' is set barely two hundred years from now, while the last story, 'Galactic North', encompasses most of the future history and slingshots into the deep, distant future. But chronological order has little to do with the order in which the pieces were written. The earliest published story in this collection, 'Dilation Sleep', is a case in point. It was sold in 1989 and published in 1990, a full ten years before my first novel. It has roots that go back another ten years: in my teens I wrote two novels (*A Union World* and *Dominant Species*, since you asked) and a slew of stories set against an unashamedly Nivenesque background, in which a United Nations-dominated humanity makes contact with a zoo-load of alien races and obtains the secret of faster-than-light travel. Although I never tried to publish any of that stuff (which isn't to say I didn't inflict it on my long-suffering friends) it was a valuable learning experience. Because I'd written two moderately long novels by the time I was eighteen, I wasn't intimidated by the idea of doing it again, and to this day I've maintained a good track record of finishing projects once I start them: good practice, I think, for any budding writer.

But by the time I finished the second novel, I was already growing dissatisfied with all the unquestioned assumptions that had gone into the melting pot. I vowed that the next novel I wrote would take a more rigorous approach, eschewing such easy cop-outs as humanoid aliens, conveniently Earth-like planets and magic faster-than-light travel. It would owe less to ideas gleaned from media SF and more to what I was reading, including scientific non-fiction by the likes of Paul Davies, John Gribbin and Carl Sagan. But those early books and stories weren't completely wasted. Some of the locations, terminology and characters in them have cropped up again in the 'Revelation Space' universe, sometimes transformed, sometimes not. Yellowstone and Chasm City, which feature as background detail in 'Dilation Sleep', go right back to that first unpublished novel.

'Dilation Sleep' itself is an example of the kind of story that – if I were to take a scrupulous approach – really ought not to be in this collection. It's that wrong jigsaw piece: a story written before I had all the large-scale details of the history nailed down. That's more or less exactly why I wanted to include it, though. I think it's of interest for the details it *does* share with the other stories, not the points of deviation. It's got the notion of colony worlds linked by slower-than-light spacecraft; it's got Yellowstone and the Melding Plague; it even has a reference to the Sylveste family (and yes, I did already know that they had an influential and ambitious scion named Dan, who'd go on to cause a bit of trouble). I could have tinkered with the story to remedy some of the more egregious points of inconsistency (change 'spacers' to 'Ultras', that kind of thing) but in the end I decided, not without misgivings, to let it stand unaltered.

The curious reader might wonder why I failed to return to the RS universe for another seven years after the publication of 'Dilation Sleep'. It wasn't for want of trying. I did write other stories, but they were never good enough to get published, even when I was selling other material. The strongest ideas from these dead stories were eventually salvaged and incorporated into later pieces, not all of them within the RS universe. In any case, 'Dilation Sleep' was part of a batch of stories I wrote before moving to the Netherlands and getting my first paid job. Settling into a new country inevitably placed constraints on my writing activities, and when I did manage to free up some time, I decided I'd be better off investing my energies in a novel.

By the time I came to write 'A Spy in Europa' and 'Galactic North', both of which were written in parallel with work on both *Revelation Space* and *Chasm City*, I was beginning to get a feel for the large-scale architecture of the future history. Here's a shocking confession: I stole a lot of good ideas from other writers. I've already mentioned Niven and Varley, but I owe an equally obvious debt to Bruce Sterling, whose 'Shaper/Mechanist' sequence blew my mind on several levels. Sterling's future history, even though it consists of only a single novel and a handful of stories, still feels utterly plausible to me twenty years after I first encountered it. Part of me wishes Sterling would write more 'Shaper/Mechanist' stories; another part of me admires him precisely for not doing so. Read *Schismatrix* if you haven't already done so: it will melt your face.

Much of the hard SF furniture of my universe – slower-than-light travel, coldsleep, machine intelligences – draws from ideas and motifs in the work of Gregory Benford, especially his 'Galactic Centre' sequence, beginning with *In the Ocean of Night* and *Across the Sea of Suns*. My fascination with cyborg spacers (and the baroque trappings of space opera in general) stems from early exposure to Samuel R. Delaney's seminal *Nova*.

The Demarchists, the faction that plays a central role in much of the history, is not my invention. Joan D. Vinge wrote about a demarchist society in her enjoyable pacey novel *The Outcasts of Heaven Belt*. It's a real political term, derived from *democratic anarchy*, but I hadn't encountered it before reading Vinge's book. Vinge's demarchists used computer networks to facilitate their real-time democratic processes; mine use neural implants, enabling the decision-making process to become rapid and subliminal.

Nor is one of my other factions, the Conjoiners, an entirely new conception. I suspect I was thinking a little of the Comprise, the human hive-mind culture from Michael Swanwick's *Vacuum Flowers*. I tried to get inside the heads of my Conjoiners in the early Clavain stories featured here, and to suggest the inner workings of a realistic hive mind. Most of the Conjoiner characters I've sketched in any detail are, like Clavain himself, tainted by some residual connection back to baseline humanity. The Conjoiners are my attempt to portray a hive mind as not necessarily an evil thing.

The Ultras, the cyborg crews who control most of the starships featured in the sequence, are, I suppose, what *Star Trek*'s Borg would be like if the Borg took an unhealthy interest in Goth subculture. I got the idea of sleek, streamlined starships from Marshall T. Savage's book *The Millennial Project*, which is a non-fiction treatise on galactic colonisation. I don't know whether Savage's arguments really stack up (I suspect not), but I did like the idea of inverting that classic SF trope of the 'ship designed only for the forgiving environment of vacuum'. In any case, even if streamlining doesn't make much sense (even if it would look wicked cool), you'd still want to make your collision cross-section as small as possible, methinks, which suggests that any future starship will tend to be considerably longer than it's wide. Savage's wonderful and frightening vision of far-future solar systems transformed into countless sun-englobing asteroid habitats, each of which would be filled with sun-filtering foliage (thereby rendering starlight green), also crops up in 'Galactic North' and *Absolution Gap*. As for ship names, I bow to no one in my admiration of Iain M. Banks. But let the record show that the unwieldy names of my ships were a direct pinch from M. John Harrison's *The Centauri Device*, not the Culture.

Okay: I don't want to give anyone the idea that I stole *everything*.

But debts must be acknowledged, and there are too many to mention here. I cannot omit Paul McAuley and Stephen Baxter, two writers who have both perpetrated future histories of their own, and who both showed great generosity to me when I was starting out. It was their short stories in the British SF magazine *Interzone* (stories with spaceships in: very much against the grain of what *Interzone* was generally publishing at the time) that encouraged me to try submitting my own material. But it was David Pringle who actually *bought* my earliest stories – including 'Dilation Sleep' and two of the other stories included here ('A Spy in Europa' and 'Galactic North') – and it's to him that I dedicate this book. Without those early sales, I'm not at all sure that I would have persevered in my efforts to become an SF writer, so in that sense I owe David and the rest of the *Interzone* team for everything that's followed. *Interzone*, incidentally, is still going strong: if you like short fiction (and if you don't, what are you doing reading this?) then you could do worse than take out a subscription.

To finish, all I can say is that if you have enjoyed my stories, and you like the form of the future history, there is a mountain of good stuff out there by other writers. I hope you have as much fun discovering it as I've had.

Enjoy your futures.